THE PENGUIN POETS

A BOOK OF ENGLISH POETRY

A BOOK OF
ENGLISH POETRY

* Chaucer to Rossetti *

COLLECTED BY
G. B. HARRISON

PENGUIN BOOKS

PENGUIN BOOKS

Published by the Penguin Group
Penguin Books Ltd, 27 Wrights Lane, London W8 5TZ, England
Penguin Putnam Inc., 375 Hudson Street, New York, New York 10014, USA
Penguin Books Australia Ltd, Ringwood, Victoria, Australia
Penguin Books Canada Ltd, 10 Alcorn Avenue, Toronto, Ontario, Canada M4V 3B2
Penguin Books (NZ) Ltd, 182–190 Wairau Road, Auckland 10, New Zealand

Penguin Books Ltd, Registered Offices: Harmondsworth, Middlesex, England

First published 1937
New enlarged edition 1950
30

This selection copyright 1937, 1950 by G. B. Harrison
All rights reserved

Printed in England by Clays Ltd, St Ives plc
Set in Monotype Fournier

Preface

IN this anthology I have aimed at gathering a gallery of poems, typical and representative of our English poets from the fourteenth to the nineteenth centuries. Most of the poems are lyrics; but, since the best work of some of our greatest poets is to be found in poems or plays too long to be given entire, I have preferred to include some extracts rather than to omit altogether such works as *The Canterbury Tales*, *The Faerie Queene*, *Hamlet*, *Paradise Lost*, *Absalom and Achitophel*, or *The Rape of the Lock*. Where an extract, and not the whole poem, is given, the title of the work is noted at the end within square brackets. Spelling and punctuation have been modernised throughout, even in the extracts from Chaucer. By students this may be regretted, though I believe that Spenser certainly, and Chaucer probably, would be more widely appreciated if their archaic spellings were rendered less uncouth to the general reader. The arrangement is roughly chronological in that the poets are set out in the order of their birth. In this way, the collection shows, in little, the progress of English poetry.

G.B.H.

Note to the Seventh Impression

AN additional forty-five poems have been added, and several of the longer poems, formerly represented by short extracts, are now printed complete.

G. B. H.

November 1949

Contents

GEOFFREY CHAUCER
  The Canterbury Pilgrims: (i) The Knight, (ii) The Squire,
    (iii) The Yeoman, (iv) The Prioress, (v) The Clerk of
    Oxford, (vi) The Wife of Bath, (vii) The Poor Parson   15

SIR THOMAS WYATT
  'And wilt thou leave me thus? . . .'   21
  'Forget not yet . . .'   22
  The Lover Complaineth the Unkindness of His Love   23
  Farewell to the Faithless   24
  'Is it possible . . .'   25

HENRY HOWARD, EARL OF SURREY
  Description of Spring   26
  The Means to attain a Happy Life   27

NICHOLAS BRETON
  A Country Song   27

EDMUND SPENSER
  To His Love (i)   28
  Easter Day   29
  To His Love (ii)   29
  Epithalamium   30
  The Garden of Adonis   42

SIR WALTER RALEGH
  'As you came from the holy land . . .'   46
  'Even such is Time . . .'   48

SIR PHILIP SIDNEY
  He Seeks Inspiration to Write Worthily to his Love   49
  The Sleepless Lover   49
  'With how sad steps, O Moon . . .'   50
  'My true-love . . .'   50

JOHN LYLY
  Cupid and Campaspe   51

THOMAS LODGE
  The Sad Lover   51
  My Phillis   52

SIR EDWARD DYER
  'My mind to me a kingdom is . . .'   53

8 CONTENTS

ROBERT SOUTHWELL
The Burning Babe   55

HENRY CONSTABLE
Diaphenia   55

SAMUEL DANIEL
'Care-charmer Sleep . . .'   56

MICHAEL DRAYTON
'Stay, stay, sweet Time . . .'   57
'Some Atheist . . .'   57
Farewell to Love   58

CHRISTOPHER MARLOWE
The Aspiring Mind   58
Beauty Inexpressible   59

WILLIAM SHAKESPEARE
The Seven Ages of Man   59
Study   60
'O Mistress mine . . .'   61
'Shall I compare thee to a summer's day? . . .'   61
'When to the sessions of sweet silent thought . . .'   62
'Full many a glorious morning . . .'   62
'Tired with all these . . .'   63
'That time of year . . .'   63
'My Mistress' eyes . . .'   64
Love and Time   64
Imagination   65
'The quality of mercy . . .'   65
The Cares of Kingship   66
'To be, or not to be . . .'   67
Neglect of Degree   68
Capricious Time   69
Antony's First Meeting with Cleopatra   70
A Requiem   71
Eternity through Poetry   72
This Insubstantial Pageant   72

THOMAS CAMPION
'Follow your saint . . .'   73
'There is a garden . . .'   73
'When to her lute Corinna sings . . .'   74
'Rose-cheeked Laura, come . . .'   74
'Thou art not fair . . .'   75

CONTENTS

SIR HENRY WOTTON
On his Mistress, the Queen of Bohemia 75
The Character of a Happy Life 76
BEN JONSON
'Still to be neat . . .' 77
To Celia 78
(i) To Charis, (ii) Her Answer 78
The Hour Glass 81
Song 81
JOHN DONNE
Song 82
The Indifferent 83
The Good-Morrow 84
The Anniversary 84
Love's Growth 85
The Funeral 86
The Relic 87
'Sweetest love . . .' 88
Death 89
GEORGE WITHER
'I loved a lass . . .' 90
ROBERT HERRICK
Upon the Loss of His Mistresses 92
'Cherry ripe . . .' 92
Corrina's Going a-Maying 93
The Night-Piece 95
Delight in Disorder 95
'Gather ye rose-buds . . .' 96
To Daffodils 96
To Anthea Who may Command him Anything 97
To Blossoms 98
Upon Julia's Clothes 99
The Hag 99
Grace for a Child 100
His Litany to the Holy Spirit 100
GEORGE HERBERT
The Collar 102
Love 103
The Gifts of God 103
EDMUND WALLER
'Go, lovely Rose . . .' 104

EDMUND WALLER *(contd)*
  The Girdle   105
JOHN MILTON
  At a Solemn Music   106
  L'Allegro   107
  Il Penseroso   111
  Lycidas   116
  Paradise Lost: The First Book   121
  'Hail, holy Light . . .'   144
  On His Blindness   146
  Paradise Lost   146
  God's Purposes Revealed   147
SIR JOHN SUCKLING
  'Why so pale and wan . . .'   147
  The Constant Lover   148
RICHARD CRASHAW
  A Hymn to the Name and Honour of the Admirable Saint
    Teresa   149
  Charitas Nimia   154
RICHARD LOVELACE
  To Althea from Prison   156
  To Lucasta, on Going Beyond the Seas   157
ABRAHAM COWLEY
  Platonic Love   158
  The Wish   159
  Life and Fame   160
ANDREW MARVELL
  The Garden   162
  To his Coy Mistress   164
HENRY VAUGHAN
  The Retreat   165
  The Morning Watch   166
  'They are all gone into the world of light! . . .'   167
  The Garland   169
  Childhood   170
JOHN BUNYAN
  The Shepherd Boy's Song   171
  The Song of Master Valiant-for-Truth   172
JOHN DRYDEN
  Achitophel   ·173
  Zimri   175

JOHN DRYDEN *(contd)*
Song for Saint Cecilia's Day 176
HENRY CAREY
Sally in our Alley 178
ALEXANDER POPE
An Essay on Man 180
Hampton Court 188
Nature and Art 189
The Critic's Task 190
The Return of Chaos 191
The Character of Atticus 192
JAMES THOMSON
Spring 192
Autumn 193
Winter 195
SAMUEL JOHNSON
Poverty 196
The Vanity of Human Wishes 196
THOMAS GRAY
Elegy Written in a Country Churchyard 197
The Bard 202
WILLIAM COLLINS
Ode written in 1746 206
To Evening 206
Ode to Simplicity 208
OLIVER GOLDSMITH
The Deserted Village 210
WILLIAM COWPER
His Mother's Picture 222
The Solitude of Alexander Selkirk 223
To Mary Unwin 225
THOMAS CHATTERTON
An Excelente Balade of Charitie 227
Minstrel's Song 229
GEORGE CRABBE
Village Life – as it is 232
WILLIAM BLAKE
To Winter 233
To the Muses 234
The Lamb 234
The Voice of the Ancient Bard 235

WILLIAM BLAKE *(contd)*

The Tiger 235
A Poison Tree 236
The Garden of Love 237
The Sick Rose 237
'Ah! Sun-flower ...' 238
Jerusalem 238

WILLIAM WORDSWORTH

'I wandered lonely as a cloud ...' 239
'I travelled among unknown men ...' 240
'Three years she grew in sun and shower ...' 240
'She dwelt among the untrodden ways ...' 242
'A slumber did my spirit seal ...' 242
Tintern Abbey Re-visited 242
The Solitary Reaper 246
'My heart leaps up ...' 247
London, 1802 247
Composed upon Westminster Bridge, September 3, 1802 247
Ode on Intimations of Immortality from Recollections of
    Early Childhood 248

SAMUEL TAYLOR COLERIDGE

The Rime of the Ancient Mariner 254
Kubla Khan 274
Frost at Midnight 276

ROBERT SOUTHEY

'My days among the Dead are passed ...' 277
After Blenheim 277

CHARLES LAMB

The Old Familiar Faces 280
A Farewell to Tobacco 280

THOMAS CAMPBELL

The Soldier's Dream 285
Hohenlinden 286
'Ye Mariners of England ...' 287

JAMES HENRY LEIGH HUNT

The Nile 288
Abou Ben Adhem 288

GEORGE GORDON NOEL BYRON, LORD BYRON

'When we two parted ...' 289
'She walks in beauty ...' 290

GEORGE GORDON NOEL BYRON, LORD BYRON (contd)

The Incantation 291
Waterloo 293
Darkness 295
'So, we'll go no more a roving . . .' 298
The Poet's Song to Don Juan and Haidee 298

CHARLES WOLFE

The Burial of Sir John Moore at Corunna 302

PERCY BYSSHE SHELLEY

Ode to the West Wind 303
The Cloud 305
Hymn to Intellectual Beauty 308
'When the lamp is shatter'd . . .' 310
Ozymandias 311
'Music, when soft voices die . . .' 312
Adonais 312

JOHN KEATS

On First Looking into Chapman's Homer 327
Ode to a Nightingale 327
Ode on a Grecian Urn 330
Ode to Autumn 331
La Belle Dame sans Merci 332

THOMAS HOOD

'I remember, I remember . . .' 334
The Song of the Shirt 335

EDWARD FITZGERALD

Rubaiyát of Omar Khayyám of Naishápúr 338

ALFRED TENNYSON, LORD TENNYSON

Mariana 348
The Lady of Shalott 350
The Lotos-Eaters 356
Ulysses 361
Tithonus 363
To Virgil 365
Morte d'Arthur 367
Crossing the Bar 374

ROBERT BROWNING

The Lost Leader 375
My Last Duchess 376
Meeting at Night 377
Home-Thoughts, from Abroad 378

ROBERT BROWNING (*contd*)
Porphyria's Lover   378
Rabbi Ben Ezra   380
Prospice   387

ARTHUR HUGH CLOUGH
'Say not the struggle nought availeth . . .'   388

MATTHEW ARNOLD
Requiescat   388
The Scholar Gipsy   389
Rugby Chapel   397
Dover Beach   403

DANTE GABRIEL ROSSETTI
The Blessed Damozel   404

INDEX OF AUTHORS   409
INDEX OF FIRST LINES   410

GEOFFREY CHAUCER
(c. 1340–1400)

The Canterbury Pilgrims

i. *The Knight*

A Knight there was and that a worthy man,
That fro the timë that he first began
To riden out, he lovëd chivalry,
Truth and honour, freedom and courtesy.
Full worthy was he in his Lordës war,
And thereto had he ridden, no man ferre,
As well in Christendom as in heathenesse,
And ever honoured for his worthinesse. . . .
At mortal battles had he been fifteen,
And foughten for our faith at Tramysene
In listës thriës, and ay slain his foe.
This ilkë worthy knight had been also
Sometimë with the Lord of Palaty
Against another heathen in Turkey;
And ever more he had a sovereign price
And though that he were worthy, he was wise,
And of his port as meek as is a maid.
He never yet no villainy ne sayd,
In all his life, unto no manner wight.
He was a very parfit gentle knight.

ii. *The Squire*

With him there was his son, a young Squire,
A lover and a lusty bachelor,
With lockës curl, as they were laid in press,
Of twenty year of age he was, I guess.
Of his stature he was of even length,
And wonderly deliver, and great of strength.

And he had been some time in chivachy,
In Flanders, in Artois, and Picardy,
And born him well, as of so little space,
In hope to standen in his lady's grace.
Embroidered was he, as it were a mead
All full of freshë flowers, white and red.
Singing he was or fluting all the day;
He was as fresh as is the month of May.
Short was his gown, with sleevës long and
    wide.
Well could he sit on horse, and fairë ride.
He couldë songës make and well endite,
Joust and eke dance, and well portray and
    write.
So hot he lovéd that by nightertale
He sleep no more than doth a nightingale.
Courteous he was, lowly, and serviceable,
And carve before his father at the table.

iii. *The Yeoman*

A Yeoman had he, and servants no mo
At that time, for him listë ridë so;
And he was clad in coat and hood of green;
A sheaf of peacock arrows, bright and keen,
Under his belt he bare full thriftily;
Well could he dress his tackle yeomanly;
His arrows droopéd not with feathers low;
And in his hand he bare a mighty bow.
A nut-head had he, with a brown visage.
Of wood-craft well could he all the usage.
Upon his arm he bare a gay bracer,
And by his side a sword and a buckler,
And on that other side a gay dagger,
Harnesséd well, and sharp as point of spear;
A Christopher on his breast of silver sheen;
An horn he bare, the baldrick was of green;
A forester was he, soothly as I guess.

iv. *The Prioress*

There was also a Nun, a Prioress,
That of her smiling was full simple and coy;
Her greatest oath was but by Saintë Loy;
And she was clepéd Madame Eglantine.
Full well she song the servicë divine,
Entunéd in her nose full seemëly;
And French she spake full fair and fetishly,
After the school of Stratford-attë-Bowe,
For French of Paris was to her unknow.
At meatë well y-taught was she withal;
She let no morsel from her lippës fall,
Ne wet her fingers in her saucë deep.
Well could she carry a morsel, and well keep
That no dropë ne fell upon her breast.
In courtesy was set full much her lest.
Her over-lippë wiped she so clean,
That in her cup there was no ferthing seen
Of greasë, when she drunken had her draught.
Full seemëly after her meat she raught,
And sickerly she was of great disport,
And full pleasánt, and amiable of port,
And painéd her to counterfeitë cheer
Of Court, and been estately of manner,
And to be holden dign of reverence.
But for to speaken of her conscience,
She was so charitable and so piteous,
She wouldë weep, if that she saw a mouse
Caught in a trap, if it were dead or bled.
Of smallë houndës had she that she fed
With roasted flesh, or milk, and wastel bread.
But sorë wept she if one of them were dead,
Or if men smote it with a roddë smart;
And all was conscience and tender heart.
Full seemëly her wimple pinchéd was;
Her nose tretise, her eyen grey as glass,

Her mouth full small, and thereto soft and red;
But sickerly she had a fair forehead.
It was almost a spannë broad, I trow;
For, hardily, she was not undergrown.
Full fetish was her cloak, as I was ware.
Of small coral about her arm she bare
A pair of beadës, gauded all with green;
And thereon hung a brooch of gold full sheen,
On which there was first writ a crownéd A,
And after, *Amor vincit omnia.*

v. *The Clerk of Oxford*

A Clerk there was of Oxenford also,
That unto logic haddë long y-go.
As leanë was his horse as is a rake,
And he was not right fat, I undertake:
But lookéd hollow, and thereto soberly.
Full threadbare was his overest courtepy;
For he had getten him yet no benefice,
Ne was so worldly for to have office.
For him was lever have at his bed's head
Twenty bookës, clad in black or red,
Of Aristotle and his philosophy,
Than robës rich, or fiddle, or gay psaltery.
But all be that he was a philosopher,
Yet haddë he but little of gold in coffer;
But all that he might of his friends hent,
On bookës and his learning he it spent,
And busily gan he for the soulës pray
Of them that gave him wherewith to scholey.
Of study took he most cure and most heed.
Nought one word spake he morë than was need,
And that was said in form and reverence,
And short and quick, and full of high senténce.
Sowning in moral virtue was his speech,
And gladly would he learn and gladly teach.

vi. *The Wife of Bath*

A good wife was there of besidë Bath,
But she was somedel deaf, and that was scath.
Of cloth-making she haddë such a haunt
She passëd them of Yprës and of Gaunt.
In all the parish wife ne was there none
That to the offering before her shouldë gone;
And if there did, certain so wroth was she,
That she was out of allë charity.
Her coverchiefs full finë weren of ground –
I durstë swear they weyëden ten pound –
That on a Sunday weren upon her head.
Her hosen weren of fine scarlet red,
Full straight y-tied, and shoes full moist
    and new;
Bold was her face, and fair, and red of hew.
She was a worthy woman all her life,
Husbands at churchë door she haddë five,
Withouten other company in youth –
But thereof needeth not to speak as nowth –
And thriës had she been at Jerusalem;
She haddë passëd many a strangë stream;
At Rome she haddë been, and at Boulogne,
In Galice at Saint James, and at Cologne,
She couldë muchel of wandring by the way.
Goat-toothëd was she, soothly for to say.
Upon an ambler easily she sat,
Y-wimplëd well, and on her head an hat
As broad as is a buckler or a targe;
A foot mantle about her hipës large,
And on her feet a pair of spurrës sharp.
In fellowship well could she laugh and carp;
Of remedies of love she knew perchance,
For she could of that art the oldë dance.

vii. *The Poor Parson*

A good man was there of religion,
And was a poorë Parson of a town;
But rich he was of holy thought and work;
He was also a learnëd man, a clerk,
That Christës Gospel trewëly would preach:
His parishens devoutly would he teach.
Benign he was, and wonder diligent,
And in adversity full patient;
And such he was y-provëd oftë sithes.
Full loth were him to cursen for his tithes,
But rather would he givën, out of doubt,
Unto his poorë parishens about,
Of his offring and eke of his substance:
He could in little thing have suffisance.
Wide was his parish, and houses far asunder,
But he ne leftë not for rain ne thunder,
In sickness nor in mischief to visite
The farthest in his parish, much and light,
Upon his feet, and in his hand a staff.
This noble example to his sheep he gave
That first he wrought and afterward he taught.
Out of the Gospel he those wordës caught,
And this figure he added eke thereto,
That if gold rustë what shall iron do?
For if a priest be foul, on whom we trust,
No wonder is a lewëd man to rust;
And shame it is, if a priest takë keep,
A shiten shepherd, and a cleanë sheep.
Well ought a priest ensample for to give
By his cleanness how that his sheep should live.
He settë not his benefice to hire
And left his sheep encumbered in the mire,
And ran to London, unto Saïnt Paul's,
To seeken him a chauntery for souls;
Or with a brotherhood to been withhold,

But dwelt at home and keptë well his fold,
So that the wolf ne made it not miscarry, –
He was a shepherd, and not a mercenary:
And though he holy were and virtuous,
He was to sinful man not despitous,
Nor of his speechë dangerous ne digne,
But in his teaching discreet and benign
To drawen folk to Heaven by fairnesse,
By good example, this was his businesse:
But it were any person obstinate,
What so he were, of high or low estate,
Him would he snybben sharply for the nonce.
A better priest I trow that nowhere none is;
He waited after no pomp and reverence,
Ne maked him a spicëd conscience,
But Christës lore, and his Apostles twelve,
He taught, but first he followed it himself.

[From *The Prologue to the Canterbury Tales*]

SIR THOMAS WYATT
(c. 1503–1542)

'And wilt thou leave me thus? . . .'

And wilt thou leave me thus?
Say nay, say nay, for shame!
To save thee from the blame
Of all my grief and grame.
And wilt thou leave me thus?
Say nay, say nay.

And wilt thou leave me thus,
That hath loved thee so long
In wealth and woe among:
And is thy heart so strong

As for to leave me thus?
Say nay, say nay.

And wilt thou leave me thus,
That hath given thee my heart
Never for to depart
Neither for pain nor smart:
And wilt thou leave me thus?
Say nay, say nay.

And wilt thou leave me thus
And have no more pity
Of him that loveth thee?
Alas, thy cruelty!
And wilt thou leave me thus?
Say nay, say nay.

'Forget not yet . . .'

Forget not yet the tried intent
Of such a truth as I have meant;
My great travail so gladly spent
     Forget not yet.

Forget not yet when first began
The weary life ye know, since whan
The suit, the service none tell can;
     Forget not yet.

Forget not yet the great assays,
The cruel wrong, the scornful ways,
The painful patience in delays,
     Forget not yet.

Forget not, O forget not this,
How long ago hath been, and is
The mind that never meant amiss –
     Forget not yet.

Forget not then thine own approved,
The which so long hath thee so loved,
Whose steadfast faith yet never moved;
                                     Forget not this.

The Lover Complaineth the Unkindness of His Love

My lute, awake, perform the last
Labour that thou and I shall waste,
And end that I have now begun,
And when this song is sung and past,
My lute, be still, for I have done.

As to be heard where ear is none,
As lead to grave in marble stone,
My song may pierce her heart as soon.
Should we then sigh, or sing, or moan?
No, no, my lute, for I have done.

The rocks do not so cruelly
Repulse the waves continually,
As she my suit and affection;
So that I am past remedy,
Whereby my lute and I have done.

Proud of the spoil that thou hast got
Of simple hearts through Lovës shot,
By whom unkind thou hast them won,
Think not he hath his bow forgot,
Although my lute and I have done.

Vengeance shall fall on thy disdain
That makest but game on earnest pain.
Think not alone under the sun
Unquit to cause thy lovers playn,
Although my lute and I have done.

May chance thee lie withered and old
In winter nights that are so cold,
Playning in vain unto the moon;
Thy wishes then dare not be told,
Care then who list, for I have done.

And then may chance thee to repent
The time that thou hast lost and spent
To cause thy lovers sigh and swoon;
Then shalt thou know beauty but lent,
And wish and want, as I have done.

Now cease, my lute, this is the last
Labour that thou and I shall waste,
And ended is that we begun.
Now is the song both sung and past.
My lute, be still, for I have done.

Farewell to the Faithless

What should I say,
    Since faith is dead,
And truth away
    From you is fled?
    Should I be led
       With doubleness?
       Nay, nay, mistress.

I promised you,
    And you promised me,
To be as true,
    As I would be.
    But since I see
       Your double heart,
       Farewell my part.

Though for to take
  It is not my mind,
But to forsake
  One so unkind,
  And as I find
    So will I trust,
    Farewell, unjust.

Can ye say nay,
  But that you said
That I always
  Should be obeyed?
  And thus betrayed,
    Or that I wist,
    Farewell, unkissed.

'Is it possible . . .'

Is it possible
  That so high debate,
  So sharp, so sore, and of such rate,
  Should end so soon that was begun so late?
Is it possible?

Is it possible
  So cruel intent,
  So hasty heat and so soon spent,
  From love to hate, and thence for to relent?
Is it possible?

Is it possible
  That any may find
  Within one heart so diverse mind,
  To change or turn as weather and wind?
Is it possible?

Is it possible
    To spy it in an eye
    That turns as oft as chance on die,
    The truth whereof can any try,
Is it possible?

Is it possible
    For to turn so oft,
    To bring that lowest that was most aloft,
    And to fall highest, yet to light soft.
Is it possible.

All is possible,
    Who so list believe;
    Trust therefore, first, and after preve,
    As men wed ladies by licence and leave,
All is possible.

HENRY HOWARD, EARL OF SURREY
(c. 1517–1547)

Description of Spring

The soote season, that bud and bloom forth brings,
With green hath clad the hill, and eke the vale:
The nightingale with feathers new she sings;
The turtle to her mate hath told her tale;
Summer is come, for every spray now springs,
The hart hath hung his old head on the pale;
The buck in brake his winter coat he flings;
The fishes float with new repaired scale;
The adder all her slough away she slings;
The swift swallow pursueth the flies small;
The busy bee her honey now she mings;
Winter is worn that was the flowers' bale.
    And thus I see among these pleasant things
    Each care decays, and yet my sorrow springs.

The Means to attain a Happy Life

My friend, the things that do attain
　　The happy life be these, I find;
The riches left, not got with pain;
　　The fruitful ground, the quiet mind;

The equal friend; no grudge, no strife;
　　No charge of rule, nor governance;
Without disease the healthy life;
　　The household of continuance;

The mean diet, no dainty fare;
　　Wisdom joined with simpleness;
The night discharged of all care,
　　Where wine the wit may not oppress;

The faithful wife, without debate;
　　Such sleeps as may beguile the night;
　　Content thyself with thine estate;
　　Neither wish death, nor fear his might.

NICHOLAS BRETON
(c. 1545–c. 1626)

A Country Song

In the merry month of May,
In a morn by break of day,
Forth I walked by the wood side,
Whereas May was in his pride.
There I spied all alone
Phyllida and Corydon.
Much ado there was, God wot,
He would love and she would not.

She said, never man was true;
He said, none was false to you.
He said, he had loved her long;
She said, love should have no wrong.
Corydon would kiss her then;
She said, maids must kiss no men,
Till they did for good and all.
Then she made the shepherd call
All the heavens to witness truth,
Never loved a truer youth.
Thus with many a pretty oath,
Yea and nay, and faith and troth,
Such as silly shepherds use,
When they will not love abuse,
Love, which had been long deluded,
Was with kisses sweet concluded:
And Phyllida with garlands gay
Was made the Lady of the May.

EDMUND SPENSER
(c. 1552–1599)

To His Love (i)

Mark when she smiles with amiable cheer,
    And tell me whereto can ye liken it:
    When on each eyelid sweetly do appear
    An hundred graces as in shade to sit.
Likest it seemeth in my simple wit
    Unto the fair sunshine in summer's day:
    That when a dreadful storm away is flit,
    Through the broad world doth spread his goodly ray:
At sight whereof each bird that sits on spray,
    And every beast that to his den was fled

Comes forth afresh out of their late dismay,
And to the light lift up their drooping head.
So my storm beaten heart likewise is cheered,
  With that sunshine when cloudy looks are cleared.
                              [From *Amoretti*. Sonnet XL]

Easter Day

Most glorious Lord of life, that on this day,
  Didst make Thy triumph over death and sin:
  And having harrow'd hell, didst bring away
  Captivity thence captive, us to win:
This joyous day, dear Lord, with joy begin,
  And grant that we for whom Thou diddest die
  Being with Thy dear blood clean wash'd from sin,
  May live for ever in felicity.
And that Thy love we weighing worthily,
  May likewise love Thee for the same again:
  And for Thy sake that all like dear didst buy,
  With love may one another entertain.
So let us love, dear love, like as we ought,
  Love is the lesson which the Lord us taught.
                           [From *Amoretti*. Sonnet LXVIII]

To His Love (ii)

One day I wrote her name upon the strand,
  But came the waves and washed it away:
Again I wrote it with a second hand,
  But came the tide, and made my pains his prey.
Vain man, said she, that doest in vain assay
  A mortal thing so to immortalize,
  For I myself shall like to this decay,
  And eek my name be wiped out likewise.
Not so (quoth I), let baser things devise
  To die in dust, but you shall live by fame:

My verse your virtues rare shall eternize,
And in the heavens write your glorious name.
Where whenas Death shall all the world subdue,
Our love shall live, and later life renew.

[From *Amoretti*. Sonnet LXXV

Epithalamium

Ye learned sisters which have oftentimes
Been to me aiding, others to adorn,
Whom ye thought worthy of your graceful rimes,
That even the greatest did not greatly scorn
To hear their names sung in your simple lays,
But joyed in their praise:
And when ye list your own mishaps to mourn,
Which death, or love, or fortune's wreck did raise,
Your string could soon to sadder tenour turn,
And teach the woods and waters to lament
Your doleful dreariment;
Now lay those sorrowful complaints aside,
And having all your heads with garland crowned,
Help me mine own love's praises to resound,
Ne let the same of any be envied:
So Orpheus did for his own bride,
So I unto myself alone will sing;
The woods shall to me answer and my echo ring.

Early before the world's light-giving lamp
His golden beam upon the hills doth spread,
Having dispersed the night's uncheerful damp,
Do ye awake, and with fresh lustihead
Go to the bower of my beloved love,
My truest turtle dove;
Bid her awake; for Hymen is awake,
And long since ready forth his mask to move,
With his bright tead that flames with many a flake,

And many a bachelor to wait on him,
In their fresh garments trim.
Bid her awake therefore and soon her dight,
For lo! the wished day is come at last,
That shall for all the pains and sorrows past
Pay to her usury of long delight;
And whilst she doth her dight,
Do ye to her of joy and solace sing,
That all the woods may answer and your echo ring.

Bring with you all the nymphs that you can hear
Both of the rivers and the forests green,
And of the sea that neighbours to her near,
All with gay garlands goodly well beseen.
And let them also with them bring in hand
Another gay garland
For my fair love of lilies and of roses,
Bound true-love-wise with a blue silk ribband.
And let them make great store of bridal posies,
And let them eke bring store of other flowers
To deck the bridal bowers.
And let the ground whereas her foot shall tread,
For fear the stones her tender foot should wrong,
Be strewed with fragrant flowers all along,
And diapered like the discoloured mead.
Which done, do at her chamber door await,
For she will waken straight,
The whiles do ye this song unto her sing;
The woods shall to you answer and your echo ring.

Ye nymphs of Mulla, which with careful heed
The silver scaly trouts do tend full well,
And greedy pikes which use therein to feed,
(Those trouts and pikes all others do excel)
And ye likewise which keep the rushy lake,
Where none do fishes take,
Bind up the locks the which hang scattered light,

And in his waters, which your mirror make,
Behold your faces as the crystal bright,
That when you come whereas my love doth lie,
No blemish she may spy.
And eke ye lightfoot maids which keep the deer,
That on the hoary mountain use to tower,
And the wild wolves, which seek them to devour,
With your steel darts do chase from coming near,
Be also present here,
To help to deck her and to help to sing,
That all the woods may answer and your echo ring.

Wake now, my love, awake; for it is time;
The rosy morn long since left Tithon's bed,
All ready to her silver coach to climb,
And Phoebus 'gins to shew his glorious head.
Hark how the cheerful birds do chant their lays
And carol of love's praise.
The merry lark her matins sings aloft,
The thrush replies, the mavis descant plays,
The ouzel shrills, the ruddock warbles soft,
So goodly all agree with sweet consent,
To this day's merriment.
Ah! my dear love, why do ye sleep thus long,
When meeter were that ye should now awake,
T' await the coming of your joyous make,
And hearken to the birds' love-learned song,
The dewy leaves among?
For they of joy and pleasance to you sing,
That all the woods them answer and their echo ring.

My love is now awake out of her dream,
And her fair eyes, like stars that dimmed were
With darksome cloud, now shew their goodly beams
More bright than Hesperus his head doth rear.
Come now ye damsels, daughters of delight,
Help quickly her to dight,

But first come ye, fair hours, which were begot
In love's sweet paradise, of day and night,
Which do the seasons of the year allot,
And all that ever in this world is fair
Do make and still repair.
And ye three handmaids of the Cyprian queen,
The which do still adorn her beauty's pride,
Help to adorn my beautifullest bride;
And as ye her array, still throw between
Some graces to be seen,
And as ye use to Venus, to her sing,
The whiles the woods shall answer and your echo ring.

 Now is my love all ready forth to come;
Let all the virgins therefore well await,
And ye fresh boys that tend upon her groom
Prepare yourselves; for he is coming straight.
Set all your things in seemly good array
Fit for so joyful day,
The joyful'st day that ever sun did see.
Fair sun, shew forth thy favourable ray,
And let thy lifeful heat not fervent be,
For fear of burning her sunshiny face,
Her beauty to disgrace.
O fairest Phoebus, father of the Muse,
If ever I did honour thee aright,
Or sing the thing, that mote thy mind delight,
Do not thy servant's simple boon refuse,
But let this day, let this one day, be mine,
Let all the rest be thine.
Then I thy sovereign praises loud will sing,
That all the woods shall answer and their echo ring.

 Hark how the minstrels 'gin to shrill aloud
Their merry music that resounds from far,
The pipe, the tabor, and the trembling crowd,
That well agree withouten breach or jar,

But most of all the damsels do delight,
When they their timbrels smite,
And thereunto do dance and carol sweet,
That all the senses they do ravish quite,
The whiles the boys run up and down the street,
Crying aloud with strong confused noise,
As if it were one voice.
Hymen, lo Hymen, Hymen, they do shout,
That even to the heavens their shouting shrill
Doth reach, and all the firmament doth fill,
To which the people standing all about,
As in approvance do thereto applaud
And loud advance her laud,
And evermore they Hymen, Hymen, sing,
That all the woods them answer and their echo ring.

Lo! where she comes along with portly pace
Like Phoebe from her chamber of the east,
Arising forth to run her mighty race,
Clad all in white, that seems a virgin best.
So well it her beseems that ye would ween
Some angel she had been.
Her long loose yellow locks like golden wire,
Sprinkled with pearl, and pearling flowers a-tween,
Do like a golden mantle her attire,
And being crowned with a garland green,
Seem like some maiden queen.
Her modest eyes abashed to behold
So many gazers, as on her do stare,
Upon the lowly ground affixed are.
Ne dare lift up her countenance too bold,
But blush to hear her praises sung so loud,
So far from being proud.
Nathless do ye still loud her praises sing,
That all the woods may answer and your echo ring.

Tell me, ye merchants' daughters, did ye see
So fair a creature in your town before,

So sweet, so lovely, and so mild as she,
Adorned with beauty's grace and virtue's store?
Her goodly eyes like sapphires shining bright,
Her forehead ivory white,
Her cheeks like apples which the sun hath rudded,
Her lips like cherries charming men to bite,
Her breast like to a bowl of cream uncrudded,
Her paps like lilies budded,
Her snowy neck like to a marble tower,
And all her body like a palace fair,
Ascending up with many a stately stair,
To honour's seat and chastity's sweet bower.
Why stand ye still, ye virgins, in amaze,
Upon her so to gaze,
Whiles ye forget your former lay to sing,
To which the woods did answer and your echo ring?

But if ye saw that which no eyes can see,
The inward beauty of her lively spright,
Garnished with heavenly gifts of high degree,
Much more then would ye wonder at that sight,
And stand astonished like to those which read
Medusa's mazeful head.
There dwells sweet love and constant chastity,
Unspotted faith and comely womanhood,
Regard of honour and mild modesty;
There virtue reigns as queen in royal throne,
And giveth laws alone,
The which the base affections do obey,
And yield their services unto her will;
Ne thought of thing uncomely ever may
Thereto approach to tempt her mind to ill.
Had ye once seen these her celestial treasures,
And unrevealed pleasures.
Then would ye wonder and her praises sing,
That all the woods should answer and your echo ring.

Open the temple gates unto my love,
Open them wide that she may enter in,
And all the posts adorn as doth behove,
And all the pillars deck with garlands trim,
For to receive this saint with honour due,
That cometh in to you,
With trembling steps and humble reverence,
She cometh in, before th' Almighty's view.
Of her ye virgins learn obedience,
When so ye come into those holy places,
To humble your proud faces:
Bring her up to th' high altar, that she may
The sacred ceremonies there partake,
The which do endless matrimony make,
And let the roaring organs loudly play
The praises of the Lord in lively notes,
The whiles with hollow throats
The choristers the joyous anthem sing,
That all the woods may answer and their echo ring.

Behold whiles she before the altar stands,
Hearing the holy priest that to her speaks
And blesseth her with his two happy hands,
How the red roses flush up in her cheeks,
And the pure snow with goodly vermeil stain,
Like crimson dyed in grain,
That even th' angels which continually
About the sacred altar do remain,
Forget their service and about her fly,
Oft peeping in her face that seems more fair,
The more they on it stare.
But her sad eyes, still fastened on the ground,
Are governed with goodly modesty,
That suffers not one look to glance awry,
Which may let in a little thought unsound.
Why blush ye, love, to give to me your hand,
The pledge of all our band?

Sing, ye sweet angels, Alleluia sing,
That all the woods may answer and your echo ring.

Now all is done; bring home the bride again,
Bring home the triumph of our victory,
Bring home with you the glory of her gain,
With joyance bring her and with jollity.
Never had man more joyful day than this,
Whom heaven would heap with bliss.
Make feast therefore now all this live-long day,
This day for ever to me holy is;
Pour out the wine without restraint or stay,
Pour not by cups, but by the bellyful,
Pour out to all that wull,
And sprinkle all the posts and walls with wine,
That they may sweat and drunken be withal.
Crown ye god Bacchus with a coronal,
And Hymen also crown with wreaths of vine,
And let the Graces dance unto the rest;
For they can do it best:
The whiles the maidens do their carol sing,
To which the woods shall answer and their echo ring.

Ring ye the bells, ye young men of the town,
And leave your wonted labours for this day:
This day is holy; do ye write it down,
That ye for ever it remember may.
This day the sun is in his chiefest height,
With Barnaby the bright,
From whence declining daily by degrees,
He somewhat loseth of his heat and light,
When once the Crab behind his back he sees.
But for this time it ill ordained was,
To choose the longest day in all the year,
And shortest night, when longest fitter were:
Yet never day so long, but late would pass.
Ring ye the bells, to make it wear away,

And bonfires make all day,
And dance about them, and about them sing,
That all the woods may answer and your echo ring.

   Ah! when will this long weary day have end,
And lend me leave to come unto my love?
How slowly do the hours their numbers spend!
How slowly does sad Time his feathers move!
Haste thee, O fairest planet, to thy home
Within the western foam;
Thy tired steeds long since have need of rest.
Long though it be, at last I see it gloom,
And the bright evening star with golden crest
Appear out of the east.
Fair child of beauty, glorious lamp of love
That all the host of heaven in ranks dost lead,
And guidest lovers through the nightës dread,
How cheerfully thou lookest from above,
And seem'st to laugh atween thy twinkling light,
As joying in the sight
Of these glad many which for joy do sing,
That all the wood them answer and their echo ring.

   Now cease, ye damsels, your delights forepast;
Enough is it, that all the day was yours;
Now day is done, and night is nighing fast;
Now bring the bride into the bridal bowers.
Now night is come, now soon her disarray,
And in her bed her lay;
Lay her in lilies and in violets,
And silken curtains over her display,
And odoured sheets, and Arras coverlets.
Behold how goodly my fair love does lie
In proud humility;
Like unto Maia, when as Jove her took,
In Tempe, lying on the flowery grass,
'Twixt sleep and wake, after she weary was,

With bathing in the Acidalian brook.
Now it is night, ye damsels may be gone,
And leave my love alone,
And leave likewise your former lay to sing;
The woods no more shall answer, nor your echo ring.

Now welcome, night, thou night so long expected,
That long day's labour dost at last defray,
And all my cares, which cruel love collected,
Hast summed in one, and cancelled for aye:
Spread thy broad wing over my love and me,
That no man may us see,
And in thy sable mantle us enwrap,
From fear of peril and foul horror free.
Let no false treason seek us to entrap,
Nor any dread disquiet once annoy
The safety of our joy:
But let the night be calm and quietsome,
Without tempestuous storms or sad affray;
Like as when Jove with fair Alcmena lay,
When he begot the great Tirynthian groom;
Or like as when he with thyself did lie,
And begot majesty.
And let the maids and young men cease to sing;
Ne let the woods them answer, nor their echo ring.

Let no lamenting cries, nor doleful tears,
Be heard all night within nor yet without;
Ne let false whispers, breeding hidden fears,
Break gentle sleep with misconceived doubt.
Let no deluding dreams nor dreadful sights
Make sudden sad affrights;
Ne let housefires, nor lightning's helpless harms,
Ne let the Puck, nor other evil sprights,
Ne let mischievous witches with their charms,
Ne let hobgoblins, names whose sense we see not,
Fray us with things that be not.

Let not the screech owl, nor the stork be heard;
Nor the night raven that still deadly yells,
Nor damned ghosts called up with mighty spells,
Nor grisly vultures make us once affeared:
Ne let th' unpleasant quire of frogs still croaking
Make us to wish their choking.
Let none of these their dreary accents sing;
Ne let the woods them answer, nor their echo ring.

But let still silence true night watches keep,
That sacred peace may in assurance reign,
And timely sleep, when it is time to sleep,
May pour his limbs forth on your pleasant plain,
The whiles as hundred little winged loves,
Like divers feathered doves,
Shall fly and flutter round about your bed,
And in the secret dark, that none reproves,
Their pretty stealths shall work, and snares shall spread
To filch away sweet snatches of delight,
Concealed through covert night.
Ye sons of Venus, play your sports at will,
For greedy pleasure, careless of your toys,
Thinks more upon her paradise of joys,
That what ye do, albeit good or ill,
All night therefore attend your merry play,
For it will soon be day:
Now none doth hinder you, that say or sing;
Ne will the woods now answer, nor your echo ring.

Who is the same, which at my window peeps,
Or whose is that fair face, that shines so bright?
Is it not Cynthia, she that never sleeps,
But walks about high heaven all the night?
O fairest goddess, do thou not envy
My love with me to spy;
For thou likewise didst love, though now unthought,
And for a fleece of wool, which privily

The Latmian shepherd once unto thee brought,
His pleasures with thee wrought.
Therefore to us be favourable now;
And sith of women's labours thou hast charge,
And generation goodly dost enlarge,
Incline thy will t' effect our wishful vow,
And the chaste womb inform with timely seed,
That may our comfort breed:
Till which we cease our hopeful hap to sing;
Ne let the woods us answer, nor our echo ring.

And thou great Juno, which with awful might
The laws of wedlock still dost patronize,
And the religion of the faith first plight
With sacred rites hast taught to solemnize,
And eke for comfort often called art
Of women in their smart,
Eternally bind thou this lovely band,
And all thy blessings unto us impart.
And thou glad Genius, in whose gentle hand
The bridal bower and genial bed remain,
Without blemish or stain,
And the sweet pleasures of their love's delight
With secret aid dost succour and supply,
Till they bring forth the fruitful progeny,
Send us the timely fruit of this same night.
And thou fair Hebe, and thou Hymen free,
Grant that it may so be.
Till which we cease your further praise to sing,
Ne any woods shall answer, nor your echo ring.

And ye high heavens, the temple of the gods,
In which a thousand torches flaming bright
Do burn, that to us wretched earthly clods
In dreadful darkness lend desired light;
And all ye powers which in the same remain,
More than we men can feign,

Pour out your blessing on us plenteously,
And happy influence upon us rain,
That we may raise a large posterity,
Which from the earth, which they may long possess,
With lasting happiness,
Up to your haughty palaces may mount,
And for the guerdon of their glorious merit
May heavenly tabernacles there inherit,
Of blessed saints for to increase the count.
So let us rest, sweet love, in hope of this,
And cease till then our timely joys to sing;
The woods no more us answer, nor our echo ring.

Song, made in lieu of many ornaments,
With which my love should duly have been decked,
Which cutting off through hasty accidents,
Ye would not stay your due time to expect,
But promised both to recompense,
Be unto her a goodly ornament,
And for short time an endless monument.

The Garden of Adonis

In that same Garden all the goodly flowers,
Wherewith Dame Nature doth her beautify,
And decks the garlands of her paramours,
Are fetched: there is the first seminary
Of all things, that are born to live and die,
According to their kinds. Long work it were,
Here to account the endless progeny
Of all the weeds, that bud and blossom there;
But so much as doth need, must needs be counted here.

It sited was in fruitful soil of old,
And girt in with two walls on either side;
The one of iron, the other of bright gold,
That none might thorough break, nor overstride:

And double gates it had, which opened wide,
By which both in and out men moten pass;
Th' one fair and fresh, the other old and dried:
Old Genius the porter of them was,
Old Genius, the which a double nature has.

He letteth in, he letteth out to wend,
All that to come into the world desire;
A thousand thousand naked babes attend
About him day and night, which do require,
That he with fleshly weeds would them attire:
Such as him list, such as eternal fate
Ordained hath, he clothes with sinful mire,
And sendeth forth to live in mortal state,
Till they again return back by the hinder gate.

After that they again returned been,
They in that Garden planted be again;
And grow afresh, as they had never seen
Fleshly corruption, nor mortal pain.
Some thousand years so do they there remain;
And then of him are clad with other hue,
Or sent into the changeful world again,
Till thither they return, where first they grew:
So like a wheel around they run from old to new.

Ne needs there Gardener to set, or sow,
To plant or prune: for of their own accord
All things, as they created were, do grow,
And yet remember well the mighty word,
Which first was spoken by th' Almighty Lord,
That bade them to increase and multiply:
Ne do they need with water of the ford,
Or of the clouds to moisten their roots dry;
For in themselves eternal moisture they imply.

Infinite shapes of creatures there are bred,
And uncouth forms, which none yet ever knew,

And every sort is in a sundry bed
Set by itself, and rank'd in comely rew:
Some fit for reasonable souls t' indue,
Some made for beasts, some made for birds to wear,
And all the fruitful spawn of fishes hue
In endless ranks along enranged were,
That seem'd the Ocean could not contain them there.

Daily they grow, and daily forth are sent
Into the world, it to replenish more;
Yet is the stock not lessened, nor spent,
But still remains in everlasting store,
As it at first created was of yore.
For in the wide womb of the world there lies,
In hateful darkness, and in deep horror,
An huge eternal Chaos which supplies
The substances of nature's fruitful progenies.

All things from thence do their first being fetch,
And borrow matter, whereof they are made,
Which when as form and feature it does ketch,
Becomes a body, and doth then invade
The state of life, out of the grisly shade.
That substance is eterne, and bideth so,
Ne when the life decays, and form does fade,
Doth it consume, and into nothing go,
But changed is, and often altered to and fro.

The substance is not changed, nor altered,
But th' only form and outward fashion;
For every substance is conditioned
To change her hue, and sundry forms to don,
Meet for her temper and complexion:
For forms are variable and decay,
By course of kind, and by occasion;
And that fair flower of beauty fades away,
As doth the lily fresh before the sunny ray.

Great enemy to it, and to all the rest,
That in the Garden of Adonis springs,
Is wicked Time, who with his scythe addrest,
Does mow the flow'ring herbs and goodly things,
And all their glory to the ground down flings,
Where they do wither, and are foully marr'd:
He flies about, and with his flaggy wings
Beats down both leaves and buds without regard,
Ne ever pity may relent his malice hard.

Yet pity often did the gods relent,
To see so fair things marr'd, and spoiled quite;
And their great Mother Venus did lament
The loss of her dear brood, her dear delight:
Her heart was pierc'd with pity at the sight,
When walking through the Garden, them she spied,
Yet no'te she finds redress for such despite.
For all that lives, is subject to that law:
All things decay in time, and to their end do draw.

But were it not, that Time their troubler is,
All that in this delightful Garden grows,
Should happy be, and have immortal bliss;
For here all plenty and all pleasure flows,
And sweet love gentle fits amongst them throws,
Without fell rancour, or fond jealousy;
Frankly each paramour his leman knows,
Each bird his mate, ne any does envy
Their goodly merriment, and gay felicity.

There is continual spring, and harvest there
Continual, both meeting at one time:
For both the boughs do laughing blossoms bear,
And with fresh colours deck the wanton prime,
And eke attonce the heavy trees they climb,
Which seem to labour under their fruit's load:
The whiles the joyous birds make their pastime

Amongst the shady leaves, their sweet abode,
And their true loves without suspicion tell abroad.

Right in the middest of that Paradise,
There stood a stately Mount, on whose round top
A gloomy grove of myrtle trees did rise,
Whose shady boughs sharp steel did never lop,
Nor wicked beats their tender buds did crop,
But like a garland compassed the height,
And from their fruitful sides sweet gum did drop,
That all the ground with precious dew bedight,
Threw forth most dainty odours, and most sweet delight.

And in the thickest covert of that shade,
There was a pleasant arbour, not by art,
But of the trees' own inclination made,
Which knitting their rank branches part to part,
With wanton ivy twine entrail'd athwart,
And eglantine, and caprifole among,
Fashion'd above within their inmost part,
That neither Phoebus' beams could through
    them throng,
Nor Aeolus' sharp blast could work them any wrong.
                    [From *The Faerie Queene.* Book III. Canto VI]

SIR WALTER RALEGH
(c. 1552–1618)

'*As you came from the holy land . . .*'

'As you came from the holy land
    Of Walsingham,
Met you not with my true love
    By the way as you came?'

'How shall I know your true love,
    That have met many one,
 As I went to the holy land,
    That have come, that have gone?'

'She is neither white nor brown,
    But as the heavens fair;
 There is none hath a form so divine
    In the earth or the air.'

'Such an one did I meet, good sir,
    Such an angelic face,
 Who like a queen, like a nymph, did appear,
    By her gate, by her grace.'

'She hath left me here all alone,
    All alone, as unknown,
 Who sometimes did me lead with herself,
    And me loved as her own.'

'What's the cause that she leaves you alone,
    And a new way doth take,
 Who loved you once as her own,
    And her joy did you make?'

'I have loved her all my youth,
    But now old, as you see:
 Love likes not the falling fruit
    From the withered tree.

'Know that Love is a careless child,
    And forgets promise past;
 He is blind, he is deaf when he list,
    And in faith never fast.

'His desire is a dureless content,
    And a trustless joy;
 He is won with a world of despair,
    And is lost with a toy.

'Of womenkind such indeed is the love,
　　Or the word love abused,
Under which many childish desires
　　And conceits are excused.

'But true love is a durable fire,
　　In the mind ever burning,
Never sick, never old, never dead,
　　From itself never turning.'

'Even such is Time . . .'

Even such is Time, that takes in trust
　　Our youth, our joys, our all we have,
And pays us but with earth and dust;
　　Who, in the dark and silent grave,
When we have wandered all our ways,
Shuts up the story of our days;
But from this earth, this grave, this dust,
My God shall raise me up, I trust.

[Found in his Bible after his death]

SIR PHILIP SIDNEY
(1554–1586)

He Seeks Inspiration to Write Worthily to his Love

Loving in truth, and fain my love in verse to show,
That the dear She might take some pleasure of my pain:
Pleasure might cause her read, reading might make her know,
Knowledge might pity win, and pity grace obtain,
I sought fit words, to paint the blackest face of woe,
Studying inventions fine, her wits to entertain,
Oft turning others' leaves, to see if thence would flow,
Some fresh and fruitful shower, upon my sunburnt brain.
But words came halting out, wanting Invention's stay,
Invention, Nature's child, fled stepdame Study's blows;
And others' feet still seem'd but strangers in my way;
Thus great with child to speak, and helpless in my throes,
Biting my tongue and pen, beating myself for spite,
'Fool,' said my Muse to me, 'look in thy heart and write.'

The Sleepless Lover

Come Sleep, O Sleep, the certain knot of peace,
The baiting place of wits, the balm of woe,
The poor man's wealth, the prisoner's release,
Th' indifferent judge between the high and low;
With shield of proof, shield me from out the prease
Of these fierce darts, Despair at me doth throw;
O make in me those civil wars to cease:
I will good tribute pay if thou do so.
Take thou of me smooth pillows, sweetest bed,
A chamber deaf of noise, and blind of light,
A rosy garland, and a weary head;
And if these things (as being thine in right)
Move not thy heavy grace, thou shalt in me,
(Livelier than else) rare Stella's image see.

49

'With how sad steps, O Moon . . .'

With how sad steps, O Moon, thou climb'st the skies!
How silently, and with how wan a face!
What! may it be that even in heavenly place
That busy archer with his sharp arrows tries?
Sure, if that long-with-love-acquainted eyes
  Can judge of love, thou feel'st a lover's case;
  I read it in thy looks; thy languished grace
To me, that feel the like, my state descries.
Then, even of fellowship, O Moon, tell me,
Is constant love deemed there but want of wit?
Are beauties there as proud as here they be?
Do they above love to be loved, and yet
  Those lovers scorn whom that love doth possess?
  Do they call virtue there ungratefulness?

'My true-love . . .'

My true-love hath my heart, and I have his,
By just exchange one for another given:
I hold his dear, and mine he cannot miss,
There never was a better bargain driven:
  My true-love hath my heart, and I have his.

His heart in me keeps him and me in one,
My heart in him his thoughts and senses guides:
He loves my heart, for once it was his own,
I cherish his because in me it bides:
  My true-love hath my heart, and I have his.

JOHN LYLY
(c. 1554–1606)

Cupid and Campaspe

Cupid and my Campaspe play'd
At cards for kisses; Cupid paid:
He stakes his quiver, bow, and arrows,
His mother's doves, and team of sparrows;
Loses them too; then down he throws
The coral of his lip, the rose
Growing on 's cheek (but none knows how);
With these, the crystal of his brow,
And then the dimple on his chin;
All these did my Campaspe win.
At last he set her both his eyes:
She won, and Cupid blind did rise.
    O Love, has she done this to thee?
    What shall, alas, become of me?

THOMAS LODGE
(c. 1557–1625)

The Sad Lover

The earth, late chok'd with showers,
    Is now array'd in green;
Her bosom springs with flowers,
    The air dissolves her teen:
The heavens laugh at her glory,
Yet bide I sad and sorry.

The woods are deck'd with leaves,
   And trees are clothed gay;
And Flora, crown'd with sheaves,
   With oaken boughs doth play:
Where I am clad in black,
The token of my wrack.

The birds upon the trees
   Do sing with pleasant voices,
And chant in their degrees
   Their loves and lucky choices:
When I, whilst they are singing,
With sighs mine arms am wringing.

The thrushes seek the shade,
   And I my fatal grave;
Their flight to heaven is made,
   My walk on earth I have:
They free, I thrall; they jolly,
I sad and pensive wholly.

My Phillis

My Phillis hath the morning sun
   At first to look upon her;
And Phillis hath morn-waking birds
   Her risings for to honour.
My Phillis hath prime-feather'd flowers
   That smile when she treads on them;
And Phillis hath a gallant flock
   That leaps since she doth own them.
But Phillis hath so hard a heart –
   Alas, that she should have it –
As yields no mercy to desert,
   Nor grace to those that crave it.
   Sweet sun, when thou look'st on,
   Pray her regard my moan;

Sweet birds, when you sing to her,
　　To yield some pity, woo her;
Sweet flowers, when as she treads on,
　　Tell her, her beauty deads one:
And if in life her love she nill agree me,
Pray her, before I die she will come see me.

SIR EDWARD DYER
(1550?–1607)

'My mind to me a kingdom is . . .'

My mind to me a kingdom is,
　　Such present joys therein I find
That it excels all other bliss
　　That earth affords or grows by kind:
Though much I want which most would have,
Yet still my mind forbids to crave.

No princely pomp, no wealthy store,
　　No force to win the victory,
No wily wit to salve a sore,
　　No shape to feed a loving eye;
To none of these I yield as thrall:
For why? My mind doth serve for all.

I see how plenty surfeits oft,
　　And hasty climbers soon do fall;
I see that those which are aloft
　　Mishap doth threaten most of all;
They get with toil, they keep with fear:
Such cares my mind could never bear.

Content to live, this is my stay;
  I seek no more than may suffice:
I press to bear no haughty sway;
  Look, what I lack my mind supplies:
Lo, thus I triumph like a king,
Content with that my mind doth bring.

Some have too much, yet still do crave;
  I little have, and seek no more.
They are but poor, though much they have,
  And I am rich with little store:
They poor, I rich; they beg, I give;
They lack, I leave; they pine, I live.

I laugh not at another's loss;
  I grudge not at another's pain;
No worldly waves my mind can toss;
  My state at one doth still remain:
I fear no foe, I fawn no friend;
I loathe not life, nor dread my end.

Some weigh their pleasure by their lust,
  Their wisdom by their rage of will;
Their treasure is their only trust;
  A cloaked craft their store of skill:
But all the pleasure that I find
Is to maintain a quiet mind.

My wealth is health and perfect ease;
  My conscience clear my chief defence;
I neither seek by bribes to please,
  Nor by deceit to breed offence:
Thus do I live; thus will I die;
Would all did so as well as I!

ROBERT SOUTHWELL
(c. 1561–1595)

The Burning Babe

As I in hoary winter's night stood shivering in the snow,
Surpris'd I was with sudden heat which made my heart to glow;
And lifting up a fearful eye to view what fire was near,
A pretty Babe all burning bright did in the air appear;
Who, scorched with excessive heat, such floods of tears did shed,
As though his floods should quench his flames which with his tears
   were fed.
'Alas!' quoth he, 'but newly born in fiery heats I fry,
Yet none approach to warm their hearts or feel my fire but I.
My faultless breast the furnace is, the fuel wounding thorns;
Love is the fire, and sighs the smoke, the ashes shame and scorns;
The fuel Justice layeth on, and Mercy blows the coals;
The metal in this furnace wrought are men's defiled souls;
For which, as now on fire I am to work them to their good,
So will I melt into a bath to wash them in my blood.'
With this he vanish'd out of sight and swiftly shrunk away,
And straight I called unto mind that it was Christmas Day.

HENRY CONSTABLE
(1562–1613)

Diaphenia

   Diaphenia like the daffadowndilly,
    White as the sun, fair as the lily,
Heigh ho, how I do love thee!
    I do love thee as my lambs
    Are beloved of their dams;
How blest were I if thou wouldst prove me

Diaphenia like the spreading roses,
That in thy sweets all sweets encloses,
Fair sweet, how I do love thee!
I do love thee as each flower
Loves the sun's life-giving power;
For dead, thy breath to life might move me.

Diaphenia like to all things blessed
When all thy praises are expressed,
Dear joy, how I do love thee!
As the birds do love the spring,
Or the bees their careful king:
Then in requite, sweet virgin, love me!

SAMUEL DANIEL
(1562–1619)

'Care-charmer Sleep ...'

Care-charmer Sleep, son of the sable Night,
Brother to Death, in silent darkness born,
Relieve my languish, and restore the light,
With dark forgetting of my cares return.
And let the day be time enough to mourn
The shipwreck of my ill-adventur'd youth;
Let waking eyes suffice to wail their scorn,
Without the torment of the night's untruth.
Cease, dreams, the images of day-desires,
To model forth the passions of the morrow;
Never let rising sun approve you liars,
To add more grief to aggravate my sorrow.
    Still let me sleep, embracing clouds in vain;
    And never wake to feel the day's disdain.

MICHAEL DRAYTON
(1563–1631)

'Stay, stay, sweet Time . . .'

Stay, stay, sweet Time; behold, or ere thou pass
From world to world, thou long hast sought to see,
That wonder now wherein all wonders be,
Where heaven beholds her in a mortal glass.
Nay, look thee, Time, in this celestial glass,
And thy youth past in this fair mirror see:
Behold world's beauty in her infancy.
What she was then, and thou, or ere she was.
Now pass on, Time: to after-worlds tell this,
Tell truly, Time, what in thy time hath been,
That they may tell more worlds what Time hath seen,
And Heaven may joy to think on past world's bliss.
    Here make a period, Time, and say, for me,
    She was the like that never was, nor never more shall be.

'Some Atheist . . .'

Some Atheist or vile Infidel in love,
When I do speak of thy divinity,
May blaspheme thus, and say I flatter thee,
And only write my skill in verse to prove.
See miracles, ye unbelieving! See
A dumb-born Muse, made to express the mind,
A cripple hand to write, yet lame by kind,
One by thy name, the other touching thee.
Blind were mine eyes, till they were seen of thine,
And mine ears deaf by thy fame healed be;
My vices cur'd by virtues sprung from thee,
My hopes reviv'd, which long in grave had lain:
    All unclean thoughts, foul spirits, cast out in me
    By thy great power, and by strong faith in thee.

Farewell to Love

Since there's no help, come let us kiss and part;
Nay I have done, you get no more of me;
And I am glad, yea, glad with all my heart,
That thus so cleanly I myself can free;
Shake hands for ever, cancel all our vows,
And when we meet at any time again,
Be it not seen in either of our brows
That we one jot of former love retain.
Now at the last gasp of love's latest breath,
When his pulse failing, passion speechless lies,
When faith is kneeling by his bed of death,
And innocence is closing up his eyes,
    Now if thou would'st, when all have given him over,
    From death to life thou might'st him yet recover.

CHRISTOPHER MARLOWE
(1564–1593)

The Aspiring Mind

Nature, that fram'd us of four elements
Warring within our breasts for regiment,
Doth teach us all to have aspiring minds:
Our souls, whose faculties can comprehend
The wondrous architecture of the world,
And measure every wandering planet's course,
Still climbing after knowledge infinite,
And always moving as the restless spheres,
Wills us to wear ourselves and never rest,
Until we reach the ripest fruit of all,
That perfect bliss and sole felicity,
The sweet fruition of an earthly crown.

[From the First Part of *Tamburlaine the Great*]

Beauty Inexpressible

What is beauty, saith my sufferings, then?
If all the pens that ever poets held
Had fed the feeling of their masters' thoughts,
And every sweetness that inspir'd their hearts,
Their minds, and muses on admired themes;
If all the heavenly quintessence they still
From their immortal flowers of poesy,
Wherein as in a mirror we perceive
The highest reaches of a human wit —
If these had made one poem's period,
And all combin'd in beauty's worthiness,
Yet should there hover in their restless heads
One thought, one grace, one wonder, at the least,
Which unto words no virtue can digest.

[From the First Part of *Tamburlaine the Great*]

WILLIAM SHAKESPEARE
(1564–1616)

The Seven Ages of Man

All the world's a stage,
And all the men and women merely players:
They have their exits and their entrances;
And one man in his time plays many parts,
His acts being seven ages. At first the infant,
Mewling and puking in the nurse's arms.
And then the whining school-boy, with his satchel,
And shining morning face, creeping like snail
Unwillingly to school. And then the lover
Sighing like furnace, with a woeful ballad

Made to his mistress' eyebrow. Then a soldier,
Full of strange oaths, and bearded like a pard,
Jealous in honour, sudden and quick in quarrel
Seeking the bubble reputation
Even in the cannon's mouth. And then the justice,
In fair round belly with good capon lin'd,
With eyes severe, and beard of formal cut,
Full of wise saws and modern instances;
And so he plays his part. The sixth age shifts
Into the lean and slipper'd pantaloon,
With spectacles on nose and pouch on side,
His youthful hose well sav'd, a world too wide
For his shrunk shank; and his big manly voice,
Turning again toward childish treble, pipes
And whistles in his sound. Last scene of all,
That ends this strange eventful history,
Is second childishness and mere oblivion
Sans teeth, sans eyes, sans taste, sans everything.

[From *As You Like It*]

Study

Why, all delights are vain; but that most vain,
Which with pain purchased doth inherit pain:
As, painfully to pore upon a book
　　To see the light of truth; while truth the while
Doth falsely blind the eyesight of his look:
　　Light seeking light doth light of light beguile:
So, ere you find where light in darkness lies,
Your light grows dark by losing of your eyes.
Study me how to please the eye indeed
　　By fixing it upon a fairer eye,
Who dazzling so, that eye shall be his heed
　　And give him light that it was blinded by.
Study is like the heaven's glorious sun
　　That will not be deep-search'd with saucy looks:
Small have continual plodders ever won

Save base authority from others' books.
These earthly godfathers of heaven's lights
    That give a name to every fixed star
Have no more profit of their shining nights
    That those that walk and wot not what they are.
Too much to know is to know nought but fame;
And every godfather can give a name.

                     [From *Love's Labour's Lost*]

'O Mistress mine . . .'

O Mistress mine, where are you roaming?
O stay and hear! your true-love's coming,
    That can sing both high and low.
Trip no further, pretty sweeting;
Journeys end in lovers' meeting.
    Every wise man's son doth know.

What is love? 'tis not hereafter;
Present mirth hath present laughter;
    What's to come is still unsure:
In delay there lies no plenty;
Then come kiss me, sweet and twenty,
    Youth's a stuff will not endure.

                     [From *Twelfth Night*]

'Shall I compare thee to a summer's day? . . .'

Shall I compare thee to a summer's day?
Thou art more lovely and more temperate:
Rough winds do shake the darling buds of May,
And summer's lease hath all too short a date:
Sometime too hot the eye of heaven shines
And often is his gold complexion dimmed;
And every fair from fair sometime declines,
By chance or nature's changing course untrimmed;
But thy eternal summer shall not fade

Nor lose possession of that fair thou owest;
Nor shall Death brag thou wanderest in his shade,
When in eternal lines to time thou growest:
    So long as men can breathe or eyes can see,
    So long lives this and this gives life to thee.

                    [*Sonnet* XVIII]

'When to the sessions of sweet silent thought . . .'

When to the sessions of sweet silent thought
I summon up remembrance of things past,
I sigh the lack of many a thing I sought,
And with old woes new wail my dear time's waste:
Then can I drown an eye, unused to flow,
For precious friends hid in death's dateless night,
And weep afresh love's long-since-cancell'd woe,
And moan the expense of many a vanish'd sight.
Then can I grieve at grievances foregone,
And heavily from woe to woe tell o'er
The sad account of fore-bemoanéd moan,
Which I new pay as if not paid before:
    But if the while I think on thee, dear friend,
    All losses are restored, and sorrows end.

                    [*Sonnet* XXX]

'Full many a glorious morning . . .'

Full many a glorious morning have I seen
Flatter the mountain-tops with sovereign eye,
Kissing with golden face the meadows green,
Gilding pale streams with heavenly alchemy;
Anon permit the basest clouds to ride
With ugly rack on his celestial face,
And from the forlorn world his visage hide,
Stealing unseen to west with this disgrace:
Even so my sun one early morn did shine
With all-triumphant splendour on my brow;

But out, alack! he was but one hour mine;
The region cloud hath masked him from me now.
    Yet him for this my love no white disdaineth;
    Suns of the world may stain when heaven's
        sun staineth.

                                        [*Sonnet* XXXIII]

'Tired with all these ...'

Tired with all these, for restful death I cry, –
As, to behold desert a beggar born,
And needy nothing trimmed in jollity,
And purest faith unhappily forsworn,
And gilded honour shamefully misplaced,
And maiden virtue rudely strumpeted,
And right perfection wrongfully disgraced,
And strength by limping sway disablèd,
And art made tongue-tied by authority,
And folly doctor-like controlling skill,
And simple truth miscalled simplicity,
And captive good attending captain ill:
    Tired with all these, from these would I be gone,
    Save that, to die, I leave my love alone.

                                        [*Sonnet* LXVI]

'That time of year ...'

That time of year thou mayst in me behold
When yellow leaves, or none, or few, do hang
Upon those boughs which shake against the cold,
Bare ruined choirs, where late the sweet birds sang.
In me thou see'st the twilight of such day
As after sunset fadeth in the west,
Which by and by black night doth take away,
Death's second self, that seals up all in rest.
In me thou see'st the glowing of such fire

That on the ashes of his youth doth lie,
As the death-bed whereon it must expire,
Consumed with that which it was nourished by.
    Thus thou perceiv'st, which makes thy love more
      strong,
    To love that well which thou must leave ere long.

                                  [*Sonnet* LXXIII]

'My Mistress' eyes . . .'

My Mistress' eyes are nothing like the sun;
Coral is far more red than her lips' red;
If snow be white, why then her breasts are dun;
If hairs be wires, black wires grow on her head.
I have seen roses damasked, red and white,
But no such roses see I in her cheeks;
And in some perfumes is there more delight
Than in the breath that from my mistress reeks.
I love to hear her speak, yet well I know
That music hath a far more pleasing sound;
I grant I never saw a goddess go;
My mistress, when she walks, treads on the ground:
    And yet, by heaven, I think my love as rare
    As any she belied with false compare.

                                  [*Sonnet* CXXX]

Love and Time

Let me not to the marriage of true minds
Admit impediments. Love is not love
Which alters when it alteration finds,
Or bends with the remover to remove:
O no! it is an ever-fixéd mark
That looks on tempests, and is never shaken;
It is the star to every wandering bark,
Whose worth's unknown, although his height be taken.

Love's not Time's fool, though rosy lips and cheeks
Within his bending sickle's compass come;
Love alters not with his brief hours and weeks,
But hears it out ev'n to the edge of doom: –
   If this be error, and upon me proved,
    I never writ, nor no man ever loved.

[*Sonnet* CXVI]

Imagination

The lunatic, the lover, and the poet,
Are of imagination all compact;
One sees more devils than vast hell can hold,
That is, the madman; the lover, all as frantic,
Sees Helen's beauty in a brow of Egypt:
The poet's eye, in a fine frenzy rolling,
Doth glance from heaven to earth, from earth
    to heaven;
And, as imagination bodies forth
The forms of things unknown, the poet's pen
Turns them to shapes, and gives to airy nothing
A local habitation and a name.

[From *A Midsummer Night's Dream*]

'The quality of mercy . . .'

The quality of mercy is not strain'd,
It droppeth as the gentle rain from heaven
Upon the place beneath: it is twice bless'd;
It blesseth him that gives and him that takes:
'Tis mightiest in the mightiest; it becomes
The throned monarch better than his crown;
His sceptre shows the force of temporal power,
The attribute to awe and majesty,
Wherein doth sit the dread and fear of kings;
But mercy is above this sceptred sway,

It is enthroned in the hearts of kings,
It is an attribute to God himself,
And earthly power doth then show likest God's
When mercy seasons justice.

[From *The Merchant of Venice*]

The Cares of Kingship

How many thousand of my poorest subjects
Are at this hour asleep! O sleep, O gentle sleep,
Nature's soft nurse, how have I frighted thee,
That thou no more wilt weigh my eyelids down
And steep my senses in forgetfulness?
Why rather, sleep, liest thou in smoky cribs,
Upon uneasy pallets stretching thee,
And hush'd with buzzing night-flies to thy slumber,
Than in the perfum'd chambers of the great,
Under the canopies of costly state,
And lull'd with sound of sweetest melody?
O thou dull god, why liest thou with the vile
In loathsome beds, and leavest the kingly couch
A watch-case or a common 'larum bell?
Wilt thou upon the high and giddy mast
Seal up the ship-boy's eyes, and rock his brains
In cradle of the rude imperious surge
And in the visitation of the winds,
Who take the ruffian billows by the top,
Curling their monstrous heads and hanging them
With deafening clamour in the slippery clouds,
That, with the hurly, death itself awakes?
Canst thou, O partial sleep, give thy repose
To the wet sea-boy in an hour so rude,
And in the calmest and most stillest night,
With all appliances and means to boot,
Deny it to a king? Then happy low, lie down!
Uneasy lies the head that wears a crown.

[From the Second Part of *Henry IV*]

'To be, or not to be . . .'

To be, or not to be: that is the question:
Whether 'tis nobler in the mind to suffer
The slings and arrows of outrageous fortune,
Or to take arms against a sea of troubles,
And by opposing end them? To die: to sleep;
No more; and, by a sleep to say we end
The heart-ache and the thousand natural shocks
That flesh is heir to, 'tis a consummation
Devoutly to be wish'd. To die, to sleep;
To sleep: perchance to dream: ay, there's the rub;
For in that sleep of death what dreams may come
When we have shuffled off this mortal coil,
Must give us pause. There's the respect
That makes calamity of so long life;
For who would bear the whips and scorns of time,
The oppressor's wrong, the proud man's contumely,
The pangs of dispriz'd love, the law's delay,
The insolence of office, and the spurns
That patient merit of the unworthy takes,
When he himself might his quietus make
With a bare bodkin? who would fardels bear,
To grunt and sweat under a weary life,
But that the dread of something after death,
The undiscover'd country from whose bourn
No traveller returns, puzzles the will,
And makes us rather bear those ills we have
Than fly to others that we know not of?
Thus conscience does makes cowards of us all;
And thus the native hue of resolution
Is sicklied o'er with the pale cast of thought,
And enterprises of great pith and moment
With this regard their currents turn awry,
And lose the name of action.

[From *Hamlet*]

Neglect of Degree

            Degree being vizarded,
The unworthiest shows as fairly in the mask.
The heavens themselves, the planets, and this centre,
Observe degree, priority, and place,
Insisture, course, proportion, season, form,
Office, and custom, in all line of order.
And therefore is the glorious planet Sol
In noble eminence enthroned and sphered
Amidst the other, whose medicinable eye
Corrects the ill aspects of planets evil,
And posts like the commandment of a king,
Sans check to good and bad. But when the planets
In evil mixture to disorder wander,
What plagues and what portents, what mutiny,
What raging of the sea, shaking of earth,
Commotion in the winds, frights, changes, horrors,
Divert and crack, rend and deracinate
The unity and married calm of states
Quite from their fixure! Oh, when degree is shaked,
Which is the ladder to all high designs,
The enterprise is sick! How could communities,
Degrees in schools, and brotherhoods in cities,
Peaceful commerce from dividable shores,
The primogenitive and due of birth,
Prerogative of age, crowns, sceptres, laurels,
But by degree, stand in authentic place?
Take but degree away, untune that string,
And hark, what discord follows! Each thing meets
In mere oppugnancy. The bounded waters
Should lift their bosoms higher than the shores,
And make a sop of all this solid globe.
Strength should be lord of imbecility,
And the rude son should strike his father dead.
Force should be right, or rather, right and wrong,

Between whose endless jar justice resides,
Should lose their names, and so should justice too.
Then everything includes itself in power,
Power into will, will into appetite,
And appetite, a universal wolf,
So doubly seconded with will and power,
Must make perforce a universal prey,
And last eat up himself.

[From *Troilus and Cressida*]

Capricious Time

ULYSSES ADVISES ACHILLES NOT TO LET
SLIP OPPORTUNITY

Time hath, my Lord, a wallet at his back,
Wherein he puts alms for oblivion,
A great-siz'd monster of ingratitudes:
Those scraps are good deeds past; which are devour'd
As fast as they are made, forgot as soon
As done: perseverance, dear my Lord,
Keeps honour bright: to have done, is to hang
Quite of fashion, like a rusty mail
In monumental mockery. Take the instant way;
For honour travels in a strait so narrow
Where one but goes abreast: keep, then, the path;
For emulation hath a thousand sons
That one by one pursue: if you give way,
Or hedge aside from the direct forthright,
Like to an enter'd tide they all rush by
And leave you hindmost;
Or, like a gallant horse fall'n in first rank,
Lie there for pavement to the abject rear,
O'errun and trampled on: then what they do in present,
Though less than yours in past, must o'ertop yours;
For time is like a fashionable host,
That slightly shakes his parting guest by the hand,

And with his arms outstretched, as he would fly,
Grasps in the comer: welcome ever smiles,
And farewell goes out sighing. O! let not virtue seek
Remuneration for the thing it was;
For beauty, wit,
High birth, vigour of bone, desert in service,
Love, friendship, charity, are subjects all
To envious and calumniating time.
One touch of nature makes the whole world kin,
That all with one consent praise new-born gawds,
Though they are made and moulded of things past,
And give to dust that is a little gilt
More laud than gilt o'er-dusted.

                              [From *Troilus and Cressida*]

Antony's First Meeting with Cleopatra

The barge she sat in, like a burnish'd throne,
Burn'd on the water; the poop was beaten gold:
Purple the sails, and so perfumed that
The winds were love-sick with them; the oars were silver,
Which to the tune of flutes kept stroke, and made
The water which they beat to follow faster,
As amorous of their strokes. For her own person,
It beggar'd all description; she did lie
In her pavilion – cloth-of-gold of tissue –
O'er-picturing that Venus where we see
The fancy outwork nature; on each side her
Stood pretty-dimpled boys, like smiling Cupids,
With divers-colour'd fans, whose wind did seem
To glow the delicate cheeks which they did cool,
And what they undid did . . .
Her gentlewomen, like the Nereides,
So many mermaids, tended her i' the eyes,
And made their bends adornings; at the helm
A seeming mermaid steers; the silken tackle

Swell with the touches of those flower-soft hands,
That yarely frame the office. From the barge
A strange invisible perfume hits the sense
Of the adjacent wharfs. The city cast
Her people out upon her, and Antony,
Enthron'd i' the market-place, did sit alone,
Whistling to the air; which, but for vacancy,
Had gone to gaze on Cleopatra too
And made a gap in nature.

[From *Antony and Cleopatra*]

A Requiem

Fear no more the heat o' the sun
    Nor the furious winter's rages;
Thou thy worldly task hast done,
    Home art gone, and ta'en thy wages:
Golden lads and girls all must,
As chimney-sweepers, come to dust.

Fear no more the frown o' the great,
    Thou art past the tyrant's stroke;
Care no more to clothe and eat;
    To thee the reed is as the oak:
The sceptre, learning, physic, must
All follow this, and come to dust.

Fear no more the lightning-flash,
    Nor the all-dreaded thunder-stone;
Fear not slander, censure rash;
    Thou hast finish'd joy and moan:
All lovers young, all lovers must
Consign to thee, and come to dust.

[From *Cymbeline*]

Eternity through Poetry

Not marble, nor the gilded monuments
Of princes, shall outlive this powerful rime;
But you shall shine more bright in these contents
Than unswept stone, besmear'd with sluttish time.
When wasteful war shall statues overturn,
And broils root out the work of masonry,
Nor Mars his sword nor war's quick fire shall burn
The living record of your memory.
'Gainst death and all-oblivious enmity
Shall you pace forth; your praise shall still find room
Even in the eyes of all posterity
That wear this world out to the ending doom.
　　So, till the judgement that yourself arise,
　　You live in this, and dwell in lovers' eyes.

[*Sonnet* LV]

This Insubstantial Pageant

Our revels now are ended. These our actors,
As I foretold you, were all spirits and
Are melted into air, into thin air:
And, like the baseless fabric of this vision,
The cloud-capp'd towers, the gorgeous palaces,
The solemn temples, the great globe itself,
Yea, all which it inherit, shall dissolve
And, like this insubstantial pageant faded,
Leave not a rack behind. We are such stuff
As dreams are made on, and our little life
Is rounded with a sleep.

[From *The Tempest*]

THOMAS CAMPION
(1567–1620)

'Follow your saint . . .'

Follow your saint, follow with accents sweet;
Haste you, sad notes, fall at her flying feet.
There, wrapped in cloud of sorrow, pity move,
And tell the ravisher of my soul I perish for her love.
But if she scorns my never-ceasing pain,
Then burst with sighing in her sight, and ne'er return again.

All that I sung still to her praise did tend.
Still she was first, still she my songs did end.
Yet she my love and music doth both fly,
The music that her echo is, and beauty's sympathy.
Then let my notes pursue her scornful flight;
It shall suffice that they were breathed, and died for her
      delight.

'There is a garden . . .'

There is a garden in her face,
    Where roses and white lilies grow;
A heavenly paradise is that place,
    Wherein all pleasant fruits do flow.
There cherries grow which none can buy,
Till 'Cherry-ripe' themselves do cry.

Those cherries fairly do enclose
    Of orient pearl a double row,
Which when her lovely laughter shows,
    They look like rosebuds filled with snow.
Yet them nor peer nor prince can buy,
Till 'Cherry-ripe' themselves do cry.

Her eyes like angels watch them still,
   Her brows like bended bows do stand,
Threatening with piercing frowns to kill
   All that attempt with eye or hand
Those sacred cherries to come nigh,
Till 'Cherry-ripe' themselves do cry.

'When to her lute Corinna sings . . .'

When to her lute Corinna sings,
Her voice revives the leaden strings,
And doth in highest notes appear
As any challenged echo clear;
But when she doth of mourning speak,
Even with her sighs the strings do break.

And as her lute doth live or die,
Led by her passion, so must I:
For when of pleasure she doth sing,
My thoughts enjoy a sudden spring,
But if she doth of sorrow speak,
Even from my heart the strings do break.

'Rose-cheeked Laura, come . . .'

Rose-cheeked Laura, come;
Sing thou smoothly with thy beauty's
Silent music, either other
   Sweetly gracing.

Lovely forms do flow
From concent divinely framed;
Heaven is music, and thy beauty's
   Birth is heavenly.

These dull notes we sing
Discords need for helps to grace them,
Only beauty purely loving
    Knows no discord,

But still moves delight,
Like clear springs renewed by flowing,
Ever perfect, ever in them-
    selves eternal.

'Thou art not fair . . .'

Thou art not fair, for all thy red and white,
For all those rosy ornaments in thee;
Thou art not sweet, though made of mere delight,
Not fair nor sweet, unless thou pity me.
I will not soothe thy fancies: thou shalt prove
That beauty is no beauty without love.

Yet love not me, nor seek thou to allure
My thoughts with beauty, were it more divine:
Thy smiles and kisses I cannot endure,
I'll not be wrapt up in those arms of thine:
Now show it, if thou be a woman right, –
Embrace, and kiss, and love me, in despite!

SIR HENRY WOTTON
(1568–1639)

On his Mistress, the Queen of Bohemia

You meaner beauties of the night,
    Which poorly satisfy our eyes
More by your number than your light,
    You common people of the skies,
What are you, when the Moon shall rise?

Ye violets that first appear,
  By your pure purple mantles known
Like the proud virgins of the year
  As if the spring were all your own,
What are you, when the Rose is blown?

Ye curious chanters of the wood
  That warble forth dame Nature's lays,
Thinking your passions understood
  By your weak accents; what's your praise
When Philomel her voice doth raise?

So when my Mistress shall be seen
  In sweetness of her looks and mind,
By virtue first, then choice, a Queen,
  Tell me, if she were not design'd
Th' eclipse and glory of her kind?

The Character of a Happy Life

How happy is he born and taught
  That serveth not another's will;
Whose armour is his honest thought,
  And simple truth his utmost skill;

Whose passions not his masters are;
  Whose soul is still prepar'd for death,
Untied unto the world by care
  Of public fame or private breath;

Who envies none that chance doth raise,
  Nor vice; who never understood
How deepest wounds are given by praise;
  Nor rules of state, but rules of good;

Who hath his life from rumours freed,
    Whose conscience is his strong retreat;
Whose state can neither flatterers feed,
    Nor ruin make accusers great;

Who God doth late and early pray
    More of His grace than gifts to lend;
And entertains the harmless day
    With a well-chosen book or friend;

This man is freed from servile bands
    Of hope to rise, or fear to fall;
Lord of himself, though not of lands;
    And having nothing, yet hath all.

BEN JONSON
(1573–1637)

'*Still to be neat . . .*'

Still to be neat, still to be drest
As you were going to a feast;
Still to be powder'd, still perfum'd;
Lady, it is to be presum'd,
Though art's hid causes are not found,
All is not sweet, all is not sound.

Give me a look, give me a face
That makes simplicity a grace;
Robes loosely flowing, hair as free:
Such sweet neglect more taketh me
Than all th' adulteries of art;
They strike mine eyes, but not my heart.

To Celia

Drink to me only with thine eyes,
    And I will pledge with mine;
Or leave a kiss but in the cup
    And I'll not look for wine.
The thirst that from the soul doth rise
    Doth ask a drink divine;
But might I of Jove's nectar sup,
    I would not change for thine.

I sent thee late a rosy wreath,
    Not so much honouring thee
As giving it a hope that there
    It could not wither'd be;
But thou thereon didst only breathe,
    And sent'st it back to me;
Since when it grows, and smells, I swear,
    Not of itself, but thee!

i. *To Charis*

URGING HER TO KEEP HER PROMISE TO
DESCRIBE HER MAN

Charis one day in discourse
Had of Love, and of his force,
Lightly promis'd she would tell
What a man she could love well;
And that promise set on fire
All that heard her with desire.
With the rest, I long expected
When the work would be effected;
But we find that cold delay,
And excuse spun every day,
As, until she tell her one,
We all fear she loveth none.

Therefore, Charis, you must do 't,
For I will so urge you to 't,
You shall neither eat nor sleep,
No, nor forth your window peep,
With your emissary eye,
To fetch in the forms go by,
And pronounce, which band or lace
Better fits him than his face:
Nay, I will not let you sit
'Fore your idol glass a whit,
To say over every purl
 There; or to reform a curl;
Or with Secretary Cis
To consult, if fucus this
Be as good as was the last: –
All your sweet of life is past;
Make account, unless you can,
And that quickly, speak your Man.

ii. *Her Answer*

Of your trouble, BEN, to ease me,
I will tell what Man would please me.
I would have him, if I could,
Noble; or of greater blood;
Titles, I confess, do take me,
And a woman God did make me;
French to boot, at least in fashion,
And his manners of that nation.
   Young I'd have him too, and fair,
Yet a man; with crisped hair,
Cast in thousand snares or rings,
For Love's fingers, or his wings:
Chestnut colour, or more slack,
Gold, upon a ground of black.
Venus' or Minerva's eyes,
For he must look wanton-wise.

Eyebrows bent like Cupid's bow,
Front, an ample field of snow;
Even nose, and cheek withal,
Smooth as is the billiard-ball:
Chin as woolly as the peach;
And his lip should kissing teach,
Till he cherished too much beard,
And make Love or me afeard.

He should have a hand as soft
As the down, and show it oft;
Skin as smooth as any rush,
And so thin to see a blush
Rising through it ere it came;
All his blood should be a flame
Quickly fired, as in beginners
In Love's school, and yet no sinners.

'Twere too long to speak of all:
What we harmony do call
In a body should be there.
Well he should his clothes, too, wear,
Yet no tailor help to make him;
Drest, you still for man should take him.
And not think h' had eat a stake,
Or were set up in a brake.

Valiant he should be as fire,
Showing danger more than ire.
Bounteous as the clouds to earth,
And as honest as his birth;
All his actions to be such,
As to do no thing too much:
Nor o'er-praise not yet condemn,
Nor out-value, nor contemn;
Nor do wrongs, nor wrongs receive,
Nor tie knots, nor knots unweave;
And from baseness to be free,
As he durst love Truth and me.

Such a man, with every part,

I could give my very heart;
But of one if short he came,
I can rest me where I am.

The Hour Glass

Consider this small dust, here in the glass,
    By atoms mov'd:
Could you believe that this the body was
    Of one that lov'd;
And in his mistress' flame playing like a fly,
Was turned to cinders by her eye:
Yes; and in death, as life unblest,
    To have 't exprest,
Even ashes of lovers find no rest.

Song

That Women are but Men's Shadows

Follow a shadow, it still flies you,
    Seem to fly it, it will pursue:
So court a mistress, she denies you;
    Let her alone, she will court you.
Say, are not women truly, then,
Styled but the shadows of us men?

At morn and even shades are longest;
    At noon they are or short or none:
So men at weakest, they are strongest,
    But grant us perfect, they're not known.
Say, are not women truly, then,
Styled but the shadows of us men?

JOHN DONNE
(1573–1631)

Song

Go and catch a falling star,
    Get with child a mandrake root,
Tell me where all past years are,
    Or who cleft the devil's foot,
Teach me to hear mermaids singing,
Or to keep off envy's stinging,
        And find
        What wind
Serves to advance an honest mind.

If thou be'st born to strange sights,
    Things invisible to see,
Ride ten thousand days and nights,
    Till age snow white hairs on thee.
Thou, when thou return'st, wilt tell me,
All strange wonders that befell thee,
        And swear
        No where
Lives a woman true and fair.

If thou find'st one, let me know;
    Such a pilgrimage were sweet.
Yet do not, I would not go,
    Though at next door we might meet.
Though she were true when you met her,
And last till you write your letter,
        Yet she
        Will be
False, ere I come, to two or three.

The Indifferent

I can love both fair and brown;
Her whom abundance melts, and her whom want betrays;
Her who loves loneness best, and her who masks and plays;
Her whom the country formed, and whom the town;
Her who believes, and her who tries;
Her who still weeps with spongy eyes,
And her who is dry cork and never cries.
I can love her, and her, and you, and you;
I can love any, so she be not true.

Will no other vice content you?
Will it not serve your turn to do as did your mothers?
Or have you all old vices spent, and now would find out
    others?
Or doth a fear that men are true torment you?
O we are not, be not you so;
Let me – and do you – twenty know;
Rob me, but bind me not, and let me go.
Must I, who came to travel thorough you,
Grow your fixed subject, because you are true?

Venus heard me sigh this song;
And by love's sweetest part, variety, she swore,
She heard not this till now; it should be so no more.
She went, examined, and returned ere long,
And said, 'Alas! some two or three
Poor heretics in love there be,
Which think to stablish dangerous constancy.
But I have told them, "Since you will be true,
You shall be true to them who're false to you." '

The Good-Morrow

I wonder, by my troth, what thou and I
Did, till we lov'd? Were we not wean'd till then?
But suck'd on country pleasures, childishly?
Or snorted we in the Seven Sleepers' den?
'Twas so; but this, all pleasures fancies be;
If ever any beauty I did see,
Which I desir'd, and got, 'twas but a dream of thee.

And now good-morrow to our waking souls,
Which watch not one another out of fear;
For love all love of other sights controls,
And makes one little room an everywhere.
Let sea-discoverers to new worlds have gone;
Let maps to other, worlds on worlds have shown;
Let us possess one world; each hath one, and is one.

My face in thine eyes, thine in mine appears,
And true plain hearts do in the faces rest;
Where can we find two better hemispheres
Without sharp north, without declining west?
Whatever dies, was not mix'd equally;
If our two loves be one, or thou and I
Love so alike that none do slacken, none can die.

The Anniversary

All kings, and all their favourites,
All glory of honours, beauties, wits,
The sun itself, which makes times, as they pass,
Is elder by a year now than it was
When thou and I first one another saw.
All other things to their destruction draw,
    Only our love hath no decay;

This no to-morrow hath, nor yesterday.
Running it never runs from us away,
But truly keeps his first, last, everlasting day.

    Two graves must hide thine and my corse;
      If one might, death were no divorce.
Alas! as well as other princes, we
– Who prince enough in one another be –
Must leave at last in death these eyes and ears,
Oft fed with true oaths, and with sweet salt tears;
    But souls where nothing dwells but love
– All other thoughts being inmates – then shall prove
This or a love increasèd there above,
When bodies to their graves, souls from their graves
      remove.

    And then we shall be throughly blest;
      But we no more than all the rest.
Here upon earth we're kings, and none but we
Can be such kings, nor of such subjects be.
Who is so safe as we? where none can do
Treason to us, except one of us two.
    True and false fears let us refrain,
Let us love nobly, and live, and add again
Years and years unto years, till we attain
To write threescore; this is the second of our reign.

Love's Growth

    I scarce believe my love to be so pure
        As I had thought it was,
        Because it doth endure
Vicissitude, and season, as the grass;
Methinks I lied all winter, when I swore
My love was infinite, if spring make it more.

But if this medicine, love, which cures all sorrow
　　With more, not only be no quintessence,
　　But mix'd of all stuffs, vexing soul, or sense,
And of the sun his active vigour borrow,
Love's not so pure, and abstract, as they use
To say, which have no mistress but their Muse;
But as all else, being elemented too,
Love sometimes would contemplate, sometimes do.

And yet no greater, but more eminent,
　　Love by the spring is grown;
　　As in the firmament
Stars by the sun are not enlarged, but shown,
Gentle love deeds, as blossoms on a bough,
From love's awaken'd root do bud out now.

If, as in water stirr'd more circles be
　　Produced by one, love such additions take,
　　Those like so many spheres but one heaven make,
For they are all concentric unto thee;
And though each spring do add to love new heat,
As princes do in times of action get
New taxes, and remit them not in peace,
No winter shall abate the spring's increase.

The Funeral

Whoever comes to shroud me, do not harm
　　Nor question much
That subtle wreath of hair, which crowns my arm;
The mystery, the sign you must not touch;
For 'tis my outward soul,
Viceroy to that, which unto heaven being gone,
　　Will leave this to control
And keep these limbs, her provinces, from
　　dissolution.

For if the sinewy thread my brain lets fall
    Through every part
Can tie those parts, and make me one of all,
Those hairs which upward grew, and strength and art
    Have from a better brain,
Can better do 't; except she meant that I
    By this should know my pain,
As prisoners then are manacled, when they're
  condemn'd to die.

Whate'er she meant by it, bury it with me,
    For since I am
Love's martyr, it might breed idolatry,
If into others' hands these relics came.
    As 'twas humility
To afford to it all that a soul can do,
    So 'tis some bravery,
That since you would save none of me, I bury
  some of you.

The Relic

When my grave is broke up again
Some second guest to entertain,
  – For graves have learn'd that woman-head,
To be to more than one a bed –
    And he that digs it, spies
A bracelet of bright hair about the bone,
    Will not he let us alone,
And think that there a loving couple lies,
Who thought that this device might be some way
To make their souls at the last busy day
Meet at this grave, and make a little stay?

If this fall in a time, or land,
Where mass-devotion doth command,

Then he that digs us up will bring
    Us to the bishop or the king,
        To make us relics; then
Thou shalt be a Mary Magdalen, and I
        A something else thereby;
All women shall adore us, and some men.
And, since at such time miracles are sought,
I would have that age by this paper taught
What miracles we harmless lovers wrought.

First we loved well and faithfully,
    Yet knew not what we loved, nor why;
    Difference of sex we never knew,
    No more than guardian angels do;
        Coming and going we
Perchance might kiss, but not between those meals;
        Our hands ne'er touch'd the seals,
Which nature, injured by late law, sets free.
These miracles we did; but now alas!
All measure, and all language, I should pass,
Should I tell what a miracle she was.

'Sweetest love . . .'

Sweetest love, I do not go,
    For weariness of thee,
Nor in hope the world can show
    A fitter love for me;
        But since that I
At the last must part, 'tis best,
Thus to use myself in jest
    By feigned deaths to die.

Yesternight the sun went hence,
    And yet is here to-day;
He hath no desire nor sense,
    Nor half so short a way;

Then fear not me,
But believe that I shall make
Speedier journeys, since I take
   More wings and spurs than he.

O how feeble is man's power,
   That if good fortune fall,
Cannot add another hour,
   Nor a lost hour recall;
     But come bad chance,
And we join to it our strength,
And we teach it art and length,
   Itself o'er us to advance.

When thou sigh'st, thou sigh'st not wind,
   But sigh'st my soul away;
When thou weep'st, unkindly kind,
   My life's blood doth decay.
     It cannot be
That thou lovest me, as thou say'st,
If in thine my life thou waste,
   That art the best of me.

Let not thy divining heart
   Forethink me any ill;
Destiny may take thy part,
   And may thy fears fulfil.
     But think that we
Are but turn'd aside to sleep.
They who one another keep
   Alive, ne'er parted be.

Death

Death, be not proud, though some have callèd thee
Mighty and dreadful, for thou art not so;
For those whom thou think'st thou dost overthrow
Die not, poor Death; nor yet canst thou kill me.

From rest and sleep, which but thy pictures be,
Much pleasure; then from thee much more must flow;
And soonest our best men with thee do go –
Rest of their bones, and souls' delivery!
Thou'rt slave to fate, chance, kings, and desperate men,
And dost with poison, war, and sickness dwell;
And poppy or charms can make us sleep as well
And better than thy stroke. Why swell'st thou then?
One short sleep past, we wake eternally,
And Death shall be no more: Death, thou shalt die!

GEORGE WITHER
(1588–1667)

'I loved a lass ...'

I loved a lass, a fair one,
    As fair as e'er was seen;
She was indeed a rare one,
    Another Sheba Queen:
But, fool as then I was,
    I thought she loved me too:
But now, alas! she's left me,
    Falero, lero, loo!

Her hair like gold did glister,
    Each eye was like a star,
She did surpass her sister,
    Which pass'd all others far;
She would me honey call,
    She'd – O she'd kiss me too!
But now, alas! she's left me,
    Falero, lero, loo!

Many a merry meeting
  My love and I have had;
She was my only sweeting,
  She made my heart full glad;
The tears stood in her eyes
  Like to the morning dew:
But now, alas! she's left me,
  Falero, lero, loo!

Her cheeks were like the cherry,
  Her skin was white as snow;
When she was blithe and merry
  She angel-like did show;
Her waist exceeding small,
  The fives did fit her shoe:
But now, alas! she's left me,
  Falero, lero, loo!

In summer time or winter
  She had her heart's desire;
I still did scorn to stint her
  From sugar, sack, or fire;
The world went round about,
  No cares we ever knew:
But now, alas! she's left me,
  Falero, lero, loo!

To maidens' vows and swearing
  Henceforth no credit give;
You may give them the hearing
  But never them believe;
They are as false as fair,
  Unconstant, frail, untrue:
For mine, alas! hath left me,
  Falero, lero, loo!

ROBERT HERRICK
(1591–1674)

Upon the Loss of His Mistresses

I have lost, and lately, these
Many dainty mistresses;
Stately Julia, prime of all;
Sapho next, a principal:
Smooth Anthea, for a skin
White, and Heaven-like crystalline:
Sweet Electra, and the choice
Myrrha, for the lute, and voice.
Next, Corinna, for her wit,
And for the graceful use of it:
With Perilla: all are gone;
Only Herrick's left alone,
For to number sorrow by
Their departures hence, and die.

'Cherry ripe . . .'

Cherry ripe, ripe, ripe, I cry,
Full and fair ones; come and buy:
If so be, you ask me where
They do grow? I answer, 'There,
Where my Julia's lips do smile
There's the land, or Cherry Isle:
Whose plantations fully show
All the year, where Cherries grow.'

Corinna's Going a-Maying

Get up, get up for shame, the blooming morn
Upon her wings presents the god unshorn.
    See how Aurora throws her fair
    Fresh-quilted colours through the air;
    Get up, sweet slug-a-bed, and see
    The dew bespangling herb and tree.
Each flower has wept and bowèd toward the east
Above an hour since: yet you not dressed;
    Nay! not so much as out of bed?
    When all the birds have matins said
    And sung their thankful hymns, 'tis sin,
    Nay, profanation, to keep in,
Whenas a thousand virgins on this day
Spring, sooner than the lark, to fetch in May.

Rise, and put on your foliage, and be seen
To come forth, like the spring-time, fresh and green,
    And sweet as Flora. Take no care
    For jewels for your gown or hair:
    Fear not; the leaves will strew
    Gems in abundance upon you:
Besides, the childhood of the day has kept,
Against you come, some orient pearls unwept;
    Come and receive them while the light
    Hangs on the dew-locks of the night:
    And Titan on the eastern hill
    Retires himself, or else stands still
Till you come forth. Wash, dress, be brief in praying:
Few beads are best when once we go a-Maying.

Come, my Corinna, come; and, coming mark
How each field turns a street, each street a park
    Made green and trimmed with trees; see how
    Devotion gives each house a bough
    Or branch: each porch, each door ere this
    An ark, a tabernacle is,

Made up of white-thorn, neatly interwove;
As if here were those cooler shades of love.
   Can such delights be in the street
   And open fields and we not see 't?
   Come, we'll abroad; and let's obey
   The proclamation made for May:
And sin no more, as we have done, by staying:
But, my Corinna, come, let's go a-Maying.

There's not a budding boy or girl this day
But is got up, and gone to bring in May.
   A deal of youth, ere this, is come
   Back, and with white-thorn laden home.
   Some have despatched their cakes and cream
   Before that we have left to dream:
And some have wept, and wooed, and plighted troth,
And chose their priest, ere we can cast off sloth:
   Many a green-gown has been given;
   Many a kiss, both odd and even:
   Many a glance too has been sent
   From out the eye, love's firmament;
Many a jest told of the keys betraying
This night, and locks picked, yet we're not a-Maying.

Come, let us go while we are in our prime;
And take the harmless folly of the time.
   We shall grow old apace, and die
   Before we know our liberty.
   Our life is short, and our days run
   As fast away as does the sun;
And, as a vapour or a drop of rain,
Once lost, can n'er be found again,
   So when or you or I are made
   A fable, song, or fleeting shade,
   All love, all liking, all delight
   Lies drowned with us in endless night.
Then while time serves, and we are but decaying,
Come, my Corinna, come, let's go a-Maying.

The Night-Piece

Her eyes the glow-worm lend thee,
The shooting stars attend thee;
    And the elves also,
    Whose little eyes glow,
Like the sparks of fire, befriend thee.

No will-o'-th'-wisp mis-light thee;
Nor snake, or slow-worm bite thee;
    But on, on thy way
    Not making a stay,
Since ghost there's none to affright thee.

Let not the dark thee cumber;
What though the Moon does slumber?
    The Stars of the night
    Will lend thee their light,
Like tapers clear without number.

Then Julia let me woo thee,
Thus, thus to come unto me:
    And when I shall meet
    Thy silv'ry feet,
My soul I'll pour into thee.

Delight in Disorder

A sweet disorder in the dress
Kindles in clothes a wantonness:
A lawn about the shoulders thrown
Into a fine distraction,
An erring lace, which here and there
Enthrals the crimson stomacher,
A cuff neglectful, and thereby
Ribbands to flow confusedly,

A winning wave, deserving note,
In the tempestuous petticoat,
A careless shoe-string, in whose tie
I see a wild civility,
Do more bewitch me, than when art
Is too precise in every part.

'Gather ye rose-buds . . .'

Gather ye rose-buds while ye may,
    Old Time is still a-flying:
And this same flower that smiles to-day,
To-morrow will be dying.

The glorious Lamp of Heaven, the Sun,
    The higher he's a-getting
The sooner will his race be run,
    And nearer he's to setting.

That age is best which is the first,
    When youth and blood are warmer:
But being spent, the worse, and worst
    Times, still succeed the former.

Then, be not coy, but use your time;
    And while ye may, go marry:
For having lost but once your prime,
    You may for ever tarry.

To Daffodils

Fair Daffodils, we weep to see
    You haste away so soon;
As yet the early rising sun
    Has not attained his noon.
        Stay, stay,
        Until the hasting day

    Has run
    But to the even-song;
And, having prayed together, we
    Will go with you along.

We have short time to stay, as you,
    We have as short a spring;
As quick a growth to meet decay,
    As you, or anything.
      We die
    As your hours do, and dry
      Away,
    Like to the summer's rain;
Or as the pearls of morning's dew,
    Ne'er to be found again.

To Anthea Who may Command him Anything

Bid me to live, and I will live,
    Thy Protestant to be:
Or bid me love, and I will give
    A loving heart to thee.

A heart as soft, a heart as kind,
    A heart as sound and free
As in the whole world thou canst find,
    That heart I'll give to thee.

Bid that heart stay, and it will stay,
    To honour thy decree:
Or bid it languish quite away,
    And 't shall do so for thee.

Bid me to weep, and I will weep
    While I have eyes to see:
And having none, yet I will keep
    A heart to weep for thee.

Bid me despair, and I'll despair,
    Under that cypress tree:
Or bid me die, and I will dare
    E'en Death, to die for thee.

Thou art my life, my love, my heart,
    The very eyes of me,
And hast command of every part,
    To live and die for thee.

To Blossoms

Fair pledges of a fruitful tree,
        Why do ye fall so fast?
        Your date is not so past,
But you may stay yet here awhile
        To blush and gently smile,
            And go at last.

What, were ye born to be
        An hour or half's delight,
        And so to bid good-night?
'Twas pity Nature brought ye forth
        Merely to show your worth,
            And lose you quite.

But you are lovely leaves, where we
        May read how soon things have
        Their end, though ne'er so brave:
And after they have shown their pride
        Like you, awhile, they glide
            Into the grave.

Upon Julia's Clothes

Whenas in silks my Julia goes,
Then, then, me thinks how sweetly flows
That liquefaction of her clothes.

Next, when I cast mine eyes and see
That brave vibration each way free;
O how that glittering taketh me!

The Hag

The Hag is astride,
This night for to ride;
The Devil and she together:
Through thick, and through thin,
Now out, and then in,
Though ne'er so foul be the weather.

A thorn or a burr
She takes for a spur:
With a lash of bramble she rides now,
Through brakes and through briars,
O'er ditches, and mires,
She follows the spirit that guides now.

No beast, for his food,
Dares now range the wood;
But hush'd in his lair he lies lurking
While mischiefs, by these,
On land and on seas,
At noon of night are a-working.

The storm will arise,
And trouble the skies;
This night, and more for the wonder,
The ghost from the tomb
Affrighted shall come,
'Call'd out by the clap of the thunder.

Grace for a Child

Here, a little child, I stand,
Heaving up my either hand;
Cold as paddocks though they be,
Here I lift them up to thee,
For a benison to fall
On our meat, and on us all.
        Amen.

His Litany to the Holy Spirit

In the hour of my distress,
When temptations me oppress,
And when I my sins confess,
    Sweet Spirit comfort me!

When I lie within my bed,
Sick in heart, and sick in head,
And with doubts discomforted,
    Sweet Spirit comfort me!

When the house doth sigh and weep,
And the world is drown'd in sleep,
Yet mine eyes the watch do keep;
    Sweet Spirit comfort me!

When the artless doctor sees
No one hope, but of his fees,
And his skill runs on the lees;
    Sweet Spirit comfort me!

When his potion and his pill,
Has, or none, or little skill,
Meet for nothing, but to kill;
    Sweet Spirit comfort me!

When the passing-bell doth toll,
And the Furies in a shoal
Come to fright a parting soul;
    Sweet Spirit comfort me!

When the tapers now burn blue,
And the comforters are few,
And that number more than true;
    Sweet Spirit comfort me!

When the Priest his last hath prayed,
And I nod to what is said,
'Cause my speech is now decayed;
    Sweet Spirit comfort me!

When, God knows, I'm toss'd about,
Either with despair, or doubt;
Yet before the glass be out,
    Sweet Spirit comfort me!

When the Tempter me pursu'th
With the sins of all my youth,
And half damns me with untruth;
    Sweet Spirit comfort me!

When the flames and hellish cries
Fright mine ears, and fright mine eyes,
And all terrors me surprise;
    Sweet Spirit comfort me!

When the Judgment is reveal'd,
And that open'd which was seal'd
When to Thee I have appeal'd;
    Sweet Spirit comfort me!

GEORGE HERBERT
(1593–1633)

The Collar

I struck the board, and cried 'No more:
    I will abroad.
  What, shall I ever sigh and pine?
My lines and life are free; free as the road,
  Loose as the wind, as large as store.
    Shall I be still in suit?
Have I no harvest but a thorn
  To let me blood, and not restore
What I have lost with cordial fruit?
  Sure there was wine
Before my sighs did dry it; there was corn
  Before my tears did drown it;
Is the year only lost to me?
  Have I no bays to crown it,
No flowers, no garlands gay? all blasted,
    All wasted?
Not so, my heart; but there is fruit,
    And thou hast hands.
  Recover all thy sigh-blown age
On double pleasures; leave thy cold dispute
  Of what is fit and not; forsake thy cage,
    Thy rope of sands
Which petty thoughts have made; and made to thee
  Good cable, to enforce and draw,
    And be thy law,
While thou didst wink and wouldst not see.
    Away! take heed;
    I will abroad.
  Call in thy death's-head there, tie up thy fears;
    He that forbears
  To suit and serve his need

Deserves his load.'
But as I rav'd and grew more fierce and wild
        At every word,
    Methought I heard one calling 'Child';
        And I replied, 'My Lord.'

Love

Love bade me welcome; yet my soul drew back,
        Guilty of dust and sin.
But quick-ey'd Love, observing me grow slack
        From my first entrance in,
Drew nearer to me, sweetly questioning
        If I lack'd anything.

'A guest,' I answer'd, 'worthy to be here';
        Love said, 'You shall be he.'
'I, the unkind, ungrateful? Ah, my dear,
        I cannot look on Thee.'
Love took my hand, and smiling did reply.
        'Who made the eyes but I?'

'Truth, Lord; but I have marr'd them; let my shame
        Go where it doth deserve.'   .
'And know you not,' says Love, 'Who bore the blame?'
        'My dear, then I will serve.'
'You must sit down,' says Love, 'and taste My meat.'
        So I did sit and eat.

The Gifts of God

When God at first made Man,
Having a glass of blessings standing by;
'Let us,' said He, 'pour on him all we can:
Let the world's riches, which dispersèd lie,
        Contract into a span.'

So strength first made a way;
Then beauty flow'd, then wisdom, honour, pleasure:
When almost all was out, God made a stay,
Perceiving that alone, of all His treasure,
     Rest in the bottom lay.

     'For if I should,' said He,
'Bestow this jewel also on My creature,
He would adore My gifts instead of Me,
And rest in Nature, not the God of Nature:
     So both should losers be.

     Yet let him keep the rest,
But keep them with repining restlessness:
Let him be rich and weary, that at least,
If goodness lead him not, yet weariness
     May toss him to My breast.'

EDMUND WALLER
(1606–1687)

'Go, lovely Rose . . .'

Go, lovely Rose,
Tell her, that wastes her time and me,
     That now she knows,
When I resemble her to thee,
How sweet and fair she seems to be.

     Tell her that's young
And shuns to have her graces spied,
     That hadst thou sprung
In deserts, where no men abide,
Thou must have uncommended died.

Small is the worth
Of beauty from the light retired;
   Bid her come forth,
Suffer herself to be desired,
And not blush so to be admired.

Then die! that she
The common fate of all things rare
   May read in thee:
How small a part of time they share
That are so wondrous sweet and fair!

The Girdle

That which her slender waist confin'd
Shall now my joyful temples bind;
No monarch but would give his crown
His arms might do what this has done.

It was my Heaven's extremest sphere,
The pale which held that lovely dear:
My joy, my grief, my hope, my love,
Did all within this circle move.

A narrow compass! and yet there
Dwelt all that's good, and all that's fair;
Give me but what this ribband bound,
Take all the rest the sun goes round!

JOHN MILTON
(1608–1674)

At a Solemn Music

Blest pair of Sirens, pledges of Heaven's joy,
Sphere-born harmonious Sisters, Voice and Verse!
Wed your divine sounds, and mixt power employ,
Dead things with inbreathed sense able to pierce;
And to our high-raised phantasy present
That undisturbed Song of pure concent
Ay sung before the sapphire-colour'd throne
    To Him that sits thereon
With saintly shout and solemn jubilee;
Where the bright Seraphim in burning row
Their loud uplifted angel-trumpets blow;
And the Cherubic host in thousand quires
Touch their immortal harps of golden wires,
With those just Spirits that wear victorious palms,
    Hymns devout and holy psalms
    Singing everlastingly:
Thus we on earth, with undiscording voice
May rightly answer that melodious noise;
As once we did, till disproportion'd sin
Jarr'd against nature's chime, and with harsh din
Broke the fair music that all creatures made
To their great Lord, whose love their motion sway'd
In perfect diapason, whilst they stood
In first obedience, and their state of good.
  O may we soon again renew that Song,
    And keep in tune with Heaven, till God ere long
    To His celestial concert us unite,
To live with Him, and sing in endless morn of light!

L'Allegro

Hence loathed Melancholy
  Of Cerberus and blackest midnight born,
In Stygian Cave forlorn
  'Mongst horrid shapes, and shrieks, and
    sights unholy,
Find out some uncouth cell,
  Where brooding darkness spreads his jealous
    wings,
And the night-raven sings;
  There, under ebon shades, and low-brow'd
    rocks,
As ragged as thy locks,
  In dark Cimmerian desert ever dwell.
But come thou Goddess fair and free,
In Heaven yclept Euphrosyne,
And by men, heart-easing Mirth,
Whom lovely Venus at a birth
With two sister Graces more
To ivy-crownéd Bacchus bore;
Or whether (as some sager sing)
The frolic wind that breathes the spring,
Zephyr, with Aurora playing,
As he met her once a-Maying –
There on beds of violets blue
And fresh-blown roses wash'd in dew
Fill'd her with thee, a daughter fair,
So buxom, blithe, and debonair.
  Haste thee, Nymph, and bring with thee
Jest, and youthful jollity,
Quips, and cranks, and wanton wiles,
Nods, and becks, and wreathéd smiles
Such as hang on Hebe's cheek,
And love to live in dimple sleek;
Sport that wrinkled Care derides,

And Laughter holding both his sides: —
Come, and trip it as you go
On the light fantastic toe;
And in thy right hand lead with thee
The mountain nymph, sweet Liberty;
And if I give thee honour due,
Mirth, admit me of thy crew,
To live with her, and live with thee
In unreprovéd pleasures free;
To hear the lark begin his flight
And singing startle the dull night
From his watch-tower in the skies,
Till the dappled dawn doth rise;
Then to come, in spite of sorrow,
And at my window bid good-morrow
Through the sweetbriar, or the vine,
Or the twisted eglantine:
While the cock with lively din
Scatters the rear of darkness thin,
And to the stack, or the barn-door,
Stoutly struts his dames before:
Oft listening how the hounds and horn
Cheerly rouse the slumbering morn,
From the side of some hoar hill,
Through the high wood echoing shrill.
Sometime walking, not unseen,
By hedge-row elms, on hillocks green,
Right against the eastern gate
Where the great Sun begins his state
Robed in flames and amber light,
The clouds in thousand liveries dight.
While the ploughman, near at hand,
Whistles o'er the furrow'd land,
And the milkmaid singeth blithe,
And the mower whets his scythe,
And every shepherd tells his tale
Under the hawthorn in the dale.

Straight mine eye hath caught new pleasures
Whilst the landscape round it measures;
Russet lawns, and fallows grey,
Where the nibbling flocks do stray;
Mountains, on whose barren breast
The labouring clouds do often rest;
Meadows trim with daisies pied,
Shallow brooks and rivers wide;
Towers and battlements it sees
Bosom'd high in tufted trees,
Where perhaps some Beauty lies,
The Cynosure of neighbouring eyes.
Hard by, a cottage chimney smokes
From betwixt two aged oaks,
Where Corydon and Thyrsis, met,
Are at their savoury dinner set
Of herbs, and other country messes
Which the neat-handed Phillis dresses;
And then in haste her bower she leaves
With Thestylis to bind the sheaves;
Or, if the earlier season lead,
To the tann'd haycock in the mead.
Sometimes with secure delight
The upland hamlets will invite,
When the merry bells ring round,
And the jocund rebecks sound
To many a youth and many a maid,
Dancing in the chequer'd shade;
And young and old come forth to play
On a sunshine holy-day,
Till the livelong daylight fail:
Then to the spicy nut-brown ale,
With stories told of many a feat,
How Faery Mab the junkets eat;
She was pinch'd, and pull'd, she said;
And he, by Friar's lantern led,
Tells how the drudging Goblin sweat

To earn his cream-bowl duly set,
When in one night, ere glimpse of morn,
His shadowy flail hath thresh'd the corn
That ten day-labourers could not end;
Then lies him down the lubber fiend,
And, stretch'd out all the chimney's length,
Basks at the fire his hairy strength;
And crop-full out of doors he flings,
Ere the first cock his matin rings.
   Thus done the tales, to bed they creep,
By whispering winds soon lull'd asleep.
   Tower'd cities please us then
And the busy hum of men,
Where throngs of knights and barons bold,
In weeds of peace high triumphs hold,
With store of ladies, whose bright eyes
Rain influence, and judge the prize
Of wit or arms, while both contend
To win her grace, whom all commend.
There let Hymen oft appear
In saffron robe, with taper clear,
And pomp, and feast, and revelry,
With masks, and antique pageantry;
Such sights as youthful poets dream
On summer eves by haunted stream.
Then to the well-trod stage anon,
If Jonson's learned sock be on,
Or sweetest Shakespeare, Fancy's child,
Warble his native wood-notes wild,
And ever against eating cares
Lap me in soft Lydian airs
Married to immortal verse,
Such as the meeting soul may pierce
In notes, with many a winding bout
Of linkéd sweetness long drawn out,
With wanton heed and giddy cunning,
The melting voice through mazes running,

Untwisting all the chains that tie
The hidden soul of harmony;
That Orpheus' self may heave his head
From golden slumber, on a bed
Of heap'd Elysian flowers, and hear
Such strains as would have won the ear
Of Pluto, to have quite set free
His half-regain'd Eurydice.

These delights if thou canst give,
Mirth, with thee I mean to live.

Il Penseroso

Hence vain deluding joys,
  The brood of folly without father bred,
How little you bested,
  Or fill the fixed mind with all your toys;
Dwell in some idle brain,
  And fancies fond with gaudy shapes possess,
As thick and numberless
  As the gay motes that people the sunbeams,
Or likest hovering dreams,
  The fickle pensioners of Morpheus' train.
But hail thou Goddess, sage and holy
Hail divinest Melancholy,
Whose saintly visage is too bright
To hit the sense of human sight;
And therefore to our weaker view,
O'er laid with black staid Wisdom's hue.
Black, but such as in esteem,
Prince Memnon's sister might beseem,
Or that starr'd Ethiop queen that strove
To set her beauty's praise above
The sea-nymphs, and their powers offended:
Yet thou art higher far descended:

Thee bright-hair'd Vesta, long of yore,
To solitary Saturn bore;
His daughter she; in Saturn's reign
Such mixture was not held a stain:
Oft in glimmering bowers and glades
He met her, and in secret shades
Of woody Ida's inmost grove,
While yet there was no fear of Jove.
　　Come, pensive nun, devout and pure,
Sober, steadfast, and demure,
All in a robe of darkest grain
Flowering with majestic train,
And sable stole of cypress lawn
Over thy decent shoulders drawn:
Come, but keep thy wonted state,
With even step, and musing gait,
And looks commercing with the skies,
Thy rapt soul sitting in thine eyes:
There, held in holy passion still,
Forget thyself to marble, till
With a sad leaden downward cast
Thou fix them on the earth as fast:
And join with thee calm Peace and Quiet,
Spare Fast, that oft with gods doth diet,
And hears the Muses in a ring
Ay round about Jove's altar sing;
And add to these retired Leisure
That in trim gardens takes his pleasure: –
But first, and chiefest, with thee bring
Him that yon soars on golden wing
Guiding the fiery-wheeléd throne,
The cherub Contemplation;
And the mute Silence hist along,
'Less Philomel will deign a song
In her sweetest saddest plight,
Smoothing the rugged brow of Night,
While Cynthia checks her dragon yoke

Gently o'er the accustom'd oak.
– Sweet bird, that shunn'st the noise of folly,
Most musical, most melancholy!
Thee, chauntress, oft, the woods among
I woo, to hear thy even-song;
And missing thee, I walk unseen
On the dry smooth-shaven green,
To behold the wandering Moon
Riding near her highest noon,
Like one that had been led astray
Through the heaven's wide pathless way,
And oft, as if her head she bow'd,
Stooping through a fleecy cloud.
    Oft, on a plat of rising ground
I hear the far-off curfew sound
Over some wide-water'd shore,
Swinging slow with sullen roar:
Or, if the air will not permit,
Some still removéd place will fit,
Where glowing embers through the room
Teach light to counterfeit a gloom;
Far from all resort of mirth,
Save the cricket on the hearth,
Or the bellman's drowsy charm
To bless the doors from nightly harm.
Or let my lamp at midnight hour
Be seen in some high lonely tower,
Where I may oft out-watch the Bear
With thrice-great Hermes, or unsphere
The spirit of Plato, to unfold
What worlds or what vast regions hold
The immortal mind, that hath forsook
Her mansion in this fleshly nook:
And of those demons that are found
In fire, air, flood, or under ground,
Whose power hath a true consent
With planet, or with element.

Sometime let gorgeous Tragedy
In sceptre'd pall come sweeping by,
Presenting Thebes, or Pelops' line,
Or the tale of Troy divine;
Or what (though rare) of later age
Ennobled hath the buskin'd stage.

But, O sad Virgin, that thy power
Might raise Musaeus from his bower,
Or bid the soul of Orpheus sing
Such notes as, warbled to the string,
Drew iron tears down Pluto's cheek
And made Hell grant what Love did seek!
Or call up him that left half-told
The story of Cambuscan bold,
Of Camball, and of Algarsife,
And who had Canacé to wife,
That own'd the virtuous ring and glass,
And of the wondrous horse of brass
On which the Tartar king did ride:
And if aught else great bards beside
In sage and solemn tunes have sung
Of tourneys, and of trophies hung,
Of forests and enchantments drear,
Where more is meant than meets the ear.

Thus, Night, oft see me in thy pale career,
Till civil-suited Morn appear,
Not trick'd and frounced as she was wont
With the Attic Boy to hunt,
But kercheft in a comely cloud
While rocking winds are piping loud,
Or usher'd with a shower still,
When the gust hath blown his fill,
Ending on the rustling leaves
With minute drops from off the eaves.
And when the sun begins to fling
His flaring beams, me, goddess, bring
To archéd walks of twilight groves,

And shadows brown, that Sylvan loves,
Of pine, or monumental oak,
Where the rude axe, with heavéd stroke,
Was never heard the nymphs to daunt
Or fright them from their hallow'd haunt.
There in close covert by some brook
Where no profaner eye may look,
Hide me from day's garnish eye.
While the bee with honey'd thigh
That at her flowery work doth sing,
And the waters murmuring,
With such consort as they keep
Entice the dewy-feather'd Sleep;
And let some strange mysterious dream
Wave at his wings in airy stream
Of lively portraiture display'd,
Softly on my eyelids laid:
And, as I wake, sweet music breathe
Above, about, or underneath,
Sent by some Spirit to mortals good,
Or the unseen Genius of the wood.
    But let my due feet never fail
To walk the studious cloister's pale,
And love the high-embowéd roof,
With antique pillars massy proof,
And storied windows richly dight
Casting a dim religious light:
There let the pealing organ blow
To the full-voiced quire below
In service high and anthems clear,
As may with sweetness, through mine ear,
Dissolve me into ecstasies,
And bring all Heaven before mine eyes.
    And may at last my weary age
Find out the peaceful hermitage,
The hairy gown and mossy cell
Where I may sit and rightly spell

Of every star that heaven doth show,
And every herb that sips the dew:
Till old experience do attain
To something like prophetic strain.

These pleasures, Melancholy, give,
And I with thee will choose to live.

Lycidas

Yet once more, O ye laurels, and once more,
Ye myrtles brown, with ivy never sere,
I come, to pluck your berries harsh and crude,
    And with forced fingers rude
Shatter your leaves before the mellowing year.
Bitter constraint and sad occasion dear
Compels me to disturb your season due;
For Lycidas is dead, dead ere his prime,
Young Lycidas, and hath not left his peer;
Who would not sing for Lycidas? He knew
Himself to sing, and build the lofty rime.
He must not float upon his watery bier
Unwept, and welter to the parching wind
Without the meed of some melodious tear.

Begin, then, sisters of the sacred well
That from beneath the seat of Jove doth spring:
Begin, and somewhat loudly sweep the string;
Hence with denial vain, and coy excuse:
    So may some gentle muse
With lucky words favour my destined urn.
    And as he passes, turn,
And bid fair peace to be my sable shroud!

For we were nursed upon the self-same hill,
Fed the same flock, by fountain, shade, and rill.

Together both, ere the high lawns appeared
Under the opening eyelids of the morn,
We drove afield, and both together heard
What time the grey-fly winds her sultry horn,
Battening our flocks with the fresh dews of night,
Oft till the star that rose at evening bright
Toward heaven's descent had sloped his westering wheel.
Meanwhile the rural ditties were not mute;
  Tempered to the oaten flute
Rough satyrs danced, and fauns with cloven heel
From the glad sound would not be absent long:
And old Damoetas loved to hear our song.

 But, oh! the heavy change, now thou art gone,
Now thou art gone and never must return!
Thee, shepherd, thee the woods, and desert caves,
With wild thyme and the gadding vine o'er-grown,
  And all their echoes, mourn:
The willows, and the hazel copses green,
  Shall now no more be seen
Fanning their joyous leaves to thy soft lays.
As killing as the canker to the rose,
Or taint-worm to the weanling herds that graze,
Or frost to flowers, that their gay wardrobe wear,
  When first the white-thorn blows;
Such, Lycidas, thy loss to shepherd's ear.

 Where were ye, Nymphs, when the remorseless deep
Closed o'er the head of your loved Lycidas?
For neither were ye playing on the steep
Where your old bards, the famous Druids, lie,
Nor on the shaggy top of Mona high,
Nor yet where Deva spreads her wizard stream:
  Ay me! I fondly dream,
'Had ye been there': for what could that have done?
What could the Muse herself that Orpheus bore,
The Muse herself, for her enchanting son

Whom universal nature did lament,
When by the rout that made the hideous roar
His gory visage down the stream was sent,
Down the swift Hebrus to the Lesbian shore?

Alas! what boots it with incessant care
To tend the homely, slighted, shepherd's trade,
And strictly meditate the thankless Muse?
Were it not better done, as others use,
To sport with Amaryllis in the shade,
Or with the tangles of Neaera's hair?
Fame is the spur that the clear spirit doth raise
(That last infirmity of noble mind)
To scorn delights and live laborious days:
But the fair guerdon when we hope to find,
And think to burst out into sudden blaze,
Comes the blind Fury with the abhorrèd shears
And slits the thin-spun life. 'But not the praise,'
Phoebus replied, and touched my trembling ears:
'Fame is no plant that grows on mortal soil,
          Nor in the glistering foil
Set off to the world, nor in broad rumour lies,
But lives and spreads aloft by those pure eyes
And perfect witness of all-judging Jove:
As he pronounces lastly on each deed,
Of so much fame in heaven expect thy meed.'

O fountain Arethuse, and thou honoured flood,
Smooth-sliding Mincius, crowned with vocal reeds,
That strain I heard was of a higher mood.
          But now my oat proceeds,
And listens to the herald of the sea
          That came in Neptune's plea;
He asked the waves, and asked the felon winds,
What hard mishap hath doomed this gentle swain?
And questioned every gust, of rugged wings,
That blows from off each beakèd promontory:
          They know not of his story:

And sage Hippotades their answer brings,
That not a blast was from his dungeon strayed,
The air was calm, and on the level brine
Sleek Panopè with all her sisters played.
It was that fatal and perfidious bark,
Built in the eclipse, and rigged with curses dark,
That sunk so low that sacred head of thine.

Next, Camus, reverend sire, went footing slow,
His mantle hairy, and his bonnet sedge
Inwrought with figures dim and on the edge
Like to that sanguine flower inscribed with woe.
'Ah! who hath reft,' quoth he, 'my dearest pledge?'
      Last came, and last did go,
The pilot of the Galilean lake.
Two massy keys he bore, of metals twain,
The golden opes, the iron shuts amain.
He shook his mitred locks, and stern bespoke:
'How well could I have spared for thee, young swain,
Enow of such as, for their bellies' sake,
Creep, and intrude, and climb into the fold!
Of other care they little reckoning make
Than how to scramble at the shearers' feast
And shove away the worthy bidden guest;
Blind mouths! that scarce themselves know how to hold
A sheep-hook, or have learned aught else the least
That to the faithful herdsman's art belongs!
What recks it them? What need they? They are sped,
And, when they list, their lean and flashy songs
Grate on their scrannel pipes of wretched straw;
The hungry sheep look up, and are not fed,
But, swoln with wind and the rank mist they draw,
Rot inwardly, and foul contagion spread;
Besides what the grim wolf, with privy paw,
Daily devours apace, and nothing said.
But that two-handed engine at the door
Stands ready to smite once, and smite no more.'

Return, Alphëus, the dread voice is past,
That shrunk thy streams; return, Sicilian Muse,
And call the vales, and bid them hither cast
Their bells and flowerets of a thousand hues.
Ye valleys low, where the mild whispers use
Of shades and wanton winds, and gushing brooks,
On whose fresh lap the swart star sparely looks,
Throw hither all your quaint enamelled eyes
That on the green turf suck the honeyed showers,
And purple all the ground with vernal flowers.
Bring the rathe primrose that forsaken dies,
The tufted crow-toe, and pale jessamine,
The white pink, and the pansy freaked with jet,
    The glowing violet,
The musk-rose, and the well-attired woodbine,
With cowslips wan that hang the pensive head,
And every flower that sad embroidery wears;
Bid amaranthus all his beauty shed,
And daffodillies fill their cups with tears,
To strew the laureate hearse where Lycid lies.
For so, to interpose a little ease,
Let our frail thoughts dally with false surmise:
Ah me! whilst thee the shores and sounding seas
Wash far away, where'er thy bones are hurled;
Whether beyond the stormy Hebrides,
Where thou, perhaps under the whelming tide,
Visit'st the bottom of the monstrous world;
Or whether thou, to our moist vows denied,
Sleep'st by the fable of Bellerus old,
Where the great vision of the guarded mount
Looks toward Namancos and Bayona's hold:
Look homeward, angel, now, and melt with ruth;
And, O ye dolphins, waft the hapless youth.

Weep no more, woeful shepherds, weep no more,
For Lycidas, your sorrow, is not dead,
Sunk though he be beneath the watery floor.

So sinks the day-star in the ocean-bed,
And yet anon repairs his drooping head,
And tricks his beams, and, with new spangled ore,
Flames in the forehead of the morning sky:
So Lycidas sunk low, but mounted high,
Through the dear might of Him that walked
        the waves,
Where, other groves and other streams along,
With nectar pure his oozy locks he laves,
And hears the unexpressive nuptial song
In the blest kingdoms meek of joy and love.
There entertain him all the saints above,
In solemn troops and sweet societies
That sing, and singing, in their glory move,
And wipe the tears for ever from his eyes.
Now, Lycidas, the shepherds weep no more;
Henceforth thou art the genius of the shore
In thy large recompense, and shalt be good
To all that wander in that perilous flood.

    Thus sang the uncouth swain to the oaks and rills,
While the still morn went out with sandals grey;
He touched the tender stops of various quills,
With eager thought warbling his Doric lay;
And now the sun had stretched out all the hills.
And now was dropt into the western bay;
At last he rose, and twitched his mantle blue:
To-morrow to fresh woods, and pastures new.

Paradise Lost

The First Book

    Of Man's first disobedience, and the fruit
Of that forbidden tree, whose mortal taste
Brought death into the world, and all our woe,
With loss of Eden, till one greater Man

Restore us, and regain the blissful seat,
Sing, heavenly Muse, that on the secret top
Of Oreb, or of Sinai, did'st inspire
That shepherd, who first taught the chosen seed
In the beginning how the heavens and earth
Rose out of chaos: or, if Sion hill
Delight thee more, and Siloa's brook that flowed
Fast by the oracle of God, I thence
Invoke thy aid to my adventurous song,
That with no middle flight intends to soar
Above the Aonian mount, while it pursues
Things unattempted yet in prose or rhyme.

And chiefly thou, O Spirit, that dost prefer
Before all temples the upright heart and pure,
Instruct me, for thou know'st; thou from the first
Wast present, and, with mighty wings outspread,
Dove-like, sat'st brooding on the vast abyss,
And mad'st it pregnant: what in me is dark
Illumine; what is low, raise and support;
That to the height of this great argument
I may assert eternal Providence,
And justify the ways of God to men.

Say first – for heaven hides nothing from thy view,
Nor the deep tract of hell – say first, what cause
Moved our grand Parents, in that happy state,
Favoured of Heaven so highly, to fall off
From their Creator, and transgress his will
For one restraint, lords of the world besides.
Who first seduced them to that foul revolt?

The infernal Serpent; he it was, whose guile,
Stirred up with envy and revenge, deceived
The mother of mankind; what time his pride
Had cast him out from heaven, with all his host
Of rebel angels; by whose aid, aspiring
To set himself in glory above his peers

He trusted to have equalled the Most High,
If he opposed; and, with ambitious aim
Against the throne and monarchy of God,
Raised impious war in heaven, and battle proud,
With vain attempt. Him the Almighty Power
Hurled headlong flaming from the ethereal sky,
With hideous ruin and combustion, down
To bottomless perdition; there to dwell
In adamantine chains and penal fire,
Who durst defy the Omnipotent to arms.

    Nine times the space that measures day and night
To mortal men, he with his horrid crew
Lay vanquished, rolling in the fiery gulf,
Confounded, though immortal. But his doom
Reserved him to more wrath; for now the thought
Both of lost happiness and lasting pain
Torments him; round he throws his baleful eyes,
That witnessed huge affliction and dismay,
Mixed with obdurate pride, and steadfast hate.
At once, as far as angels' ken, he views
The dismal situation waste and wild.
A dungeon horrible, on all sides round,
As one great furnace, flamed; yet from those flames
No light; but rather darkness visible
Served only to discover sights of woe,
Regions of sorrow, doleful shades, where peace
And rest can never dwell; hope never comes
That comes to all; but torture without end
Still urges, and a fiery deluge, fed
With ever-burning sulphur unconsumed.

    Such place eternal justice had prepared
For those rebellious; here their prison ordained
In utter darkness, and their portion set
As far removed from God and light of heaven,
As from the centre thrice to the utmost pole.
O, how unlike the place from whence they fell!

There the companions of his fall, o'erwhelmed
With floods and whirlwinds of tempestuous fire,
He soon discerns; and weltering by his side
One next himself in power, and next in crime,
Long after known in Palestine, and named
Beëlzebub. To whom the arch-enemy,
And thence in heaven called Satan, with bold words
Breaking the horrid silence, thus began:

'If thou beest he – but O, how fall'n! how changed
From him who, in the happy realms of light,
Clothed with transcendent brightness, didst outshine
Myriads, though bright! If he, whom mutual league,
United thoughts and counsels, equal hope
And hazard in the glorious enterprise,
Joined with me once, now misery hath joined
In equal ruin; into what pit thou seest
From what height fall'n, so much the stronger proved
He with his thunder: and till then who knew
The force of those dire arms? Yet not for those,
Nor what the potent victor in his rage
Can else inflict, do I repent or change,
Though changed in outward lustre, that fixed mind,
And high disdain, from sense of injured merit,
That with the Mightiest raised me to contend,
And to the fierce contention brought along
Innumerable force of spirits armed,
That durst dislike his reign, and, me preferring,
His utmost power with adverse power opposed
In dubious battle on the plains of heaven,
And shook his throne. What though the field be lost?
All is not lost; the unconquerable will,
And study of revenge, immortal hate,
And courage never to submit or yield,
And what is else not to be overcome;
That glory never shall his wrath or might
Extort from me. To bow and sue for grace

With suppliant knee, and deify his power
Who from the terror of this arm so late
Doubted his empire – that were low indeed,
That were an ignominy, and shame beneath
This downfall; since, by fate, the strength of gods,
And this empyreal substance, cannot fail:
Since through experience of this great event,
In arms not worse, in foresight much advanced,
We may with more successful hope resolve
To wage by force or guile eternal war,
Irreconcilable, to our grand foe,
Who now triumphs, and, in the excess of joy
Sole reigning, holds the tyranny of heaven.'

So spake the apostate angel, though in pain,
Vaunting aloud, but racked with deep despair;
And him thus answered soon his bold compeer:

'O prince, O chief of many-thronèd powers,
That led the embattled seraphim to war
Under thy conduct, and in dreadful deeds
Fearless, endangered heaven's perpetual King,
And put to proof his high supremacy,
Whether upheld by strength, or chance, or fate;
Too well I see, and rue the dire event,
That with sad overthrow, and foul defeat,
Hath lost us heaven, and all this mighty host
In horrible destruction laid thus low,
As far as gods and heavenly essences
Can perish: for the mind and spirit remain
Invincible, and vigour soon returns,
Though all our glory extinct, and happy state
Here swallowed up in endless misery.
But what if he our Conqueror (whom I now
Of force believe Almighty, since no less
Than such could have o'erpowered such force as ours)
Have left us this our spirit and strength entire,

Strongly to suffer and support our pains,
That we may so suffice his vengeful ire,
Or do him mightier service as his thralls
By right of war, whate'er his business be,
Here in the heart of hell to work in fire,
Or do his errands in the gloomy deep?
What can it then avail, though yet we feel
Strength undiminished, or eternal being
To undergo eternal punishment?'

Whereto with speedy words the arch-fiend replied:
    'Fallen cherub, to be weak is miserable,
Doing or suffering; but of this be sure,
To do aught good never will be our task,
But ever to do ill our sole delight,
As being the contrary to his high will
Whom we resist. If then his providence
Out of our evil seek to bring forth good,
Our labour must be to pervert that end,
And out of good still to find means of evil,
Which ofttimes may succeed, so as perhaps
Shall grieve him, if I fail not, and disturb
His inmost counsels from their destined aim.
But see, the angry Victor hath recalled
His ministers of vengeance and pursuit
Back to the gates of heaven; the sulphurous hail,
Shot after us in storm, o'er blown, hath laid
The fiery surge, that from the precipice
Of heaven received us falling; and the thunder,
Winged with red lightning and impetuous rage,
Perhaps hath spent his shafts, and ceases now
To bellow through the vast and boundless deep.
Let us not slip the occasion, whether scorn
Or satiate fury yield it from our foe.
Seest thou yon dreary plain, forlorn and wild,
The seat of desolation, void of light,
Save what the glimmering of these livid flames

Casts pale and dreadful? Thither let us tend
From off the tossing of these fiery waves;
There rest, if any rest can harbour there;
And, re-assembling our afflicted powers,
Consult how we may henceforth most offend
Our enemy; our own loss how repair;
How overcome this dire calamity;
What reinforcement we may gain from hope;
If not, what resolution from despair.'

    Thus Satan, talking to his nearest mate,
With head uplift above the wave, and eyes
That sparkling blazed; his other parts besides
Prone on the flood, extended long and large,
Lay floating many a rood; in bulk as huge
As whom the fables name of monstrous size,
Titanian, or Earth-born, that warred on Jove;
Briareos or Typhon, whom the den
By ancient Tarsus held; or that sea-beast
Leviathan, which God of all his works
Created hugest that swim the ocean stream.
Him, haply, slumbering on the Norway foam,
The pilot of some small night-foundered skiff,
Deeming some island, oft, as seamen tell,
With fixèd anchor in his scaly rind
Moors by his side under the lee, while night
Invests the sea, and wishèd morn delays;
So stretched out huge in length the arch-fiend lay
Chained on the burning lake: nor ever thence
Had risen, or heaved his head; but that the will
And high permission of all-ruling Heaven
Left him at large to his own dark designs;
That with reiterated crimes he might
Heap on himself damnation, while he sought
Evil to others; and, enraged, might see
How all his malice served but to bring forth
Infinite goodness, grace, and mercy, shown

On man by him seduced; but on himself
Treble confusion, wrath, and vengeance poured.

Forthwith upright he rears from off the pool
His mighty stature; on each hand the flames,
Driven backward, slope their pointing spires, and rolled
In billows, leave i' the midst a horrid vale.
Then with expanded wings he steers his flight
Aloft, incumbent on the dusky air,
That felt unusual weight; till on dry land
He lights, if it were land that ever burned
With solid, as the lake with liquid fire;
And such appeared in hue, as when the force
Of subterranean wind transports a hill
Torn from Pelorus, or the shattered side
Of thundering Etna, whose combustible
And fuelled entrails thence conceiving fire,
Sublimed with mineral fury, aid the winds,
And leave a singèd bottom, all involved
With stench and smoke: such resting found the sole
Of unblest feet. Him followed his next mate:
Both glorying to have 'scaped the Stygian flood
As gods, and by their own recovered strength,
Not by the sufferance of supernal power.

'Is this the region, this the soil, the clime,'
Said then the lost archangel, 'this the seat
That we must change for heaven; this mournful gloom
For that celestial light? Be it so, since he,
Who now is Sovereign, can dispose and bid
What shall be right: farthest from him is best,
Whom reason hath equalled, force hath made supreme
Above his equals. Farewell, happy fields,
Where joy for ever dwells! Hail, horrors! hail
Infernal world! and thou profoundest hell,
Receive thy new possessor – one who brings
A mind not to be changed by place or time:

The mind is its own place, and in itself
Can make a heaven of hell, a hell of heaven.
What matter where, if I be still the same,
And what I should be; all but less than he
Whom thunder hath made greater? Here at least
We shall be free: the Almighty hath not built
Here for his envy, will not drive us hence:
Here we may reign secure, and, in my choice,
To reign is worth ambition, though in hell;
Better to reign in hell, than serve in heaven.
But wherefore let we then our faithful friends,
The associates and co-partners of our loss,
Lie thus astonished on the oblivious pool,
And call them not to share with us their part
In this unhappy mansion; or once more
With rallied arms to try what may be yet
Regained in heaven, or what more lost in hell?'

So Satan spake, and him Beëlzebub
Thus answered: 'Leader of those armies bright,
Which, but the Omnipotent, none could have foiled,
If once they hear that voice, their liveliest pledge
Of hope in fears and dangers, heard so oft
In worst extremes, and on the perilous edge
Of battle when it raged, in all assaults
Their surest signal, they will soon resume
New courage and revive; though now they lie
Grovelling and prostrate on yon lake of fire,
As we erewhile, astounded and amazed;
No wonder, fall'n such a pernicious height.'

He scarce had ceased, when the superior fiend
Was moving toward the shore: his ponderous shield,
Ethereal temper, massy, large, and round,
Behind him cast; the broad circumference
Hung on his shoulders like the moon, whose orb
Through optic glass the Tuscan artist views

At evening, from the top of Fesolè,
Or in Valdarno, to descry new lands,
Rivers, or mountains, in her spotty globe.
His spear, to equal which the tallest pine
Hewn on Norwegian hills, to be the mast
Of some great admiral, were but a wand,
He walked with, to support uneasy steps
Over the burning marl, not like those steps
On heaven's azure, and the torrid clime
Smote on him sore besides, vaulted with fire:
Nathless he so endured, till on the beach
Of that inflamèd sea he stood, and called
His legions, angel forms, who lay entranced,
Thick as autumnal leaves, that strew the brooks
In Vallombrosa, where the Etrurian shades,
High over-arched, embower; or scattered sedge
Afloat, when with fierce winds Orion armed
Hath vexed the Red Sea coast, whose waves o'erthrew
Busiris and his Memphian chivalry,
While with perfidious hatred they pursued
The sojourners of Goshen, who beheld
From the safe shore their floating carcasses
And broken chariot-wheels; so thick bestrewn,
Abject and lost lay these, covering the flood,
Under amazement of their hideous change.

He called so loud, that all the hollow deep
Of hell resounded. 'Princes, potentates,
Warriors, the flower of heaven, once yours, now lost,
If such astonishment as this can seize
Eternal spirits; or have ye chosen this place
After the toil of battle to repose
Your wearied virtue, for the ease you find
To slumber here, as in the vales of heaven?
Or in this abject posture have ye sworn
To adore the Conqueror? who now beholds
Cherub and seraph rolling in the flood

With scattered arms and ensigns, till anon
His swift pursuers from heaven-gates discern
The advantage, and descending, tread us down
Thus drooping, or with linkèd thunderbolts
Transfix us to the bottom of this gulf?
Awake, arise, or be for ever fall'n!'

They heard, and were abashed, and up they sprung
Upon the wing; as when men, wont to watch
On duty, sleeping found by whom they dread,
Rouse and bestir themselves ere well awake.
Nor did they not perceive the evil plight
In which they were, or the fierce pains not feel;
Yet to their general's voice they soon obeyed,
Innumerable. As when the potent rod
Of Amram's son, in Egypt's evil day,
Waved round the coast, up called a pitchy cloud
Of locusts, warping on the eastern wind,
That o'er the realm of impious Pharaoh hung
Like night, and darkened all the land of Nile:
So numberless were those bad angels seen
Hovering on wing under the cope of hell,
'Twixt upper, nether, and surrounding fires;
Till, at a signal given, the uplifted spear
Of their great sultan waving to direct
Their course, in even balance down they light
On the firm brimstone, and fill all the plain:
A multitude like which the populous north
Poured never from her frozen loins, to pass
Rhine or the Danube, when her barbarous sons
Came like a deluge on the south, and spread
Beneath Gibraltar to the Libyan sands.

Forthwith from every squadron and each band
The heads and leaders thither haste where stood
Their great commander; godlike shapes and forms
Excelling human; princely dignities;

And powers that erst in heaven sat on thrones,
Though of their names in heav'nly records now
Be no memorial; blotted out and rased
By their rebellion from the books of life.
Nor had they yet among the sons of Eve
Got them new names; till, wandering o'er the earth,
Through God's high sufferance, for the trial of man,
By falsities and lies the greater part
Of mankind they corrupted to forsake
God their Creator, and the invisible
Glory of him that made them, to transform
Oft to the image of a brute, adorned
With gay religions, full of pomp and gold,
And devils to adore for deities:
Then were they known to men by various names,
And various idols through the heathen world.

   Say, Muse, their names then known, who first,
     who last,
Roused from the slumber on that fiery couch,
At their great emperor's call, as next in worth,
Came singly where he stood on the bare strand,
While the promiscuous crowd stood yet aloof.

   The chief were those who from the pit of hell,
Roaming to seek their prey on earth, durst fix
Their seats long after next the seat of God,
Their altars by his altar, gods adored
Among the nations round, and durst abide
Jehovah thundering out of Sion, throned
Between the cherubim; yea, often placed
Within his sanctuary itself their shrines,
Abominations; and with cursèd things
His holy rites and solemn feasts profaned,
And with their darkness durst affront his light.
First, Moloch, horrid king, besmeared with blood
Of human sacrifice, and parents' tears;
Though, for the noise of drums and timbrels loud,

Their children's cries unheard, that passed through fire
To his grim idol. Him the Ammonite
Worshipped in Rabba and her watery plain,
In Argob and in Basan, to the stream
Of utmost Arnon. Nor content with such
Audacious neighbourhood, the wisest heart
Of Solomon he led by fraud to build
His temple right against the temple of God,
On that opprobrious hill; and made his grove
The pleasant valley of Hinnom, Tophet thence
And black Gehenna called, the type of hell.

Next, Chemos, the obscene dread of Moab's sons,
From Aroer to Nebo, and the wild
Of southmost Abarim; in Hesebon
And Horonáim, Seon's realm, beyond
The flowery dale of Sibma clad with vines,
And Eleälè to the asphaltic pool;
Peor his other name, when he enticed
Israel in Sittim, on their march from Nile,
To do him wanton rites, which cost them woe.
Yet thence his lustful orgies he enlarged
Even to that hill of scandal, by the grove
Of Moloch homicide: lust hard by hate;
Till good Josiah drove them thence to hell.

With these came they who, from the bordering flood
Of old Euphrates to the brook that parts
Egypt from Syrian ground, had general names
Of Baälim and Ashtaroth; those male,
These feminine; for spirits, when they please,
Can either sex assume, or both; so soft
And uncompounded is their essence pure;
Not tied or manacled with joint or limb,
Nor founded on the brittle strength of bones,
Like cumbrous flesh; but, in what shape they choose,
Dilated or condensed, bright or obscure,
Can execute their aëry purposes,

And works of love or enmity fulfil.
For those the race of Israel oft forsook
Their living Strength, and unfrequented left
His righteous altar, bowing lowly down
To bestial gods; for which their heads as low
Bowed down in battle, sunk before the spear
Of despicable foes.
                With these in troop
Came Astoreth, whom the Phenicians called
Astartè, queen of heaven, with crescent horns;
To whose bright image nightly by the moon
Sidonian virgins paid their vows and songs;
In Sion also not unsung, where stood
Her temple on the offensive mountain, built
By that uxorious king, whose heart, though large,
Beguiled by fair idolatresses, fell
To idols foul. Thammuz came next behind,
Whose annual wound in Lebanon allured
The Syrian damsels to lament his fate
In amorous ditties all a summer's day;
While smooth Adonis from his native rock
Ran purple to the sea, supposed with blood
Of Thammuz yearly wounded; the love-tale
Infected Sion's daughters with like heat;
Whose wanton passions in the sacred porch
Ezekiel saw, when, by the vision led,
His eye surveyed the dark idolatries
Of alienated Judah. Next came one
Who mourned in earnest, when the captive ark
Maimed his brute image, head and hands lopped off
In his own temple, on the grunsel edge,
Where he fell flat, and shamed his worshippers;
Dagon his name, sea-monster, upward man
And downward fish; yet had his temple high
Reared in Azotus, dreaded through the coast
Of Palestine, in Gath and Ascalon,
And Accaron and Gaza's frontier bounds.

Him followed Rimmon, whose delightful seat
Was fair Damascus, on the fertile banks
Of Abbana and Pharphar, lucid streams.
He also 'gainst the house of God was bold:
A leper once he lost, and gained a king;
Ahas his sottish conqueror, whom he drew
God's altar to disparage and displace
For one of Syrian mode, whereon to burn
His odious offerings, and adore the gods
Whom he had vanquished.
                              After these appeared
A crew who, under names of old renown,
Osiris, Isis, Orus, and their train,
With monstrous shapes and sorceries abused
Fanatic Egypt and her priests, to seek
Their wandering gods disguised in brutish forms
Rather than human. Nor did Israel 'scape
The infection, when their borrowed gold composed
The calf in Oreb; and the rebel king
Doubled that sin in Bethel and in Dan,
Likening his Maker to the grazèd ox –
Jehovah, who in one night, when he passed
From Egypt marching, equalled with one stroke
Both her first-born and all her bleating gods.

    Belial came last, than whom a spirit more lewd
Fell not from heaven, or more gross to love
Vice for itself; to him no temple stood,
Or altar smoked; yet who more oft than he
In temples and at altars, when the priest
Turns atheist, as did Eli's sons, who filled
With lust and violence the house of God?
In courts and palaces he also reigns,
And in luxurious cities, where the noise
Of riot ascends above their loftiest towers,
And injury and outrage: and when night
Darkens the streets, then wander forth the sons

Of Belial, flown with insolence and wine.
Witness the streets of Sodom, and that night
In Gibeah, when the hospitable door
Exposed a matron, to avoid worse rape.

These were the prime in order and in might:
The rest were long to tell, though far renowned;
The Ionian gods – of Javan's issue held
Gods, yet confessed later than Heaven and Earth,
Their boasted parents: Titan, Heaven's first-born
With his enormous brood, and birthright seized
By younger Saturn; he from mightier Jove,
His own and Rhea's son, like measure found;
So Jove usurping reigned: these first in Crete
And Ida known, thence on the snowy top
Of cold Olympus ruled the middle air,
Their highest heaven; or on the Delphian cliff,
Or in Dodona, and through all the bounds
Of Doric land: or who with Saturn old
Fled over Adria to the Hesperian fields,
And o'er the Celtic roamed the utmost isles.

All these and more came flocking, but with looks
Downcast and damp; yet such wherein appeared
Obscure some glimpse of joy, to have found their chief
Not in despair, to have found themselves not lost
In loss itself; which on his countenance cast
Like doubtful hue; but he, his wonted pride
Soon recollecting, with high words, that bore
Semblance of worth, not substance, gently raised
Their fainting courage, and dispelled their fears.
Then straight commands that at the warlike sound
Of trumpets loud and clarions be upreared
His mighty standard; that proud honour claimed
Azazel as his right, a cherub tall;
Who forthwith from the glittering staff unfurled
The imperial ensign; which, full high advanced,

Shone like a meteor, streaming to the wind,
With gems and golden lustre rich emblazed,
Seraphic arms and trophies, all the while
Sonorous metal blowing martial sounds:
At which the universal host up-sent
A shout, that tore hell's concave, and beyond
Frighted the reign of Chaos and old Night.

All in a moment through the gloom were seen
Ten thousand banners rise into the air
With orient colours waving; with them rose
A forest huge of spears; and thronging helms
Appeared, and serried shields in thick array
Of depth immeasurable; anon they move
In perfect phalanx to the Dorian mood
Of flutes and soft recorders; such as raised
To height of noblest temper heroes old
Arming to battle, and instead of rage,
Deliberate valour breathed, firm and unmoved
With dread of death to flight or foul retreat;
Nor wanting power to mitigate and 'suage
With solemn touches troubled thoughts, and chase
Anguish, and doubt, and fear, and sorrow, and pain
From mortal or immortal minds. Thus they,
Breathing united force, with fixèd thought,
Moved on in silence, to soft pipes, that charmed
Their painful steps o'er the burnt soil: and now
Advanced in view they stand; a horrid front
Of dreadful length and dazzling arms, in guise
Of warriors old with ordered spear and shield,
Awaiting what command their mighty chief
Had to impose: he through the armèd files
Darts his experienced eye, and soon traverse
The whole battalion views, their order due,
Their visages and stature as of gods;
Their number last and he sums. And now his heart
Distends with pride, and hardening in his strength

Glories: for never since created man
Met such embodied force as, named with these,
Could merit more than that small infantry
Warred on by cranes: though all the giant brood
Of Phlegra with the heroic race were joined
That fought at Thebes and Ilium, on each side
Mixed with auxiliar gods; and what resounds
In fable or romance of Uther's son
Begirt with British and Armoric knights;
And all who since, baptized or infidel,
Jousted in Aspramont, or Montalban,
Damascus, or Morocco, or Trebizond,
Or whom Biserta sent from Afric shore,
When Charlemagne with all his peerage fell
By Fontarabbia.

                    Thus far these beyond
Compare of mortal prowess, yet observed
Their dread commander; he, above the rest
In shape and gesture proudly eminent,
Stood like a tower; his form had yet not lost
All its original brightness; nor appeared
Less than archangel ruined, and the excess
Of glory obscured: as when the sun, new risen,
Looks through the horizontal misty air
Shorn of his beams, or from behind the moon,
In dim eclipse, disastrous twilight sheds
On half the nations, and with fear of change
Perplexes monarchs. Darkened so, yet shone
Above them all the archangel; but his face
Deep scars of thunder had entrenched; and care
Sat on his faded cheek; but under brows
Of dauntless courage, and considerate pride.
Waiting revenge; cruel his eye, but cast
Signs of remorse and passion, to behold
The fellows of his crime, the followers rather
(Far other once beheld in bliss), condemned
For ever now to have their lot in pain;

Millions of spirits for his fault amerced
Of heaven, and from eternal splendours flung
For his revolt; yet faithful now they stood,
Their glory withered; as when heaven's fire
Hath scathed the forest oaks, or mountain pines,
With singèd top their stately growth, though bare,
Stands on the blasted heath. He now prepared
To speak; whereat their doubled ranks they bend
From wing to wing, and half enclose him round
With all his peers: attention held them mute.
Thrice he essayed, and thrice, in spite of scorn,
Tears, such as angels weep, burst forth; at last
Words, interwove with sighs, found out their way.

'O myriads of immortal spirits! O powers
Matchless but with the Almighty; and that strife
Was not in glorious, though the event was dire,
At this place testifies, and this dire change,
Hateful to utter! but what power of mind,
Foreseeing or presaging, from the depth
Of knowledge, past or present, could have feared
How such united force of gods, how such
As stood like these, could ever know repulse?
For who can yet believe, though after loss,
That all these puissant legions, whose exile
Hath emptied heaven, shall fail to reascend
Self-raised, and repossess their native seat?
For me, be witness all the host of heaven,
If counsels different, or danger shunned
By me, have lost our hopes. But he who reigns
Monarch in heaven, till then as one secure
Sat on his throne upheld by old repute,
Consent or custom; and his regal state
Put forth at full, but still his strength concealed,
Which tempted our attempt, and wrought our fall.
Henceforth his might we know, and know our own;
So as not either to provoke, or dread

New war, provoked; our better part remains,
To work in close design, by fraud or guile,
What force effected not; that he no less
At length from us may find, who overcomes
By force, hath overcome but half his foe.
Space may produce new worlds; whereof so rife
There went a fame in heaven that he ere long
Intended to create, and therein plant
A generation, whom his choice regard
Should favour equal to the sons of heaven:
Thither, if but to pry, shall be perhaps
Our first eruption; thither, or elsewhere;
For this infernal pit shall never hold
Celestial spirits in bondage, nor the abyss
Long under darkness cover. But these thoughts
Full counsel must mature; peace is despaired;
For who can think submission? War, then, war,
Open or understood, must be resolved.'

He spake; and, to confirm his words, outflew
Millions of flaming swords, drawn from the thighs
Of mighty cherubim; the sudden blaze
Far round illumined hell; highly they raged
Against the Highest, and fierce with graspèd arms
Clashed on their sounding shields the din of war,
Hurling defiance toward the vault of heaven.

There stood a hill not far, whose grisly top
Belched fire and rolling smoke; the rest entire
Shone with a glossy scurf, undoubted sign
That in his womb was hid metallic ore,
The work of sulphur. Thither, winged with speed,
A numerous brigade hastened: as when bands
Of pioneers, with spade and pickaxe armed,
Forerun the royal camp, to trench a field,
Or cast a rampart. Mammon led them on:
Mammon, the least erected spirit that fell

From heaven; for even in heaven his looks and
    thoughts
Were always downward bent, admiring more
The riches of heaven's pavement, trodden gold,
Than aught, divine or holy, else enjoyed
In vision beatific; by him first
Men also, and by his suggestion taught,
Ransacked the centre, and with impious hands
Rifled the bowels of their mother earth
For treasures, better hid. Soon had his crew
Opened into the hill a spacious wound,
And digged out ribs of gold. Let none admire
That riches grow in hell; that soil may best
Deserve the precious bane. And here let those
Who boast in mortal things, and wondering tell
Of Babel, and the works of Memphian kings,
Learn how their greatest monuments of fame,
And strength and art, are easily outdone
By spirits reprobate, and in an hour
What in an age they with incessant toil
And hands innumerable scarce perform.

    Nigh on the plain, in many cells prepared,
That underneath had veins of liquid fire
Sluiced from the lake, a second multitude
With wondrous art founded the massy ore,
Severing each kind, and scummed the bullion dross;
A third as soon had formed within the ground
A various mould, and from the boiling cells,
By strange conveyance, filled each hollow nook,
As in an organ, from one blast of wind,
To many a row of pipes the sound-board breathes.
Anon, out of the earth a fabric huge
Rose like an exhalation, with the sound
Of dulcet symphonies and voices sweet,
Built like a temple, where pilasters round
Were set, and Doric pillars overlaid

With golden architrave; nor did there want
Cornice or frieze, with bossy sculptures graven:
The roof was fretted gold. Not Babylon,
Nor great Alcairo, such magnificence
Equalled in all their glories, to enshrine
Belus or Serapis their gods, or seat
Their kings, when Egypt with Assyria strove
In wealth and luxury. The ascending pile
Stood fixed her stately height: and straight the doors,
Opening their brazen folds, discover, wide
Within, her ample spaces, o'er the smooth
And level pavement; from the archèd roof,
Pendent by subtle magic, many a row
Of starry lamps and blazing cressets, fed
With naphtha and asphaltus, yielded light
As from a sky. The hasty multitude
Admiring entered; and the work some praise,
And some the architect: his hand was known
In heaven by many a towered structure high
Where sceptered angels held their residence,
And sat as princes; whom the supreme King
Exalted to such power, and gave to rule,
Each in his hierarchy, the orders bright.
Nor was his name unheard or unadored
In ancient Greece; and in Ausonian land
Men called him Mulciber; and how he fell
From heaven they fabled, thrown by angry Jove
Sheer o'er the crystal battlements: from morn
To noon he fell, from noon to dewy eve,
A summer's day; and with the setting sun
Dropped from the zenith like a falling star,
On Lemnos, th' Aegean isle: thus they relate,
Erring; for he with this rebellious rout
Fell long before; nor aught availed him now
To have built in heaven high towers; nor did he 'scape
By all his engines, but was headlong sent
With his industrious crew to build in hell.

Meanwhile, the wingèd heralds, by command
Of sovereign power, with awful ceremony
And trumpet's sound, throughout the host proclaim
A solemn council, forthwith to be held
At Pandemonium, the high capital
Of Satan and his peers: their summons called
From every band and squarèd regiment
By place or choice the worthiest; they anon,
With hundreds and with thousands, trooping came,
Attended; all access was thronged; the gates
And porches wide, but chief the spacious hall
(Though like a covered field, where champions bold
Wont ride in armed, and at the soldan's chair
Defied the best of paynim chivalry
To mortal combat, or career with lance),
Thick swarmed, both on the ground and in the air,
Brushed with the hiss of rustling wings. As bees
In spring-time, when the sun with Taurus rides,
Pour forth their populous youth about the hive
In clusters; they among fresh dews and flowers
Fly to and fro, or on the smoothèd plank,
The suburb of their straw-built citadel,
New rubbed with balm, expatiate, and confer
Their state affairs; so thick the aëry crowd
Swarmed and were straightened; till, the signal given,
Behold a wonder! They, but now who seemed
In bigness to surpass earth's giant sons,
Now less than smallest dwarfs, in narrow room
Throng numberless, like that Pygmëan race
Beyond the Indian mount, or faëry elves
Whose midnight revels, by a forest side
Or fountain, some belated peasant sees,
Or dreams he sees, while over head the moon
Sits arbitress, and nearer to the earth
Wheels her pale course; they, on their mirth and dance
Intent, with jocund music charm his ear;
At once with joy and fear his heart rebounds.

Thus incorporeal spirits to smallest forms
Reduced their shapes immense, and were at large,
Though without number still, amidst the hall
Of that infernal court. But far within,
And in their own dimensions, like themselves,
The great seraphic lords and cherubim
In close recess and secret conclave sat;
A thousand demi-gods on golden seats
Frequent and full. After short silence then,
And summons read, the great consult began.

'Hail, holy Light . . .'

Hail, holy Light, offspring of Heaven first-born,
Or of th' Eternal coeternal beam
May I express thee unblam'd? since God is light,
And never but in unapproached light
Dwelt from eternity, dwelt then in thee,
Bright effluence of bright essence increate.
Or hear'st thou rather pure ethereal stream,
Whose fountain who shall tell? Before the Sun,
Before the Heavens thou wert, and at the voice
Of God, as with a mantle didst invest
The rising world of waters dark and deep,
Won from the void and formless Infinite.
Thee I revisit now with bolder wing,
Escap'd the Stygian Pool, though long detain'd
In that obscure sojourn, while in my flight
Through utter and through middle darkness borne,
With other notes than to th' Orphean lyre
I sung of Chaos and eternal Night,
Taught by the heav'nly Muse to venture down
The dark descent, and up to reascend,
Though hard and rare: thee I revisit safe,
And feel thy sovran vital lamp; but thou
Revisit'st not these eyes, that roll in vain

To find thy piercing ray, and find no dawn;
So thick a drop serene hath quencht their orbs,
Or dim suffusion veil'd. Yet not the more
Cease I to wander where the Muses haunt
Clear spring, or shady grove, or sunny hill,
Smit with the love of sacred song; but chief
Thee Sion and the flowery brooks beneath,
That wash thy hallow'd feet, and warbling flow,
Nightly I visit: nor sometimes forget
Those other two equall'd with me in fate,
So were I equall'd with them in renown,
Blind Thamyris and blind Maeonides,
And Tiresias and Phineus prophets old.
Then feed on thoughts, that voluntary move
Harmonious numbers; as the wakeful bird
Sings darkling, and in shadiest covert hid
Tunes her nocturnal note. Thus with the year
Seasons return, but not to me returns
Day, or the sweet approach of ev'n or morn,
Or sight of vernal bloom, or summer's rose,
Or flocks, or herds, or human face divine;
But cloud instead, and ever-during dark
Surrounds me, from the cheerful ways of men
Cut off, and for the book of knowledge fair
Presented with a universal blank
Of Nature's works to me expung'd and ras'd
And wisdom at one entrance quite shut out.
So much the rather thou Celestial Light
Shine inward, and the mind through all her powers
Irradiate, there plant eyes, all mist from thence
Purge and disperse, that I may see and tell
Of things invisible to mortal sight.

[From *Paradise Lost*, Book III]

On His Blindness

When I consider how my light is spent,
  Ere half my days, in this dark world and wide,
  And that one talent which is death to hide,
  Lodg'd with me useless, though my soul more bent
To serve therewith my Maker, and present
  My true account, lest He returning chide,
  Doth God exact day-labour, light denied,
  I fondly ask; but patience to prevent
That murmur, soon replies, God doth not need
  Either man's work or His own gifts; who best
  Bear His mild yoke, they serve Him best. His state
Is kingly. Thousands at His bidding speed
  And post o'er land and ocean without rest;
  They also serve who only stand and wait.

Paradise Lost

     High in front advanc'd,
The brandish'd sword of God before them blaz'd
Fierce as a comet; which with torrid heat,
And vapour as the Libyan air adust,
Began to parch that temperate clime: whereat
In either hand the hast'ning Angel caught
Our ling'ring parents, and to th' eastern gate
Led them direct, and down the cliff as fast
To the subjected plain; then disappear'd.
They looking back, all th' eastern side beheld
Of Paradise, so late their happy seat,
Wav'd over by that flaming brand, the gate
With dreadful faces throng'd and fiery arms:
Some natural tears they dropp'd, but wip'd them soon;
The world was all before them, where to choose
Their place of rest, and Providence their guide:
They hand in hand with wand'ring steps and slow,
Through Eden took their solitary way.

[From *Paradise Lost*, Book XII]

God's Purposes Revealed

All is best, though we oft doubt,
What th' unsearchable dispose
Of highest Wisdom brings about,
And ever best found in the close.
Oft he seems to hide his face,
But unexpectedly returns
And to his faithful Champion hath in place
Bore witness gloriously; whence Gaza mourns
And all that band them to resist
His uncontrollable intent,
His servants he with new acquist
Of true experience from this great event
With peace and consolation hath dismiss'd,
And calm of mind all passion spent.

[From *Samson Agonistes*]

SIR JOHN SUCKLING
(1609–1642)

'*Why so pale and wan . . .*'

Why so pale and wan, fond lover?
    Prithee, why so pale?
Will, when looking well can't move her,
    Looking ill prevail?
    Prithee, why so pale?

Why so dull and mute, young sinner?
    Prithee, why so mute?
Will, when speaking well can't win her,
    Saying nothing do 't?
    Prithee, why so mute?

Quit, quit for shame! This will not move;
　　This cannot take her.
If of herself she will not love,
　　Nothing can make her:
　　The devil take her!

The Constant Lover

Out upon it! I have lov'd
　　Three whole days together;
And am like to love three more,
　　If it prove fair weather.

Time shall moult away his wings,
　　Ere he shall discover
In the whole wide world again
　　Such a constant lover.

But the spite on 't is, no praise
　　Is due at all to me:
Love with me had made no stays,
　　Had it any been but she.

Had it any been but she,
　　And that very face,
There had been at least ere this
　　A dozen dozen in her place.

RICHARD CRASHAW
(1613?–1649)

A Hymn to the Name and Honour of the Admirable Saint Teresa

Love, thou art absolute, sole lord
O Life and Death. To prove the word,
We'll now appeal to none of all
Those thy old soldiers, great and tall,
Ripe men of martyrdom, that could reach down
With strong arms their triumphant crown;
Such as could with lusty breath
Speak loud into the face of death
Their great Lord's glorious name; to none
Of those whose spacious bosoms spread a throne
For Love at large to fill; spare blood and sweat;
We'll see him take a private seat,
And make his mansion in the mild
And milky soul of a soft child.

    Scarce has she learnt to lisp the name
Of martyr; yet she thinks it shame
Life should so long play with that breath
Which spent can buy so brave a death.
She never undertook to know
What death with love should have to do;
Nor has she e'er yet understood
Why to show love, she should shed blood;
Yet though she cannot tell you why,
She can love, and she can die.

    Scarce has she blood enough to make
A guilty sword blush for her sake;
Yet has a heart dares hope to prove
How much less strong is Death than Love.

Be love but there; let poor six years
Be pos'd with the maturest fears
Man trembles at, we straight shall find
Love knows no nonage, nor the mind.
'Tis love, not years or limbs that can
Make the martyr, or the man.
Love touch'd her heart, and lo it beats
High, and burns with such brave heats;
Such thirst to die, as dares drink up,
A thousand cold deaths in one cup.
Good reason. For she breathes all fire.
Her weak breast heaves with strong desire
Of what she may with fruitless wishes
Seek for amongst her mother's kisses.

   Since 'tis not to be had at home,
She'll travel to a martyrdom.
No home for her confesses she
But where she may a martyr be.

   She'll to the Moors; and trade with them,
For this unvalued diadem.
She'll offer them her dearest breath,
With Christ's Name in 'it, in change for death.
She'll bargain with them; and will give
Them God; and teach them how to live
In Him: or, if they this deny,
For Him she'll teach them how to die.
So shall she leave amongst them sown
Her Lord's Blood; or at least her own.

   Farewell then, all the world! Adieu.
Teresa is no more for you.
Farewell, all pleasures, sports, and joys,
(Never till now esteemed toys)
Farewell whatever dear may be,
Mother's arms or father's knee.
Farewell house, and farewell home!
She's for the Moors, and martyrdom.

   Sweet, not so fast! lo, thy fair Spouse

Whom thou seek'st with so swift vows,
Calls thee back, and bids thee come
T'embrace a milder martyrdom.

    Blest powers forbid, thy tender life
Should bleed upon a barbarous knife;
Or some base hand have power to rase
Thy breast's chast cabinet, and uncase
A soul kept there so sweet. O no;
Wise heav'n will never have it so.
Thou art love's victim; and must die
A death more mystical and high.
Into love's arms, thou shalt let fall
A still-surviving funeral.
His is the dart must make the death
Whose stroke will taste thy hallow'd breath;
A dart thrice dipt in that rich flame
Which writes thy spouse's radiant Name
Upon the roof of Heav'n; where aye
It shines, and with a sovereign ray
Beats bright upon the burning faces
Of souls which in that name's sweet graces
Find everlasting smiles. So rare,
So spiritual, pure, and fair
Must be th' immortal instrument
Upon whose choice point shall be spent
A life so lov'd; and that there be
Fit executioners for thee,
The fairest first-born sons of fire
Blest Seraphim, shall leave their quire
And turn love's soldiers, upon thee
To exercise their archery.

    O how oft shall thou complain
Of a sweet and subtle pain,
Of intolerable joys;
Of a death, in which who dies
Loves his death, and dies again,
And would for ever be so slain,

And lives, and dies; and knows not why
To live, but that he still may die.
    How kindly will thy gentle heart
Kiss the sweetly-killing dart!
And close in his embraces keep
Those delicious wounds, that weep
Balsam to heal themselves with, thus
When these thy deaths, so numerous,
Shall all at once die into one,
And melt thy soul's sweet mansion;
Like a soft lump of incense, hasted
By too hot a fire, and wasted
Into perfuming clouds, so fast
Shalt thou exhale to Heav'n at last
In a resolving sigh, and then
O what? Ask not the tongues of men.
    Angels cannot tell; suffice
Thyself shalt feel thine own full joys
And hold them fast for ever there,
So soon as thou shalt first appear,
The Moon of maiden stars, thy white
Mistress, attended by such bright
Souls as thy shining self, shall come
And in her first ranks make thee room;
Where 'mongst her snowy family
Immortal welcomes wait for thee.
    O what delight, when she shall stand
And teach thy lips heav'n with her hand;
On which thou now mayest to thy wishes
Heap up thy consecrated kisses.
What joy shall seize thy soul, when she
Bending her blessed eyes on thee
Those second smiles of Heav'n shall dart
Her mild rays through thy melting heart!
    Angels, thy old friends, there shall greet thee
Glad at their own home now to meet thee.
All thy good works which went before

And waited for thee, at the door,
Shall own thee there; and all in one
Weave a constellation
Of crowns, with which the King thy spouse
Shall build up thy triumphant brows.

　　All thy old woes shall now smile on thee,
And thy pains sit bright upon thee,
All thy sorrows here shall shine,
And thy suff'rings be divine
Tears shall take comfort, and turn gems,
And wrongs repent to diadems.
Ev'n thy death shall live: and new
Dress the soul which late they slew.
Thy wounds shall blush to such bright scars
As keep account of the Lamb's wars.

　　Those rare works where thou shalt leave writ
Love's noble history, with wit
Taught thee by none by Him, while here
They feed our souls, shall clothe thine there.
Each heavenly word by whose hid flame
Our hard hearts shall strike fire, the same
Shall flourish on thy brows, and be
Both fire to us and flame to thee;
Whose light shall live bright in thy face
By glory, in our hearts by grace.

　　Thou shalt look round about, and see
Thousands of crown'd souls throng to be
Themselves thy crown, sons of thy vows,
The virgin-births with which thy spouse
Made fruitful thy fair soul, go now
And with them all about thee bow
To Him, put on (he'll say) put on
My rosy love, that thy rich zone
Sparkling with the sacred flames
Of thousand souls, whose happy names
Heav'n keeps upon thy score: Thy bright
Life brought them first to kiss the light

That kindled them to stars; and so
Thou with the Lamb, thy Lord, shalt go;
And whereso'er He sets His white
Steps, walk with Him those ways of light
Which who in death would live to see,
Must learn in life to die like thee.

Charitas Nimia

OR, THE DEAR BARGAIN

Lord, what is man? why should he cost Thee
So dear? what had his ruin lost Thee?
Lord, what is man? that Thou hast overbought
So much a thing of nought?

Love is too kind, I see, and can
Make but a simple merchantman.
'Twas for such sorry merchandise
Bold painters have put out his eyes.

Alas, sweet Lord! what were 't to Thee
If there were no such worms as we?
Heav'n ne'ertheless still heav'n would be.
    Should mankind dwell
    In the deep hell,
What have his woes to do with Thee?

    Let him go weep
    O'er his own wounds;
    Seraphim will not sleep,
Nor spheres let fall their faithful rounds.

Still would the youthful spirits sing,
And still Thy spacious palace ring;
Still would those beauteous ministers of light
    Burn all as bright.

And bow their flaming heads before Thee;
Still thrones and dominations would adore Thee;
Still would those ever-wakeful sons of fire
          Keep warm Thy praise,
          Both nights and days,
And teach Thy loved name to their noble lyre.

    Let froward dust then do its kind,
And give itself for sport to the proud wind.
Why should a piece of peevish clay plead shares
In the eternity of Thy old cares?
Why should'st Thou bow Thy awful breast to see
What mine own madnesses have done with me?

    Should not the king still keep his throne
Because some desperate fool's undone?
Or will the world's illustrious eyes
Weep for every worm that dies?

          Will the gallant sun
          E'er the less glorious run?
Will he hang down his golden head,
Or e'er the sooner seek his western bed,
          Because some foolish fly
          Grows wanton, and will die?

    If I were lost in misery,
What was it to Thy heav'n, and Thee?
What was it to Thy precious blood
If my foul heart call'd for a flood?

    What if my faithless soul and I
          Would need fall in
          With guilt and sin,
What did the Lamb that He should die?
What did the Lamb that He should need,
When the wolf sins, Himself to bleed?

                    If my base lust
Bargain'd with death and well-beseeming dust,
                    Why should the white
                    Lamb's bosom write
                    The purple name
                    Of my sin's shame?

    Why should His unstain'd breast make good
My blushes with His own heart blood?

    O, my Saviour, make me see
How dearly Thou hast paid for me,

    That, lost again, my life may prove
As then in death, so now in love!

RICHARD LOVELACE
(1618–1658)

To Althea from Prison

When Love with unconfined wings
    Hovers within my gates,
And my divine Althea brings
    To whisper at the grates;
When I lie tangled in her hair
    And fetter'd to her eye,
The birds that wanton in the air
    Know no such liberty.

When flowing cups run swiftly round
    With no allaying Thames,
Our careless heads with roses crown'd,
    Our hearts with loyal flames;

When thirsty grief in wine we steep,
 When healths and draughts go free,
Fishes that tipple in the deep
 Know no such liberty.

When, linnet-like confined, I
 With shriller throat shall sing
The sweetness, mercy, majesty
 And glories of my King;
When I shall voice aloud how good
 He is, how great should be,
Enlarged winds, that curl the flood,
 Know no such liberty.

Stone walls do not a prison make,
 Nor iron bars a cage;
Minds innocent and quiet take
 That for an hermitage:
If I have freedom in my love
 And in my soul am free,
Angels alone, that soar above,
 Enjoy such liberty.

To Lucasta, on Going Beyond the Seas

If to be absent were to be
  Away from thee;
 Or that when I am gone
 You or I were alone;
Then, my Lucasta, might I crave
Pity from blustering wind, or swallowing wave.

Though seas and land be 'twixt us both,
  Our faith and troth,
 Like separated souls,
 All time and space controls:
Above the highest sphere we meet
Unseen, unknown, and greet as Angels greet.

So then we do anticipate
          Our after-fate,
     And are alive i' the skies,
     If thus our lips and eyes
Can speak like spirits unconfin'd
In Heaven, their earthy bodies left behind.

ABRAHAM COWLEY
(1618–1667)

Platonic Love

Indeed I must confess,
     When souls mix, 'tis an happiness;
But not complete till bodies too combine,
And closely as our minds together join;
But half of Heaven the souls in glory taste,
     Till by Love in Heaven at last
          Their bodies too are plac'd.

In thy immortal part
     Man, as well as I, thou art.
But something 'tis that differs thee and me;
And we must one even in that difference be.
I thee, both as a man, and woman prize;
     For a perfect Love implies
          Love in all capacities.

Can that for true love pass
     When a fair woman courts her glass?
Something unlike must in Love's likeness be.
His wonder is, one, and variety.
For he, whose soul nought but a soul can move,
     Does a new Narcissus prove,
          And his own image love.

That souls do beauty know,
'Tis to the bodies help they owe;
If when they know 't, they straight abuse that trust,
And shut the body from 't, 'tis as unjust,
As if I brought my dearest friend to see
   My mistress, and at th' instant he
      Should steal her quite from me.

The Wish

Well then; I now do plainly see,
This busy world and I shall ne'er agree;
The very honey of all earthly joy
   Does of all meats the soonest cloy,
   And they, methinks, deserve my pity,
Who for it can endure the stings,
The crowd, and buzz, and murmurings
   Of this great hive, the city.

Ah, yet, e'er I descend to th' grave
May I a small house, and large garden have!
And a few friends, and many books, both true,
   Both wise, and both delightful too!
   And since love ne'er will from me flee,
A mistress moderately fair,
And good as guardian-angels are,
   Only belov'd, and loving me!

Oh, fountains, when in you shall I
My self, eas'd of unpeaceful thoughts, espy?
O fields! O woods! when, when shall I be made
   The happy tenant of your shade?
   Here's the spring-head of pleasure's flood;
Where all the riches lie, that she
   Has coin'd and stamp'd for good.

Pride and ambition here,
Only in far-fetch'd metaphors appear;
Here nought but winds can hurtful murmurs scatter;
  And nought but echo flatter.
  The gods when they descended hither
From Heav'n did always choose their way;
And therefore we may boldly say,
  That 'tis the way too thither.

How happy here should I,
And one dear She live, and embracing die?
She who is all the world, and can exclude
  In deserts solitude.
  I should have then this only fear,
Lest men, when they my pleasures see,
Should hither throng to live like me,
  And so make a city here.

Life and Fame

O Life, thou Nothing's younger brother!
  So like, that one might take one for the other.
  What's somebody, or nobody?
In all the cobwebs of the schoolmen's trade,
We no such nice distinction woven see,
  As 'tis to be, or not to be.
Dream of a shadow! A reflection made
From the false glories of the gay reflected bow,
  Is a more solid thing than thou.
Vain weak-built isthmus, which dost proudly rise
  Up betwixt two eternities;
  Yet canst nor wave nor wind sustain,
But broken and o'erwhelm'd, the endless oceans
    meet again.

And with what rare inventions do we strive,
  Ourselves then to survive?

Wise, subtle arts, and such as well befit
   That nothing man's no wit.
Some with vast costly tombs would purchase it,
And by the proofs of Death pretend to live.
Here lies the great – False marble, where?
Nothing but small, and sordid dust lies there.
Some build enormous mountain-palaces,
   The fools and architects to please:
A lasting life in well-hewn stone they rear:
   So he who on th' Egyptian shore
Was slain so many hundred years before,
   Lives still (O life most happy and most dear!
   O life that epicures envy to hear!)
Lives in the dropping ruins of his amphitheatre.

His father-in-law an higher place does claim
In the seraphic entity of fame.
   He since that toy his death,
Does fill all mouths, and breathes in all men's breath.
'Tis true, the two immortal syllables remain,
   But, oh ye learned men explain,
   What essence, what existence this,
What substance, what subsistence, what hypostasis
   In six poor letters is?
In those alone does the great Caesar live,
   'Tis all the conquer'd world could give.
   We poets madder yet than all,
With a refin'd fantastic vanity,
Think we not only have, but give eternity.
   Fain would I see that prodigal,
   Who his to-morrow would bestow,
For all old Homer's life e'er since he died till now.

ANDREW MARVELL
(1621–1678)

The Garden

How vainly men themselves amaze,
To win the palm, the oak or bays,
And their incessant labours see
Crown'd from some single herb or tree,
Whose short and narrow-verged shade
Does prudently their toils upbraid,
While all the flowers, and trees, do close,
To weave the garlands of repose!

Fair Quiet, have I found thee here,
And Innocence, thy sister dear?
Mistaken long, I sought you then
In busy companies of men,
Your sacred plants, if here below,
Only among the plants will grow;
Society is all but rude,
To this delicious solitude.

No white nor red was ever seen
So amorous as this lovely green.
Fond lovers, cruel as their flame,
Cut in these trees their mistress' name:
Little, alas! they know or heed,
How far these beauties her exceed!
Fair trees! where'er your barks I wound,
No name shall but your own be found.

When we have run our passion's heat,
Love hither makes his best retreat.
The gods, who mortal beauty chase,
Still in a tree did end their race;
Apollo hunted Daphne so,
Only that she might laurel grow;

And Pan did after Syrinx speed,
Not as a nymph, but for a reed.

What wond'rous life is this I lead!
Ripe apples drop about my head;
The luscious clusters of the vine
Upon my mouth do crush their wine;
The nectarine, and curious peach,
Into my hands themselves do reach;
Stumbling on melons, as I pass,
Insnared with flowers, I fall on grass.

Meanwhile the mind, from pleasure less,
Withdraws into its happiness; –
The mind, that ocean where each kind
Does straight its own resemblance find; –
Yet it creates, transcending these,
Far other worlds, and other seas,
Annihilating all that's made
To a green thought in a green shade.

Here at the fountain's sliding foot,
Or at some fruit-tree's mossy root,
Casting the body's vest aside,
My soul into the boughs does glide:
There, like a bird, it sits and sings,
Then whets and claps its silver wings,
And, till prepar'd for longer flight,
Waves in its plumes the various light.

Such was that happy garden-state,
While man there walked without a mate:
After a place so pure and sweet,
What other help could yet be meet!
But 'twas beyond a mortal's share
To wander solitary there:
Two paradises 'twere in one,
To live in paradise alone.

How well the skilful gardener drew
Of flowers, and herbs, this dial new,
Where, from above, the milder sun
Does through a fragrant zodiac run,
And, as it works the industrious bee
Computes its time as well as we!
How could such sweet and wholesome hours
Be reckoned but with herbs and flowers?

To his Coy Mistress

Had we but world enough, and time,
This coyness, Lady, were no crime,
We would sit down and think which way
To walk and pass our long love's day.
Thou by the Indian Ganges' side
Shouldst rubies find; I by the tide
Of Humber would complain. I would
Love you ten years before the Flood,
And you should, if you please, refuse
Till the conversion of the Jews.
My vegetable love should grow
Vaster than empires, and more slow;
An hundred years should go to praise
Thine eyes, and on thy forehead gaze,
Two hundred to adore each breast,
But thirty thousand to the rest;
An age at least to every part,
And the last age should show your heart.
For, Lady, you deserve this state,
Nor would I love at lower rate.

But at my back I always hear
Time's wingèd chariot hurrying near;
And yonder all before us lie
Deserts of vast eternity.
Thy beauty shall no more be found,
Nor, in thy marble vault shall sound

My echoing song; then worms shall try
That long preserved virginity,
And your quaint honour turn to dust,
And into ashes all my lust:
The grave's a fine and private place,
But none, I think, do there embrace.

Now therefore, while the youthful hue
Sits on thy skin like morning dew,
And while thy willing soul transpires
At every pore with instant fires,
Now let us sport us while we may,
And now, like amorous birds of prey,
Rather at once our time devour
Than languish in his slow-chapt power.
Let us roll all our strength and all
Our sweetness up into one ball,
And tear our pleasures with rough strife
Through the iron gates of life.
Thus, though we cannot make our sun
Stand still, yet we will make him run.

HENRY VAUGHAN
(1622–1695)

The Retreat

Happy those early days, when I
Shined in my Angel-infancy!
Before I understood this place
Appointed for my second race,
Or taught my soul to fancy aught
But a white, celestial thought;
When yet I had not walk'd above
A mile or two from my first Love,

And looking back, at that short space
Could see a glimpse of His bright face;
When on some gilded cloud or flower
My gazing soul would dwell an hour,
And in those weaker glories spy
Some shadows of eternity;
Before I taught my tongue to wound
My conscience with a sinful sound,
Or had the black art to dispense
A several sin to every sense,
But felt through all this fleshly dress
Bright shoots of everlastingness.
 O how I long to travel back,
And tread again that ancient track!
That I might once more reach that plain,
Where first I left my glorious train;
From whence th' enlighten'd spirit sees
That shady city of palm-trees.
But ah! my soul with too much stay
Is drunk, and staggers in the way!
Some men a forward motion love,
But I by backward steps would move,
And when this dust falls to the urn,
In that state I came, return.

The Morning Watch

O joys! infinite sweetness! with what flowers
And shoots of glory, my soul breaks and buds!
   All the long hours
   Of night and rest,
   Through the still shrouds
   Of sleep, and clouds,
  This dew fell on my breast;
   O how it bloods,

And spirits all my earth! hark! in what rings,
And hymning circulations the quick world
      Awakes and sings!
      The rising winds
      And falling springs,
     Birds, beasts, all things
   Adore Him in their kinds.
      Thus all is hurl'd
In sacred hymns and order; the great chime
And symphony of Nature. Prayer is
      The world in tune,
      A spirit-voice,
      And vocal joys,
   Whose echo is heaven's bliss.
      O let me climb
When I lie down! The pious soul by night –
Is like a clouded star, whose beams, though said
      To shed their light
      Under some cloud,
      Yet are above,
      And shine and move
   Beyond that misty shroud;
      So in my bed,
That curtain'd grave, though sleep, like ashes, hide
My lamp and life, both shall in Thee abide.

'They are all gone into the world of light! . . .'

They are all gone into the world of light!
   And I alone sit ling'ring here;
Their very memory is fair and bright,
   And my sad thoughts doth clear.

It glows and glitters in my cloudy breast,
   Like stars upon some gloomy grove,
Or those faint beams in which this hill is dress'd,
   After the sun's remove.

I see them walking in an air of glory,
    Whose light doth trample on my days:
My days, which are at best but dull and hoary,
    Mere glimmering and decays.

O holy Hope! and high Humility,
    High as the heavens above!
These are your walks, and you have show'd them me,
    To kindle my cold love.

Dear, beauteous Death! the jewel of the just,
    Shining nowhere, but in the dark;
What mysteries do lie beyond thy dust,
    Could man outlook that mark!

He that hath found some fledg'd bird's nest, may know
    At first sight, if the bird be flown;
But what fair well or grove he sings in now,
    That is to him unknown.

And yet, as angels in some brighter dreams
    Call to the soul when man doth sleep,
So some strange thoughts transcend our wonted themes,
    And into glory peep.

If a star were confin'd into a tomb,
    Her captives must needs burn there;
But when the hand that lock'd her up, gives room,
    She'll shine through all the sphere.

O Father of eternal life, and all
    Created glories under Thee!
Resume Thy spirit from this world of thrall
    Into true liberty.

Either disperse these mists, which blot and fill
    My perspective still as they pass:
Or else remove me hence unto that hill
    Where I shall need no glass.

The Garland

Thou, who dost flow and flourish here below,
   To whom a falling star and nine days' glory,
Or some frail beauty makes the bravest show,
   Hark, and make use of this ensuing story.

When first my youthful, sinful age
   Grew master of my ways,
Appointing Error for my Page,
   And Darkness for my days;
I flung away, and with full cry
   Of wild affections, rid
In post for pleasures, bent to try
   All gamesters that would bid.
I play'd with fire, did counsel spurn,
   Made life my common stake;
But never thought that fire would burn,
   Or that a soul could ache.
Glorious deceptions, gilded mists,
   False joys, fantastic flights,
Pieces of sackcloth with silk lists,
   These were my prime delights.
I sought choice bowers, haunted the spring,
   Cull'd flowers and made me posies;
Gave my fond humours their full wing,
   And crown'd my head with roses.
But at the height of this career
   I met with a dead man,
Who, noting well my vain abear,
   Thus unto me began:
Desist, fond fool, be not undone;
   What thou hast cut to-day
Will fade at night, and with this sun
   Quite vanish and decay.

Flowers gather'd in this world, die here; if thou
  Wouldst have a wreath that fades not, let them grow,
And grow for thee. Who spares them here, shall find
  A garland, where comes neither rain, nor wind.

Childhood

  I cannot reach it; and my striving eye
  Dazzles at it, as at eternity.

        Were now that chronicle alive,
  Those white designs which children drive,
  And the thoughts of each harmless hour,
  With their content too in my pow'r,
  Quickly would I make my path ev'n,
  And by mere playing go to heaven,
        Why should men love
  A wolf, more than a lamb or dove?
  Or choose hell-fire and brimstone streams
  Before bright stars and God's own beams?
  Who kisseth thorns will hurt his face,
  But flowers do both refresh and grace;
  And sweetly living – fie on men! –
  Are, when dead, medicinal then;
  If seeing much should make staid eyes,
  And long experience should make wise;
  Since all that age doth teach is ill,
  Why should I not love childhood still?
  Why, if I see a rock or shelf,
  Shall I from thence cast down myself?
  Or by complying with the world,
  From the same precipice be hurl'd?
  Those observations are but foul,
  Which make me wise to lose my soul.

  And yet the practice wordlings call
  Business, and weighty action all,
  Checking the poor child for his play,
  But gravely cast themselves away.

Dear, harmless age! the short, swift span
Where weeping Virtue parts with man;
Where love without lust dwells, and bends
What way we please without self-ends.

An age of mysteries! which he
Must live that would God's face see
Which angels guard, and with it play,
Angels! which foul men drive away.

How do I study now, and scan
Thee more than e'er I studied man,
And only see through a long night
Thy edges and thy bordering light!
O for thy centre and midday!
For sure that is the narrow way!

JOHN BUNYAN
(1628–1688)

The Shepherd Boy's Song

He that is down, needs fear no fall,
    He that is low, no pride;
He that is humble, ever shall
    Have God to be his guide.

I am content with what I have,
    Little be it, or much:
And, Lord, contentment still I crave,
    Because thou savest such.

Fullness to such a burden is
    That go on pilgrimage:
Here little, and hereafter bliss
    Is best from age to age.

        [From the Second Part of *The Pilgrim's Progress*]

The Song of Master Valiant-for-Truth

Who would true valour see,
    Let him come hither;
One here will constant be,
    Come wind, come weather.
There's no discouragement
Shall make him once relent
His first avow'd intent
        To be a pilgrim.

Whoso beset him round,
    With dismal stories,
Do but themselves confound;
    His strength the more is.
No lion can him fright,
He'll with a giant fight,
But he will have a right
        To be a pilgrim.

Hobgoblin, nor foul fiend,
    Can daunt his spirit:
He knows, he at the end
    Shall Life inherit.
Then fancies fly away,
He'll fear not what men say,
He'll labour night and day
        To be a pilgrim.

[From the Second Part of *The Pilgrim's Progress*]

JOHN DRYDEN
(1631–1700)

Achitophel

Of these the false Achitophel was first,
A name to all succeeding ages curs'd.
For close designs and crooked counsels fit,
Sagacious, bold, and turbulent of wit,
Restless, unfix'd in principles and place,
In pow'r unpleas'd, impatient of disgrace;
A fiery soul, which working out its way,
Fretted the pigmy body to decay:
And o'er inform'd the tenement of clay.
A daring pilot in extremity;
Pleas'd with the danger, when the waves went high
He sought the storms; but, for a calm unfit,
Would steer too nigh the sands to boast his wit.
Great wits are sure to madness near allied,
And thin partitions do their bounds divide;
Else, why should he, with wealth and honour blest,
Refuse his age the needful hours of rest?
Punish a body which he could not please,
Bankrupt of life, yet prodigal of ease?
And all to leave what with his toil he won
To that unfeather'd two-legg'd thing, a son;
Got, while his soul did huddled notions try,
And born a shapeless lump, like anarchy;
In friendship false, implacable in hate,
Resolv'd to ruin or to rule the State;
To compass this the triple bond he broke;
The pillars of the public safety shook,
And fitted Israel for a foreign yoke;
Then, seiz'd with fear, yet still affecting fame,
Usurp'd a Patriot's all-atoning name.

So easy still it proves in factious times
With public zeal to cancel private crimes.
How safe is treason, and how sacred ill,
Where none can sin against the people's will!
Where crowds can wink, and no offence be known,
Since in another's guilt they find their own!
Yet fame deserved no enemy can grudge;
The statesman we abhor, but praise the judge.
In Israel's courts ne'er sat an Abbethdin
With more discerning eyes, or hands more clean;
Unbribed, unsought, the wretched to redress;
Swift of dispatch, and easy of access.
Oh, had he been content to serve the crown,
With virtues only proper to the gown;
Or had the rankness of the soil been freed
From cockle, that oppressed the noble seed;
David for him his tuneful harp had strung,
And Heaven had wanted one immortal song.
But wild Ambition loves to slide, not stand,
And Fortune's ice prefers to Virtue's land.
Achitophel, grown weary to possess
A lawful fame, and lazy happiness,
Disdained the golden fruit to gather free,
And lent the crowd his arm to shake the tree.
Now, manifest of crimes contrived long since,
He stood at bold defiance with his prince;
Held up the buckler of the people's cause
Against the crown, and skulked behind the laws.
The wished occasion of the Plot he takes;
Some circumstances finds, but more he makes.
By buzzing emissaries fills the ears
Of listening crowds with jealousies and fears
Of arbitrary counsels brought to light,
And proves the king himself a Jebusite.
Weak arguments! which yet he knew full well
Were strong with people easy to rebel.
For, governed by the moon, the giddy Jews

Tread the same track when she the prime renews;
And once in twenty years, their scribes record,
By natural instinct they change their lord.
Achitophel still wants a chief, and none
Was found so fit as warlike Absalon.
Not that he wished his greatness to create,
(For politicians neither love nor hate),
But, for he knew his title not allowed,
Would keep him still depending on the crowd:
That kingly power, thus ebbing out, might be
Drawn to the dregs of a democracy.

[From *Absalom and Achitophel*]

Zimri

In the first rank of these did Zimri stand:
A man so various, that he seem'd to be
Not one, but all mankind's epitome.
Stiff in opinions, always in the wrong;
Was everything by starts, and nothing long:
But, in the course of one revolving moon,
Was chemist, fiddler, statesman, and buffoon;
Then all for women, painting, rhyming, drinking,
Besides ten thousand freaks that died in thinking.
Blest madman, who could every hour employ,
With something new to wish, or to enjoy!
Railing and praising were his usual themes;
And both, to show his judgment, in extremes;
So over violent, or over civil,
That every man, with him, was God or Devil,
In squand'ring wealth was his peculiar art:
Nothing went unrewarded, but desert.
Beggar'd by fools, whom still he found too late:
He had his jest, and they had his estate.
He laugh'd himself from court; then sought relief
By forming parties, but could ne'er be chief;

For, spite of him, the weight of business fell
On Absalom and wise Achitophel;
Thus wicked but in will, of means bereft,
He left not faction, but of that was left.

[From *Absalom and Achitophel*]

Song for Saint Cecilia's Day
(*November 22, 1687*)

From Harmony, from heavenly Harmony
    This universal Frame began:
  When Nature underneath a heap
    Of jarring atoms lay
  And could not heave her head,
The tuneful voice was heard from high,
    Arise, ye more than dead.
Then cold and hot and moist and dry
    In order to their stations leap,
    And MUSIC'S power obey.
From Harmony, from heavenly Harmony
    This universal Frame began:
    From Harmony to Harmony
Through all the compass of the notes it ran,
The diapason closing full in Man.

What passion cannot MUSIC raise and quell?
    When Jubal struck the chorded shell
  His listening brethren stood around,
    And, wondering, on their faces fell
  To worship that celestial sound:
Less than a god they thought there could not dwell
    Within the hollow of that shell,
    That spoke so sweetly, and so well.
What passion cannot MUSIC raise and quell?

  The TRUMPET'S loud clangor
    Excite us to arms,
  With shrill notes of anger
    And mortal alarms.

The double double double beat
　　Of the thund'ring DRUM
Cries, 'hark the foes come;
Charge, charge, 'tis too late to retreat!'

　The soft complaining FLUTE.
　In dying notes discovers
　The woes of hopeless lovers,
Whose dirge is whisper'd by the warbling LUTE.

　Sharp VIOLINS proclaim
Their jealous pangs and desperation,
Fury, frantic indignation,
Depth of pains, and height of passion,
　For the fair, disdainful Dame.

But oh! what Art can teach,
What human voice can reach
　The sacred ORGAN'S praise?
Notes inspiring holy love,
Notes that wing their heavenly ways
　To mend the choirs above.

Orpheus could lead the savage race
And trees uprooted left their place,
　Sequacious of the LYRE:
But bright CECILIA rais'd the wonder higher:
When to her Organ vocal breath was given,
An Angel heard, and straight appear'd
　Mistaking Earth for Heaven.

GRAND CHORUS

As from the power of sacred lays
　The Spheres began to move,
And sung the great Creator's praise
　To all the blest above;
So when the last and dreadful Hour
This crumbling pageant shall devour,
The TRUMPET shall be heard on high,
The dead shall live, the living die,
And MUSIC shall untune the sky.

HENRY CAREY
(1687–1743)

Sally in our Alley

Of all the girls that are so smart
   There's none like pretty Sally;
She is the darling of my heart,
   And she lives in our alley.
There is no lady in the land
   Is half so sweet as Sally;
She is the darling of my heart,
   And she lives in our alley.

Her father he makes cabbage-nets,
   And through the streets does cry 'em;
Her mother she sells laces long
   To such as please to buy 'em:
But sure such folks could ne'er beget
   So sweet a girl as Sally!
She is the darling of my heart,
   And she lives in our alley.

When she is by, I leave my work,
   I love her so sincerely;
My master comes like any Turk,
   And bangs me most severely:
But let him bang his bellyful,
   I'll bear it all for Sally;
She is the darling of my heart,
   And she lives in our alley.

Of all the days that's in the week
   I dearly love but one day –
And that's the day that comes betwixt
   A Saturday and Monday;

For then I'm dressed all in my best
   To walk abroad with Sally;
She is the darling of my heart,
   And she lives in our alley.

My master carries me to church,
   And often am I blamèd
Because I leave him in the lurch
   As soon as text is namèd;
I leave the church in sermon-time
   And slink away to Sally;
She is the darling of my heart,
   And she lives in our alley.

When Christmas comes about again,
   O, then I shall have money;
I'll hoard it up, and box it all,
   I'll give it to my honey:
I would it were ten thousand pound,
   I'd give it all to Sally;
She is the darling of my heart,
   And she lives in our alley.

My master and the neighbours all
   Make game of me and Sally,
And, but for her, I'd better be
   A slave and row a galley;
But when my seven long years are out,
   O, then I'll marry Sally;
O, then we'll wed, and then we'll bed –
   But not in our alley!

ALEXANDER POPE
(1688–1744)

An Essay on Man

EPISTLE I

Awake, my St John! leave all meaner things
To low ambition, and the pride of kings.
Let us (since life can little more supply
Than just to look about us and to die)
Expatiate free o'er all this scene of man;
A mighty maze! but not without a plan;
A wild, where weeds and flowers promiscuous shoot,
Or garden, tempting with forbidden fruit.
Together let us beat this ample field,
Try what the open, what the covert yield;
The latent tracts, the giddy heights, explore
Of all who blindly creep, or sightless soar;
Eye Nature's walks, shoot folly as it flies,
And catch the manners living as they rise;
Laugh where we must, be candid where we can;
But vindicate the ways of God to man.

Say first, of God above, or man below,
What can we reason, but from what we know?
Of man, what see we but his station here,
From which to reason, or to which refer?
Through worlds unnumbered though the God
    be known,
'Tis ours to trace him only in our own.
He, who through vast immensity can pierce,
See worlds on worlds compose one universe,
Observe how system into system runs,
What other planets circle other suns,

What varied Being peoples every star,
May tell why Heaven has made us as we are.
But of this frame the bearings, and the ties,
The strong connections, nice dependencies,
Gradations just, has thy pervading soul
Looked through? or can a part contain the whole?

Is the great chain, that draws all to agree,
And drawn supports, upheld by God, or thee?

Presumptuous man! the reason wouldst thou
    find,
Why formed so weak, so little, and so blind?
First, if thou canst, the harder reason guess,
Why formed no weaker, blinder, and no less?
Ask of thy mother earth, why oaks are made
Taller or stronger than the weeds they shade?
Or ask of yonder argent fields above,
Why Jove's satellites are less than Jove?
Of systems possible, if 'tis confessed
That Wisdom infinite must form the best,
Where all must full or not coherent be,
And all that rises, rise in due degree;
Then, in the scale of reasoning life, 'tis plain,
There must be, somewhere, such a rank as man:
And all the question (wrangle e'er so long)
Is only this, if God has placed him wrong?
Respecting man, whatever wrong we call,
May, must be right, as relative to all.
In human works, though laboured on with pain,
A thousand movements scarce one purpose gain;
In God's, one single can its end produce;
Yet serves to second too some other use.
So man, who here seems principal alone,
Perhaps acts second to some sphere unknown,
Touches some wheel, or verges to some goal;
'Tis but a part we see, and not a whole.

When the proud steed shall know why man
    restrains
His fiery course, or drives him o'er the plains;
When the dull ox, why now he breaks the clod,
Is now a victim, and now Egypt's god:
Then shall man's pride and dulness comprehend
His actions', passions', being's use and end;
Why doing, suffering, checked, impelled; and why
This hour a slave, the next a deity.

    Then say not man's imperfect, Heaven in fault;
Say rather, man's as perfect as he ought:
His knowledge measured to his state and place;
His time a moment, and a point his space.
If to be perfect in a certain sphere,
What matter, soon or late, or here or there?
The blest to-day is as completely so,
As who began a thousand years ago.

    Heaven from all creatures hides the Book of Fate,
All but the page prescribed, their present state;
From brutes what men, from men what spirits
    know:
Or who could suffer Being here below?
The lamb thy riot dooms to bleed to-day,
Had he thy reason, would he skip and play?
Pleased to the last, he crops the flowery food,
And licks the hand just raised to shed his blood.
O blindness to the future! kindly given,
That each may fill the circle marked by Heaven:
Who sees with equal eye, as God of all,
A hero perish, or a sparrow fall,
Atoms or systems into ruin hurled,
And now a bubble burst, and now a world.
    Hope humbly then; with trembling pinions soar;
Wait the great teacher Death: and God adore.
What future bliss, he gives not thee to know,
But gives that hope to be thy blessing now.

Hope springs eternal in the human breast:
Man never is, but always to be blest:
The soul, uneasy and confined from home,
Rests and expatiates in a life to come.

   Lo, the poor Indian! whose untutored mind
Sees God in clouds, or hears him in the wind;
His soul, proud Science never taught to stray
Far as the solar walk, or milky way;
Yet simple Nature to his hope has given,
Behind the cloud-topped hill, an humbler heaven;
Some safer world in depth of woods embraced,
Some happier island in the watery waste,
Where slaves once more their native land behold,
No fiends torment, no Christians thirst for gold.
To be, contents his natural desire,
He asks no angel's wing, no seraph's fire;
But thinks, admitted to that equal sky,
His faithful dog shall bear him company.

   Go, wiser thou! and, in thy scale of sense,
Weigh thy opinion against Providence;
Call imperfection what thou fanciest such,
Say, here he gives too little, there too much:
Destroy all creatures for thy sport or gust,
Yet cry, If man's unhappy, God's unjust;
If man alone engross not Heaven's high care,
Alone made perfect here, immortal there:
Snatch from his hand the balance and the rod,
Re-judge his justice, be the God of God.
In pride, in reasoning pride, our error lies;
All quit their sphere, and rush into the skies.
Pride still is aiming at the blest abodes,
Men would be angels, angels would be gods.
Aspiring to be gods, if angels fell,
Aspiring to be angels, men rebel:
And who but wishes to invert the laws
Of Order, sins against the Eternal Cause.

Ask for what end the heavenly bodies shine,
Earth for whose use? Pride answers, ''Tis for mine:
For me kind Nature wakes her genial power,
Suckles each herb, and spreads out every flower:
Annual for me, the grape, the rose, renew,
The juice nectareous, and the balmy dew;
For me, the mine a thousand treasures brings;
For me, health gushes from a thousand springs;
Seas roll to waft me, suns to light me rise;
My footstool earth, my canopy the skies.'
But errs not Nature from this gracious end,
From burning suns when livid deaths descend,
When earthquakes swallow, or when tempests sweep
Towns to one grave, whole nations to the deep?
'No,' 'tis replied, 'the first Almighty Cause
Acts not by partial, but by general laws;
The exceptions few; some change since all began;
And what created perfect?' – Why then man?
If the great end be human happiness,
Then Nature deviates; and can man do less?
As much that end a constant course requires
Of showers and sunshine, as of man's desires;
As much eternal springs and cloudless skies,
As men forever temperate, calm, and wise.
If plagues or earthquakes break not Heaven's
        design,
Why then a Borgia, or a Catiline?
Who knows but He whose hand the lightning forms,
Who heaves old ocean, and who wings the storms;
Pours fierce ambition in a Caesar's mind,
Or turns young Ammon loose to scourge mankind?
From pride, from pride, our very reasoning springs;
Account for moral, as for natural things:
Why charge we Heaven in those, in these acquit?
In both, to reason right is to submit.
Better for us, perhaps, it might appear,
Were there all harmony, all virtue here;

That never air or ocean felt the wind;
That never passion discomposed the mind.
But All subsists by elemental strife;
And passions are the elements of life.
The general Order, since the whole began,
Is kept in Nature, and is kept in man.

   What would this man? Now upward will he
     soar,
And little less than angel, would be more;
Now looking downwards, just as grieved appears
To want the strength of bulls, the fur of bears.
Made for his use all creatures if he call,
Say what their use, had he the powers of all?
Nature to these, without profusion, kind,
The proper organs, proper powers assigned;
Each seeming want compénsated of course,
Here with degrees of swiftness, there of force;
All in exact proportion to the state;
Nothing to add, and nothing to abate.
Each beast, each insect, happy in its own:
Is Heaven unkind to man, and man alone?
Shall he alone, whom rational we call,
Be pleased with nothing, if not blessed with all?
   The bliss of man (could pride that blessing
     find)
Is not to act or think beyond mankind;
No powers of body or of soul to share,
But what his nature and his state can bear.
Why has not man a microscopic eye?
For this plain reason, man is not a fly.
Say what the use, were finer optics given,
T' inspect a mite, not comprehend the heaven?
Or touch, if tremblingly alive all o'er,
To smart and agonize at every pore?
Or quick effluvia darting through the brain,
Die of a rose in aromatic pain?

If Nature thundered in his opening ears,
And stunned him with the music of the spheres,
How would he wish that Heaven had left him still
The whispering zephyr, and the purling rill?
Who finds not Providence all good and wise,
Alike in what it gives, and what denies?

Far as creation's ample range extends,
The scale of sensual, mental powers ascends:
Mark how it mounts, to man's imperial race,
From the green myriads in the peopled grass:
What modes of sight betwixt each wide extreme,
The mole's dim curtain, and the lynx's beam:
Of smell, the headlong lioness between,
And hound sagacious on the tainted green:
Of hearing, from the life that fills the flood,
To that which warbles through the vernal wood:
The spider's touch, how exquisitely fine!
Feels at each thread, and lives along the line:
In the nice bee, what sense so subtly true
From poisonous herbs extracts the healing dew?
How instinct varies in the grovelling swine,
Compared, half-reasoning elephant, with thine!
'Twixt that, and reason, what a nice barrier;
Forever separate, yet forever near!
Remembrance and reflection how allied;
What thin partitions sense from thought divide:
And middle natures, how they long to join,
Yet never pass the insuperable line!
Without this just gradation, could they be
Subjected, these to those, or all to thee?
The powers of all subdued by thee alone,
Is not thy reason all these powers in one?

See, through this air, this ocean, and this
    earth,
All matter quick, and bursting into birth.

Above, how high, progressive life may go!
Around, how wide! how deep extend below!
Vast chain of Being! which from God began,
Natures ethereal, human, angel, man,
Beast, bird, fish, insect, what no eye can see,
No glass can reach; from Infinite to thee,
From thee to Nothing. – On superior powers
Were we to press, inferior might on ours:
Or in the full creation leave a void,
Where, one step broken, the great scale's destroyed:
From Nature's chain whatever link you strike,
Tenth or ten thousandth, breaks the chain alike.

    And, if each system in gradation roll
Alike essential to the amazing Whole,
The least confusion but in one, not all
That system only, but the Whole must fall.
Let earth unbalanced from her orbit fly,
Planets and suns run lawless through the sky;
Let ruling angels from their spheres be hurled,
Being on being wrecked, and world on world;
Heaven's whole foundations to their centre nod,
And Nature trembles to the throne of God.
All this dread Order break – for whom? for thee?
Vile worm! – oh, madness! pride, impiety!

    What if the foot, ordained the dust to tread,
Or hand, to toil, aspired to be the head?
What if the head, the eye, or ear repined
To serve mere engines to the ruling Mind?
Just as absurd for any part to claim
To be another, in this general frame:
Just as absurd, to mourn the tasks or pains,
The great directing Mind of All ordains.

    All are but parts of one stupendous whole,
Whose body Nature is, and God the soul;
That, changed through all, and yet in all the same;
Great in the earth, as in the ethereal frame;

Warms in the sun, refreshes in the breeze,
Glows in the stars, and blossoms in the trees,
Lives through all life, extends through all extent,
Spreads undivided, operates unspent;
Breathes in our soul, informs our mortal part,
As full, as perfect, in a hair as heart;
As full, as perfect, in vile man that mourns,
As the rapt seraph that adores and burns:
To him no high, no low, no great, no small;
He fills, he bounds, connects, and equals all.

Cease then, nor Order imperfection name:
Our proper bliss depends on what we blame.
Know thy own point: this kind, this due degree
Of blindness, weakness, Heaven bestows on thee.
Submit. – In this, or any other sphere,
Secure to be as blest as thou canst bear:
Safe in the hand of one disposing Power,
Or in the natal, or the mortal hour.
All nature is but art, unknown to thee;
All chance, direction, which thou canst not see;
All discord, harmony not understood;
All partial evil, universal good:
And, spite of pride, in erring reason's spite,
One truth is clear, WHATEVER IS, IS RIGHT.

Hampton Court

Close by those meads, for ever crown'd with flow'rs,
Where Thames with pride surveys his rising tow'rs,
There stands a structure of majestic frame,
Which from the neighb'ring Hampton takes its name.
Here Britain's statesmen oft the fall foredoom
Of foreign Tyrants, and of Nymphs at home;
Here thou, great Anna! whom three Realms obey,
Dost sometimes counsel take – and sometimes tea.
  Hither the heroes and the nymphs resort,
To taste awhile the pleasures of a Court;

In various talk th' instructive hours they past,
Who gave the ball, or paid the visit last;
One speaks the glory of the British Queen,
And one describes a charming Indian screen;
A third interprets motions, looks, and eyes;
At every word a reputation dies.
Snuff, or the fan, supply each pause of chat,
With singing, laughing, ogling, *and all that.*

[From *The Rape of the Lock*]

Nature and Art

First follow Nature, and your judgment frame
By her just standard, which is still the same:
Unerring Nature, still divinely bright,
One clear, unchang'd, and universal light,
Life, force, and beauty, must to all impart,
At once the source, and end, and test of Art.
Art from that fund each just supply provides,
Works without show, and without pomp presides:
In some fair body thus th' informing soul
With spirits feeds, with vigour fills the whole,
Each motion guides, and ev'ry nerve sustains;
Itself unseen, but in th' effects, remains.
Some, to whom Heaven in wit has been profuse,
Want as much more to turn it to its use;
For wit and judgment often are at strife,
Tho' meant each other's aid, like man and wife.
'Tis more to guide, than spur the Muse's steed;
Restrain his fury, than provoke his speed;
The winged courser, like a gen'rous horse,
Shows most true mettle when you check his course.

Those Rules of old discover'd, not devis'd,
Are Nature still, but Nature methodiz'd;
Nature, like Liberty, is but restrain'd
By the same Laws which first herself ordain'd.

[From *The Essay on Criticism*]

The Critic's Task

A little learning is a dang'rous thing;
Drink deep, or taste not the Pierian spring:
There shallow draughts intoxicate the brain,
And drinking largely sobers us again.
Fir'd at first sight with what the Muse imparts,
In fearless youth we tempt the heights of Arts,
While from the bounded level of our mind
Short views we take, nor see the lengths behind;
But more advanc'd, behold with strange surprise
New distant scenes of endless science rise!
So pleas'd at first the tow'ring Alps we try,
Mount o'er the vales, and seem to tread the sky,
Th' eternal snows appear already past,
And the first clouds and mountains seem the last:
But, those attain'd, we tremble to survey
The growing labours of the lengthen'd way,
Th' increasing prospect tires our wand'ring eyes.
Hills peep o'er hills, and Alps on Alps arise!
A perfect Judge will read each work of Wit
With the same spirit that its author writ:
Survey the Whole, nor seek slight faults to find
Where nature moves, and rapture warms the mind;
Nor lose, for that malignant dull delight,
The gen'rous pleasure to be charm'd with Wit.
But in such lays as neither ebb, nor flow,
Correctly cold, and regularly low,
That shunning faults, one quiet tenour keep;
We cannot blame indeed – but we may sleep.
In Wit, as Nature, what affects our hearts
Is not th' exactness of peculiar parts;
'Tis not a lip, or eye, we beauty call,
But the joint force and full result of all.
Thus when we view some well-proportion'd dome
(The world's just wonder, and ev'n thine, O Rome!)

No single parts unequally surprise,
All comes united to th' admiring eyes;
No monstrous height, or breadth, or length appear;
The Whole at once is bold, and regular.

[From *The Essay on Criticism*]

The Return of Chaos

She comes! she comes! the sable Throne behold
Of Night Primaeval, and of Chaos old!
Before her, Fancy's gilded clouds decay,
And all its varying Rainbows die away,
Wit shoots in vain its momentary fires,
The meteor drops, and in a flash expires.
As one by one, at dread Medea's strain,
The sick'ning stars fade off th' ethereal plain;
As Argus' eyes, by Hermes' wand opprest,
Clos'd one by one to everlasting rest;
Thus at her felt approach, and secret might,
Art after Art goes out, and all is Night.
See skulking Truth to her old cavern fled,
Mountains of Casuistry heap'd o'er her head!
Philosophy, that lean'd on Heav'n before,
Shrinks to her second cause, and is no more.
Physic of Metaphysic begs defence,
And Metaphysic calls for aid on Sense!
See Mystery to Mathematics fly!
In vain! they gaze, turn giddy, rave, and die.
Religion blushing veils her sacred fires,
And unawares Morality expires.
Nor public Flame, nor private, dares to shine;
Nor human Spark is left, nor Glimpse divine!
Lo! thy dread Empire, CHAOS! is restor'd;
Light dies before thy uncreating word:
Thy hand, great Anarch! lets the curtain fall;
And Universal Darkness buries All.

[From *The Dunciad*]

The Character of Atticus

Peace to all such! but were there One whose fires
True Genius kindles, and fair Fame inspires;
Blest with each talent and each art to please,
And born to write, converse, and live with ease:
Should such a man, too fond to rule alone,
Bear, like the Turk, no brother near the throne,
View him with scornful, yet with jealous eyes,
And hate for arts that caus'd himself to rise;
Damn with faint praise, assent with civil leer,
And without sneering, teach the rest to sneer;
Willing to wound, and yet afraid to strike,
Just hint a fault, and hesitate dislike;
Alike reserv'd to blame, or to commend,
A tim'rous foe, and a suspicious friend;
Dreading ev'n fools, by flatterers besieg'd,
And so, obliging, that he ne'er oblig'd;
Like Cato, give his little Senate laws,
And sit attentive to his own applause;
While Wits and Templars ev'ry sentence raise,
And wonder with a foolish face of praise –
Who but must laugh, if such a man there be?
Who would not weep, if Atticus were he!

[From *The Prologue to the Satires*]

JAMES THOMSON
(1700–1748)

Spring

From the moist meadow to the wither'd hill,
Led by the breeze, the vivid verdure runs,
And swells, and deepens, to the cherish'd eye.
The hawthorn whitens; and the juicy groves

Put forth their buds, unfolding by degrees,
Till the whole leafy forest stands display'd,
In full luxuriance to the sighing gales;
Where the deer rustle thro' the twining brake,
And the birds sing conceal'd. At once, array'd
In all the colours of the flushing year,
By Nature's swift and secret-working hand,
The garden glows, and fills the liberal air
With lavish fragrance; while the promis'd fruit
Lies yet a little embryo, unperceiv'd,
Within its crimson folds. Now from the town
Buried in smoke, and sleep, and noisome damps,
Oft let me wander o'er the dewy fields,
Where freshness breathes; and dash the trembling drops
From the bent bush, as thro' the verdant maze
Of sweet-briar hedges I pursue my walk;
Or taste the smell of dairy; or ascend
Some eminence, Augusta, in thy plains;
And see the country, far diffus'd around,
One boundless blush; one white-empurpl'd shower
Of mingled blossoms; where the raptur'd eye
Hurries from joy to joy, and hid beneath
The fair profusion, yellow Autumn spies.

[From *The Seasons*]

Autumn

But see the fading many-coloured woods,
Shade deepening over shade, the country round
Imbrown; a crowded umbrage dusk and dun,
Of every hue, from wan declining green
To sooty dark. These now the lonesome muse,
Low whispering, lead into their leaf-strewn walks,
And give the season in its latest view.

Meantime, light shadowing all, a sober calm
Fleeces unbounded ether: whose least wave

Stands tremulous, uncertain where to turn
The gentle current; while illumined wide,
The dewy-skirted clouds imbibe the sun,
And through their lucid veil his softened force
Shed o'er the peaceful world. Then is the time,
For those whom virtue and whom nature charm,
To steal themselves from the degenerate crowd,
And soar above this little scene of things:
To tread low-thoughted vice beneath their feet;
To soothe the throbbing passions into peace;
And woo lone Quiet in her silent walks.

Thus solitary, and in pensive guise,
Oft let me wander o'er the russet mead,
And through the saddened grove, where scarce
      is heard
One dying strain, to cheer the woodman's toil.
Haply some widowed songster pours his plaint,
Far, in faint warblings, through the tawny copse;
While congregated thrushes, linnets, larks,
And each wild throat, whose artless strains so late
Swelled all the music of the swarming shades,
Robbed of their tuneful souls, now shivering sit
On the dead tree, a dull despondent flock:
With not a brightness waving o'er their plumes,
And nought save chattering discord in their note.
O let not, aimed from some inhuman eye,
The gun the music of the coming year
Destroy; and harmless, unsuspecting harm,
Lay the weak tribes a miserable prey
In mingled murder, fluttering on the ground!

The pale descending year, yet pleasing still,
A gentler mood inspires; for now the leaf
Incessant rustles from the mournful grove;
Oft startling such as studious walk below,
And slowly circles through the waving air.

But should a quicker breeze amid the boughs
Sob, o'er the sky the leafy deluge streams;
Till choked, and matted with the dreary shower,
The forest walks, at every rising gale,
Roll wide the withered waste, and whistle bleak.
Fled is the blasted verdure of the fields;
And, shrunk into their beds, the flowery race
Their sunny robes resign. E'en what remained
Of stronger fruits falls from the naked tree;
And woods, fields, gardens, orchards all around,
The desolated prospect thrills the soul.

[From *The Seasons*]

Winter

From pole to pole the rigid influence falls,
Thro' the still night, incessant, heavy, strong,
And seizes Nature fast. It freezes on;
Till morn, late rising o'er the drooping world,
Lifts her pale eye unjoyous. Then appears
The various labour of the silent night:
Prone from the dripping eave, and dumb cascade,
Whose idle torrents only seem to roar,
The pendant icicle; the frost-work fair,
Where transient hues, and fancy'd figures rise;
Wide-spouted o'er the hill, the frozen brook,
A livid tract, cold-gleaming on the morn;
The forest bent beneath the plumy wave;
And by the frost refin'd the whiter snow,
Incrusted hard, and sounding to the tread
Of early shepherd, as he pensive seeks
His pining flock; or from the mountain top,
Pleas'd with the slippery surface, swift descends.

[From *The Seasons*]

SAMUEL JOHNSON
(1709–1784)

Poverty

Has heaven reserv'd, in pity to the poor,
No pathless waste, or undiscover'd shore?
No secret island in the boundless main?
No peaceful desert yet unclaim'd by Spain?
Quick let us rise, the happy seats explore,
And bear oppression's insolence no more.
This mournful truth is everywhere confess'd,
SLOW RISES WORTH, BY POVERTY
    DEPRESS'D:
But here more slow, where all are slaves to gold,
Where looks are merchandise, and smiles are sold;
Where won by bribes, by flatteries implor'd,
The groom retails the favours of his lord.

    But hark! th' affrighted crowd's tumultous cries
Roll through the streets, and thunder to the skies:
Rais'd from some pleasing dream of wealth and pow'r,
Some pompous palace, or some blissful bow'r;
Aghast you start, and scarce with aching sight
Sustain th' approaching fire's tremendous light;
Swift from pursuing horrors take your way,
And leave your little ALL to flames a prey;
Then thro' the world a wretched vagrant roam,
For where can starving merit find a home?
In vain your mournful narrative disclose,
While all neglect, and most insult your woes.

[From *London*]

The Vanity of Human Wishes

Where then shall Hope and Fear their objects find?
Must dull Suspense corrupt the stagnant mind?

Must helpless man, in ignorance sedate,
Roll darkling down the torrent of his fate?
Must no dislike alarm, no wishes rise,
No cries attempt the mercies of the skies?
Inquirer, cease, petitions yet remain,
Which heaven may hear, nor deem religion vain.
Still raise for good the supplicating voice,
But leave to heaven the measure and the choice;
Safe in his power, whose eyes discern afar
The secret ambush of a specious pray'r;
Implore his aid, in his decisions rest,
Secure, whate'er he gives, he gives the best.
Yet when the sense of sacred presence fires,
And strong devotion to the skies aspires,
Pour forth thy fervours for a healthful mind,
Obedient passions, and a will resign'd;
For love, which scarce collective man can fill;
For patience, sovereign o'er transmuted ill;
For faith, that, panting for a happier seat,
Counts death kind Nature's signal of retreat:
These goods for man the laws of heaven ordain,
These goods he grants, who grants the power to gain,
With these celestial Wisdom calms the mind,
And makes the happiness she does not find.

[From *The Vanity of Human Wishes*]

THOMAS GRAY
(1716–1771)

Elegy

Written in a Country Churchyard

The curfew tolls the knell of parting day,
  The lowing herd winds slowly o'er the lea,
The ploughman homeward plods his weary way,
  And leaves the world to darkness and to me.

Now fades the glimmering landscape on the sight,
   And all the air a solemn stillness holds,
Save where the beetle wheels his droning flight,
   And drowsy tinklings lull the distant folds:

Save that from yonder ivy-mantled tower
   The moping owl does to the moon complain
Of such as, wandering near her secret bower,
   Molest her ancient solitary reign.

Beneath those rugged elms, that yew-tree's shade
   Where heaves the turf in many a mouldering heap,
Each in his narrow cell for ever laid,
   The rude Forefathers of the hamlet sleep.

The breezy call of incense-breathing morn,
   The swallow twittering from the straw-built shed,
The cock's shrill clarion, or the echoing horn,
   No more shall rouse them from their lowly bed.

For them no more the blazing hearth shall burn,
   Or busy housewife ply her evening care:
No children run to lisp their sire's return,
   Or climb his knees the envied kiss to share.

Oft did the harvest to their sickle yield,
   Their furrow oft the stubborn glebe has broke;
How jocund did they drive their team afield!
   How bow'd the woods beneath their sturdy stroke!

Let not Ambition mock their useful toil,
   Their homely joys, and destiny obscure;
Nor Grandeur hear with a disdainful smile
   The short and simple annals of the Poor.

The boast of heraldry, the pomp of power,
   And all that beauty, all that wealth e'er gave,
Awaits alike th' inevitable hour: –
   The paths of glory lead but to the grave.

Nor you, ye Proud, impute to these the fault
  If Memory o'er their tomb no trophies raise,
Where through the long-drawn aisle and fretted vault
  The pealing anthem swells the note of praise.

Can storied urn or animated bust
  Back to its mansion call the fleeting breath?
Can Honour's voice provoke the silent dust,
  Or Flattery soothe the dull cold ear of Death?

Perhaps in this neglected spot is laid
  Some heart once pregnant with celestial fire;
Hands, that the rod of empire might have sway'd,
  Or waked to ecstasy the living lyre:

But Knowledge to their eyes her ample page
  Rich with the spoils of time, did ne'er unroll;
Chill Penury repress'd their noble rage,
  And froze the genial current of the soul.

Full many a gem of purest ray serene
  The dark unfathom'd caves of ocean bear:
Full many a flower is born to blush unseen,
  And waste its sweetness on the desert air.

Some village Hampden, that with dauntless breast
  The little tyrant of his fields withstood,
Some mute inglorious Milton here may rest,
  Some Cromwell, guiltless of his country's blood.

Th' applause of list'ning senates to command,
  The threats of pain and ruin to despise,
To scatter plenty o'er a smiling land,
  And read their history in a nation's eyes,

Their lot forbade: nor circumscribed alone
  Their growing virtues, but their crimes confined;
Forbade to wade through slaughter to a throne,
  And shut the gates of mercy on mankind;

The struggling pangs of conscious truth to hide,
    To quench the blushes of ingenuous shame,
Or heap the shrine of Luxury and Pride
    With incense kindled at the Muse's flame.

Far from the madding crowd's ignoble strife,
    Their sober wishes never learn'd to stray;
Along the cool sequester'd vale of life
    They kept the noiseless tenor of their way.

Yet e'en these bones from insult to protect
    Some frail memorial still erected nigh,
With uncouth rhymes and shapeless sculpture deck'd,
    Implores the passing tribute of a sigh.

Their name, their years, spelt by th' unletter'd Muse,
    The place of fame and elegy supply:
And many a holy text around she strews,
    That teach the rustic moralist to die.

For who, to dumb forgetfulness a prey,
    This pleasing anxious being e'er resign'd,
Left the warm precincts of the cheerful day,
    Nor cast one longing lingering look behind?

On some fond breast the parting soul relies,
    Some pious drops the closing eye requires;
E'en from the tomb the voice of Nature cries,
    E'en in our ashes live their wonted fires.

For thee, who, mindful of th' unhonour'd dead,
    Dost in these lines their artless tale relate;
If chance, by lonely Contemplation led,
    Some kindred spirit shall inquire thy fate, –

Haply some hoary-headed swain may say,
    'Oft have we seen him at the peep of dawn
Brushing with hasty steps the dews away,
    To meet the sun upon the upland lawn;

There at the foot of yonder nodding beech
   That wreathes its old fantastic roots so high,
His listless length at noon-tide would he stretch,
   And pore upon the brook that babbles by.

Hard by yon wood, now smiling as in scorn,
   Muttering his wayward fancies he would rove;
Now drooping, woeful-wan, like one forlorn,
   Or crazed with care, or cross'd in hopeless love.

One morn I miss'd him on the custom'd hill,
   Along the heath, and near his favourite tree;
Another came; nor yet beside the rill,
   Nor up the lawn, nor at the wood was he;

The next with dirges due in sad array
   Slow through the church-way path we saw him
      borne, –
Approach and read (for thou canst read) the lay
   Graved on the stone beneath yon aged thorn.'

THE EPITAPH

Here rests his head upon the lap of Earth
   A Youth, to Fortune and to Fame unknown;
Fair Science frown'd not on his humble birth,
   And Melancholy mark'd him for her own.

Large was his bounty, and his soul sincere;
   Heaven did a recompense as largely send:
He gave to Misery all he had, a tear,
   He gain'd from Heaven, 'twas all he wish'd,
      a friend.

No farther seek his merits to disclose,
   Or draw his frailties from their dread abode,
(There they alike in trembling hope repose),
   The bosom of his Father and his God.

The Bard

A PINDARIC ODE

'Ruin seize thee, ruthless King!
  Confusion on thy banners wait!
Tho' fann'd by Conquest's crimson wing
  They mock the air with idle state.
Helm, nor hauberk's twisted mail,
Nor e'en thy virtues, tyrant, shall avail
To save thy secret soul from nightly fears,
From Cambria's curse, from Cambria's tears!'
– Such were the sounds that o'er the crested pride
  Of the first Edward scatter'd wild dismay,
As down the steep of Snowdon's shaggy side
  He wound with toilsome march his long array: –
Stout Glo'ster stood aghast in speechless trance;
'To arms!' cried Mortimer, and couch'd his quivering
      lance.

On a rock, whose haughty brow
Frowns o'er old Conway's foaming flood,
  Robed in the sable garb of woe
With haggard eyes the Poet stood;
(Loose his beard and hoary hair
Stream'd like a meteor to the troubled air)
And with a master's hand and prophet's fire
Struck the deep sorrows of his lyre:
  'Hark, how each giant oak and desert-cave
    Sighs to the torrent's awful voice beneath!
O'er thee, O King! their hundred arms they wave,
    Revenge on thee in hoarser murmurs breathe:
Vocal no more, since Cambria's fatal day,
To high-born Hoel's harp, or soft Llewellyn's lay.

  'Cold is Cadwallo's tongue,
  That hush'd the stormy main:
Brave Urien sleeps upon his craggy bed:

Mountains, ye mourn in vain
Modred, whose magic song
Made huge Plinlimmon bow his cloud-topt head.
On dreary Arvon's shore they lie
Smear'd with gore and ghastly pale;
Far, far aloof the affrighted ravens sail;
The famish'd eagle screams, and passes by.
Dear lost companions of my tuneful art,
Dear as the light that visits these sad eyes,
Dear as the ruddy drops that warm my heart,
Ye died amidst your dying country's cries –
No more I weep; they do not sleep;
On yonder cliffs, a grisly band,
I see them sit; they linger yet,
Avengers of their native land:
With me in dreadful harmony they join,
And weave with bloody hands the tissue of thy line.

'Weave the warp, and weave the woof,
The winding sheet of Edward's race:
Give ample room and verge enough
The characters of hell to trace.
Mark the year and mark the night
When Severn shall re-echo with affright
The shrieks of death thro' Berkley's roofs that ring,
Shrieks of an agonizing king!
She-wolf of France, with unrelenting fangs
That tear'st the bowels of thy mangled mate,
From thee be born, who o'er thy country hangs
The scourge of Heaven! What terrors round him wait!
Amazement in his van, with Flight combined,
And Sorrow's faded form, and Solitude behind.

'Mighty victor, mighty lord,
Low on his funeral couch he lies!
No pitying heart, no eye, afford
A tear to grace his obsequies.

Is the sable warrior fled?
Thy son is gone. He rests among the dead.
The swarm that in thy noon-tide beam were born?
– Gone to salute the rising morn.
Fair laughs the Morn, and soft the zephyr blows,
　While proudly riding o'er the azure realm
In gallant trim the gilded Vessel goes:
　Youth on the prow, and Pleasure at the helm:
Regardless of the sweeping Whirlwind's sway,
That hush'd in grim repose expects his evening prey.

　'Fill high the sparkling bowl,
The rich repast prepare;
　Reft of a crown, he yet may share the feast:
　Close by the regal chair
　Fell Thirst and Famine scowl
　A baleful smile upon their baffled guest.
Heard ye the din of battle bray,
　Lance to lance, and horse to horse?
　Long years of havoc urge their destined course,
And thro' the kindred squadrons mow their way.
　Ye towers of Julius, London's lasting shame,
With many a foul and midnight murder fed,
　Revere his Consort's faith, his Father's fame,
And spare the meek usurper's holy head!
Above, below, the rose of snow,
　Twined with her blushing foe, we spread:
The bristled boar in infant-gore
　Wallows beneath the thorny shade.
Now, brothers, bending o'er the accursèd loom,
Stamp we our vengeance deep, and ratify his doom.

　'Edward, lo! to sudden fate
　(Weave we the woof; The thread is spun;)
Half of thy heart we consecrate.
　(The web is wove; The work is done;)
Stay, O stay! nor thus forlorn
Leave me unbless'd, unpitied, here to mourn:

In yon bright track that fires the western skies
They melt, they vanish from my eyes.
But O! what solemn scenes on Snowdon's height
   Descending slow their glittering skirts unroll?
Visions of glory, spare my aching sight,
   Ye unborn ages, crowd not on my soul.
No more our long-lost Arthur we bewail: —
All hail, ye genuine kings! Britannia's issue, hail!

   'Girt with many a baron bold
Sublime their starry fronts they rear;
   And gorgeous dames, and statesmen old
In bearded majesty, appear.
In the midst a form divine!
Her eye proclaims her of the Briton-Line:
Her lion-port, her awe-commanding face
Attemper'd sweet to virgin grace.
What strings symphonious tremble in the air,
   What strains of vocal transport round her play?
Hear from the grave, great Talliessin, hear;
   They breathe a soul to animate thy clay.
Bright Rapture calls, and soaring as she sings,
Waves in the eye of Heaven her many-colour'd wings.

   'The verse adorn again
   Fierce War, and faithful Love,
And Truth severe, by fairy Fiction drest.
   In buskin'd measures move
Pale Grief, and pleasing Pain,
With Horror, tyrant of the throbbing breast.
A voice as of the cherub-choir
   Gales from blooming Eden bear,
   And distant warblings lessen on my ear
That lost in long futurity expire.
Fond impious man, think'st thou yon sanguine cloud
   Raised by thy breath, has quench'd the orb of day?
To-morrow he repairs the golden flood
   And warms the nations with redoubled ray.

Enough for me: with joy I see
   The different doom our fates assign:
Be thine Despair and sceptred Care;
   To triumph and to die are mine.'
– He spoke, and headlong from the mountain's height
Deep in the roaring tide he plunged to endless night.

WILLIAM COLLINS
(1721–1759)

Ode written in 1746

How sleep the Brave who sink to rest
By all their Country's wishes blest!
When Spring, with dewy fingers cold,
Returns to deck their hallow'd mould,
She there shall dress a sweeter sod
Than Fancy's feet have ever trod.

By fairy hands their knell is rung,
By forms unseen their dirge is sung:
There Honour comes, a pilgrim grey,
To bless the turf that wraps their clay;
And Freedom shall awhile repair
To dwell a weeping hermit there!

To Evening

If aught ot oaten stop or pastoral song
May hope, chaste Eve, to soothe thy modest ear
   Like thy own solemn springs,
   Thy springs, and dying gales;

O Nymph reserved, – while now the bright-
     hair'd sun
Sits in yon western tent, whose cloudy skirts,
   With brede ethereal wove,
   O'erhang his wavy bed,

Now air is hush'd, save where the weak-eyed bat
With short shrill shriek flits by on leathern wing,
   Or where the beetle winds
   His small but sullen horn,

As oft he rises 'midst the twilight path,
Against the pilgrim borne in heedless hum, –
   Now teach me, maid composed,
   To breathe some soften'd strain.

Whose numbers, stealing through thy dark'ning
    vale,
May not unseemly with its stillness suit;
   As musing slow I hail
   Thy genial loved return.

For when thy folding-star arising shows
His paly circlet, at his warning lamp
   The fragrant Hours, and Elves
   Who slept in buds the day,

And many a Nymph who wreathes her brows
    with sedge
And sheds the freshening dew, and lovelier still
   The pensive Pleasures sweet,
   Prepare thy shadowy car.

Then let me rove some wild and heathy scene;
Or find some ruin 'midst its dreary dells,
   Whose walls more awful nod
   By thy religious gleams.

Or if chill blustering winds or driving rain
Prevent my willing feet, be mine the hut
   That, from the mountain's side,
   Views wilds and swelling floods,

And hamlets brown, and dim-discover'd spires;
And hears their simple bell; and marks o'er all
    Thy dewy fingers draw
    The gradual dusky veil.

While Spring shall pour his showers, as oft he wont,
And bathe thy breathing tresses, meekest Eve!
    While Summer loves to sport
    Beneath thy lingering light;

While sallow Autumn fills thy lap with leaves;
Or Winter, yelling through the troublous air,
    Affrights thy shrinking train
    And rudely rends thy robes;

So long, regardful of thy quiet rule,
Shall Fancy, Friendship, Science, smiling Peace,
    Thy gentlest influence own,
    And love thy favourite name!

Ode to Simplicity

    O Thou, by nature taught,
    To breathe her genuine thought,
In numbers warmly pure, and sweetly strong:
    Who first, on mountains wild,
    In fancy, loveliest child,
Thy babe, or pleasure's, nursed the powers of song!

    Thou, who, with hermit heart,
    Disdain'st the wealth of art,
And gauds, and pageant weeds, and trailing pall;
    But com'st a decent maid,
    In Attic robe arrayed,
O chaste, unboastful nymph, to thee I call;

By all the honeyed store
  On Hybla's thymy shore;
By all her blooms, and mingled murmurs dear;
  By her whose lovelorn woe,
  In evening musings slow,
Soothed sweetly sad Electra's poet's ear:

  By old Cephisus deep,
  Who spread his wavy sweep,
In warbled wanderings, round thy green retreat;
  On whose enamelled side,
  When holy freedom died,
No equal haunt allured thy future feet.

  O sister meek of truth,
  To my admiring youth,
Thy sober aid and native charms infuse!
  The flowers that sweetest breathe,
  Though beauty culled the wreath,
Still ask thy hand to range their ordered hues.

  While Rome could none esteem
  But virtue's patriot theme,
You loved her hills, and led her laureat band:
  But stayed to sing alone –
  To one distinguished throne;
And turned thy face, and fled her altered land.

  No more, in hall or bower,
  The passions own thy power;
Love, only love, her forceless numbers mean:
  For thou hast left her shrine;
  Nor olive more, nor vine,
Shall gain thy feet to bless the servile scene.

  Though taste, though genius, bless
  To some divine excess,

Faints the cold work till thou inspire the whole;
  What each, what all supply,
  May court, may charm, our eye;
Thou, only thou, canst raise the meeting soul!

  Of these let others ask,
  To aid some mighty task,
I only seek to find thy temperate vale;
  Where oft my reed might sound
  To maids and shepherds round,
And all thy sons, O Nature, learn my tale.

OLIVER GOLDSMITH
(1728–1774)

The Deserted Village

Sweet Auburn! loveliest village of the plain;
Where health and plenty cheered the labouring swain,
Where smiling spring its earliest visit paid,
And parting summer's lingering blooms delayed:
Dear lovely bowers of innocence and ease,
Seats of my youth, when every sport could please,
How often have I loitered o'er thy green,
Where humble happiness endeared each scene!
How often have I paused on every charm,
The sheltered cot, the cultivated farm,
The never-failing brook, the busy mill,
The decent church that topped the neighbouring hill,
The hawthorn bush, with seats beneath the shade,
For talking age and whispering lovers made!
How often have I blest the coming day,
When toil remitting lent its turn to play,
And all the village train, from labour free,
Led up their sports beneath the spreading tree,

While many a pastime circled in the shade,
The young contending as the old surveyed;
And many a gambol frolicked o'er the ground,
And sleights of art and feats of strength went round.
And still, as each repeated pleasure tired,
Succeeding sports the mirthful band inspired;
The dancing pair that simply sought renown,
By holding out to tire each other down;
The swain mistrustless of his smutted face,
While secret laughter tittered round the place;
The bashful virgin's side-long looks of love,
The matron's glance that would those looks reprove:
These were thy charms, sweet village! sports like these,
With sweet succession, taught even toil to please:
These round thy bowers their cheerful influence shed;
These were thy charms – but all these charms are fled.

Sweet smiling village, loveliest of the lawn,
Thy sports are fled, and all thy charms withdrawn;
Amidst thy bowers the tyrant's hand is seen,
And desolation saddens all the green:
One only master grasps the whole domain,
And half a tillage stints thy smiling plain.
No more thy glassy brook reflects the day,
But, choked with sedges, works its weedy way;
Along thy glades, a solitary guest,
The hollow sounding bittern guards its nest:
Amidst thy desert walks the lapwing flies,
And tires their echoes with unvaried cries;
Sunk are thy bowers in shapeless ruin all,
And the long grass o'ertops the mouldering wall;
And trembling, shrinking from the spoiler's hand,
Far, far away thy children leave the land.

Ill fares the land, to hastening ills a prey,
Where wealth accumulates, and men decay:
Princes and lords may flourish, or may fade;
A breath can make them, as a breath has made;

But a bold peasantry, their country's pride,
When once destroyed, can never be supplied.

A time there was, ere England's griefs began,
When every rood of ground maintained its man;
For him light labour spread her wholesome store,
Just gave what life required, but gave no more:
His blest companions, innocence and health;
And his best riches, ignorance of wealth.

But times are altered; trade's unfeeling train
Usurp the land and dispossess the swain;
Along the lawn, where scattered hamlets rose,
Unwieldy wealth and cumbrous pomp repose,
And every want to opulence allied,
And every pang that folly pays to pride.
These gentle hours that plenty bade to bloom,
Those calm desires that asked but little room,
Those healthful sports that graced the peaceful scene,
Lived in each look, and brightened all the green;
These, far departing, seek a kinder shore,
And rural mirth and manners are no more.

Sweet Auburn! parent of the blissful hour,
Thy glades forlorn confess the tyrant's power.
Here, as I take my solitary rounds
Amidst thy tangling walks and ruined grounds,
And, many a year elapsed, return to view
Where once the cottage stood, the hawthorn grew,
Remembrance wakes with all her busy train,
Swells at my breast, and turns the past to pain.

In all my wanderings round this world of care,
In all my griefs – and God has given my share –
I still had hopes, my latest hours to crown,
Amidst these humble bowers to lay me down;
To husband out life's taper at the close,
And keep the flame from wasting by repose:

I still had hopes, for pride attends us still,
Amidst the swains to show my book-learned skill,
Around my fire an evening group to draw,
And tell of all I felt, and all I saw;
And, as an hare whom hounds and horns pursue,
Pants to the place from whence at first she flew,
I still had hopes, my long vexations past,
Here to return – and die at home at last.

O, blest retirement, friend to life's decline,
Retreats from care, that never must be mine,
How happy he who crowns in shades like these,
A youth of labour with an age of ease;
Who quits a world where strong temptations try,
And, since 'tis hard to combat, learns to fly!
For him no wretches, born to work and weep,
Explore the mine, or tempt the dangerous deep;
No surly porter stands in guilty state,
To spurn imploring famine from the gate;
But on he moves to meet his latter end,
Angels around befriending Virtue's friend;
Bends to the grave with unperceived decay,
While resignation gently slopes the way;
And, all his prospects brightening to the last,
His heaven commences ere the world be past!

Sweet was the sound, when oft at evening's close
Up yonder hill the village murmur rose.
There, as I passed with careless steps and slow,
The mingling notes came softened from below;
The swain responsive as the milk-maid sung,
The sober herd that lowed to meet their young,
The noisy geese that gabbled o'er the pool,
The playful children just let loose from school,
The watch-dog's voice that bayed the whispering wind,
And the loud laugh that spoke the vacant mind; –
These all in sweet confusion sought the shade,
And filled each pause the nightingale had made.

But now the sounds of population fail,
No cheerful murmurs fluctuate in the gale,
No busy steps the grass-grown foot-way tread,
For all the bloomy flush of life is fled.
All but yon widowed, solitary thing,
That feebly bends beside the plashy spring:
She, wretched matron, forced in age, for bread,
To strip the brook with mantling cresses spread,
To pick her wintry faggot from the thorn,
To seek her nightly shed, and weep till morn;
She only left of all the harmless train,
The sad historian of the pensive plain.

Near yonder copse, where once the garden smiled,
And still where many a garden flower grows wild;
There, where a few torn shrubs the place disclose,
The village preacher's modest mansion rose.
A man he was to all the country dear,
And passing rich with forty pounds a year;
Remote from towns he ran his godly race,
Nor e'er had changed, nor wished to change his place;
Unpractised he to fawn, or seek for power,
By doctrines fashioned to the varying hour;
Far other aims his heart had learned to prize,
More skilled to raise the wretched than to rise.
His house was known to all the vagrant train;
He chid their wanderings, but relieved their pain:
The long-remembered beggar was his guest,
Whose beard descending swept his aged breast;
The ruined spendthrift, now no longer proud,
Claimed kindred there, and had his claims allowed;
The broken soldier, kindly bade to stay,
Sat by the fire, and talked the night away,
Wept o'er his wounds, or, tales of sorrow done,
Shouldered his crutch and showed how fields were won.
Pleased with his guests, the good man learned to glow,
And quite forgot their vices in their woe;

Careless their merits or their faults to scan
His pity gave ere charity began.

Thus to relieve the wretched was his pride,
And e'en his failings leaned to Virtue's side;
But in his duty prompt at every call,
He watched and wept, he prayed and felt, for all;
And, as a bird each fond endearment tries
To tempt its new-fledged offspring to the skies,
He tried each art, reproved each dull delay,
Allured to brighter worlds, and led the way.

Beside the bed where parting life was laid,
And sorrow, guilt, and pain by turns dismayed,
The reverend champion stood. At his control
Despair and anguish fled the struggling soul;
Comfort came down the trembling wretch to raise,
And his last faltering accents whispered praise.

At church, with meek and unaffected grace,
His looks adorned the venerable place;
Truth from his lips prevailed with double sway,
And fools, who came to scoff, remained to pray.
The service past, around the pious man,
With steady zeal, each honest rustic ran;
Even children followed with endearing wile,
And plucked his gown, to share the good man's smile.
His ready smile a parent's warmth expressed;
Their welfare pleased him, and their cares distrest:
To them his heart, his love, his griefs were given,
But all his serious thoughts had rest in heaven.
As some tall cliff that lifts its awful form,
Swells from the vale, and midway leaves the storm,
Though round its breast the rolling clouds are spread,
Eternal sunshine settles on its head.

Beside yon straggling fence that skirts the way,
With blossomed furze unprofitably gay,
There, in his noisy mansion, skilled to rule,
The village master taught his little school.

A man severe he was, and stern to view;
I knew him well, and every truant knew;
Well had the boding tremblers learned to trace
The day's disasters in his morning face;
Full well they laughed with counterfeited glee
At all his jokes, for many a joke had he;
Full well the busy whisper circling round
Conveyed the dismal tidings when he frowned.
Yet he was kind, or, if severe in aught,
The love he bore to learning was in fault;
The village all declared how much he knew:
'Twas certain he could write, and cipher too;
Lands he could measure, terms and tides presage,
And even the story ran that he could gauge;
In arguing, too, the parson owned his skill,
For, even though vanquished, he could argue still;
While words of learned length and thundering sound
Amazed the gazing rustics ranged around;
And still they gazed, and still the wonder grew,
That one small head could carry all he knew.

But past is all his fame. The very spot
Where many a time he triumphed, is forgot.
Near yonder thorn, that lifts its head on high,
Where once the sign-post caught the passing eye,
Low lies that house where nut-brown draughts inspired,
Where greybeard mirth and smiling toil retired,
Where village statesmen talked with looks profound,
And news much older than their ale went round.
Imagination fondly stoops to trace
The parlour splendours of that festive place:
The white-washed wall, the nicely sanded floor,
The varnished clock that clicked behind the door;
The chest, contrived a double debt to pay,
A bed by night, a chest of drawers by day;
The pictures placed for ornament and use,
The twelve good rules, the royal game of goose;

The hearth, except when winter chilled the day,
With aspen boughs and flowers and fennel gay;
While broken tea-cups, wisely kept for show,
Ranged o'er the chimney, glistened in a row.

Vain transitory splendours! could not all
Reprieve the tottering mansion from its fall?
Obscure it sinks, nor shall it more impart
An hour's importance to the poor man's heart.
Thither no more the peasant shall repair
To sweet oblivion of his daily care;
No more the farmer's news, the barber's tale;
No more the woodman's ballad shall prevail;
No more the smith his dusky brow shall clear,
Relax his ponderous strength, and lean to hear;
The host himself no longer shall be found
Careful to see the mantling bliss go round;
Nor the coy maid, half willing to be prest,
Shall kiss the cup to pass it to the rest.

Yes! let the rich deride, the proud disdain
These simple blessings of the lowly train;
To me more dear, congenial to my heart,
One native charm, than all the gloss of art.
Spontaneous joys, where Nature has its play,
The soul adopts, and owns their first-born sway;
Lightly they frolic o'er the vacant mind,
Unenvied, unmolested, unconfined.
But the long pomp, the midnight masquerade,
With all the freaks of wanton wealth arrayed –
In these, ere triflers half their wish obtain,
The toiling pleasure sickens into pain;
And, even while fashion's brightest arts decoy,
The heart distrusting asks if this be joy.

Ye friends to truth, ye statesmen who survey
The rich man's joy increase, the poor's decay,

'Tis yours to judge, how wide the limits stand
Between a splendid and an happy land.
Proud swells the tide with loads of freighted ore,
And shouting Folly hails them from her shore;
Hoards even beyond the miser's wish abound,
And rich men flock from all the world around.
Yet count our gains! This wealth is but a name
That leaves our useful products still the same.
Not so the loss. The man of wealth and pride
Takes up a space that many poor supplied;
Space for his lake, his park's extended bounds,
Space for his horses, equipage, and hounds:
The robe that wraps his limbs in silken sloth
Has robbed the neighbouring fields of half their
    growth;
His seat, where solitary sports are seen,
Indignant spurns the cottage from the green:
Around the world each needful product flies,
For all the luxuries the world supplies;
While thus the land adorned for pleasure all
In barren splendour feebly waits the fall.
As some fair female unadorned and plain,
Secure to please while youth confirms her reign,
Slights every borrowed charm that dress supplies,
Nor shares with art the triumph of her eyes;
But when those charms are past, for charms are frail,
When time advances, and when lovers fail,
She then shines forth, solicitous to bless,
In all the glaring impotence of dress.
Thus fares the land by luxury betrayed:
In nature's simplest charms at first arrayed,
But verging to decline, its splendours rise,
Its vistas strike, its palaces surprise;
While, scourged by famine from the smiling land
The mournful peasant leads his humble band,
And while he sinks, without one arm to save,
The country blooms – a garden and a grave.

Where then, ah! where, shall poverty reside,
To 'scape the pressure of contiguous pride?
If to some common's fenceless limits strayed,
He drives his flock to pick the scanty blade,
Those fenceless fields the sons of wealth divide,
And even the bare-worn common is denied.

If to the city sped – what waits him there?
To see profusion that he must not share;
To see ten thousand baneful arts combined
To pamper luxury, and thin mankind;
To see those joys the sons of pleasure know
Extorted from his fellow-creature's woe.
Here while the courtier glitters in brocade,
There the pale artist plies the sickly trade;
Here while the proud their long-drawn pomps display,
There the black gibbet glooms beside the way.
The dome where pleasure holds her midnight reign,
Here, richly decked, admits the gorgeous train:
Tumultuous grandeur crowds the blazing square,
The rattling chariots clash, the torches glare.
Sure scenes like these no troubles e'er annoy!
Sure these denote one universal joy!
Are these thy serious thought? – Ah, turn thine eyes
Where the poor, houseless, shivering female lies.
She once, perhaps, in village plenty blest,
Has wept at tales of innocence distrest;
Her modest looks the cottage might adorn,
Sweet as the primrose peeps beneath the thorn;
Now lost to all; her friends, her virtue fled,
Near her betrayer's door she lays her head,
And, pinched with cold, and shrinking from the shower,
With heavy heart deplores that luckless hour,
When idly first, ambitious of the town,
She left her wheel and robes of country brown.

Do thine, sweet Auburn, thine, the loveliest train,
Do thy fair tribes participate her pain?

Even now, perhaps, by cold and hunger led,
At proud men's doors they ask a little bread!

   Ah, no! To distant climes, a dreary scene,
Where half the convex world intrudes between,
Through torrid tracts with fainting steps they go,
Where wild Altama murmurs to their woe.
Far different there from all that charmed before
The various terrors of that horrid shore;
Those blazing suns that dart a downward ray,
And fiercely shed intolerable day;
Those matted woods, where birds forget to sing,
But silent bats in drowsy clusters cling;
Those poisonous fields with rank luxuriance crowned,
Where the dark scorpion gathers death around;
Where at each step the stranger fears to wake
The rattling terrors of the vengeful snake;
Where crouching tigers wait their hapless prey,
And savage men more murderous still than they;
While oft in whirls the mad tornado flies,
Mingling the ravaged landscape with the skies.
Far different these from every former scene,
The cooling brook, the grassy vested green,
The breezy covert of the warbling grove,
That only sheltered thefts of harmless love.

   Good Heaven! what sorrows gloomed that parting
      day,
That called them from their native walks away;
When the poor exiles, every pleasure past,
Hung round the bowers, and fondly looked their last,
And took a long farewell, and wished in vain
For seats like these beyond the western main,
And shuddering still to face the distant deep,
Returned and wept, and still returned to weep.
The good old sire, the first prepared to go
To new found worlds, and wept for others' woe;

But for himself, in conscious virtue brave,
He only wished for worlds beyond the grave.
His lovely daughter, lovelier in her tears,
The fond companion of his helpless years,
Silent went next, neglectful of her charms,
And left a lover's for a father's arms.
With louder plaints the mother spoke her woes,
And blest the cot where every pleasure rose,
And kissed her thoughtless babes with many a tear,
And clasped them close, in sorrow doubly dear,
Whilst her fond husband strove to lend relief,
In all the silent manliness of grief.

   O luxury! thou curst by Heaven's decree,
How ill exchanged are things like these for thee!
How do thy potions, with insidious joy,
Diffuse their pleasure only to destroy!
Kingdoms by thee, to sickly greatness grown,
Boast of a florid vigour not their own.
At every draught more large and large they grow,
A bloated mass of rank, unwieldy woe;
Till sapped their strength, and every part unsound,
Down, down, they sink, and spread a ruin round.

   Even now the devastation is begun,
And half the business of destruction done;
Even now, methinks, as pondering here I stand,
I see the rural virtues leave the land.
Down where yon anchoring vessel spreads the sail,
That idly waiting flaps with every gale,
Downward they move, a melancholy band,
Pass from the shore, and darken all the strand.
Contented toil, and hospitable care,
And kind connubial tenderness, are there;
And piety with wishes placed above,
And steady loyalty, and faithful love.
And thou, sweet Poetry, thou loveliest maid,
Still first to fly where sensual joys invade;

Unfit in these degenerate times of shame
To catch the heart, or strike for honest fame;
Dear charming nymph, neglected and decried,
My shame in crowds, my solitary pride;
Thou source of all my bliss, and all my woe,
That found'st me poor at first, and keep'st me so;
Thou guide by which the nobler arts excel,
Thou nurse of every virtue, fare thee well!
Farewell, and oh! where'er thy voice be tried,
On Torno's cliffs, or Pambamarca's side,
Whether where equinoctial fervours glow,
Or winter wraps the polar world in snow,
Still let thy voice, prevailing over time,
Redress the rigours of the inclement clime;
Aid slighted truth with thy persuasive strain;
Teach erring man to spurn the rage of gain:
Teach him, that states of native strength possessed,
Though very poor, may still be very blest;
That trade's proud empire hastes to swift decay,
As ocean sweeps the laboured mole away;
While self-dependent power can time defy,
As rocks resist the billows and the sky.

WILLIAM COWPER
(1731–1800)

His Mother's Picture

Oh that those lips had language! Life has passed
With me but roughly since I heard thee last.
Those lips are thine – thy own sweet smiles I see,
The same, that oft in childhood solaced me;
Voice only fails, else, how distinct they say,
'Grieve not, my child, chase all thy fears away!'

The meek intelligence of those dear eyes
(Blest be the art that can immortalize,
The art that baffles time's tyrannic claim
To quench it) here shines on me still the same.
  Faithful remembrancer of one so dear,
Oh welcome guest, though unexpected, here!
Who bidd'st me honour with an artless song,
Affectionate, a mother lost so long,
I will obey, not willingly alone,
But gladly, as the precept were her own:
And, while that face renews my filial grief,
Fancy shall weave a charm for my relief,
Shall steep me in Elysian reverie,
A momentary dream, that thou art she.

[From *On The Receipt of My Mother's Picture out of Norfolk*]

The Solitude of Alexander Selkirk

I am monarch of all I survey;
My right there is none to dispute;
From the centre all round to the sea
I am lord of the fowl and the brute.
O Solitude! where are the charms
That sages have seen in thy face?
Better dwell in the midst of alarms
Than reign in this horrible place.

I am out of humanity's reach,
I must finish my journey alone,
Never hear the sweet music of speech;
I start at the sound of my own.
The beasts that roam over the plain
My form with indifference see;
They are so unacquainted with man,
Their tameness is shocking to me.

Society, Friendship, and Love
Divinely bestow'd upon man,
O had I the wings of a dove
How soon would I taste you again!
My sorrows I then might assuage
In the ways of religion and truth,
Might learn from the wisdom of age,
And be cheer'd by the sallies of youth.

Ye winds that have made me your sport,
Convey to this desolate shore
Some cordial endearing report
Of a land I shall visit no more:
My friends, do they now and then send
A wish or a thought after me?
O tell me I yet have a friend,
Though a friend I am never to see.

How fleet is a glance of the mind!
Compared with the speed of its flight,
The tempest itself lags behind,
And the swift-wingéd arrows of light.
When I think of my own native land
In a moment I seem to be there;
But alas! recollection at hand
Soon hurries me back to despair.

But the seafowl is gone to her nest,
The beast is laid down in his lair;
Even here is a season of rest,
And I to my cabin repair.
There's mercy in every place,
And mercy, encouraging thought!
Gives even affliction a grace
And reconciles man to his lot.

To Mary Unwin

The twentieth year is well nigh past
Since first our sky was overcast;
Ah, would that this might be the last!
    My Mary!

Thy spirits have a fainter flow,
I see thee daily weaker grow;
'Twas my distress that brought thee low,
    My Mary!

Thy needles, once a shining store,
For my sake restless heretofore,
Now rust disused, and shine no more,
    My Mary!

For though thou gladly wouldst fulfil
The same kind office for me still,
Thy sight now seconds not thy will,
    My Mary!

But well thou play'dst the housewife's part,
And all thy threads with magic art
Have wound themselves about this heart,
    My Mary!

Thy indistinct expressions seem
Like language utter'd in a dream;
Yet me they charm, whate'er the theme,
    My Mary!

Thy silver locks, once auburn bright,
Are still more lovely in my sight
Than golden beams of orient light,
    My Mary!

For could I view nor them nor thee,
What sight worth seeing could I see?
The sun would rise in vain for me,
    My Mary!

Partakers of thy sad decline
Thy hands their little force resign;
Yet gently press'd, press gently mine,
    My Mary!

And then I feel that still I hold
A richer store ten thousandfold
Than misers fancy in their gold,
    My Mary!

Such feebleness of limbs thou prov'st
That now at every step thou mov'st
Upheld by two; yet still thou lov'st,
    My Mary!

And still to love, though press'd with ill,
In wintry age to feel no chill,
With me is to be lovely still,
    My Mary!

But ah! by constant heed I know
How oft the sadness that I show
Transforms thy smiles to looks of woe,
    My Mary!

And should my future lot be cast
With much resemblance of the past,
Thy worn-out heart will break at last –
    My Mary!

THOMAS CHATTERTON
(1752–1770)

An Excelente Balade of Charitie

(As wroten bie the gode priest, Thomas Rowley, 1464)

In Virginè the sweltry sun 'gan sheene,
   And hot upon the mees did cast his ray;
The apple ripened from its paly green,
   And the soft pear did bend the leafy spray;
   The pied chelandre sung the livelong day;
'Twas now the pride, the manhood of the year,
And eke the ground was dressed in its most neat aumere.

The sun was gleaming in the midst of day,
   Dead-still the air, and eke the welkin blue,
When from the sea arose in drear array
   A heap of clouds of sable sullen hue,
   The which full fast unto the woodland drew,
Hiding at once the sunnis beauteous face,
And the black tempest swelled, and gathered up apace.

Beneath a holm, fast by a pathway-side,
   Which did unto Saint Godwin's convent lead,
A hapless pilgrim moaning did abide,
   Poor in his view, ungentle in his weed,
   Long filled with the miseries of need.
Where from the hailstone could the beggar fly?
He had no houses there, nor any convent nigh.

Look in his clouded face, his sprite there scan;
   How woe-begone, how withered, sapless, dead!
Haste to thy church-glebe-house, accursed man!
   Haste to thy kiste, thy only sleeping bed.
   Cold as the clay which will grow on thy head
Is charity and love among high elves;
Knights and barons live for pleasure and themselves.

The gathered storm is ripe; the big drops fall,
   The sunburnt meadows smoke, and drink the rain;
The coming ghastness do the cattle 'pall,
   And the full flocks are driving o'er the plain;
   Dashed from the clouds, the waters fly again;
The welkin opes; the yellow lightning flies
And the hot fiery steam in the wide lowings dies.

List! now the thunder's rattling noisy sound
   Moves slowly on, and then embollen clangs,
Shakes the high spire, and lost, expended, drowned,
   Still on the frighted ear of terror hangs,
   The winds are up; the lofty elmen swangs;
Again the lightning and the thunder pours,
And the full clouds are burst at once in stony showers.

Spurring his palfrey o'er the watery plain,
   The abbot of Saint Godwin's convent came;
His chapournette was drented with the rain,
   And his pencte girdle met with mickle shame;
   He backwards told his bede-roll at the same
The storm increased, and he drew aside,
With the poor alms-craver near to the holm to bide.

His cloak was all of Lincoln cloth so fine,
   With a gold button fastened near his chin,
His autremete was edged with golden twine,
   And his shoe's peak a loverde's might have been;
   Full well it shewn he thoughten cost no sin.
The trammels of his palfry pleased his sight,
For the horse-milliner his head with roses dight.

'An alms, sir priest!' the drooping pilgrim said,
   'O! let me wait within your convent-door,
Till the sun shineth high above our head,
   And the loud tempest of the air is o'er.
   Helpless and old am I, alas! and poor.
No house, no friend, no money in my pouch,
All that I call my own is this my silver crouche.'

'Varlet!' replied the Abbot, 'cease your din;
 This is no season alms and prayers to give;
My porter never lets a beggar in;
 None touch my ring who not in honour live.'
 And now the sun with the black clouds did strive,
And shedding on the ground his glaring ray;
The abbot spurred his steed, and eftsoons rode away.

Once more the sky was black, the thunder rolled,
 Fast running o'er the plain a priest was seen;
Not dight full proud, not buttoned up in gold,
 His cope and jape were grey, and eke were clean;
 A limit he was of order seen;
And from the pathway-side then turned he,
Where the poor beggar lay beneath the elmen tree.

'An alms, sir priest!' the drooping pilgrim said,
 'For sweet Saint Mary and your order sake.'
The limitour then loosened his pouch-thread,
 And did thereout a groat of silver take:
 The needly pilgrim did for halline shake,
'Here, take this silver, it may ease thy care,
We are God's stewards all, naught of our own we bear.

'But ah! unhappy pilgrim, learn of me,
 Scathe any give a rent-roll to their Lord;
Here, take my semi-cope, thou'rt bare, I see,
 'Tis thine, the saints will give me my reward.'
 He left the pilgrim, and his way aborde.
Virgin and holy saint, who sit in gloure,
Or give the mighty will, or give the good man power.

Minstrel's Song

        Oh! sing unto my roundelay:
          Oh! drop the briny tear with me;
        Dance no more at holiday;
          Like a running river be.

My love is dead,
Gone to his death-bed,
All under the willow-tree.

Black his hair as the winter night,
    White his rode as the summer snow,
Red his face as the morning light;
    Cold he lies in the grave below.
        My love is dead,
        Gone to his death-bed,
        All under the willow-tree.

Sweet his tongue as the throstle's note,
    Quick in dance as thought can be,
Deft his tabour, cudgel stout;
    Oh! he lies by the willow-tree.
        My love is dead,
        Gone to his death-bed,
        All under the willow-tree.

Hark! the raven flaps his wing,
    In the briared dell below;
Hark! the death-owl loud doth sing
    To the night-mares as they go.
        My love is dead,
        Gone to his death-bed,
        All under the willow-tree.

See! the white moon shines on high,
    Whiter is my true love's shroud,
Whiter than the morning sky,
    Whiter than the evening cloud.
        My love is dead,
        Gone to his death-bed,
        All under the willow-tree.

Here, upon my true love's grave,
  Shall the barren flowers be laid;
Not one holy saint to save
All the coldness of a maid.
    My love is dead,
    Gone to his death-bed,
    All under the willow-tree.

With my hands I'll dente the briars,
  Round his holy corse to gre,
Elfin fairy, light your fires,
  Here my body still shall be.
    My love is dead,
    Gone to his death-bed,
    All under the willow-tree.

Come, with acorn-cup and thorn,
  Drain my hartys blood away;
Life and all its good I scorn,
  Dance by night, or feast by day.
    My love is dead,
    Gone to his death-bed,
    All under the willow-tree.

Water-witches, crowned with reytes,
  Bear me to your lethal tide.
I die! I come! my true love waits; –
  Thus the damsel spake, and died.

GEORGE CRABBE
(1754–1832)

Village Life – as it is

I grant indeed that fields and flocks have charms
For him that grazes or for him that farms;
But when amid such pleasing scenes I trace
The poor laborious natives of the place,
And see the mid-day sun, with fervid ray,
On their bare heads and dewy temples play;
While some, with feebler heads and fainter hearts,
Deplore their fortune, yet sustain their parts:
Then shall I dare these real ills to hide
In tinsel trappings of poetic pride?

  No; cast by Fortune on a frowning coast,
Which neither groves nor happy valleys boast;
Where other cares than those the Muse relates,
And other shepherds dwell with other mates:
By such examples taught, I paint the Cot,
As Truth will paint it, and as Bards will not:
Nor you, ye poor, of letter'd scorn complain,
To you the smoothest song is smooth in vain;
O'ercome by labour, and bow'd down by time,
Feel you the barren flattery of a rhyme?
Can poets soothe you, when you pine for bread,
By winding myrtles round your ruin'd shed?
Can their light tales your weighty griefs o'erpower,
Or glad with airy mirth the toilsome hour?

  Lo! where the heath, with withering brake grown o'er,
Lends the light turf that warms the neighbouring poor;
From thence a length of burning sand appears,
Where the thin harvest waves its wither'd ears;
Rank weeds, that every art and care defy,
Reign o'er the land, and rob the blighted rye:

There thistles stretch their prickly arms afar,
And to the ragged infant threaten war;
There poppies nodding, mock the hope of toil;
There the blue bugloss paints the sterile soil;
Hardy and high, above the slender sheaf,
The slimy mallow waves her silky leaf;
O'er the young shoot the charlock throws a shade,
And clasping tares cling round the sickly blade;
With mingled tints the rocky coasts abound,
And a sad splendour vainly shines around,

So looks the nymph whom wretched arts adorn,
Betray'd by man, then left for man to scorn;
Whose cheek in vain assumes the mimic rose,
While her sad eyes the troubled breast disclose;
Whose outward splendour is but folly's dress,
Exposing most, when most it gilds distress.

Here joyless roam a wild amphibious race,
With sullen woe display'd in every face;
Who far from civil arts and social fly,
And scowl at strangers with suspicious eye.

[From *The Village*]

WILLIAM BLAKE
(1757–1827)

To Winter

'O Winter! bar thine adamantine doors:
The north is thine; there hast thou built thy dark
Deep-founded habitation. Shake not thy roofs,
Nor bend thy pillars with thine iron car.'

He hears me not, but o'er the yawning deep
Rides heavy; his storms are unchain'd, sheathèd
In ribbèd steel; I dare not lift mine eyes,
For he hath rear'd his sceptre o'er the world.

Lo! now the direful monster, whose skin clings
To his strong bones, strides o'er the groaning rocks:
He withers all in silence, and his hand
Unclothes the earth, and freezes up frail life.

He takes his seat upon the cliffs, – the mariner
Cries in vain. Poor little wretch, that deal'st
With storms! – till heaven smiles, and the monster
Is driv'n yelling to his caves beneath Mount Hecla.

To the Muses

Whether on Ida's shady brow,
Or in the chambers of the East,
The chambers of the sun, that now
From ancient melody have ceas'd;

Whether in Heaven ye wander fair,
Or the green corners of the earth,
Or the blue regions of the air
Where the melodious winds have birth;

Whether on crystal rocks ye rove,
Beneath the bosom of the sea
Wand'ring in many a coral grove,
Fair Nine, forsaking Poetry!

How have you left the ancient love
That bards of old enjoy'd in you!
The languid strings do scarcely move!
The sound is forced, the notes are few!

The Lamb

Little Lamb, who made thee?
Dost thou know who made thee?
Gave thee life, and bid thee feed,
By the stream and o'er the mead;

Gave thee clothing of delight,
Softest clothing, woolly, bright;
Gave thee such a tender voice,
Making all the vales rejoice?
  Little Lamb, who made thee?
  Dost thou know who made thee?

  Little Lamb, I'll tell thee,
  Little Lamb, I'll tell thee:
He is calléd by thy name,
For He calls Himself a Lamb.
He is meek, and He is mild;
He became a little child.
I a child, and thou a lamb,
We are calléd by His name.
  Little Lamb, God bless thee!
  Little Lamb, God bless thee!

The Voice of the Ancient Bard

Youth of delight, come hither,
And see the opening morn,
Image of truth new-born.
Doubt is fled, and clouds of reason,
Dark disputes and artful teasing.
Folly is an endless maze.
Tangled roots perplex her ways.
How many have fallen there!
They stumble all night over bones of the dead,
And feel they know not what but care,
And wish to lead others, when they should be led.

The Tiger

Tiger! Tiger! burning bright
In the forests of the night,
What immortal hand or eye
Could frame thy fearful symmetry?

In what distant deeps or skies
Burnt the fire of thine eyes?
On what wings dare he aspire?
What the hand dare seize the fire?

And what shoulder, and what art,
Could twist the sinews of thy heart?
And when thy heart began to beat,
What dread hand? and what dread feet?

What the hammer? what the chain?
In what furnace was thy brain?
What the anvil? what dread grasp
Dare its deadly terrors clasp?

When the stars threw down their spears,
And water'd heaven with their tears,
Did he smile his work to see?
Did he who made the Lamb make thee?

Tiger! Tiger! burning bright
In the forests of the night,
What immortal hand or eye,
Dare frame thy fearful symmetry?

A Poison Tree

I was angry with my friend:
I told my wrath, my wrath did end.
I was angry with my foe:
I told it not, my wrath did grow.

And I watered it in fears,
Night and morning with my tears;
And I sunned it with smiles,
And with soft deceitful wiles.

And it grew both day and night,
Till it bore an apple bright;

And my foe beheld it shine,
And he knew that it was mine,

And into my garden stole
When the night had veiled the pole:
In the morning glad I see
My foe outstretched beneath the tree.

The Garden of Love

I went to the Garden of Love,
And saw what I never had seen:
A chapel was built in the midst,
Where I used to play on the green.

And the gates of this chapel were shut,
And 'Thou shalt not' writ over the door;
So I turned to the Garden of Love,
That so many sweet flowers bore;

And I saw it was fillèd with graves,
And tombstones where flowers should be;
And priests in black gowns were walking
    their rounds,
And binding with briars my joys and desires.

The Sick Rose

O Rose, thou art sick!
The invisible worm,
That flies in the night,
In the howling storm,

Has found out thy bed
Of crimson joy;
And his dark secret love
Does thy life destroy.

'*Ah! Sun-flower . . .*'

Ah, Sun-flower! weary of time,
Who countest the steps of the sun;
Seeking after that sweet golden clime,
Where the traveller's journey is done;

Where the Youth pined away with desire,
And the pale Virgin shrouded in snow,
Arise from their graves, and aspire
Where my Sun-flower wishes to go.

Jerusalem

And did those feet in ancient time
    Walk upon England's mountains green?
And was the holy Lamb of God
    On England's pleasant pastures seen?

And did the Countenance Divine
    Shine forth upon our clouded hills?
And was Jerusalem builded here
    Among these dark Satanic Mills?

Bring me my bow of burning gold!
    Bring me my arrows of desire!
Bring me my spear! O clouds, unfold!
    Bring me my chariot of fire!

I will not cease from mental fight,
    Nor shall my sword sleep in my hand,
Till we have built Jerusalem
    In England's green and pleasant land.

WILLIAM WORDSWORTH
(1770–1850)

'I wandered lonely as a cloud . . .'

I wandered lonely as a cloud
That floats on high o'er vales and hills,
When all at once I saw a crowd,
A host, of golden daffodils,
Beside the lake, beneath the trees,
Fluttering and dancing in the breeze.

Continuous as the stars that shine
And twinkle on the milky way,
They stretch'd in never-ending line
Along the margin of a bay:
Ten thousand saw I at a glance
Tossing their heads in sprightly dance.

The waves beside them danced, but they
Out-did the sparkling waves in glee: –
A Poet could not but be gay
In such a jocund company!
I gazed – and gazed – but little thought
What wealth the show to me had brought;

For oft, when on my couch I lie
In vacant or in pensive mood,
They flash upon that inward eye
Which is the bliss of solitude;
And then my heart with pleasure fills
And dances with the daffodils.

'I travelled among unknown men . . .'

I travelled among unknown men
    In lands beyond the sea;
Nor, England! did I know till then
    What love I bore to thee.

'Tis past, that melancholy dream!
    Nor will I quit thy shore
A second time; for still I seem
    To love thee more and more.

Among thy mountains did I feel
    The joy of my desire;
And she I cherished turned her wheel
    Beside an English fire.

Thy mornings showed, thy nights concealed
    The bowers where Lucy played;
And thine too is the last green field
    That Lucy's eyes surveyed.

'Three years she grew in sun and shower . . .'

Three years she grew in sun and shower;
Then Nature said, 'A lovelier flower
On earth was never sown;
This child I to myself will take;
She shall be mine, and I will make
A lady of my own.

'Myself will to my darling be
Both law and impulse: and with me
The girl, in rock and plain,
In earth and heaven, in glade and bower,

Shall feel an overseeing power
To kindle or restrain.

'She shall be sportive as the fawn
That wild with glee across the lawn
Or up the mountain springs;
And hers shall be the breathing balm,
And hers the silence and the calm
Of mute insensate things.

'The floating clouds their state shall lend
To her; for her the willow bend;
Nor shall she fail to see
E'en in the motions of the storm
Grace that shall mould the maiden's form
By silent sympathy.

'The stars of midnight shall be dear
To her; and she shall lean her ear
In many a secret place
Where rivulets dance their wayward round,
And beauty born of murmuring sound
Shall pass into her face.

'And vital feelings of delight
Shall rear her form to stately height,
Her virgin bosom swell;
Such thoughts to Lucy I will give
While she and I together live
Here in this happy dell.'

Thus Nature spake – The work was done –
How soon my Lucy's race was run!
She died, and left to me
This heath, this calm and quiet scene;
The memory of what has been,
And never more will be.

'She dwelt among the untrodden ways . . .'

She dwelt among the untrodden ways
   Beside the springs of Dove,
A Maid whom there were none to praise,
   And very few to love.

A violet by a mossy stone
   Half-hidden from the eye!
Fair as a star, when only one
   Is shining in the sky.

She lived unknown, and few could know
   When Lucy ceased to be;
But she is in her grave, and, oh,
   The difference to me!

'A slumber did my spirit seal . . .'

A slumber did my spirit seal;
   I had no human fears:
She seemed a thing that could not feel
   The touch of earthly years.

No motion has show now, no force;
   She neither hears nor sees;
Rolled round in earth's diurnal course,
   With rocks, and stones, and trees.

Tintern Abbey Re-visited

Five years have passed; five summers, with the length
Of five long winters! and again I hear
These waters, rolling from their mountain-springs
With a soft inland murmur. – Once again
Do I behold these steep and lofty cliffs,
That on a wild secluded scene impress

Thoughts of more deep seclusion; and connect
The landscape with the quiet of the sky.
The day is come when I again repose
Here, under this dark sycamore, and view
These plots of cottage-ground, these orchard-tufts,
Which at this season, with their unripe fruits,
Are clad in one green hue, and lose themselves
'Mid groves and copses. Once again I see
These hedge-rows, hardly hedge-rows, little lines
Of sportive wood run wild: these pastoral farms,
Green to the very door; and wreaths of smoke
Sent up, in silence, from among the trees!
With some uncertain notice, as might seem
Of vagrant dwellers in the houseless woods,
Or of some Hermit's cave, where by his fire
The Hermit sits alone.
                                        These beauteous forms,
Through a long absence, have not been to me
As is a landscape to a blind man's eye:
But oft, in lonely rooms, and 'mid the din
Of towns and cities, I have owed to them,
In hours of weariness, sensations sweet,
Felt in the blood, and felt along the heart;
And passing even into my purer mind,
With tranquil restoration: – feelings too
Of unremembered pleasure: such, perhaps,
As have no slight or trivial influence
On that best portion of a good man's life,
His little, nameless, unremembered, acts
Of kindness and of love. Nor less, I trust,
To them I may have owed another gift,
Of aspect more sublime; that blessed mood,
In which the burthen of the mystery,
In which the heavy and the weary weight
Of all this unintelligible world,
Is lightened: – that serene and blessed mood,
In which the affections gently lead us on, –

Until, the breath of this corporeal frame
And even the motion of our human blood
Almost suspended, we are laid asleep
In body, and become a living soul:
While with an eye made quiet by the power
Of harmony, and the deep power of joy,
We see into the life of things.
                                      If this
Be but a vain belief, yet, oh! how oft –
In darkness and amid the many shapes
Of joyless daylight; when the fretful stir
Unprofitable, and the fever of the world,
Have hung upon the beatings of my heart -
How oft, in spirit, have I turned to thee,
O sylvan Wye! thou wanderer thro' the woods,
How often has my spirit turned to thee!

And now, with gleams of half-extinguished thought,
With many recognitions dim and faint,
And somewhat of a sad perplexity,
The picture of the mind revives again:
While here I stand, not only with the sense
Of present pleasure, but with pleasing thoughts
That in this moment there is life and food
For future years. And so I dare to hope,
Though changed, no doubt, from what I was
      when first
I came among these hills; when like a roe
I bounded o'er the mountains, by the sides
Of the deep rivers, and the lonely streams,
Wherever nature led: more like a man
Flying from something that he dreads than one
Who sought the thing he loved. For nature then
(The coarser pleasures of my boyish days,
And their glad animal movements all gone by)
To me was all in all. – I cannot paint
What then I was. The sounding cataract

Haunted me like a passion: the tall rock,
The mountain, and the deep and gloomy wood,
Their colours, and their forms, were then to me
An appetite; a feeling and a love,
That had no need of a remoter charm,
By thought supplied, nor any interest
Unborrowed from the eye. – That time is past,
And all its aching joys are now no more,
And all its dizzy raptures. Not for this
Faint I, nor mourn nor murmur; other gifts
Have followed; for such loss, I would believe,
Abundant recompense. For I have learned
To look on nature, not as in the hour
Of thoughtless youth; but hearing oftentimes
The still, sad music of humanity,
Nor harsh, nor grating, though of ample power
To chasten and subdue. And I have felt
A presence that disturbs me with the joy
Of elevated thoughts; a sense sublime
Of something far more deeply interfused,
Whose dwelling is the light of setting suns,
And the round ocean and the living air,
And the blue sky, and in the mind of man:
A motion and a spirit, that impels
All thinking things, all objects of all thought,
And rolls through all things. Therefore am I still
A lover of the meadows and the woods,
And mountains; and of all that we behold
From this green earth; of all the mighty world
Of eye, and ear, – both what they half create,
And what perceive; well pleased to recognise
In nature and the language of the sense,
The anchor of my purest thoughts, the nurse,
The guide, the guardian of my heart, and soul
Of all my moral being.

[From LINES *Composed a few miles above Tintern Abbey, on re-visiting the banks of the Wye during a tour, July 13, 1798*]

The Solitary Reaper

Behold her, single in the field,
Yon solitary Highland Lass!
Reaping and singing by herself;
Stop here, or gently pass!
Alone she cuts and binds the grain,
And sings a melancholy strain;
O listen! for the vale profound
Is overflowing with the sound.

No nightingale did ever chaunt
More welcome notes to weary bands
Of travellers in some shady haunt,
Among Arabian sands:
A voice so thrilling ne'er was heard
In spring-time from the cuckoo-bird,
Breaking the silence of the seas
Among the farthest Hebrides.

Will no one tell me what she sings?
Perhaps the plaintive numbers flow
For old, unhappy, far-off things,
And battles long ago:
Or is it some more humble lay,
Familiar matter of to-day?
Some natural sorrow, loss or pain,
That has been, and may be again?

Whate'er the theme, the maiden sang
As if her song could have no ending;
I saw her singing at her work,
And o'er the sickle bending;
I listen'd, motionless and still;
And, as I mounted up the hill,
The music in my heart I bore,
Long after it was heard no more.

'My heart leaps up . . .'

My heart leaps up when I behold
   A rainbow in the sky:
So was it when my life began,
So is it now I am a man,
So be it when I shall grow old,
    Or let me die!
The Child is father of the Man:
And I could wish my days to be
Bound each to each by natural piety.

London, 1802

Milton! thou shouldst be living at this hour:
England hath need of thee; she is a fen
Of stagnant waters; altar, sword, and pen,
Fireside, the heroic wealth of hall and bower,
Have forfeited their ancient English dower
Of inward happiness. We are selfish men;
Oh! raise us up, return to us again;
And give us manners, virtue, freedom, power.
Thy soul was like a star, and dwelt apart;
Thou hadst a voice whose sound was like the sea:
Pure as the naked heavens, majestic, free,
So didst thou travel on life's common way,
In cheerful godliness; and yet thy heart
The lowliest duties on herself did lay.

Composed upon Westminster Bridge
September 3, 1802

Earth has not anything to show more fair:
Dull would he be of soul who could pass by
A sight so touching in its majesty:
This city now doth like a garment wear
The beauty of the morning; silent, bare,

Ships, towers, domes, theatres, and temples lie
Open unto the fields, and to the sky;
All bright and glittering in the smokeless air.
Never did sun more beautifully steep
In his first splendour valley, rock, or hill;
Ne'er saw I, never felt, a calm so deep!
The river glideth at his own sweet will:
Dear God! the very houses seem asleep;
And all that mighty heart is lying still!

Ode on Intimations of Immortality from Recollections of Early Childhood

There was a time when meadow, grove, and stream,
The earth, and every common sight
                    To me did seem
                Apparelled in celestial light,
The glory and the freshness of a dream.
It is not now as it hath been of yore; –
                Turn wheresoe'er I may,
                    By night or day,
The things which I have seen I now can see no more.

                The rainbow comes and goes,
                And lovely is the rose;
                The moon doth with delight
Look round her when the heavens are bare;
                Waters on a starry night
                Are beautiful and fair;
The sunshine is a glorious birth;
But yet I know, where'er I go,
That there hath past away a glory from the earth.

Now, while the birds thus sing a joyous song,
                And while the young lambs bound
                As to the tabor's sound,
To me alone there came a thought of grief:

A timely utterance gave that thought relief,
      And I again am strong.
The cataracts blow their trumpets from the steep, –
No more shall grief of mine the season wrong:
I hear the echoes through the mountains throng.
The winds come to me from the fields of sleep,
      And all the earth is gay;
        Land and sea
    Give themselves up to jollity,
      And with the heart of May
Doth every beast keep holiday; –
       Thou child of joy,
Shout round me, let me hear thy shouts, thou happy
    Shepherd-boy!

Ye blesséd Creatures, I have heard the call
     Ye to each other make; I see
The heavens laugh with you in your jubilee;
     My heart is at your festival,
     My head hath its coronal,
The fulness of your bliss, I feel – I feel it all.
      O evil day! if I were sullen
      While Earth herself is adorning
        This sweet May-morning;
      And the children are culling
        On every side
      In a thousand valleys far and wide
      Fresh flowers; while the sun shines warm,
And the babe leaps up on his mother's arm: –
     I hear, I hear, with joy I hear!
     – But there's a tree, of many, one,
A single field which I have look'd upon,
Both of them speak of something that is gone:
       The pansy at my feet
       Doth the same tale repeat:
Whither is fled the visionary gleam?
Where is it now, the glory and the dream?

Our birth is but a sleep and a forgetting;
The Soul that rises with us, our life's Star,
            Hath had elsewhere its setting
            And cometh from afar;
        Not in entire forgetfulness,
        And not in utter nakedness,
But trailing clouds of glory do we come
            From God, who is our home:
Heaven lies about us in our infancy!
Shades of the prison-house begin to close
            Upon the growing Boy,
But he beholds the light, and whence it flows,
            He sees it in his joy;
The Youth, who daily farther from the east
        Must travel, still is Nature's priest,
            And by the vision splendid
            Is on his way attended;
At length the Man perceives it die away,
And fade into the light of common day.

Earth fills her lap with pleasures of her own;
Yearnings she hath in her own natural kind,
And, even with something of a mother's mind,
            And no unworthy aim,
            The homely nurse doth all she can
To make her foster-child, her inmate, Man,
            Forget the glories he hath known,
And that imperial palace whence he came.

Behold the Child among his new-born blisses,
A six years' darling of a pigmy size!
See, where 'mid work of his own hand he lies,
Fretted by sallies of his mother's kisses,
With light upon him from his father's eyes!
See, at his feet, some little plan or chart,
Some fragment from his dream of human life,
Shaped by himself with newly-learned art;

A wedding or a festival,
A mourning or a funeral;
    And this hath now his heart,
And unto this he frames his song:
    Then will he fit his tongue
To dialogues of business, love, or strife;
    But it will not be long
    Ere this be thrown aside,
    And with new joy and pride
The little actor cons another part;
Filling from time to time his 'humorous stage'
With all the Persons, down to palsied Age,
That life brings with her in her equipage;
    As if his whole vocation
    Were endless imitation.

Thou, whose exterior semblance doth belie
    Thy soul's immensity;
Thou best philosopher, who yet dost keep
Thy heritage, thou eye among the blind,
That, deaf and silent, read'st the eternal deep,
Haunted for ever by the eternal Mind, –
    Mighty Prophet! Seer blest!
    On whom those truths do rest
Which we are toiling all our lives to find,
In darkness lost, the darkness of the grave;
Thou, over whom thy Immortality
Broods like the day, a master o'er a slave,
A Presence which is not to be put by;
    To whom the grave
Is but a lonely bed, without the sense of sight
Of day or the warm light,
A place of thoughts where we in waiting lie;
Thou little child, yet glorious in the might
Of heaven-born freedom on thy being's height,
Why with such earnest pains dost thou provoke
The years to bring the inevitable yoke,

Thus blindly with thy blessedness at strife?
Full soon thy soul shall have her earthly freight,
And custom lie upon thee with a weight
Heavy as frost, and deep almost as life!

     O joy! that in our embers
     Is something that doth live,
     That Nature yet remembers
     What was so fugitive!
The thought of our past years in me doth breed
Perpetual benediction: not indeed
For that which is most worthy to be blest,
Delight and liberty, the simple creed
Of Childhood, whether busy or at rest,
With new-fledged hope still fluttering in his breast: —
     — Not for these I raise
     The song of thanks and praise;
     But for those obstinate questionings
     Of sense and outward things,
     Fallings from us, vanishings,
     Blank misgivings of a creature
Moving about in worlds not realized,
High instincts, before which our mortal nature
Did tremble like a guilty thing surprised:
     But for those first affections,
     Those shadowy recollections,
     Which, be they what they may,
Are yet the fountain-light of all our day,
Are yet a master-light of all our seeing;
     Uphold us — cherish — and have power to make
Our noisy years seem moments in the being
Of the eternal Silence: truths that wake,
     To perish never;
Which neither listlessness, nor mad endeavour,
     Nor man nor boy,
Nor all that is at enmity with joy,
Can utterly abolish or destroy!
   Hence, in a season of calm weather

Though inland far we be,
Our souls have sight of that immortal sea
               Which brought us hither;
               Can in a moment travel thither –
And see the children sport upon the shore,
And hear the mighty waters rolling evermore.

Then, sing, ye birds, sing, sing a joyous song!
               And let the young lambs bound
               As to the tabor's sound!
     We, in thought, will join your throng,
               Ye that pipe and ye that play,
               Ye that through your hearts to-day
               Feel the gladness of the May!
What though the radiance which was once so bright
Be now for ever taken from my sight,
               Though nothing can bring back the hour
Of splendour in the grass, of glory in the flower;
               We will grieve not, rather find
               Strength in what remains behind;
               In the primal sympathy
               Which having been must ever be;
               In the soothing thoughts that spring
               Out of human suffering;
               In the faith that looks through death,
In years that bring the philosophic mind.

And O, ye Fountains, Meadows, Hills, and Groves,
Forebode not any severing of our loves!
Yet in my heart of hearts I feel your might;
I only have relinquish'd one delight
To live beneath your more habitual sway;
I love the brooks which down their channels fret
Even more than when I tripp'd lightly as they;
The innocent brightness of a new-born day
               Is lovely yet;
The clouds that gather round the setting sun
Do take a sober colouring from an eye

That hath kept watch o'er man's mortality;
Another race hath been, and other palms are won.
 Thanks to the human heart by which we live,
 Thanks to its tenderness, its joys, and fears,
 To me the meanest flower that blows can give
 Thoughts that do often lie too deep for tears.

SAMUEL TAYLOR COLERIDGE
(1772–1834)

The Rime of the Ancient Mariner

PART I

It is an ancient Mariner,
And he stoppeth one of three.
'By thy long grey beard and glittering eye,
Now wherefore stopp'st thou me?

'The Bridegroom's doors are opened wide,
And I am next of kin;
The guests are met, the feast is set:
May'st hear the merry din.'

He holds him with his skinny hand,
'There was a ship,' quoth he.
'Hold off! unhand me, greybeard loon!'
Eftsoons his hand dropped he.

He holds him with his glittering eye –
The Wedding-Guest stood still,
And listens like a three years' child:
The Mariner hath his will.

The Wedding-Guest sat on a stone:
He cannot choose but hear;
And thus spake on that ancient man,
The bright-eyed Mariner.

'The ship was cheered, the harbour cleared,
Merrily did we drop
Below the kirk, below the hill,
Below the lighthouse top.

'The Sun came up upon the left,
Out of the sea came he!
And he shone bright, and on the right
Went down into the sea.

'Higher and higher every day,
Till over the mast at noon – '
The Wedding-Guest here beat his breast,
For he heard the loud bassoon.

The bride hath paced into the hall,
Red as a rose is she;
Nodding their heads before her goes
The merry minstrelsy.

The Wedding-Guest he beat his breast,
Yet he cannot choose but hear;
And thus spake on that ancient man,
The bright-eyed Mariner:

'And now the Storm-blast came, and he
Was tyrannous and strong:
He struck with his o'ertaking wings,
And chased us south along.

'With sloping masts and dipping prow,
As who pursued with yell and blow
Still treads the shadow of his foe,
And forward bends his head,
The ship drove fast, loud roared the blast,
And southward aye we fled.

'And now there came both mist and snow,
And it grew wondrous cold;
And ice, mast-high, came floating by,
As green as emerald.

'And through the drifts the snowy clifts
Did send a dismal sheen:
Nor shapes of men nor beasts we ken –
The ice was all between.

'The ice was here, the ice was there,
The ice was all around:
It cracked and growled, and roared and howled,
Like noises in a swound!

'At length did cross an Albatross:
Through the fog it came:
As if it had been a Christian soul,
We hailed it in God's name.

'It ate the food it ne'er had eat,
And round and round it flew.
The ice did split with a thunder-fit;
The helmsman steered us through!

'And a good south wind sprung up behind;
The Albatross did follow,
And every day, for food or play,
Came to the mariner's hollo!

'In mist or cloud, on mast or shroud,
It perched for vespers nine;
Whiles all the night, through fog-smoke white,
Glimmeréd the white Moon-shine.'

'God save thee, ancient Mariner!
From the fiends, that plague thee thus! –
Why look'st thou so?' – 'With my cross-bow
I shot the Albatross!'

PART II

'The Sun now rose upon the right:
Out of the sea came he,
Still hid in mist, and on the left
Went down into the sea.

'And the good south wind still blew behind,
But no sweet bird did follow,
Nor any day, for food or play,
Came to the mariner's hollo!

'And I had done a hellish thing,
And it would work 'em woe;
For all averred, I had killed the bird
That made the breeze to blow.
Ah, wretch! said they, the bird to slay
That made the breeze to blow!

'Nor dim nor red, like God's own head,
The glorious Sun uprist:
Then all averred, I had killed the bird
That brought the fog and mist.
'T was right, said they, such birds to slay,
That bring the fog and mist.

'The fair breeze blew, the white foam flew,
The furrow followed free:
We were the first that ever burst
Into that silent sea.

'Down dropped the breeze, the sails dropped down,
'T was sad as sad could be;
And we did speak only to break
The silence of the sea!

'All in a hot and copper sky,
The bloody Sun, at noon,
Right up above the mast did stand,
No bigger than the Moon.

'Day after day, day after day,
We stuck, nor breath nor motion;
As idle as a painted ship
Upon a painted ocean.

'Water, water, everywhere,
And all the boards did shrink;
Water, water, everywhere,
Nor any drop to drink.

'The very deep did rot: O Christ!
That ever this should be!
Yea, slimy things did crawl with legs
Upon the slimy sea.

'About, about, in reel and rout,
The death-fires danced at night;
The water, like a witch's oils,
Burnt green, and blue, and white.

'And some in dreams assurèd were
Of the Spirit that plagued us so:
Nine fathoms deep he had followed us,
From the land of mist and snow.

'And every tongue, through utter drought,
Was withered at the root;
We could not speak, no more than if
We had been choked with soot.

'Ah! well-a-day! what evil looks
Had I from old and young!
Instead of the cross, the Albatross
About my neck was hung.

PART III

'There passed a weary time. Each throat
Was parched, and glazed each eye.
A weary time! A weary time!
How glazed each weary eye!
When looking westward I beheld
A something in the sky.

'At first it seemed a little speck,
And then it seemed a mist:
It moved and moved, and took at last
A certain shape, I wist.

'A speck, a mist, a shape, I wist!
And still it neared and neared:
As if it dodged a water-sprite,
It plunged and tacked and veered.

'With throats unslaked, with black lips baked,
We could nor laugh nor wail;
Through utter drought all dumb we stood!
I bit my arm, I sucked the blood,
And cried, "A sail! a sail!"

'With throats unslaked, with black lips baked,
Agape they heard me call:
Gramercy! they for joy did grin,
And all at once their breath drew in,
As they were drinking all.

'"See! see (I cried) she tacks no more!
Hither to work us weal;
Without a breeze, without a tide,
She steadies with upright keel!"

'The western wave was all a-flame:
The day was well nigh done:
Almost upon the western wave
Rested the broad bright Sun;
When that strange shape drove suddenly
Betwixt us and the Sun.

'And straight the Sun was flecked with bars,
(Heaven's Mother send us grace!)
As if through a dungeon grate he peered,
With broad and burning face.

'Alas (thought I, and my heart beat loud)
How fast she nears and nears!
Are those her sails that glance in the Sun,
Like restless gossameres?

'Are those her ribs through which the Sun
Did peer, as through a grate?
And is that Woman all her crew?
Is that a Death? and are there two?
Is Death that woman's mate?

'Her lips were red, her looks were free,
Her locks were yellow as gold:
Her skin was as white as leprosy,
The Nightmare Life-in-Death was she,
Who thicks man's blood with cold.

'The naked hulk alongside came,
And the twain were casting dice;
"The game is done! I've won, I've won!"
Quoth she, and whistled thrice.

'The Sun's rim dips; the stars rush out:
At one stride comes the dark;
With far-heard whisper, o'er the sea,
Off shot the spectre-bark.

'We listened and looked sideways up!
Fear at my heart, as at a cup,
My life-blood seemed to sip!
The stars were dim, and thick the night,
The steersman's face by his lamp gleamed white;
From the sails the dew did drip –
Till clomb above the eastern bar
The hornèd Moon with one bright star
Within the nether tip.

'One after one, by the star-dogged Moon,
Too quick for groan or sigh,
Each turned his face with a ghastly pang,
And cursed me with his eye.

'Four times fifty living men
(And I heard nor sigh nor groan)
With heavy thump, a lifeless lump,
They dropped down one by one.

'The souls did from their bodies fly –
They fled to bliss or woe!
And every soul, it passed me by,
Like the whiz of my cross-bow!'

PART IV

'I fear thee, ancient Mariner!
I fear thy skinny hand!
And thou art long, and lank, and brown,
As is the ribbed sea-sand.

'I fear thee and thy glittering eye,
And thy skinny hand, so brown.' –
'Fear not, fear not, thou Wedding-Guest!
This body dropped not down.

'Alone, alone, all, all alone,
Alone on a wide, wide sea!
And never a saint took pity on
My soul in agony.

'The many men, so beautiful!
And they all dead did lie:
And a thousand thousand slimy things
Lived on; and so did I.

'I looked upon the rotting sea,
And drew my eyes away;
I looked upon the rotting deck,
And there the dead men lay.

'I looked to heaven, and tried to pray;
But or ever a prayer had gusht,
A wicked whisper came, and made
My heart as dry as dust.

'I closed my lids, and kept them close,
And the balls like pulses beat;
For the sky and the sea, and the sea and the sky,
Lay like a load on my weary eye,
And the dead were at my feet.

'The cold sweat melted from their limbs,
Nor rot nor reek did they:
The look with which they looked on me
Had never passed away.

'An orphan's curse would drag to hell
A spirit from on high;
But oh! more horrible than that
Is the curse in a dead man's eye!
Seven days, seven nights, I saw that curse,
And yet I could not die.

'The moving Moon went up the sky,
And nowhere did abide:
Softly she was going up,
And a star or two beside –

'Her beams bemocked the sultry main,
Like April hoar-frost spread;
But where the ship's huge shadow lay,
The charmèd water burnt alway
A still and awful red.

'Beyond the shadow of the ship,
I watched the water-snakes:
They moved in tracks of shining white,
And when they reared, the elfish light
Fell off in hoary flakes.

'Within the shadow of the ship
I watched their rich attire:
Blue, glossy green, and velvet black,
They coiled and swam; and every track
Was a flash of golden fire.

'O happy living things! no tongue
Their beauty might declare:
A spring of love gushed from my heart,
And I blessed them unaware!
Sure my kind saint took pity on me,
And I blessed them unaware.

'The selfsame moment, I could pray;
And from my neck so free
The Albatross fell off, and sank
Like lead into the sea.

PART V

'Oh, sleep! it is a gentle thing,
Beloved from pole to pole!

To Mary Queen the praise be given!
She sent the gentle sleep from Heaven,
That slid into my soul.

'The silly buckets on the deck,
That had so long remained,
I dreamt that they were filled with dew;
And when I awoke, it rained.

'My lips were wet, my throat was cold,
My garments all were dank;
Sure I had drunken in my dreams,
And still my body drank.

'I moved, and could not feel my limbs:
I was so light – almost
I thought that I had died in sleep,
And was a blessèd ghost.

'And soon I heard a roaring wind:
It did not come anear;
But with its sound it shook the sails,
That were so thin and sere.

'The upper air burst into life!
And a hundred fire-flags sheen,
To and fro they were hurried about;
And to and fro, and in and out,
The wan stars danced between.

'And the coming wind did roar more loud,
And the sails did sigh like sedge;
And the rain poured down from one black cloud;
The Moon was at its edge.

'The thick black cloud was cleft, and still
The Moon was at its side:
Like waters shot from some high crag,
The lightning fell with never a jag,
A river steep and wide.

'The loud wind never reached the ship,
Yet now the ship moved on!
Beneath the lightning and the Moon
The dead men gave a groan.

'They groaned, they stirred, they all uprose,
Nor spake nor moved their eyes;
It had been strange, even in a dream,
To have seen those dead men rise.

'The helmsman steered, the ship moved on;
Yet never a breeze up-blew;
The mariners all 'gan work the ropes,
Where they were wont to do:
They raised their limbs like lifeless tools –
We were a ghastly crew.

'The body of my brother's son
Stood by me, knee to knee;
The body and I pulled at one rope,
But he said nought to me.'

'I fear thee, ancient Mariner!'
'Be calm, thou Wedding-Guest!
'T was not those souls that fled in pain,
Which to their corses came again,
But a troop of spirits blest:

'For when it dawned – they dropped their arms,
And clustered round the mast;
Sweet sounds rose slowly through their mouths,
And from their bodies passed.

'Around, around, flew each sweet sound,
Then darted to the Sun;
Slowly the sounds came back again,
Now mixed, now one by one.

'Sometimes a-dropping from the sky
I heard the skylark sing;
Sometimes all little birds that are,
How they seemed to fill the sea and air
With their sweet jargoning!

'And now 't was like all instruments,
Now like a lonely flute;
And now it is an angel's song,
That makes the heavens be mute.

'It ceased; yet still the sails made on
A pleasant noise till noon,
A noise like of a hidden brook
In the leafy month of June,
That to the sleeping woods all night
Singeth a quiet tune.

'Till noon we quietly sailed on,
Yet never a breeze did breathe:
Slowly and smoothly went the ship,
Moved onwards from beneath.

'Under the keel nine fathom deep,
From the land of mist and snow,
The spirit slid; and it was he
That made the ship to go.
The sails at noon left off their tune,
And the ship stood still also.

'The Sun, right up above the mast,
Had fixed her to the ocean;
But in a minute she 'gan stir,
With a short uneasy motion –
Backwards and forwards half her length,
With a short uneasy motion.

'Then like a pawing horse let go,
She made a sudden bound:
It flung the blood into my head,
And I fell down in a swound.

'How long in that same fit I lay,
I have not to declare;
But ere my living life returned,
I heard, and in my soul discerned
Two voices in the air.

'"Is it he?" quoth one, "is this the man?
By Him who died on cross,
With his cruel bow he laid full low
The harmless Albatross.

'"The spirit who bideth by himself
In the land of mist and snow,
He loved the bird that loved the man
Who shot him with his bow."

'The other was a softer voice,
As soft as honey-dew:
Quoth he, "The man hath penance done,
And penance more will do."

PART VI

First Voice

'"But tell me, tell me! speak again
Thy soft response renewing –
What makes that ship drive on so fast?
What is the ocean doing?"

Second Voice

'"Still as a slave before his lord,
The ocean hath no blast;

His great bright eye most silently
Up to the Moon is cast –

'"If he may know which way to go;
For she guides him, smooth or grim.
See, brother, see! how graciously
She looketh down on him."

First Voice

'"But why drives on that ship so fast,
Without or wave or wind?"

Second Voice

'"The air is cut away before,
And closes from behind.

'"Fly brother, fly! more high, more high!
Or we shall be belated:
For slow and slow that ship will go,
When the Mariner's trance is abated."

'I woke, and we were sailing on,
As in a gentle weather:
'T was night, calm night, the moon was high;
The dead men stood together.

'All stood together on the deck,
For a charnel-dungeon fitter:
All fixed on me their stony eyes,
That in the Moon did glitter.

'The pang, the curse, with which they died,
Had never passed away:
I could not draw my eyes from theirs,
Nor turn them up to pray.

'And now this spell was snapped: once more
I viewed the ocean green,
And looked far forth, yet little saw
Of what had else been seen –

'Like one, that on a lonesome road
Doth walk in fear and dread,
And having once turned round, walks on,
And turns no more his head;
Because he knows a frightful fiend
Doth close behind him tread.

'But soon there breathed a wind on me,
Nor sound nor motion made:
Its path was not upon the sea,
In ripple or in shade.

'It raised my hair, it fanned my cheek
Like a meadow-gale of spring –
It mingled strangely with my fears,
Yet it felt like a welcoming.

'Swiftly, swiftly flew the ship,
Yet she sailed softly too:
Sweetly, sweetly blew the breeze –
On me alone it blew.

'Oh! dream of joy! is this indeed
The lighthouse top I see?
Is this the hill? is this the kirk?
Is this mine own countree?

'We drifted o'er the harbour-bar,
And I with sobs did pray
"O let me be awake, my God!
Or let me sleep alway."

'The harbour-bay was clear as glass,
So smoothly it was strewn!
And on the bay the moonlight lay,
And the shadow of the Moon.

'The rock shone bright, the kirk no less,
That stands above the rock:

The moonlight steeped in silentness
The steady weathercock.

'And the bay was white with silent light,
Till rising from the same,
Full many shapes, that shadows were,
In crimson colours came.

'A little distance from the prow
Those crimson shadows were:
I turned my eyes upon the deck –
Oh, Christ! what saw I there!

'Each corse lay flat, lifeless and flat,
And by the holy rood!
A man all light, a seraph-man,
On every corse there stood.

'This seraph-band, each waved his hand:
It was a heavenly sight!
They stood as signals to the land,
Each one a lovely light:

'This seraph-band, each waved his hand,
No voice did they impart –
No voice; but oh! the silence sank
Like music on my heart.

'But soon I heard the dash of oars,
I heard the Pilot's cheer;
My head was turned perforce away,
And I saw a boat appear.

'The Pilot, and the Pilot's boy,
I heard them coming fast:
Dear Lord in Heaven! it was a joy
The dead men could not blast.

'I saw a third – I heard his voice:
It is the Hermit good!
He singeth loud his godly hymns
That he makes in the wood.
He'll shrive my soul, he'll wash away
The Albatross's blood.

PART VII

'This Hermit good lives in that wood
Which slopes down to the sea.
How loudly his sweet voice he rears!
He loves to talk with marineres
That come from a far countree.

'He kneels at morn, and noon, and eve –
He hath a cushion plump:
It is the moss that wholly hides
The rotted old oak-stump.

'The skiff-boat neared: I heard them talk,
"Why, this is strange, I trow!
Where are those lights so many and fair,
That signal made but now?"

'"Strange, by my faith!" the Hermit said –
"And they answered not our cheer!
The planks looked warped! and see those sails,
How thin they are and sere!
I never saw aught like to them,
Unless perchance it were

'"Brown skeletons of leaves that lag
My forest-brook along:
When the ivy-tod is heavy with snow,
And the owlet whoops to the wolf below,
That eats the she-wolf's young."

'"Dear Lord! it hath a fiendish look" –
(The Pilot made reply)
"I am a-feared" – "Push on, push on!"
Said the Hermit cheerily.

'The boat came closer to the ship,
But I nor spake nor stirred;
The boat came close beneath the ship,
And straight a sound was heard.

'Under the water it rumbled on,
Still louder and more dread:
It reached the ship, it split the bay;
The ship went down like lead.

'Stunned by that loud and dreadful sound,
Which sky and ocean smote,
Like one that hath been seven days drowned,
My body lay afloat;
But swift as dreams, myself I found
Within the Pilot's boat.

'Upon the whirl, where sank the ship,
The boat spun round and round;
And all was still, save that the hill
Was telling of the sound.

'I moved my lips – The Pilot shrieked,
And fell down in a fit;
The holy Hermit raised his eyes,
And prayed where he did sit.

'I took the oars: the Pilot's boy,
Who now doth crazy go,
Laughed loud and long, and all the while
His eyes went to and fro.
"Ha! ha!" quoth he, "full plain I see,
The Devil knows how to row."

'And now, all in my own countree,
I stood on the firm land!
The Hermit stepped forth from the boat,
And scarcely he could stand.

'"O shrive me, shrive me, holy man!"
The Hermit crossed his brow.
"Say quick," quoth he, "I bid thee say –
What manner of man art thou?"

'Forthwith this frame of mine was wrenched
With a woeful agony,
Which forced me to begin my tale;
And then it left me free.

'Since then at an uncertain hour,
That agony returns;
And till my ghastly tale is told,
This heart within me burns.

'I pass, like night, from land to land;
I have strange power of speech;
That moment that his face I see,
I know the man that must hear me:
To him my tale I teach.

'What loud uproar bursts from that door!
The wedding-guests are there;
But in the garden-bower the bride
And bride-maids singing are;
And hark the little vesper bell,
Which biddeth me to prayer!

'O Wedding-Guest! this soul hath been
Alone on a wide wide sea:
So lonely 't was, that God himself
Scarce seemèd there to be.

'O sweeter than the marriage-feast,
'T is sweeter far to me,
To walk together to the kirk
With a goodly company! –

'To walk together to the kirk,
And all together pray,
While each to his great Father bends,
Old men, and babes, and loving friends,
And youths and maidens gay!

'Farewell, farewell! but this I tell
To thee, thou Wedding-Guest!
He prayeth well, who loveth well
Both man and bird and beast.

'He prayeth best, who loveth best
All things both great and small;
For the dear God who loveth us,
He made and loveth all.'

The Mariner, whose eye is bright,
Whose beard with age is hoar,
Is gone; and now the Wedding-Guest
Turned from the bridegroom's door.

He went like one that hath been stunned,
And is of sense forlorn:
A sadder and a wiser man
He rose the morrow morn.

Kubla Khan

In Xanadu did Kubla Khan
A stately pleasure-dome decree:
Where Alph, the sacred river, ran
Through caverns measureless to man
    Down to a sunless sea.
So twice five miles of fertile ground
With walls and towers were girdled round:

And there were gardens bright with sinuous rills,
Where blossomed many an incense-bearing tree;
And here were forests ancient as the hills,
Enfolding sunny spots of greenery.

But oh! that deep romantic chasm which slanted
Down the green hill athwart a cedarn cover!
A savage place! as holy and enchanted
As e'er beneath a waning moon was haunted
By woman wailing for her demon-lover!
And from this chasm, with ceaseless turmoil seething,
As if this earth in fast thick pants were breathing,
A mighty fountain momently was forced:
Amid whose swift half-intermitted burst
Huge fragments vaulted like rebounding hail,
Or chaffy grain beneath the thresher's flail:
And 'mid these dancing rocks at once and ever
It flung up momently the sacred river.
Five miles meandering with a mazy motion
Through wood and dale the sacred river ran,
Then reached the caverns measureless to man,
And sank in tumult to a lifeless ocean:
And 'mid this tumult Kubla heard from far
Ancestral voices prophesying war!
    The shadow of the dome of pleasure
    Floated midway on the waves;
    Where was heard the mingled measure
    From the fountain and the caves.
It was a miracle of rare device,
A sunny pleasure-dome with caves of ice!

    A damsel with a dulcimer
    In a vision once I saw:
    It was an Abyssinian maid,
    And on her dulcimer she played,
    Singing of Mount Abora.
    Could I revive within me
    Her symphony and song,

To such a deep delight 'twould win me,
That with music loud and long,
I would build that dome in air,
That sunny dome! those caves of ice!
And all who heard should see them there,
And all should cry, "Beware! Beware!
His flashing eyes, his floating hair!
Weave a circle round him thrice,
And close your eyes with holy dread,
For he on honey-dew hath fed,
And drunk the milk of Paradise."

Frost at Midnight

The Frost performs its secret ministry,
Unhelped by any wind. The owlet's cry
Came loud – and hark, again! loud as before.
The inmates of my cottage, all at rest,
Have left me to that solitude, which suits
Abstruser musings: save that at my side
My cradled infant slumbers peacefully.
'Tis calm indeed! so calm, that it disturbs
And vexes meditation with its strange
And extreme silentness. Sea, hill, and wood,
This populous village! Sea, and hill, and wood,
With all the numberless goings-on of life,
Inaudible as dreams! the thin blue flame
Lies on my low-burnt fire, and quivers not;
Only that film, which fluttered on the grate,
Still flutters there, the sole unquiet thing.
Methinks, its motion in this hush of nature
Gives it dim sympathies with me who live,
Making it a companionable form,
Whose puny flaps and freaks the idling Spirit
By its own moods interprets, everywhere
Echo or mirror seeking of itself,
And makes a toy of Thought.

                 [From *Frost at Midnight*]

ROBERT SOUTHEY
(1774–1843)

'My days among the Dead are passed . . .'

My days among the Dead are passed;
Around me I behold,
Where'er these casual eyes are cast,
The mighty minds of old:
My never-failing friends are they,
With whom I converse day by day.

With them I take delight in weal
And seek relief in woe;
And while I understand and feel
How much to them I owe,
My cheeks have often been bedew'd
With tears of thoughtful gratitude.

My thoughts are with the Dead; with them
I live in long-past years,
Their virtues love, their faults condemn,
Partake their hopes and fears,
And from their lessons seek and find
Instruction with an humble mind.

My hopes are with the Dead; anon
My place with them will be,
And I with them shall travel on
Through all Futurity;
Yet leaving here a name, I trust,
That will not perish in the dust.

After Blenheim

It was a summer evening,
   Old Kaspar's work was done,
And he before his cottage door
   Was sitting in the sun:

And by him sported on the green
His little grandchild Wilhelmine.

She saw her brother Peterkin
   Roll something large and round
Which he beside the rivulet
   In playing there had found:
He came to ask what he had found
That was so large and smooth and round.

Old Kaspar took it from the boy
   Who stood expectant by;
And then the old man shook his head,
   And with a natural sigh,
''Tis some poor fellow's skull,' said he,
'Who fell in the great victory.

'I find them in the garden,
   For there's many here about;
And often when I go to plough
   The ploughshare turns them out.
For many thousand men,' said he,
'Were slain in that great victory.'

'Now tell us what 'twas all about,'
   Young Peterkin he cries;
And little Wilhelmine looks up
   With wonder-waiting eyes;
'Now tell us all about the war,
And what they fought each other for.'

'It was the English,' Kaspar cried,
   'Who put the French to rout;
But what they fought each other for
   I could not well make out.
But everybody said,' quoth he,
'That 'twas a famous victory.

'My father lived at Blenheim then,
  Yon little stream hard by;
They burnt his dwelling to the ground,
  And he was forced to fly;
So with his wife and child he fled,
Nor had he where to rest his head.

'With fire and sword the country round
  Was wasted far and wide,
And many a childing mother then
  And newborn baby died:
But things like that, you know, must be
At every famous victory.

'They say it was a shocking sight
  After the field was won;
For many thousand bodies here
  Lay rotting in the sun;
But things like that, you know, must be
After a famous victory.

'Great praise the Duke of Marlboro' won
  And our good Prince Eugene.'
'Why, 'twas a very wicked thing!'
  Said little Wilhelmine;
'Nay . . . nay . . . my little girl,' quoth he,
'It was a famous victory.

'And everybody praised the Duke
  Who this great fight did win.'
'But what good came of it at last?'
  Quoth little Peterkin: —
'Why that I cannot tell,' said he,
'But 'twas a famous victory.'

CHARLES LAMB
(1775-1834)

The Old Familiar Faces

I have had playmates, I have had companions
In my days of childhood, in my joyful school-days;
All, all are gone, the old familiar faces.

I have been laughing, I have been carousing,
Drinking late, sitting late, with my bosom cronies;
All, all are gone, the old familiar faces.

I loved a Love once, fairest among women:
Closed are her doors on me, I must not see her –
All, all are gone, the old familiar faces.

I have a friend, a kinder friend has no man:
Like an ingrate, I left my friend abruptly;
Left him, to muse on the old familiar faces.

Ghost-like I paced round the haunts of my childhood,
Earth seem'd a desert I was bound to traverse,
Seeking to find the old familiar faces.

Friend of my bosom, thou more than a brother,
Why wert not thou born in my father's dwelling?
So might we talk of the old familiar faces.

How some they have died, and some they have left me,
And some are taken from me; all are departed;
All, all are gone, the old familiar faces.

A Farewell to Tobacco

May the Babylonish curse
Straight confound my stammering verse,
If I can a passage see
In this world-perplexity,

Or a fit expression find,
Or a language to my mind,
(Still the phrase is wide or scant)
To take leave of thee, GREAT PLANT!
Or in any terms relate
Half my love, or half my hate:
For I hate, yet love, thee so,
That, whichever thing I show,
The plain truth will seem to be
A constrain'd hyperbole,
And the passion to proceed
More from a mistress than a weed.

Sooty retainer to the vine,
Bacchus' black servant, negro fine;
Sorcerer, that mak'st us dote upon
Thy begrimed complexion,
And, for thy pernicious sake,
More and greater oaths to break
Than reclaimed lovers take
'Gainst women: thou thy siege dost lay
Much too in the female way,
While thou suck'st the lab'ring breath
Faster than kisses or than death.

Thou in such a cloud dost bind us,
That our worst foes cannot find us,
And ill fortune, that would thwart us,
Shoots at rovers, shooting at us;
While each man, through thy height'ning steam,
Does like a smoking Etna seem,
And all about us does express
(Fancy and wit in richest dress)
A Sicilian fruitfulness.

Thou through such a mist dost show us,
That our best friends do not know us,
And, for those allowed features,
Due to reasonable creatures,

Liken'st us to fell Chimeras,
Monsters that, who see us, fear us:
Worse than Cerberus or Geryon,
Or, who first loved a cloud, Ixion.

Bacchus we know, and we allow
His tipsy rites. But what art thou,
That but by reflex canst show
What his deity can do,
As the false Egyptian spell
Aped the true Hebrew miracle?
Some few vapours thou may'st raise,
The weak brain may serve to amaze,
But to the reins and nobler heart
Canst nor life nor heat impart.

Brother of Bacchus, later born,
The old world was sure forlorn
Wanting thee, that aidest more
The god's victories than before
All his panthers, and the brawls
Of his piping Bacchanals.
These, as stale, we disallow,
Or judge of *thee* meant: only thou
His true Indian conquest art;
And, for ivy round his dart,
The reformed god now weaves
A finer thyrsus of thy leaves.

Scent to match thy rich perfume
Chemic art did ne'er presume
Through her quaint alembic strain,
None so sov'reign to the brain.
Nature, that did in thee excel,
Framed again no second smell.
Roses, violets, but toys
For the smaller sort of boys,

Or for greener damsels meant;
Thou art the only manly scent.

Stinking'st of the stinking kind,
Filth of the mouth and fog of the mind,
Africa, that brags her foison,
Breeds no such prodigious poison
Henbane, nightshade, both together,
Hemlock, aconite –
                    Nay, rather,
Plant divine, of rarest virtue;
Blisters on the tongue would hurt you.
'Twas but in a sort I blamed thee;
None e'er prosper'd who defamed thee.
Irony all, and feign'd abuse,
Such as perplex'd lovers use,
At a need, when, in despair
To paint forth their fairest fair,
Or in part but to express
That exceeding comeliness
Which their fancies doth so strike,
They borrow language of dislike;
And, instead of Dearest Miss,
Jewel, Honey, Sweetheart, Bliss,
And those forms of old admiring,
Call her Cockatrice and Siren,
Basilisk, and all that's evil,
Witch, Hyena, Mermaid, Devil,
Ethiop, Wench, and Blackamoor,
Monkey, Ape, and twenty more;
Friendly Trait'ress, loving Foe, –
Not that she is truly so,
But no other way they know
A contentment to express,
Borders so upon excess,
That they do not rightly wot
Whether it be pain or not.

Or, as men, constrain'd to part
With what's nearest to their heart,
While their sorrow's at the height,
Lose discrimination quite,
And their hasty wrath let fall,
To appease their frantic gall,
On the darling thing whatever,
Whence they feel it death to sever,
Though it be, as they, perforce,
Guiltless of the sad divorce.
For I must (nor let it grieve thee,
Friendliest of plants, that I must) leave thee
For thy sake, TOBACCO, I
Would do anything but die,
And but seek to extend my days
Long enough to sing thy praise.
But, as she, who once hath been
A king's consort, is a queen
Ever after, nor will bate
Any tittle of her state,
Though a widow, or divorced,
So I, from thy converse forced,
The old name and style retain,
A right Katherine of Spain;
And a seat, too, 'mongst the joys
Of the blest Tobacco Boys;
Where, though I, by sour physician,
Am debarr'd the full fruition
Of thy favours, I may catch
Some collateral sweets, and snatch
Sidelong odours, that give life
Like glances from a neighbour's wife;
And still live in the by-places
And the suburbs of thy graces;
And in thy borders take delight,
An unconquer'd Canaanite.

THOMAS CAMPBELL
(1777–1844)

The Soldier's Dream

Our bugles sang truce, for the night-cloud had lower'd,
   And the sentinel stars set their watch in the sky;
And thousands had sunk on the ground overpower'd,
   The weary to sleep, and the wounded to die.

When reposing that night on my pallet of straw
   By the wolf-scaring faggot that guarded the slain,
At the dead of the night a sweet Vision I saw;
   And thrice ere the morning I dreamt it again.

Methought from the battle-field's dreadful array
   Far, far, I had roam'd on a desolate track:
'Twas Autumn, – and sunshine arose on the way
   To the home of my fathers, that welcomed me back.

I flew to the pleasant fields traversed so oft
   In life's morning march, when my bosom was young;
I heard my own mountain-goats bleating aloft,
   And knew the sweet strain that the corn-reapers sung.

Then pledged we the wine-cup, and fondly I swore
   From my home and my weeping friends never to part;
My little ones kiss'd me a thousand times o'er,
   And my wife sobb'd aloud in her fullness of heart.

'Stay – stay with us! – rest! – thou art weary and worn!' –
   And fain was their war-broken soldier to stay; –
But sorrow return'd with the dawning of morn,
   And the voice in my dreaming ear melted away.

Hohenlinden

On Linden, when the sun was low,
All bloodless lay the untrodden snow;
And dark as winter was the flow
    Of Iser, rolling rapidly.

But Linden saw another sight,
When the drum beat at dead of night
Commanding fires of death to light
    The darkness of her scenery.

By torch and trumpet fast array'd,
Each horseman drew his battle-blade,
And furious every charger neigh'd
    To join the dreadful revelry.

Then shook the hills with thunder riven;
Then rush'd the steed, to battle driven;
And louder than the bolts of Heaven
    Far flash'd the red artillery.

But redder yet that light shall glow
On Linden's hills of stainéd snow;
And bloodier yet the torrent flow
    Of Iser, rolling rapidly.

'Tis morn, but scarce yon level sun
Can pierce the war-clouds, rolling dun,
Where furious Frank, and fiery Hun,
    Shout in their sulph'rous canopy.

The combat deepens. On, ye brave,
Who rush to glory, or the grave!
Wave, Munich! all thy banners wave,
    And charge with all thy chivalry!

Few, few, shall part where many meet!
The snow shall be their winding-sheet,
And every turf beneath their feet
    Shall be a soldier's sepulchre.

'Ye Mariners of England . . .'

Ye Mariners of England
That guard our native seas!
Whose flag has braved, a thousand years,
The battle and the breeze!
Your glorious standard launch again
To match another foe:
And sweep through the deep,
While the stormy winds do blow;
While the battle rages loud and long
And the stormy winds do blow.

The spirits of your fathers
Shall start from every wave –
For the deck it was their field of fame,
And Ocean was their grave:
Where Blake and mighty Nelson fell
Your manly hearts shall glow,
As ye sweep through the deep,
While the stormy winds do blow;
While the battle rages loud and long
And the stormy winds do blow.

Britannia needs no bulwarks,
No towers along the steep;
Her march is o'er the mountain-waves,
Her home is on the deep.
With thunders from her native oak
She quells the floods below –
As they roar on the shore,
When the stormy winds do blow;
When the battle rages loud and long,
And the stormy winds do blow.

The meteor flag of England
Shall yet terrific burn;
Till danger's troubled night depart
And the star of peace return

Then, then, ye ocean-warriors!
Our song and feast shall flow
To the fame of your name,
When the storm has ceased to blow;
When the fiery fight is heard no more,
And the storm has ceased to blow.

JAMES HENRY LEIGH HUNT
(1784–1859)

The Nile

It flows through old hushed Egypt and its sands,
    Like some grave mighty thought threading a dream,
    And times and things, as in that vision, seem
Keeping along it their eternal stands, –
Caves, pillars, pyramids, the shepherd bands
    That roamed through the young world, the glory extreme
    Of high Sesostris, and that southern beam,
The laughing queen that caught the world's great hands.

Then comes a mightier silence, stern and strong,
As of a world left empty of its throng,
    And the void weighs on us; and then we wake,
And hear the fruitful stream lapsing along
    'Twixt villages, and think how we shall take
    Our own calm journey on for human sake.

Abou Ben Adhem

Abou Ben Adhem (may his tribe increase!)
Awoke one night from a deep dream of peace,
And saw, within the moonlight in his room,
Making it rich, and like a lily in bloom,

An angel writing in a book of gold: –
Exceeding peace had made Ben Adhem bold,
And to the presence in the room he said,
'What writest thou?' – The vision raised its head,
And with a look made of all sweet accord,
Answered, 'The names of those who love the Lord.'
'And is mine one?' said Abou. 'Nay, not so,'
Replied the angel. Abou spoke more low,
But cheerly still; and said, 'I pray thee then,
Write me as one that loves his fellow-men.'

The angel wrote, and vanished. The next night
It came again with a great wakening light,
And showed the names whom love of God had blessed,
And lo! Ben Adhem's name led all the rest.

GEORGE GORDON NOEL BYRON
LORD BYRON
(1788–1824)

'When we two parted . . .'

When we two parted
In silence and tears,
Half broken-hearted,
To sever for years,
Pale grew thy cheek and cold,
Colder thy kiss;
Truly that hour foretold
Sorrow to this!

The dew of the morning
Sunk chill on my brow;
It felt like the warning
Of what I feel now.

Thy vows are all broken,
And light is thy fame:
I hear thy name spoken
And share in its shame.

They name thee before me,
A knell to mine ear;
A shudder comes o'er me –
Why wert thou so dear?
They know not I knew thee
Who knew thee too well:
Long, long shall I rue thee
Too deeply to tell.

In secret we met:
In silence I grieve
That thy heart could forget,
Thy spirit deceive.
If I should meet thee
After long years,
How should I greet thee? –
With silence and tears.

'She walks in beauty . . .'

She walks in beauty, like the night
    Of cloudless climes and starry skies;
And all that's best of dark and bright
    Meet in her aspect and her eyes:
Thus mellowed to that tender light
    Which heaven to gaudy day denies.

One shade the more, one ray the less,
    Had half impaired the nameless grace
Which waves in every raven tress
    Or softly lightens o'er her face;

Where thoughts serenely sweet express
   How pure, how dear their dwelling-place.

And on that cheek, and o'er that brow
   So soft, so calm, yet eloquent,
The smiles that win, the tints that glow,
   But tell of days in goodness spent,
A mind at peace with all below,
   A heart whose love is innocent!

The Incantation

When the moon is on the wave,
   And the glow-worm in the grass,
And the meteor on the grave,
   And the wisp on the morass;
When the falling stars are shooting,
And the answer'd owls are hooting,
And the silent leaves are still
In the shadow of the hill,
Shall my soul be upon thine,
With a power and with a sign.

   Though thy slumber may be deep,
Yet thy spirit shall not sleep;
There are shades which will not vanish,
There are thoughts thou canst not banish;
By a power to thee unknown,
Thou canst never be alone;
Thou art wrapt as with a shroud,
Thou art gather'd in a cloud;
And for ever shalt thou dwell
In the spirit of this spell.

Though thou seest me not pass by,
Thou shalt feel me with thine eye

As a thing that, though unseen,
Must be near thee, and hath been;
And when in that secret dread
Thou hast turn'd around thy head,
Thou shalt marvel I am not
As thy shadow on the spot,
And the power which thou dost feel
Shall be what thou must conceal.

And a magic voice and verse
Hath baptized thee with a curse;
And a spirit of the air
Hath begirt thee with a snare;
In the wind there is a voice
Shall forbid thee to rejoice;
And to thee shall night deny
All the quiet of her sky;
And the day shall have a sun,
Which shall make thee wish it done.

From thy false tears I did distil
An essence which hath strength to kill;
From thy own heart I then did wring
The black blood in its blackest spring;
From thy own smile I snatch'd the snake,
For there it coil'd as in a brake;
From thy own lip I drew the charm
Which gave all these their chiefest harm;
In proving every poison known,
I found the strongest was thine own.

By thy cold breast and serpent smile,
By thy unfathom'd gulfs of guile,
By that most seeming virtuous eye,
By thy shut soul's hypocrisy;
By the perfection of thine art
Which pass'd for human thine own heart;

By thy delight in others' pain,
And by thy brotherhood of Cain,
I call upon thee! and compel
Thyself to be thy proper Hell!

    And on thy head I pour the vial
Which doth devote thee to this trial;
Nor to slumber, nor to die,
Shall be in thy destiny;
Though thy death shall still seem near
To thy wish, but as a fear;
Lo! the spell now works around thee,
And the clankless chain hath bound thee;
O'er thy heart and brain together
Hath the word been pass'd – now wither!

[From Manfred]

Waterloo

There was a sound of revelry by night,
And Belgium's capital had gather'd then
Her Beauty and her Chivalry, and bright
The lamps shone o'er fair women and brave men;
A thousand hearts beat happily; and when
Music arose with its voluptuous swell,
Soft eyes look'd love to eyes which spake again,
And all went merry as a marriage bell;
But hush! hark! a deep sound strikes like a rising knell!

Did ye not hear it? – No; 'twas but the wind,
Or the car rattling o'er the stony street;
On with the dance! let joy be unconfined;
No sleep till morn, when Youth and Pleasure meet
To chase the glowing Hours with flying feet –
But hark! – that heavy sound breaks in once more,
As if the clouds its echo would repeat;
And nearer, clearer, deadlier than before!
Arm! Arm! it is – it is – the cannon's opening roar!

Within a window'd niche of that high hall
Sate Brunswick's fated chieftain; he did hear
That sound the first amidst the festival,
And caught its tone with Death's prophetic ear;
And when they smiled because he deem'd it near,
His heart more truly knew that peal too well
Which stretch'd his father on a bloody bier,
And roused the vengeance blood alone could quell;
He rush'd into the field, and, foremost fighting, fell.

Ah! then and there was hurrying to and fro,
And gathering tears, and tremblings of distress,
And cheeks all pale, which but an hour ago
Blush'd at the praise of their own loveliness;
And there were sudden partings, such as press
The life from out young hearts, and choking sighs
Which ne'er might be repeated; who could guess
If ever more should meet those mutual eyes,
Since upon night so sweet such awful morn could rise!

And there was mounting in hot haste: the steed,
The mustering squadron, and the clattering car,
Went pouring forward with impetuous speed,
And swiftly forming in the ranks of war;
And the deep thunder peal on peal afar;
And near, the beat of the alarming drum
Roused up the soldier ere the morning star;
While throng'd the citizens with terror dumb,
Or whispering, with white lips – 'The foe! they come!
    they come!'

And wild and high the 'Cameron's gathering' rose!
The war-note of Lochiel, which Albyn's hills
Have heard, and heard, too, have her Saxon foes: –
How in the noon of night that pibroch thrills,

Savage and shrill! But with the breath which fills
Their mountain-pipe, so fill the mountaineers
With the fierce native daring which instils
The stirring memory of a thousand years,
And Evan's, Donald's fame rings in each clansman's ears!

And Ardennes waves above them her green leaves,
Dewy with nature's tear-drops as they pass,
Grieving, if aught inanimate e'er grieves,
Over the unreturning brave, – alas!
Ere evening to be trodden like the grass
Which now beneath them, but above shall grow
In its next verdure, when this fiery mass
Of living vapour, rolling on the foe
And burning with high hope, shall moulder cold and low.

Last noon beheld them full of lusty life,
Last eve in Beauty's circle proudly gay,
The midnight brought the signal-sound of strife,
The morn the marshalling in arms, – the day
Battle's magnificently stern array!
The thunder-clouds close o'er it, which when rent
The earth is cover'd thick with other clay,
Which her own clay shall cover, heap'd and pent,
Rider and horse, – friend, foe, – in one red burial blent!

[From *Childe Harold's Pilgrimage*. Canto III]

Darkness

I had a dream, which was not all a dream.
The bright sun was extinguish'd, and the stars
Did wander darkling in the eternal space,
Rayless, and pathless, and the icy earth
Swung blind and blackening in the moonless air;
Morn came and went – and came, and brought no day,
And men forgot their passions in the dread
Of this their desolation; and all hearts

Were chill'd into a selfish prayer for light:
And they did live by watchfires – and the thrones,
The palaces of crowned kings – the huts,
The habitations of all things which dwell,
Were burnt for beacons; cities were consumed,
And men were gather'd round their blazing homes
To look once more into each other's face;
Happy were those who dwelt within the eye
Of the volcanoes, and their mountain-torch:
A fearful hope was all the world contain'd;
Forests were set on fire – but hour by hour
They fell and faded – and the crackling trunks
Extinguish'd with a crash – and all was black.
The brows of men by the despairing light
Wore an unearthly aspect, as by fits
The flashes fell upon them; some lay down
And hid their eyes and wept; and some did rest
Their chins upon their clenched hands, and smiled;
And others hurried to and fro, and fed
Their funeral piles with fuel, and look'd up
With mad disquietude on the dull sky,
The pall of a past world; and then again
With curses cast them down upon the dust,
And gnash'd their teeth and howl'd; the wild birds shriek'd
And, terrified, did flutter on the ground,
And flap their useless wings; the wildest brutes
Came tame and tremulous; and vipers crawl'd
And twined themselves among the multitude,
Hissing, but stingless – they were slain for food!
And War, which for a moment was no more,
Did glut himself again: – a meal was bought
With blood, and each sate sullenly apart
Gorging himself in gloom: no love was left;
All earth was but one thought – and that was death
Immediate and inglorious; and the pang
Of famine fed upon all entrails – men
Died, and their bones were tombless as their flesh;

The meagre by the meagre were devour'd,
Even dogs assail'd their masters, all save one,
And he was faithful to a corse, and kept
The birds and beasts and famish'd men at bay,
Till hunger clung them, or the dropping dead
Lured their lank jaws; himself sought out no food.
But with a piteous eye and perpetual moan,
And a quick desolate cry, licking the hand
Which answer'd not with a caress – he died.
The crowd was famish'd by degrees; but two
Of an enormous city did survive,
And they were enemies; they met beside
The dying embers of an altar-place
Where had been heap'd a mass of holy things
For an unholy usage; they raked up,
And shivering scraped with their cold skeleton hands
The feeble ashes, and their feeble breath
Blew for a little life, and made a flame
Which was a mockery; then they lifted up
Their eyes, as it grew lighter, and beheld
Each other's aspects – saw, and shriek'd, and died –
Even of their mutual hideousness they died,
Unknowing who he was upon whose brow
Famine had written Fiend. The world was void,
The populous and the powerful was a lump
Seasonless, herbless, treeless, manless, lifeless,
A lump of death – a chaos of hard clay.
The rivers, lakes, and ocean all stood still,
And nothing stirr'd within their silent depths;
Ships sailorless lay rotting on the sea,
And their masts fell down piecemeal: as they dropp'd
They slept on the abyss without a surge –
The waves were dead; the tides were in their grave,
The moon, their mistress, had expired before;
The winds were wither'd in the stagnant air,
And the clouds perish'd; Darkness had no need
Of aid from them – She was the Universe.

'So, we'll go no more a roving . . .'

So, we'll go no more a roving
   So late into the night,
Though the heart be still as loving,
   And the moon be still as bright.

For the sword outwears its sheath,
   And the soul wears out the breast,
And the heart must pause to breathe,
   And love itself have rest.

Though the night was made for loving,
   And the day returns too soon,
Yet we'll go no more a roving
   By the light of the moon.

The Poet's Song to Don Juan and Haidee

'The isles of Greece, the isles of Greece!
   Where burning Sappho loved and sung,
Where grew the arts of war and peace,
   Where Delos rose, and Phoebus sprung!
Eternal summer gilds them yet,
But all, except their sun, is set.

'The Scian and the Teian muse,
   The hero's harp, the lover's lute,
Have found the fame your shores refuse:
   Their place of birth alone is mute
To sounds which echo further west
Than your sires' "Islands of the blest".

'The mountains look on Marathon –
   And Marathon looks on the sea;
And musing there an hour alone,
   I dreamed that Greece might still be free;

For standing on the Persian's grave,
I could not deem myself a slave.

'A king sate on the rocky brow
    Which looks o'er sea-born Salamis;
And ships, by thousands, lay below,
    And men in nations; – all were his!
He counted them at break of day –
And when the sun set where were they?

'And where are they, and where art thou,
    My country? On thy voiceless shore
The heroic lay is tuneless now –
    The heroic bosom beats no more!
And must thy lyre, so long divine,
Degenerate into hands like mine?

''Tis something, in the dearth of fame,
    Though link'd among a fetter'd race,
To feel at least a patriot's shame,
    Even as I sing, suffuse my face;
For what is left the poet here?
For Greeks a blush – for Greece a tear.

'Must *we* but weep o'er days more blest?
    Must *we* but blush? – Our fathers bled.
Earth! render back from out thy breast
    A remnant of our Spartan dead!
Of the three hundred grant but three,
To make a new Thermopylae!

'What, silent still? and silent all?
    Ah! no; – the voices of the dead
Sound like a distant torrent's fall,
    And answer, "Let one living head,
But one arise, – we come, we come!"
'Tis but the living who are dumb.

'In vain – in vain: strike other chords;
    Fill high the cup with Samian wine!
Leave battles to the Turkish hordes,
    And shed the blood of Scio's vine!
Hark! rising to the ignoble call –
How answers each bold Bacchanal!

'You have the Pyrrhic dance as yet;
    Where is the Pyrrhic phalanx gone?
Of two such lessons, why forget
    The nobler and the manlier one?
You have the letters Cadmus gave –
Think ye he meant them for a slave?

'Fill high the bowl with Samian wine!
    We will not think of themes like these!
It made Anacreon's song divine:
    He served – but served Polycrates –
A tyrant; but our masters then
Were still, at least, our countrymen.

'The tyrant of the Chersonese
    Was freedom's best and bravest friend;
That tyrant was Miltiades!
    Oh! that the present hour would lend
Another despot of the kind!
Such chains as his were sure to bind.

'Fill high the bowl with Samian wine!
    On Suli's rock, and Parga's shore,
Exists the remnant of a line
    Such as the Doric mothers bore;
And there, perhaps, some seed is sown,
The Heracleidian blood might own.

'Trust not for freedom to the Franks –
    They have a king who buys and sells;
In native swords, and native ranks,
    The only hope of courage dwells:

But Turkish force, and Latin fraud
Would break your shield, however broad.

'Fill high the bowl with Samian wine!
    Our virgins dance beneath the shade –
I see their glorious black eyes shine;
    But gazing on each glowing maid,
My own the burning tear-drop laves,
To think such breasts must suckle slaves.

'Place me on Sunium's marbled steep,
    Where nothing, save the waves and I,
May hear our mutual murmurs sweep;
    There, swan-like, let me sing and die:
A land of slaves shall ne'er be mine –
Dash down yon cup of Samian wine!'

————

Thus sung, or would, or could, or should have sung,
    The modern Greek, in tolerable verse;
If not like Orpheus quite, when Greece was young,
    Yet in these times he might have done much worse:
His strain display'd some feeling – right or wrong;
    And feeling, in a poet, is the source
Of others' feeling; but they are such liars,
And take all colours – like the hands of dyers.

But words are things, and a small drop of ink,
    Falling, like dew, upon a thought, produces
That which makes thousands, perhaps millions, think;
    'Tis strange, the shortest letter which man uses,
Instead of speech, may form a lasting link
    Of ages; to what straits old Time reduces
Frail man, when paper – even a rag like this.
Survives himself, his tomb, and all that's his!

[From *Don Juan.* Canto III]

CHARLES WOLFE
(1791–1823)

The Burial of Sir John Moore at Corunna

Not a drum was heard, not a funeral note,
    As his corse to the rampart we hurried;
Not a soldier discharged his farewell shot
    O'er the grave where our hero we buried.

We buried him darkly at dead of night,
    The sods with our bayonets turning;
By the struggling moonbeam's misty light,
    And the lantern dimly burning.

No useless coffin enclosed his breast,
    Not in sheet nor in shroud we wound him,
But he lay like a warrior taking his rest
    With his martial cloak around him.

Few and short were the prayers we said,
    And we spoke not a word of sorrow;
But we steadfastly gazed on the face that was dead,
    And we bitterly thought of the morrow.

We thought as we hollowed his narrow bed,
    And smoothed down his lonely pillow,
That the foe and the stranger would tread o'er
        his head,
    And we far away on the billow!

Lightly they'll talk of the spirit that's gone,
    And o'er his cold ashes upbraid him, –
But little he'll reck, if they let him sleep on
    In the grave where a Briton has laid him.

But half of our heavy task was done
    When the clock struck the hour for retiring;
And we heard the distant and random gun
    That the foe was sullenly firing.

Slowly and sadly we laid him down,
    From the field of his fame fresh and gory;
We carved not a line, and we raised not a stone –
    But we left him alone with his glory.

PERCY BYSSHE SHELLEY
(1792–1822)

Ode to the West Wind

O wild West Wind, thou breath of Autumn's being,
Thou, from whose unseen presence the leaves dead
Are driven, like ghosts from an enchanter fleeing,
Yellow, and black, and pale, and hectic red,
Pestilence-stricken multitudes: O thou
Who chariotest to their dark wintry bed
The wingéd seeds, where they lie cold and low,
Each like a corpse within its grave, until
Thine azure sister of the Spring shall blow
Her clarion o'er the dreaming earth, and fill
(Driving sweet buds like flocks to feed in air)
With living hues and odours plain and hill:
Wild Spirit, which art moving everywhere;
Destroyer and Preserver; Hear, oh, hear!

Thou on whose stream, 'mid the steep sky's
        commotion,
Loose clouds like earth's decaying leaves are shed,
Shook from the tangled boughs of Heaven and Ocean,
Angels of rain and lightning; there are spread

On the blue surface of thine airy surge,
Like the bright hair uplifted from the head
Of some fierce Maenad, ev'n from the dim verge
Of the horizon to the zenith's height –
The locks of the approaching storm. Thou dirge
Of the dying year, to which this closing night
Will be the dome of a vast sepulchre,
Vaulted with all thy congregated might
Of vapours, from whose solid atmosphere
Black rain, and fire, and hail, will burst; oh, hear!

Thou who didst waken from his summer-dreams
The blue Mediterranean, where he lay,
Lull'd by the coil of his crystalline streams,
Beside a pumice isle in Baiae's bay,
And saw in sleep old palaces and towers
Quivering within the wave's intenser day,
All overgrown with azure moss and flowers
So sweet, the sense faints picturing them! Thou
For whose path the Atlantic's level powers
Cleave themselves into chasms, while far below
The sea-blooms and the oozy woods which wear
The sapless foliage of the ocean, know
Thy voice, and suddenly grow grey with fear
And tremble and despoil themselves: oh, hear!

If I were a dead leaf thou mightest bear;
If I were a swift cloud to fly with thee;
A wave to pant beneath thy power, and share
The impulse of thy strength, only less free
Than thou, O uncontrollable! If even
I were as in my boyhood, and could be
The comrade of thy wanderings over heaven,
As then, when to outstrip thy skiey speed
Scarce seem'd a vision, I would ne'er have striven
As thus with thee in prayer in my sore need.
Oh, lift me as a wave, a leaf, a cloud!

I fall upon the thorns of life! I bleed!
A heavy weight of hours has chain'd and bow'd –
One too like thee: tameless, and swift, and proud.

Make me thy lyre, ev'n as the forest is:
What if my leaves are falling like its own?
The tumult of thy mighty harmonies
Will take from both a deep autumnal tone,
Sweet though in sadness. Be thou, Spirit fierce,
My spirit! be thou me, impetuous one!
Drive my dead thoughts over the universe
Like wither'd leaves to quicken a new birth;
And, by the incantation of this verse,
Scatter, as from an unextinguish'd hearth
Ashes and sparks, my words among mankind!
Be through my lips to unawaken'd earth
The trumpet of a prophecy! O Wind,
If Winter comes, can Spring be far behind?

The Cloud

I bring fresh showers for the thirsting flowers,
    From the seas and the streams;
I bear light shade for the leaves when laid
    In their noonday dreams.
From my wings are shaken the dews that waken
    The sweet buds every one,
When rocked to rest on their mother's breast,
    As she dances about the sun.
I wield the flail of the lashing hail,
    And whiten the green plains under,
And then again I dissolve it in rain,
    And laugh as I pass in thunder.

I sift the snow on the mountains below,
    And their great pines groan aghast;
And all the night 'tis my pillow white,
    While I sleep in the arms of the blast.

Sublime on the towers of my skiey bowers,
    Lightning my pilot sits;
In a cavern under is fettered the thunder,
    It struggles and howls at fits;
Over earth and ocean, with gentle motion,
    This pilot is guiding me,
Lured by the love of the genii that move
    In the depths of the purple sea;
Over the rills, and the crags, and the hills,
    Over the lakes and the plains,
Wherever he dream, under mountain or stream,
    The Spirit he loves remains;
And I all the while bask in Heaven's blue smile,
    Whilst he is dissolving in rains.

The sanguine Sunrise, with his meteor eyes,
    And his burning plumes outspread,
Leaps on the back of my sailing rack,
    When the morning star shines dead;
As on the jag of a mountain crag,
    Which an earthquake rocks and swings,
An eagle alit one moment may sit
    In the light of its golden wings.
And when Sunset may breathe, from the lit sea beneath,
    Its ardours of rest and of love,
And the crimson pall of eve may fall
    From the depths of Heaven above.
With wings folded I rest, on mine aëry nest,
    As still as a brooding dove.

That orbed maiden with white fire laden,
    Whom mortals call the Moon,
Glides glimmering o'er my fleece-like floor,
    By the midnight breezes strewn;
And wherever the beat of her unseen feet,
    Which only the angels hear,
May have broken the woof of my tent's thin roof,
    The stars peep behind her and peer;

And I laugh to see them whirl and flee,
   Like a swarm of golden bees,
When I widen the rent in my wind-built tent,
   Till the calm rivers, lakes, and seas,
Like strips of the sky fallen through me on high,
   Are each paved with the moon and these.

I bind the Sun's throne with a burning zone,
   And the Moon's with a girdle of pearl;
The volcanoes are dim, and the stars reel and swim,
   When the whirlwinds my banner unfurl.
From cape to cape, with a bridge-like shape,
   Over a torrent sea,
Sunbeam-proof, I hang like a roof, –
   The mountains its columns be.
The triumphal arch through which I march
   With hurricane, fire, and snow,
When the Powers of the air are chained to my chair,
   Is the million-coloured bow;
The sphere-fire above its soft colours wove,
   While the moist Earth was laughing below.

I am the daughter of Earth and Water,
   And the nursling of the Sky;
I pass through the pores of the ocean and shores;
   I change, but I cannot die.
For after the rain when with never a stain
   The pavilion of Heaven is bare,
And the winds and sunbeams with their convex
    gleams
   Build up the blue dome of air,
I silently laugh at my own cenotaph,
   And out of the caverns of rain,
Like a child from the womb, like a ghost from
    the tomb,
   I arise and unbuild it again.

Hymn to Intellectual Beauty

The awful shadow of some unseen Power
  Floats though unseen among us, – visiting
  This various world with as inconstant wing
As summer winds that creep from flower to flower: –
Like moonbeams that behind some piny mountain
      shower,
    It visits with inconstant glance
    Each human heart and countenance:
Like hues and harmonies of evening, –
    Like clouds in starlight widely spread, –
    Like memory of music fled, –
    Like aught that for its grace may be
Dear, and yet dearer for its mystery.

Spirit of Beauty, that dost consecrate
  With thine own hues all thou dost shine upon
  Of human thought or form, – where art thou gone?
Why dost thou pass away and leave our state,
This dim vast vale of tears, vacant and desolate?
    Ask why the sunlight not forever
    Weaves rainbows o'er yon mountain river,
Why aught should fail and fade that once is shown,
    Why fear and dream and death and birth
    Cast on the daylight of this earth
    Such gloom, – why man has such a scope
For love and hate, despondency and hope?

No voice from some sublimer world hath ever
  To sage or poet these responses given –
  Therefore the names of Daemon, Ghost, and Heaven,
Remain the records of their vain endeavour,
Frail spells – whose uttered charm might not avail to sever,
    From all we hear and all we see,
    Doubt, chance, and mutability.

Thy light alone – like mist o'er mountains driven,
    Or music by the night wind sent
    Through strings of some still instrument,
    Or moonlight on a midnight stream,
Gives grace and truth to life's unquiet dream.

Love, Hope, and Self-esteem, like clouds depart
    And come, for some uncertain moments lent.
    Man were immortal, and omnipotent,
Didst thou, unknown and awful as thou art,
Keep with thy glorious train firm state within his heart.
    Thou messenger of sympathies,
    That wax and wane in lovers' eyes –
Thou – that to human thought art nourishment,
    Like darkness to a dying flame!
    Depart not as thy shadow came,
    Depart not – lest the grave should be,
Like life and fear, a dark reality.

While yet a boy I sought for ghosts, and sped
    Through many a listening chamber, cave and ruin,
    And starlight wood, with fearful steps pursuing
Hopes of high talk with the departed dead.
I called on poisonous names with which our youth is fed;
    I was not heard – I saw them not –
    When musing deeply on the lot
Of life, at that sweet time when winds are wooing
    All vital things that wake to bring
    News of birds and blossoming, –
    Sudden, thy shadow fell on me;
I shrieked, and clasped my hands in ecstasy!

I vowed that I would dedicate my powers
    To thee and thine - have I not kept the vow?
    With beating heart and streaming eyes, even now
I call the phantoms of a thousand hours
Each from his voiceless grave: they have in visioned
      bowers

Of studious zeal or love's delight
Outwatched with me the envious night –
They know that never joy illumed my brow
Unlinked with hope that thou wouldst free
This world from its dark slavery,
That thou – O awful Loveliness,
Wouldst give whate'er these words cannot express.

The day becomes more solemn and serene
When noon is past – there is a harmony
In autumn, and a lustre in its sky,
Which through the summer is not heard or seen,
As if it could not be, as if it had not been!
Thus let thy power, which like the truth
Of nature on thy passive youth
Descended, to my onward life supply
Its calm – to one who worships thee,
And every form containing thee,
Whom, Spirit fair, thy spells did bind
To fear himself, and love all human kind.

'When the lamp is shatter'd . . .'

When the lamp is shatter'd
The light in the dust lies dead –
When the cloud is scatter'd,
The rainbow's glory is shed.
When the lute is broken,
Sweet tones are remember'd not;
When the lips have spoken,
Loved accents are soon forgot.

As music and splendour
Survive not the lamp and the lute,
The heart's echoes render
No song when the spirit is mute –

No song but sad dirges,
Like the wind through a ruin'd cell,
    Or the mournful surges
That ring the dead seaman's knell.

When hearts have once mingled,
Love first leaves the well-built nest;
    The weak one is singled
To endure what it once possess'd.
    O Love! who bewailest
The frailty of all things here,
    Why choose you the frailest
For your cradle, your home, and your bier?

    Its passions will rock thee
As the storms rock the ravens on high;
    Bright reason will mock thee
Like the sun from a wintry sky.
    From thy nest every rafter
Will rot, and thine eagle home
    Leave thee naked to laughter,
When leaves fall and cold winds come.

Ozymandias

I met a traveller from an antique land
Who said: Two vast and trunkless legs of stone
Stand in the desert. Near them, on the sand,
Half sunk, a shattered visage lies, whose frown,
And wrinkled lip, and sneer of cold command,
Tell that its sculptor well those passions read
Which yet survive (stamped on these lifeless things),
The hand that mocked them and the heart that fed;
And on the pedestal these words appear:
'My name is Ozymandias, king of kings;
Look on my works, ye Mighty, and despair!'
Nothing beside remains. Round the decay
Of that colossal wreck, boundless and bare,
The lone and level sands stretch far away.

'Music, when soft voices die . . .'

Music, when soft voices die,
Vibrates in the memory –
Odours, when sweet violets sicken,
Live within the sense they quicken.

Rose leaves, when the rose is dead,
Are heap'd for the beloved's bed;
And so thy thoughts, when thou are gone,
Love itself shall slumber on.

Adonais

I weep for Adonais – he is dead!
O, weep for Adonais! though our tears
Thaw not the frost which binds so dear a head!
And thou, sad Hour, selected from all years
To mourn our loss, rouse thy obscure compeers,
And teach them thine own sorrow! Say: 'With me
Died Adonais; till the Future dares
Forget the Past, his fate and fame shall be
An echo and a light unto eternity!'

Where wert thou, mighty Mother, when he lay,
When thy Son lay, pierced by the shaft which flies
In darkness? where was lorn Urania
When Adonais died? With veilèd eyes,
'Mid listening Echoes, in her Paradise
She sate, while one, with soft enamoured breath,
Rekindled all the fading melodies,
With which, like flowers that mock the corse beneath,
He had adorned and hid the coming bulk of death.

O, weep for Adonais – he is dead!
Wake, melancholy Mother, wake and weep!
Yet wherefore? Quench within their burning bed
Thy fiery tears, and let thy loud heart keep
Like his, a mute and uncomplaining sleep;
For he is gone, where all things wise and fair
Descend; – oh, dream not that the amorous Deep
Will yet restore him to the vital air;
Death feeds on his mute voice, and laughs at our despair.

Most musical of mourners, weep again!
Lament anew, Urania! – He died,
Who was the Sire of an immortal strain,
Blind, old, and lonely, when his country's pride,
The priest, the slave, and the liberticide,
Trampled and mocked with many a loathèd rite
Of lust and blood; he went, unterrified,
Into the gulf of death; but his clear Sprite
Yet reigns o'er earth: the third among the sons of light.

Most musical of mourners, weep anew!
Not all to that bright station dared to climb;
And happier they their happiness who knew,
Whose tapers yet burn through that night of time
In which suns perished; others more sublime,
Struck by the envious wrath of man or God,
Have sunk, extinct in their refulgent prime;
And some yet live, treading the thorny road,
Which leads, through toil and hate, to Fame's serene abode.

But now, thy youngest, dearest one has perished,
The nursling of thy widowhood, who grew,
Like a pale flower by some sad maiden cherished,
And fed with true-love tears, instead of dew;
Most musical of mourners, weep anew!

Thy extreme hope, the loveliest and the last,
The bloom, whose petals, nipped before they blew,
Died on the promise of the fruit, is waste;
The broken lily lies – the storm is overpast.

To that high Capital, where kingly Death
Keeps his pale court in beauty and decay,
He came; and bought, with price of purest breath,
A grave among the eternal. – Come away!
Haste, while the vault of blue Italian day
Is yet his fitting charnel-roof! while still
He lies, as if in dewy sleep he lay;
Awake him not! surely he takes his fill
Of deep and liquid rest, forgetful of all ill.

He will awake no more, oh, never more! –
Within the twilight chamber spreads apace
The shadow of white Death, and at the door
Invisible Corruption waits to trace
His extreme way to her dim dwelling-place;
The eternal Hunger sits, but pity and awe
Soothe her pale rage, nor dares she to deface
So fair a prey, till darkness, and the law
Of change, shall o'er his sleep the mortal curtain draw.

O, weep for Adonais! – The quick Dreams,
The passion-wingèd Ministers of thought,
Who were his flocks, whom near the living streams
Of his young spirit he fed, and whom he taught
The love which was its music, wander not, –
Wander no more, from kindling brain to brain,
But droop there, whence they sprung; and mourn
     their lot
Round the cold heart, where, after their sweet pain,
They ne'er will gather strength, or find a home again.

And one with trembling hands clasps his cold head,
And fans him with her moonlight wings, and cries:
'Our love, our hope, our sorrow, is not dead;
See, on the silken fringe of his faint eyes,

Like dew upon a sleeping flower, there lies
A tear some Dream has loosened from his brain.'
Lost Angel of a ruined Paradise!
She knew not 'twas her own; as with no stain
She faded, like a cloud which had outwept its rain.

One from a lucid urn of starry dew
Washed his light limbs as if embalming them;
Another clipped her profuse locks, and threw
The wreath upon him, like an anadem,
Which frozen tears instead of pearls begem;
Another in her wilful grief would break
Her bow and wingèd reeds, as if to stem
A greater loss with one which was more weak;
And dull the barbèd fire against his frozen cheek.

Another Splendour on his mouth alit,
That mouth, whence it was wont to draw the breath
Which gave it strength to pierce the guarded wit,
And pass into the panting heart beneath
With lightning and with music: the damp death
Quenched its caress upon his icy lips;
And, as a dying meteor stains a wreath
Of moonlight vapour, which the cold night clips,
It flushed through his pale limbs, and passed to its eclipse.

And others came . . . Desires and Adorations,
Wingèd Persuasions and veiled Destinies,
Splendours, and Glooms, and glimmering Incarnations
Of hopes and fears, and twilight Phantasies;
And Sorrow, with her family of Sighs,
And Pleasure, blind with tears, led by the gleam
Of her own dying smile instead of eyes,
Came in slow pomp; – the moving pomp might seem
Like pageantry of mist on an autumnal stream.

All he had loved, and moulded into thought,
From shape, and hue, and odour, and sweet sound,
Lamented Adonais. Morning sought
Her eastern watch-tower, and her hair unbound,

Wet with the tears which should adorn the ground,
Dimmed the aërial eyes that kindle day;
Afar the melancholy thunder moaned,
Pale Ocean in unquiet slumber lay,
And the wild winds flew round, sobbing in their dismay.

Lost Echo sits amid the voiceless mountains,
And feeds her grief with his remembered lay,
And will no more reply to winds or fountains,
Or amorous birds perched on the young green spray,
Or herdsman's horn, or bell as closing day;
Since she can mimic not his lips, more dear
Than those for whose disdain she pined away
Into a shadow of all sounds; – a drear
Murmur, between their songs, is all the woodmen hear.

Grief made the young Spring wild, and she threw down
Her kindling buds, as if she Autumn were,
Or they dead leaves; since her delight is flown,
For whom should she have waked the sullen year?
To Phoebus was not Hyacinth so dear
Nor to himself Narcissus, as to both
Thou, Adonais: wan they stand and sere
Amid the faint companions of their youth,
With dew all turned to tears; odour to sighing ruth.

Thy spirit's sister, the lorn nightingale,
Mourns not her mate with such melodious pain;
Not so the eagle, who like thee could scale
Heaven, and could nourish in the sun's domain
Her mighty youth with morning, doth complain,
Soaring and screaming round her empty nest,
As Albion wails for thee: the curse of Cain
Light on his head who pierced thy innocent breast,
And scared the angel soul that was its earthly guest!

Ah, woe is me! Winter is come and gone,
But grief returns with the revolving year;
The airs and streams renew their joyous tone;
The ants, the bees, the swallows, reappear;
Fresh leaves and flowers deck the dead Seasons' bier;
The amorous birds now pair in every brake,
And build their mossy homes in field and brere;
And the green lizard, and the golden snake,
Like unimprisoned flames, out of their trance awake.

Through wood and stream and field and hill and Ocean
A quickening life from the Earth's heart has burst,
As it has ever done, with change and motion
From the great morning of the world when first
God dawned on Chaos; in its stream immersed
The lamps of Heaven flash with a softer light;
All baser things pant with life's sacred thirst;
Diffuse themselves; and spend in love's delight
The beauty and the joy of their renewèd might.

The leprous corpse, touched by this spirit tender,
Exhales itself in flowers of gentle breath;
Like incarnations of the stars, when splendour
Is changed to fragrance, they illumine death
And mock the merry worm that wakes beneath;
Naught we know, dies. Shall that alone which knows
Be as a sword consumed before the sheath
By sightless lightning? – the intense atom glows
A moment, then is quenched in a most cold repose.

Alas! that all we loved of him should be,
But for our grief, as if it had not been,
And grief itself be mortal! Woe is me!
Whence are we, and why are we? of what scene
The actors or spectators? Great and mean

Meet massed in death, who lends what life must
    borrow.
As long as skies are blue, and fields are green,
Evening must usher night, night urge the morrow,
Month follow month with woe, and year wake year
      to sorrow.

He will awake no more, oh, never more!
'Wake thou,' cried Misery, 'childless Mother, rise
Out of thy sleep, and slake, in thy heart's core,
A wound more fierce than his with tears and sighs.'
And all the Dreams that watched Urania's eyes,
And all the Echoes whom their sister's song
Had held in holy silence, cried: 'Arise!'
Swift as a Thought by the snake Memory stung,
From her ambrosial rest the fading Splendour sprung.

She rose like an autumnal Night, that springs
Out of the East, and follows wild and drear
The golden Day, which, on eternal wings,
Even as a ghost abandoning a bier,
Had left the Earth a corpse. Sorrow and fear
So struck, so roused, so rapt Urania;
So saddened round her like an atmosphere
Of stormy mist; so swept her on her way
Even to the mournful place where Adonais lay.

Out of her secret Paradise she sped,
Through camps and cities rough with stone and steel,
And human hearts, which to her aëry tread
Yielding not, wounded the invisible
Palms of her tender feet where'er they fell:
And barbèd tongues, and thoughts more sharp than
    they,
Rent the soft Form they never could repel,
Whose sacred blood, like the young tears of May,
Paved with eternal flowers that undeserving way.

In the death-chamber for a moment Death,
Shamed by the presence of that living Might,
Blushed to annihilation, and the breath
Revisited those lips, and life's pale light
Flashed through those limbs, so late her dear delight.
'Leave me not wild and drear and comfortless,
As silent lightning leaves the starless night!
Leave me not!' cried Urania: her distress
Roused Death: Death rose and smiled, and met her
    vain caress.

'Stay yet awhile! speak to me once again;
Kiss me, so long but as a kiss may live;
And in my heartless breast and burning brain
That word, that kiss, shall all thoughts else survive,
With food of saddest memory kept alive,
Now thou art dead, as if it were a part
Of thee, my Adonais! I would give
All that I am to be as thou now art!
But I am chained to Time, and cannot thence depart!

'Oh gentle child, beautiful as thou wert,
Why didst thou leave the trodden paths of men
Too soon, and with weak hands though mighty heart
Dare the unpastured dragon in his den?
Defenceless as thou wert, oh, where was then
Wisdom the mirrored shield, or scorn the spear?
Or hadst thou waited the full cycle, when
Thy spirit should have filled its crescent sphere,
The monsters of life's waste had fled from thee like deer.

'The herded wolves, bold only to pursue;
The obscene ravens, clamorous o'er the dead;
The vultures to the conqueror's banner true,
Who feed where Desolation first has fed,
And whose wings rain contagion; – how they fled,
When like Apollo, from his golden bow,
The Pythian of the age one arrow sped

And smiled! – The spoilers tempt no second blow;
They fawn on the proud feet that spurn them lying low.

'The sun comes forth, and many reptiles spawn;
He sets, and each ephemeral insect then
Is gathered into death without a dawn,
And the immortal stars awake again;
So is it in the world of living men:
A godlike mind soars forth, in its delight
Making earth bare and veiling heaven, and when
It sinks, the swarms that dimmed or shared its light
Leave to its kindred lamps the spirit's awful night.'

Thus ceased she: and the mountain shepherds came,
Their garlands sere, their magic mantles rent;
The Pilgrim of Eternity, whose fame
Over his living head like Heaven is bent,
An early but enduring monument,
Came, veiling all the lightnings of his song
In sorrow: from her wilds Ierne sent
The sweetest lyrist of her saddest wrong,
And love taught grief to fall like music from his tongue.

Midst others of less note, came one frail Form,
A phantom among men, companionless
As the last cloud of an expiring storm
Whose thunder is its knell; he, as I guess,
Had gazed on Nature's naked loveliness,
Actaeon-like, and now he fled astray
With feeble steps o'er the world's wilderness,
And his own thoughts, along that rugged way,
Pursued, like raging hounds, their father and their prey.

A pardlike Spirit beautiful and swift –
A Love in desolation masked; – a Power
Girt round with weakness; – it can scarce uplift
The weight of the superincumbent hour;

It is a dying lamp, a falling shower,
A breaking billow; – even whilst we speak
Is it not broken? On the withering flower
The killing sun smiles brightly; on a cheek
The life can burn in blood, even while the heart may break.

His head was bound with pansies overblown,
And faded violets, white, and pied, and blue;
And a light spear topped with a cypress cone,
Round whose rude shaft dark ivy tresses grew
Yet dripping with the forest's noonday dew,
Vibrated, as the ever-beating heart
Shook the weak hand that grasped it; of that crew
He came the last, neglected and apart;
A herd-abandoned deer, struck by the hunter's dart.

All stood aloof, and at his partial moan
Smiled through their tears; well knew that gentle band
Who in another's fate now wept his own,
As, in the accents of an unknown land,
He sung new sorrow; sad Urania scanned
The Stranger's mien, and murmured: 'Who art thou?'
He answered not, but with a sudden hand
Made bare his branded and ensanguined brow,
Which was like Cain's or Christ's – Oh! that it should be so!

What softer voice is hushed over the dead?
Athwart what brow is that dark mantle thrown?
What form leans sadly o'er the white death-bed,
In mockery of monumental stone,
The heavy heart heaving without a moan?
If it be He, who, gentlest of the wise,
Taught, soothed, loved, honoured the departed one,
Let me not vex with inharmonious sighs
The silence of that heart's accepted sacrifice.

Our Adonais has drunk poison – oh!
What deaf and viperous murderer could crown

Life's early cup with such a draught of woe?
The nameless worm would now itself disown:
It felt, yet could escape, the magic tone
Whose prelude held all envy, hate, and wrong,
But what was howling in one breast alone,
Silent with expectation of the song,
Whose master's hand is cold, whose silver lyre unstrung.

Live thou, whose infamy is not thy fame!
Live! fear no heavier chastisement from me,
Thou noteless blot on a remembered name!
But be thyself, and know thyself to be:
And ever at thy season be thou free
To spill the venom when thy fangs o'erflow:
Remorse and Self-contempt shall cling to thee;
Hot Shame shall burn upon thy secret brow,
And like a beaten hound tremble thou shalt – as now.

Nor let us weep that our delight is fled
Far from these carrion kites that scream below;
He wakes or sleeps with the enduring dead;
Thou canst not soar where he is sitting now. –
Dust to the dust! but the pure spirit shall flow
Back to the burning fountain whence it came,
A portion of the Eternal, which must glow
Through time and change, unquenchably the same,
Whilst thy cold embers choke the sordid hearth of shame.

Peace, peace! he is not dead, he doth not sleep –
He hath awakened from the dream of life –
'T is we who, lost in stormy visions, keep
With phantoms an unprofitable strife,
And in mad trance strike with our spirit's knife
Invulnerable nothings. – *We* decay
Like corpses in a charnel; fear and grief
Convulse us and consume us day by day,
And cold hopes swarm like worms within our living clay.

He has outsoared the shadow of our night;
Envy and calumny and hate and pain,
And that unrest which men miscall delight,
Can touch him not and torture not again;
From the contagion of the world's slow stain
He is secure, and now can never mourn
A heart grown cold, a head grown grey in vain;
Nor, when the spirit's self has ceased to burn,
With sparkless ashes load an unlamented urn.

He lives, he wakes – 't is Death is dead, not he;
Mourn not for Adonais. – Thou young Dawn,
Turn all thy dew to splendour, for from thee
The spirit thou lamentest is not gone;
Ye caverns and ye forests, cease to moan!
Cease, ye faint flowers and fountains, and thou Air,
Which like a mourning veil thy scarf hadst thrown
O'er the abandoned Earth, now leave it bare
Even to the joyous stars which smile on its despair!

He is made one with Nature: there is heard
His voice in all her music, from the moan
Of thunder, to the song of night's sweet bird;
He is a presence to be felt and known
In darkness and in light, from herb and stone,
Spreading itself where'er that Power may move
Which has withdrawn his being to its own;
Which wields the world with never-wearied love,
Sustains it from beneath, and kindles it above.

He is a portion of the loveliness
Which once he made more lovely: he doth bear
His part, while the one Spirit's plastic stress
Sweeps through the dull dense world, compelling there
All new successions to the forms they wear;
Torturing the unwilling dross that checks its flight
To its own likeness, as each mass may bear;

And bursting in its beauty and its might
From trees and beasts and men into the Heaven's light.

The splendours of the firmament of time
May be eclipsed, but are extinguished not;
Like stars to their appointed height they climb
And death is a low mist which cannot blot
The brightness it may veil. When lofty thought
Lifts a young heart above its mortal lair,
And love and life contend in it, for what
Shall be its earthly doom, the dead live there
And move like winds of light on dark and stormy air.

The inheritors of unfulfilled renown
Rose from their thrones, built beyond mortal thought,
Far in the Unapparent. Chatterton
Rose pale; his solemn agony had not
Yet faded from him: Sidney, as he fought
And as he fell, and as he lived and loved,
Sublimely mild, a Spirit without spot,
Arose; and Lucan, by his death approved:
Oblivion, as they rose, shrank like a thing reproved.

And many more, whose names on Earth are dark
But whose transmitted effluence cannot die
So long as fire outlives the parent spark,
Rose, robed in dazzling immortality.
'Thou art become as one of us,' they cry,
'It was for thee yon kingless sphere has long
Swung blind in unascended majesty,
Silent alone amid an Heaven of Song.
Assume thy wingèd throne, thou Vesper of our throng!

Who mourns for Adonais? oh, come forth,
Fond wretch! and know thyself and him aright.
Clasp with thy panting soul the pendulous Earth;
As from a centre, dart thy spirit's light

Beyond all worlds, until its spacious might
Satiate the void circumference; then shrink
Even to a point within our day and night;
And keep thy heart light, lest it make thee sink,
When hope has kindled hope, and lured thee to the brink.

Or go to Rome, which is the sepulchre,
Oh, not of him, but of our joy; 't is nought
That ages, empires, and religions there
Lie buried in the ravage they have wrought;
For such as he can lend, – they borrow not
Glory from those who made the world their prey;
And he is gathered to the kings of thought
Who waged contention with their time's decay,
And of the past are all that cannot pass away.

Go thou to Rome, – at once the Paradise,
The grave, the city, and the wilderness;
And where its wrecks like shattered mountains rise
And flowering weeds and fragrant copses dress
The bones of Desolation's nakedness
Pass, till the Spirit of the spot shall lead
Thy footsteps to a slope of green access
Where, like an infant's smile, over the dead,
A light of laughing flowers along the grass is spread.

And grey walls moulder round, on which dull Time
Feeds, like slow fire upon a hoary brand,
And one keen pyramid with wedge sublime,
Pavilioning the dust of him who planned
This refuge for his memory, doth stand
Like flame transformed to marble; and beneath,
A field is spread, on which a newer band
Have pitched in Heaven's smile their camp of death,
Welcoming him we lose with scarce extinguished breath.

Here pause: these graves are all too young as yet
To have outgrown the sorrow which consigned

Its charge to each; and if the seal is set,
Here, on one fountain of a mourning mind,
Break it not thou! too surely shalt thou find
Thine own well full, if thou returnest home,
Of tears and gall. From the world's bitter wind
Seek shelter in the shadow of the tomb.
What Adonais is, why fear we to become?

The One remains, the many change and pass;
Heaven's light forever shines, Earth's shadows fly;
Life, like a dome of many-coloured glass,
Stains the white radiance of Eternity,
Until Death tramples it to fragments. – Die,
If thou wouldst be with that which thou dost seek!
Follow where all is fled! – Rome's azure sky,
Flowers, ruins, statues, music, words, are weak
The glory they transfuse with fitting truth to speak.

Why linger? why turn back, why shrink, my Heart?
Thy hopes are gone before: from all things here
They have departed; thou shouldst now depart!
A light is past from the revolving year,
And man, and woman; and what still is dear
Attracts to crush, repels to make thee wither.
The soft sky smiles, – the low wind whispers near;
'T is Adonais calls! oh, hasten thither,
No more let Life divide what Death can join together.

That Light whose smile kindles the Universe,
That Beauty in which all things work and move,
That Benediction which the eclipsing Curse
Of birth can quench not, that sustaining Love
Which, through the web of being blindly wove
By man and beast and earth and air and sea,
Burns bright or dim, as each are mirrors of
The fire for which all thirst, now beams on me,
Consuming the last clouds of cold mortality.

The breath whose might I have invoked in song
Descends on me; my spirit's bark is driven,
Far from the shore, far from the trembling throng
Whose sails were never to the tempest given;
The massy earth and spherèd skies are riven!
I am borne darkly, fearfully, afar:
Whilst burning through the inmost veil of Heaven,
The soul of Adonais, like a star,
Beacons from the abode where the Eternal are.

JOHN KEATS
(1795–1821)

On First Looking into Chapman's Homer

Much have I travelled in the realms of gold
And many goodly states and kingdoms seen;
Round many western islands have I been
Which bards in fealty to Apollo hold.
Oft of one wide expanse had I been told
That deep-browed Homer ruled as his demesne;
Yet did I never breathe its pure serene
Till I heard Chapman speak out loud and bold:
Then felt I like some watcher of the skies
When a new planet swims into his ken;
Or like stout Cortez when with eagle eyes
He stared at the Pacific – and all his men
Looked at each other with a wild surmise –
Silent, upon a peak in Darien.

Ode to a Nightingale

My heart aches, and a drowsy numbness pains
    My sense, as though of hemlock I had drunk,
Or emptied some dull opiate to the drains

One minute past, and Lethe-wards had sunk:
'Tis not through envy of thy happy lot,
    But being too happy in thy happiness, –
            That thou, light-wingéd Dryad of the trees,
                In some melodious plot
    Of beechen green, and shadows numberless,
        Singest of summer in full-throated ease.

O for a draught of vintage! that hath been
    Cool'd a long age in the deep-delvéd earth,
Tasting of Flora and the country-green,
    Dance, and Provençal song, and sunburnt mirth.
O for a beaker full of the warm South,
    Full of the true, the blushful Hippocrene,
        With beaded bubbles winking at the brim
            And purple-stainéd mouth;
    That I might drink, and leave the world unseen,
        And with thee fade away into the forest dim:

Fade far away, dissolve, and quite forget
    What thou among the leaves hast never known,
The weariness, the fever, and the fret
    Here, where men sit and hear each other groan;
Where palsy shakes a few, sad, last grey hairs,
    Where youth grows pale, and spectre-thin, and dies;
        Where but to think is to be full of sorrow
            And leaden-eyed despairs;
    Where Beauty cannot keep her lustrous eyes,
        Or new Love pine at them beyond to-morrow.

Away! away! for I will fly to thee,
    Not charioted by Bacchus and his pards,
But on the viewless wings of Poesy,
    Though the dull brain perplexes and retards:
Already with thee! tender is the night,
    And haply the Queen-Moon is on her throne,

Cluster'd around by all her starry Fays;
    But here there is no light
Save what from heaven is with the breezes blown
  Through verdurous glooms and winding mossy ways.

I cannot see what flowers are at my feet,
  Nor what soft incense hangs upon the boughs,
But, in embalméd darkness, guess each sweet
  Wherewith the seasonable month endows
The grass, the thicket, and the fruit-tree wild;
  White hawthorn, and the pastoral eglantine;
    Fast-fading violets cover'd up in leaves;
      And mid-May's eldest child,
  The coming musk-rose, full of dewy wine,
    The murmurous haunt of flies on summer eves.

Darkling I listen; and for many a time
  I have been half in love with easeful Death,
Call'd him soft names in many a muséd rhyme,
  To take into the air my quiet breath;
Now more than ever seems it rich to die,
  To cease upon the midnight with no pain,
    While thou art pouring forth thy soul abroad
      In such an ecstasy!
  Still wouldst thou sing, and I have ears in vain –
    To thy high requiem become a sod.

Thou wast not born for death, immortal Bird!
  No hungry generations tread thee down;
The voice I hear this passing night was heard
  In ancient days by emperor and clown:
Perhaps the selfsame song that found a path
  Through the sad heart of Ruth, when, sick for home,
    She stood in tears amid the alien corn;
      The same that oft-times hath
  Charm'd magic casements, opening on the foam
  Of perilous seas, in faery lands forlorn.

Forlorn! the very word is like a bell
　　To toll me back from thee to my sole self!
Adieu! the fancy cannot cheat so well
　　As she is famed to do, deceiving elf.
Adieu! adieu! thy plaintive anthem fades
　　Past the near meadows, over the still stream,
　　　Up the hillside; and now 'tis buried deep
　　　　In the next valley-glades:
　　Was it a vision, or a waking dream?
　　　Fled is that music: – do I wake or sleep?

Ode to a Grecian Urn

Thou still unravish'd bride of quietness,
　　Thou foster-child of silence and slow time,
Sylvan historian, who canst thus express
　　A flowery tale more sweetly than our rhyme;
What leaf-fring'd legend haunts about thy shape
　　Of deities or mortals, or of both,
　　　In Tempe or the dales of Arcady?
What men or gods are these? What maidens loth?
　　What mad pursuit? What struggle to escape?
　　　What pipes and timbrels? What wild ecstasy?

Heard melodies are sweet, but those unheard
　　Are sweeter; therefore, ye soft pipes, play on;
Not to the sensual ear, but, more endear'd,
　　Pipe to the spirit ditties of no tone:
Fair youth beneath the trees, thou canst not leave
　　Thy song, nor ever can those trees be bare;
　　　Bold Lover, never, never canst thou kiss,
Though winning near the goal – yet, do not grieve;
　　She cannot fade, though thou hast not thy bliss,
　　　For ever wilt thou love, and she be fair!

Ah, happy, happy boughs! that cannot shed
　　Your leaves, nor ever bid the Spring adieu;
And, happy melodist, unwearied,

For ever piping songs for ever new;
More happy love! more happy, happy love!
    For ever warm and still to be enjoy'd,
        For ever panting, and for ever young;
All breathing human passions far above,
    That leaves a heart high-sorrowful and cloy'd,
        A burning forehead, and a parching tongue.

Who are these coming to the sacrifice?
    To what green altar, O mysterious priest,
Lead'st thou that heifer lowing at the skies,
    And all her silken flanks with garlands drest?
What little town by river or sea shore,
    Or mountain-built with peaceful citadel,
        Is emptied of its folk, this pious morn?
And, little town, thy streets for evermore
    Will silent be; and not a soul to tell
        Why thou art desolate, can e'er return.

O Attic shape! Fair attitude! with brede
    Of marble men and maidens overwrought,
With forest branches and the trodden weed;
    Thou, silent form, dost tease us out of thought
As doth eternity: Cold Pastoral!
    When old age shall this generation waste,
        Thou shalt remain, in midst of other woe
Than ours, a friend to man, to whom thou say'st,
    'Beauty is truth, truth beauty,' – that is all
        Ye know on earth, and all ye need to know.

Ode to Autumn

Season of mists and mellow fruitfulness!
    Close bosom-friend of the maturing sun;
Conspiring with him how to load and bless
    With fruit the vines that round the thatch-eaves
        run;

To bend with apples the moss'd cottage-trees,
    And fill all fruit with ripeness to the core;
        To swell the gourd, and plump the hazel shells
    With a sweet kernel; to set budding more
And still more, later flowers for the bees,
Until they think warm days will never cease;
    For summer has o'er-brimm'd their clammy cells.

Who hath not seen thee oft amid thy store?
    Sometimes whoever seeks abroad may find
Thee sitting careless on a granary floor,
    Thy hair soft-lifted by the winnowing wind;
Or on a half-reap'd furrow sound asleep,
    Drowsed with the fume of poppies, while thy hook
        Spares the next swath and all its twinéd flowers;
    And sometimes like a gleaner thou dost keep
Steady thy laden head across a brook;
Or by a cider-press, with patient look,
    Thou watchest the last oozings, hours by hours.

Where are the songs of Spring? Aye, where are they?
    Think not of them, – thou hast thy music too,
While barréd clouds bloom the soft-dying day
    And touch the stubble-plains with rosy hue;
Then in a wailful choir the small gnats mourn
    Among the river-sallows, borne aloft
        Or sinking as the light wind lives or dies;
    And full-grown lambs loud bleat from hilly bourn;
Hedge-crickets sing, and now with treble soft
The redbreast whistles from a garden-croft;
    And gathering swallows twitter in the skies.

La Belle Dame sans Merci

'O what can ail thee, knight-at-arms,
    Alone and palely loitering?
The sedge has wither'd from the lake,
    And no birds sing.

'O what can ail thee, knight-at-arms!
  So haggard and so woe-begone?
The squirrel's granary is full,
  And the harvest's done.

'I see a lily on thy brow
  With anguish moist and fever-dew,
And on thy cheeks a fading rose
  Fast withereth too.'

'I met a lady in the meads,
  Full beautiful – a faery's child,
Her hair was long, her foot was light,
  And her eyes were wild.

'I made a garland for her head,
  And bracelets too, and fragrant zone;
She look'd at me as she did love,
  And made sweet moan.

'I set her on my pacing steed
  And nothing else saw all day long,
For sidelong would she bend, and sing
  A faery's song.

'She found me roots of relish sweet,
  And honey wild and manna-dew,
And sure in language strange she said
  "I love thee true."

'She took me to her elfin grot,
  And there she wept, and sigh'd full sore,
And there I shut her wild wild eyes
  With kisses four.

'And there she lulled me asleep,
  And there I dream'd – Ah! woe betide!
The latest dream I ever dream'd
  On the cold hill's side.

'I saw pale kings and princes too,
  Pale warriors, death-pale were they all;
They cried – "La belle Dame sans Merci
  Hath thee in thrall!"

'I saw their starv'd lips in the gloam
  With horrid warning gaped wide,
And I awoke and found me here
  On the cold hill's side.

'And this is why I sojourn here
  Alone and palely loitering,
Though the sedge is wither'd from the lake
  And no birds sing.'

THOMAS HOOD
(1799–1845)

'I remember, I remember . . .'

I remember, I remember
The house where I was born,
The little window where the sun
Came peeping in at morn;
He never came a wink too soon
Nor brought too long a day;
But now, I often wish the night
Had borne my breath away.

  I remember, I remember
The roses, red and white,
The violets, and the lily-cups –
Those flowers made of light!
The lilacs where the robin built,
And where my brother set
The laburnum on his birthday, –
The tree is living yet!

I remember, I remember
Where I was used to swing,
And thought the air must rush as fresh
To swallows on the wing;
My spirit flew in feathers then
That is so heavy now,
And summer pools could hardly cool
The fever on my brow.

I remember, I remember
The fir trees dark and high;
I used to think their slender tops
Were close against the sky:
It was a childish ignorance,
But now 'tis little joy
To know I'm farther off from Heaven
Than when I was a boy.

The Song of the Shirt

With fingers weary and worn,
   With eyelids heavy and red,
A Woman sat, in unwomanly rags,
   Plying her needle and thread –
Stitch! stitch! stitch!
   In poverty, hunger, and dirt,
And still with a voice of dolorous pitch
   She sang the 'Song of the Shirt!'

'Work! work! work!
   While the cock is crowing aloof!
And work – work – work,
   Till the stars shine through the roof!
It's O! to be a slave
   Along with the barbarous Turk,
Where woman has never a soul to save,
   If this is Christian work!

'Work – work – work
   Till the brain begins to swim,
Work – work – work
   Till the eyes are heavy and dim!
Seam, and gusset, and band,
   Band, and gusset, and seam,
Till over the buttons I fall asleep
   And sew them on in a dream!

'O, Men with Sisters dear!
   O Men! with Mothers and Wives!
It is not linen you're wearing out,
   But human creatures' lives!
Stitch – stitch – stitch,
   In poverty, hunger, and dirt,
Sewing at once, with a double thread,
   A Shroud as well as a Shirt.

'But why do I talk of Death?
   That Phantom of grisly bone,
I hardly fear this terrible shape,
   It seems so like my own –
It seems so like my own
   Because of the fasts I keep;
O God! that bread should be so dear,
   And flesh and blood so cheap!

'Work – work – work!
   My labour never flags;
And what are its wages? A bed of straw,
   A crust of bread – and rags.
That shatter'd roof – and this naked floor –
   A table – a broken chair –
And a wall so blank, my shadow I thank
   For sometimes falling there!

'Work – work – work!
   From weary chime to chime,
Work – work – work –
   As prisoners work for crime!

Band, and gusset, and seam,
  Seam, and gusset, and band,
Till the heart is sick, and the brain benumb'd,
  As well as the weary hand.

'Work – work – work,
  In the dull December light,
And work – work – work,
  When the weather is warm and bright –
While underneath the eaves
  The brooding swallows cling,
As if to show me their sunny backs
  And twit me with the spring.

'O, but to breathe the breath
  Of the cowslip and primrose sweet! –
With the sky above my head,
  And the grass beneath my feet;
For only one short hour
  To feel as I used to feel,
Before I knew the woes of want
  And the walk that costs a meal!

'O but for one short hour!
  A respite however brief!
No blessed leisure for Love or Hope,
  But only time for Grief!
A little weeping would ease my heart,
  But in their briny bed
My tears must stop, for every drop
  Hinders needle and thread.

'Seam, and gusset, and band,
  Band, and gusset, and seam,
Work, work, work,
  Like the Engine that works by Steam!
A mere machine of iron and wood
  That toils for Mammon's sake –
Without a brain to ponder and craze,
  Or a heart to feel – and break!'

– With fingers weary and worn,
  With eyelids heavy and red,
A Woman sat, in unwomanly rags,
  Plying her needle and thread –
Stitch! stitch! stitch!
  In poverty, hunger, and dirt,
And still with a voice of dolorous pitch, –
Would that its tone could reach the Rich! –
  She sang this 'Song of the Shirt!'

EDWARD FITZGERALD
(1809–1883)

Rubaiyát of Omar Khayyám of Naishápúr

Awake! for Morning in the Bowl of Night
Has flung the Stone that puts the Stars to Flight:
  And Lo! the Hunter of the East has caught
The Sultan's Turret in a Noose of Light.

Dreaming when Dawn's Left Hand was in the Sky
I heard a Voice within the Tavern cry,
  'Awake, my Little ones, and fill the Cup
'Before Life's Liquor in its Cup be dry.'

And, as the Cock crew, those who stood before
The Tavern shouted – 'Open then the Door!
  'You know how little while we have to stay,
'And, once departed, may return no more.'

Now the New Year reviving old Desires,
The thoughtful Soul to Solitude retires,
  Where the WHITE HAND OF MOSES on the Bough
Puts out, and Jesus from the ground suspires.

Irám indeed is gone with all its Rose,
And Jamshýd's Sev'n-ring'd Cup where no one knows;
   But still the Vine her ancient Ruby yields,
And still a Garden by the Water blows.

And David's Lips are lock't; but in divine
High-piping Pehleví, with 'Wine! Wine! Wine!
   Red Wine!' – the Nightingale cries to the Rose
That yellow Cheek of hers to incarnadine.

Come, fill the Cup, and in the Fire of Spring
The Winter Garment of Repentance fling:
   The Bird of Time has but a little way
To fly – and Lo! the Bird is on the Wing.

And look – a thousand Blossoms with the Day
Woke – and a thousand scatter'd into Clay:
   And this first Summer Month that brings the Rose
Shall take Jamshýd and Kaikobád away.

But come with old Khayyám, and leave the Lot
Of Kaikobád and Kaikhosru forgot:
   Let Rustum lay about him as he will,
Or Hátim Tai cry Supper – heed them not.

With me along some Strip of Herbage strown
That just divides the desert from the sown,
   Where name of Slave and Sultan scarce is known,
And pity Sultán Máhmúd on his Throne.

Here with a Loaf of Bread beneath the Bough,
A Flask of Wine, a Book of Verse – and Thou
   Beside me singing in the Wilderness –
And Wilderness is Paradise enow.

'How sweet is mortal Sovranty' – think some:
Others – 'How blest the Paradise to come!'
   Ah, take the Cash in hand and waive the Rest;
Oh, the brave Music of a *distant* Drum!

Look to the Rose that blows about us – 'Lo,
'Laughing,' she says, 'into the World I blow:
  'At once the silken Tassel of my Purse
'Tear, and its Treasure on the Garden throw.'

The Worldly Hope men set their Hearts upon
Turns Ashes – or it prospers; and anon,
  Like Snow upon the Desert's dusty Face
Lighting a little Hour or two – is gone.

And those who husbanded the Golden Grain,
And those who flung it to the Winds like Rain,
  Alike to no such aureate Earth are turn'd
As, buried once, Men want dug up again.

Think, in this batter'd Caravanserai
Whose Doorways are alternate Night and Day,
  How Sultán after Sultán with his Pomp
Abode his Hour or two, and went his way.

They say the Lion and the Lizard keep
The Courts where Jamshýd gloried and drank deep;
  And Bahrám, that great Hunter – the Wild Ass
Stamps o'er his Head, and he lies fast asleep.

I sometimes think that never blows so red
The Rose as where some buried Caesar bled;
  That every Hyacinth the Garden wears
Dropt in its Lap from some once lovely Head.

And this delightful Herb whose tender Green
Fledges the River's Lip on which we lean –
  Ah, lean upon it lightly! for who knows
From what once lovely Lip it springs unseen!

Ah, my Belovéd, fill the Cup that clears
TO-DAY of past Regrets and future Fears –
  To-morrow? – Why, To-morrow I may be
Myself with Yesterday's Sev'n Thousand Years.

Lo! some we loved, the loveliest and best
That Time and Fate of all their Vintage prest,
    Have drunk their Cup a Round or two before,
And one by one crept silently to Rest.

And we, that now make merry in the Room
They left, and Summer dresses in new Bloom,
    Ourselves must we beneath the Couch of Earth
Descend, ourselves to make a Couch – for whom?

Ah, make the most of what we yet may spend,
Before we too into the Dust descend;
    Dust into Dust, and under Dust, to lie,
Sans Wine, sans Song, sans Singer, and – sans End!

Alike for those who for TO-DAY prepare,
And those that after a TO-MORROW stare,
    A Muezzín from the Tower of Darkness cries
'Fools! your Reward is neither Here nor There!'

Why, all the Saints and Sages who discuss'd
Of the Two Worlds so learnedly, are thrust
    Like foolish Prophets forth; their Words to Scorn
Are scatter'd, and their Mouths are stopt with Dust.

Oh, come with old Khayyám, and leave the Wise
To talk; one thing is certain, that Life flies;
    One thing is certain, and the Rest is Lies;
The Flower that once has blown for ever dies.

Myself when young did eagerly frequent
Doctor and Saint, and heard great Argument
    About it and about: but evermore
Came out by the same Door as in I went.

With them the Seed of Wisdom did I sow,
And with my own hand labour'd it to grow:
    And this was all the Harvest that I reap'd –
'I came like Water, and like Wind I go.'

Into this Universe, and *why* not knowing,
Nor *whence*, like Water willy-nilly flowing:
   And out of it, as Wind along the Waste,
I know not *whither*, willy-nilly blowing.

What, without asking, hither hurried *whence?*
And, without asking, *whither* hurried hence?
   Another and another Cup to drown
The Memory of this Impertinence!

Up from Earth's Centre, through the Seventh Gate
I rose, and on the Throne of Saturn sate,
   And many Knots unravel'd by the Road;
But not the knot of Human Death and Fate.

There was a Door to which I found no Key:
There was a Veil past which I could not see:
   Some little Talk awhile of ME and THEE
There seem'd – and then no more of THEE and ME.

Then to the rolling Heav'n itself I cried,
Asking, 'What Lamp had Destiny to guide
   'Her little Children stumbling in the Dark?'
And – 'A blind Understanding!' Heav'n replied.

Then to this earthen Bowl did I adjourn
My Lip the secret Well of Life to learn:
   And Lip to Lip it murmur'd – 'While you live
'Drink! – for once dead you never shall return.'

I think the Vessel, that with fugitive
Articulation answer'd, once did live,
   And merry-make; and the cold Lip I kiss'd
How many Kisses might it take – and give!

For in the Market-place, one Dusk of Day,
I watch'd the Potter thumping his wet Clay:
   And with its all obliterated Tongue
It murmured – 'Gently, Brother, gently, pray!'

Ah, fill the Cup: – what boots it to repeat
How Time is slipping underneath our Feet:
    Unborn TO-MORROW and dead YESTERDAY,
Why fret about them if TO-DAY be sweet!

One Moment in Annihilation's Waste,
One Moment, of the Well of Life to taste –
    The Stars are setting and the Caravan
Starts for the Dawn of Nothing – Oh, make haste!

How long, how long, in infinite Pursuit
Of This and That endeavour and dispute?
    Better be merry with the fruitful Grape
Than sadder after none, or bitter, Fruit.

You know, my Friends, how long since in my House
For a new Marriage I did make Carouse:
    Divorced old barren Reason from my Bed,
And took the Daughter of the Vine to Spouse.

For 'Is' and 'IS-NOT' though *with* Rule and Line,
And 'UP-AND-DOWN' *without*, I could define,
    I yet in all I only cared to know,
Was never deep in anything but – Wine.

And lately, by the Tavern Door agape,
Came stealing through the Dusk an Angel Shape
    Bearing a Vessel on his Shoulder; and
He bid me taste of it; and 'twas – the Grape!

The Grape that can with Logic absolute
The Two-and-Seventy jarring Sects confute:
    The subtle Alchemist that in a Trice
Life's leaden Metal into Gold transmute.

The mighty Máhmúd, the victorious Lord,
That all the misbelieving and black Horde
    Of Fears and Sorrows that infest the Soul
Scatters and slays with his enchanted Sword.

But leave the Wise to wrangle, and with me
The Quarrel of the Universe let be:
    And, in some corner of the Hubbub coucht,
Make Game of that which makes as much of Thee.

For in and out, above, about, below,
'Tis nothing but a Magic Shadow-show,
    Play'd in a Box whose Candle is the Sun,
Round which we Phantom Figures come and go.

And if the Wine you drink, the Lip you press,
End in the Nothing all Things end in – Yes –
    Then fancy while Thou art, Thou art but what
Thou shalt be – Nothing – Thou shalt not be less.

While the Rose blows along the River Brink,
With old Khayyám the Ruby Vintage drink:
    And when the Angel with his darker Draught
Draws up to Thee – take that, and do not shrink.

'Tis all a Chequer-board of Nights and Days
Where Destiny with Men for Pieces plays:
    Hither and thither moves, and mates, and slays,
And one by one back in the Closet lays.

The Ball no Question makes of Ayes and Noes,
But Right or Left as strikes the Player goes;
    And he that toss'd Thee down into the Field,
He knows about it all – He knows – HE knows!

The Moving Finger writes; and, having writ,
Moves on: nor all thy Piety nor Wit
    Shall lure it back to cancel half a Line,
Nor all thy Tears wash out a Word of it.

And that inverted Bowl we call The Sky,
Whereunder crawling coop't we live and die,
    Lift not thy hands to *It* for help – for it
Rolls impotently on as Thou or I.

With Earth's first Clay They did the last Man's knead,
And then of the Last Harvest sow'd the Seed:
   Yea, the first Morning of Creation wrote
What the Last Dawn of Reckoning shall read.

I tell Thee this – When, starting from the Goal,
Over the shoulders of the flaming Foal
   Of Heav'n Parwin and Mishtarí they flung,
In my predestin'd Plot of Dust and Soul.

The Vine had struck a Fibre; which about
If clings my Being – let the Súfi flout;
   Of my Base Metal may be filed a Key
That shall unlock the Door he howls without.

And this I know: whether the one True Light,
Kindle to Love, or Wrath consume me quite,
   One glimpse of It within the Tavern caught
Better than in the Temple lost outright.

Oh, Thou, who did'st with Pitfall and with Gin
Beset the Road I was to wander in,
   Thou wilt not with Predestination round
Enmesh me, and impute my Fall to Sin?

Oh, Thou, who Man of baser Earth didst make,
And who with Eden didst devise the Snake;
   For all the Sin wherewith the Face of Man
Is blacken'd, Man's Forgiveness give – and take!

     .   .   .   .   .

KÚZA-NMAÁ

Listen again. One evening at the close
Of Ramazán, ere the better Moon arose,
   In that old Potter's Shop I stood alone
With the clay Population round in Rows.

And, strange to tell, among the Earthen Lot
Some could articulate, while others not;
 And suddenly one more impatient cried –
'Who *is* the Potter, pray, and who the Pot?'

Then said another – 'Surely not in vain
'My substance from the common Earth was ta'en,
 'That He who subtly wrought me into Shape
'Should stamp me back to common Earth again.'

Another said – 'Why, ne'er a peevish Boy,
'Would break the Bowl from which he drank in Joy;
 'Shall He that *made* the Vessel in pure Love
'And Fancy, in an after Rage destroy!'

None answer'd this; but after Silence spake
A Vessel of a more ungainly Make:
 'They sneer at me for leaning all awry;
'What! did the Hand then of the Potter shake?'

Said one – 'Folks of a surly Tapster tell,
'And daub his Visage with the Smoke of Hell;
 'They talk of some strict Testing of us – Pish!
'He's a Good Fellow, and 'twill all be well.'

Then said another with a long-drawn Sigh,
'My Clay with long oblivion is gone dry:
 'But, fill me with the old familiar Juice,
'Methinks I might recover by and by!'

So while the Vessels one by one were speaking,
One spied the little Crescent all were seeking:
 And then they jogg'd each other, 'Brother, Brother!
'Hark to the Porter's Shoulder-knot a-creaking!'

  . . . . .

Ah, with the Grape my fading Life provide,
And wash my Body whence the life has died,
 And in a Windingsheet of Vine-leaf wrapt,
So bury me by some sweet Garden-side.

That ev'n my buried Ashes such a Snare
Of Perfume shall fling up into the Air,
   As not a True Believer passing by
But shall be overtaken unaware.

Indeed, the Idols I have loved so long
Have done my Credit in Men's Eye much wrong:
   Have drown'd my Honour in a shallow Cup,
And sold my Reputation for a Song.

Indeed, indeed, Repentance oft before
I swore – but was I sober when I swore?
   And then and then came Spring, and Rose-in-hand
My thread-bare Penitence apieces tore.

And much as Wine has play'd the Infidel,
And robb'd me of my Robe of Honour – well,
   I often wonder what the Vintners buy
One half so precious as the Goods they sell.

Alas, that Spring should vanish with the Rose!
That Youth's sweet-scented Manuscript should close!
   The Nightingale that in the Branches sang,
Ah, whence, and whither flown again, who knows!

Ah Love! could thou and I with Fate conspire
To grasp this sorry Scheme of Things entire,
   Would not we shatter it to bits – and then
Re-mould it nearer to the Heart's Desire!

Ah, Moon of my Delight who know'st no wane,
The Moon of Heav'n is rising once again:
   How oft hereafter rising shall she look
Through this same Garden after me – in vain!

And when Thyself with shining Foot shall pass
Among the Guests Star-scatter'd on the Grass,
   And in the joyous Errand reach the Spot
Where I made one – turn down an empty Glass!

TAMÁM SHUD

ALFRED TENNYSON, LORD TENNYSON
(1809–1892)

Mariana

'Mariana in the moated grange' – *Measure for measure*

With blackest moss the flower-plots
  Were thickly crusted, one and all:
The rusted nails fell from the knots
  That held the pear to the gable-wall.
The broken sheds looked sad and strange;
  Unlifted was the clinking latch;
  Weeded and worn the ancient thatch
Upon the lonely moated grange.
    She only said, '*My life is dreary,*
      He cometh not,' she said:
    She said, '*I am aweary, aweary,*
      I would that I were dead!'

Her tears fell with the dews at even;
  Her tears fell ere the dews were dried;
She could not look on the sweet heaven,
  Either at morn or eventide.
After the flitting of the bats,
  When thickest dark did trance the sky,
  She drew her casement-curtain by,
And glanced athwart the glooming flats.
    She only said, '*The night is dreary,*
      He cometh not,' she said;
    She said, '*I am aweary, aweary,*
      I would that I were dead!'

Upon the middle of the night,
  Waking she heard the night-fowl crow:
The cock sung out an hour ere light;
  From the dark fen the oxen's low

Came to her: without hope of change,
  In sleep she seemed to walk forlorn,
  Till cold wings woke the grey-eyed morn
About the lonely moated grange.
    She only said, '*My life is dreary,*
        He cometh not,' she said;
    She said, '*I am aweary, aweary,*
        I would that I were dead!'

About a stone-cast from the wall
  A sluice with blackened waters slept
And o'er it many, round and small,
  The clustered marish-mosses crept.
Hard by a poplar shook alway,
  All silver-green with gnarlèd bark:
For leagues no other tree did mark
The level waste, the rounding grey.
    She only said, '*The night is dreary,*
        He cometh not,' she said;
    She said, '*I am aweary, aweary,*
        I would that I were dead!'

And ever when the moon was low,
  And the shrill winds were up and away,
In the white curtain, to and fro,
  She saw the gusty shadow sway.
But when the moon was very low,
  And wild winds bound within their cell,
  The shadow of the poplar fell
Upon her bed, across her brow.
    She only said, '*My life is dreary,*
        He cometh not,' she said;
    She said, '*I am aweary, aweary,*
        I would that I were dead!'

All day within the dreamy house,
  The doors upon their hinges creaked;
The blue fly sung in the pane; the mouse
  Behind the mouldering wainscot shrieked,

Or from the crevice peered about,
   Old faces glimmered through the doors,
   Old footsteps trod the upper floors,
Old voices called her from without.
     She only said, '*My life is dreary,*
       He cometh not,' she said;
     She said, '*I am aweary, aweary,*
       I would that I were dead!'

The sparrow's chirrup on the roof,
   The slow clock ticking, and the sound
Which to the wooing wind aloof
   The poplar made, did all confound
Her sense; but most she loathed the hour
   When the thick-moated sunbeam lay
   Athwart the chambers, and the day
Was sloping toward his western bower.
     Then, said she, '*I am very dreary,*
       He will not come,' she said;
     She wept, '*I am aweary, aweary,*
       O God, that I were dead!'

The Lady of Shalott

PART I

On either side the river lie
Long fields of barley and of rye,
That clothe the wold and meet the sky;
And through the field the road runs by
     To many-towered Camelot;
And up and down the people go,
Gazing where the lilies blow
Round an island there below,
     The island of Shalott.

Willows whiten, aspens quiver,
Little breezes dusk and shiver
Through the wave that runs for ever
By the island in the river
    Flowing down to Camelot.
Four grey walls, and four grey towers,
Overlook a space of flowers,
And the silent isle imbowers
    The Lady of Shalott.

By the margin, willow-veiled,
Slide the heavy barges trailed
By slow horses; and unhailed
The shallop flitteth silken-sailed
    Skimming down to Camelot;
But who hath seen her wave her hand?
Or at the casement seen her stand?
Or is she known in all the land,
    The Lady of Shalott?

Only reapers, reaping early
In among the bearded barley,
Hear a song that echoes cheerly
From the river winding clearly,
    Down to towered Camelot;
And by the moon the reaper weary,
Piling sheaves in uplands airy,
Listening, whispers, ''T is the fairy
    Lady of Shalott.'

PART II

There she weaves by night and day
A magic web with colours gay.
She has heard a whisper say,
A curse is on her if she stay
    To look down to Camelot.

She knows not what the curse may be,
And so she weaveth steadily,
And little other care hath she,
    The Lady of Shalott.

And moving through a mirror clear
That hangs before her all the year,
Shadows of the world appear.
There she sees the highway near
    Winding down to Camelot;
There the river eddy whirls,
And there the surly village-churls,
And the red cloaks of market girls,
    Pass onward from Shalott.

Sometimes a troop of damsels glad,
An abbot on an ambling pad,
Sometimes a curly shepherd-lad,
Or long-haired page in crimson clad,
    Goes by to towered Camelot;
And sometimes through the mirror blue
The knights come riding two and two:
She hath no loyal knight and true,
    The Lady of Shalott.

But in her web she still delights
To weave the mirror's magic sights,
For often through the silent nights
A funeral, with plumes and lights
    And music, went to Camelot;
Or when the moon was overhead,
Came two young lovers lately wed;
'I am half sick of shadows,' said
    The Lady of Shalott.

PART III

A bow-shot from her bower-eaves,
He rode between the barley-sheaves,

The sun came dazzling through the leaves,
And flamed upon the brazen greaves
    Of bold Sir Lancelot.
A red-cross knight for ever kneeled
To a lady in his shield,
That sparkled in the yellow field,
    Beside remote Shalott.

The gemmy bridle glittered free,
Like to some branch of stars we see
Hung in the golden Galaxy.
The bridle bells rang merrily
    As he rode down to Camelot;
And from his blazoned baldric slung
A mighty silver bugle hung,
And as he rode his armour rung,
    Beside remote Shalott.

All in the blue unclouded weather
Thick-jewelled shone the saddle-leather,
The helmet and the helmet-feather
Burned like one burning flame together,
    As he rode down to Camelot;
As often through the purple night,
Below the starry clusters bright,
Some bearded meteor, trailing light,
    Moves over still Shalott.

His broad clear brow in sunlight glowed;
On burnished hooves his war-horse trode;
From underneath his helmet flowed
His coal-black curls as on he rode,
    As he rode down to Camelot.
From the bank and from the river
He flashed into the crystal mirror,
'Tirra lirra,' by the river
    Sang Sir Lancelot.

She left the web, she left the loom,
She made three paces through the room,
She saw the water-lily bloom,
She saw the helmet and the plume,
    She looked down to Camelot.
Out flew the web and floated wide;
The mirror cracked from side to side;
'The curse is come upon me,' cried
    The Lady of Shalott.

PART IV

In the stormy east-wind straining,
The pale yellow woods were waning,
The broad stream in his banks complaining,
Heavily the low sky raining
    Over towered Camelot;
Down she came and found a boat
Beneath a willow left afloat,
And round about the prow she wrote
    The Lady of Shalott.

And down the river's dim expanse
Like some bold seër in a trance,
Seeing all his own mischance –
With a glassy countenance
    Did she look to Camelot.
And at the closing of the day
She loosed the chain, and down she lay;
The broad stream bore her far away,
    The Lady of Shalott.

Lying, robed in snowy white
That loosely flew to left and right –
The leaves upon her falling light –
Through the noises of the night
    She floated down to Camelot;

And as the boat-head wound along
The willowy hills and fields among,
They heard her singing her last song,
    The Lady of Shalott.

Heard a carol, mournful, holy,
Chanted loudly, chanted lowly,
Till her blood was frozen slowly
And her eyes were darkened wholly,
    Turned to towered Camelot.
For ere she reached upon the tide
The first house by the water-side.
Singing in her song she died,
    The Lady of Shalott.

Under tower and balcony,
By garden-wall and gallery,
A gleaming shape she floated by,
Dead-pale between the houses high,
    Silent into Camelot.
Out upon the wharfs they came,
Knight and burgher, lord and dame,
And round the prow they read her name,
    The Lady of Shalott.

Who is this? and what is here?
And in the lighted palace near
Died the sound of royal cheer;
And they crossed themselves for fear,
    All the knights at Camelot;
But Lancelot mused a little space;
He said, 'She has a lovely face;
God in his mercy lend her grace,
    The Lady of Shalott.'

The Lotos-Eaters

'Courage!' he said, and pointed toward the land,
'This mounting wave will roll us shoreward soon.'
In the afternoon they came unto a land
In which it seemed always afternoon.
All round the coast the languid air did swoon,
Breathing like one that hath a weary dream.
Full-faced above the valley stood the moon;
And like a downward smoke, the slender stream
Along the cliff to fall and pause and fall did seem.

A land of streams! some, like a downward smoke,
Slow-dropping veils of thinnest lawn, did go;
And some thro' wavering lights and shadows broke,
Rolling a slumbrous sheet of foam below.
They saw the gleaming river seaward flow
From the inner land: far off, three mountain-tops,
Three silent pinnacles of aged snow,
Stood sunset-flush'd; and, dew'd with showery drops,
Up-clomb the shadowy pine above the woven copse.

The charmed sunset linger'd low adown
In the red West: thro' mountain clefts the dale
Was seen far inland, and the yellow down
Border'd with palm, and many a winding vale
And meadow, set with slender galingale;
A land where all things always seem'd the same!
And round about the keel with faces pale,
Dark faces pale against that rosy flame,
The mild-eyed melancholy Lotos-eaters came.

Branches they bore of that enchanted stem,
Laden with flower and fruit, whereof they gave
To each, but whoso did receive of them,
And taste, to him the gushing of the wave

Far far away did seem to mourn and rave
On alien shores; and if his fellow spake,
His voice was thin, as voices from the grave;
And deep-asleep he seem'd, yet all awake,
And music in his ears, his beating heart did make.

They sat them down upon the yellow sand,
Between the sun and moon upon the shore;
And sweet it was to dream of Fatherland,
Of child, and wife, and slave; but evermore
Most weary seemed the sea, weary the oar,
Weary the wandering fields of barren foam.
Then someone said, 'We will return no more';
And all at once they sang, 'Our island home
Is far beyond the wave; we will no longer roam.'

CHORIC SONG

There is sweet music here that softer falls
Than petals from blown roses on the grass,
Or night-dews on still waters between walls
Of shadowy granite, in a gleaming pass;
Music that gentlier on the spirit lies,
Than tir'd eyelids upon tir'd eyes;
Music that brings sweet sleep down from the blissful
    skies.
Here are cool mosses deep,
And thro' the moss the ivies creep,
And in the stream the long-leaved flowers weep,
And from the craggy ledge the poppy hangs in sleep.

Why are we weigh'd upon with heaviness,
And utterly consumed with sharp distress,
While all things else have rest from weariness?
All things have rest: why should we toil alone,
We only toil, who are the first of things,
And make perpetual moan,
Still from one sorrow to another thrown:

Nor ever fold our wings,
And cease from wanderings,
Nor steep our brows in slumber's holy balm;
Nor harken what the inner spirit sings,
'There is no joy but calm!'
Why should we only toil, the roof and crown of
   things?

   Lo! in the middle of the wood,
The folded leaf is woo'd from out the bud
With winds upon the branch, and there
Grows green and broad, and takes no care,
Sun-steep'd at noon, and in the moon
Nightly dew-fed; and turning yellow
Falls, and floats adown the air.
Lo! sweeten'd with the summer light,
The full-juiced apple, waxing over-mellow,
Drops in a silent autumn night.
All is allotted length of days,
The flower ripens in its place,
Ripens and fades, and falls, and hath no toil,
Fast-rooted in the fruitful soil.

   Hateful is the dark-blue sky,
Vaulted o'er the dark-blue sea.
Death is the end of life; ah, why
Should life all labour be?
Let us alone. Time driveth onward fast,
And in a little while our lips are dumb.
Let us alone. What is it that will last?
All things are taken from us, and become
Portions and parcels of the dreadful Past.
Let us alone. What pleasure can we have
To war with evil? Is there any peace
In ever climbing up the climbing wave?
All things have rest, and ripen toward the grave
In silence; ripen, fall and cease:
Give us long rest or death, dark death, or dreamful
   ease.

How sweet it were, hearing the downward stream,
With half-shut eyes ever to seem
Falling asleep in a half-dream!
To dream and dream, like yonder amber light
Which will not leave the myrrh-bush on the height;
To hear each other's whisper'd speech;
Eating the Lotos day by day,
To watch the crisping ripples on the beach,
And tender curving lines of creamy spray;
To lend our hearts and spirits wholly
To the influence of mild-minded melancholy;
To muse and brood and live again in memory,
With those old faces of our infancy
Heap'd over with a mound of grass,
Two handfuls of white dust, shut in an urn of brass!

Dear is the memory of our wedded lives,
And dear the last embraces of our wives
And their warm tears: but all hath suffer'd change:
For surely now our household hearths are cold:
Our sons inherit us: our looks are strange:
And we should come like ghosts to trouble joy.
Or else the island princes over-bold
Have eat our substance, and the minstrel sings
Before them of the ten years' war in Troy,
And our great deeds, as half-forgotten things.
Is there confusion in the little isle?
Let what is broken so remain.
The Gods are hard to reconcile:
'Tis hard to settle order once again.
There *is* confusion worse than death,
Trouble on trouble, pain on pain,
Long Labour unto aged breath,
Sore task to hearts worn out by many wars,
And eyes grown dim with gazing on the pilot-stars.

But, propp'd on beds of amaranth and moly, –
How sweet (while warm airs lull us, blowing lowly)

With half-dropp'd eyelids still,
Beneath a heaven dark and holy,
To watch the long bright river drawing slowly
His waters from the purple hill –
To hear the dewy echoes calling
From cave to cave thro' the thick-twined vine –
To watch the emerald-colour'd water falling
Thro' many a wov'n acanthus-wreath divine!
Only to hear and see the far-off sparkling brine,
Only to hear were sweet, stretch'd out beneath the pine.

   The Lotos blooms below the barren peak:
The Lotos blows by every winding creek:
All day the wind breathes low with mellower tone:
Thro' every hollow cave and alley lone
Round and round the spicy downs the yellow Lotos-dust is blown.
We have had enough of action, and of motion we,
Roll'd to starboard, roll'd to larboard, when the surge was seething
      free,
Where the wallowing monster spouted his foam-fountains in the sea.
Let us swear an oath, and keep it with an equal mind,
In the hollow Lotos-land to live and lie reclined
On the hills like Gods together, careless of mankind.
For they lie beside their nectar, and the bolts are hurl'd
Far below them in the valleys, and the clouds are lightly curl'd
Round their golden houses, girdled with the gleaming world:
Where they smile in secret, looking over wasted lands,
Blight and famine, plague and earthquake, roaring deeps and fiery
      sands,
Clanging fights, and flaming towns, and sinking ships, and praying
      hands.
But they smile, they find a music centred in a doleful song
Steaming up, a lamentation and an ancient tale of wrong,
Like a tale of little meaning tho' the words are strong;
Chanted from an ill-used race of men that cleave the soil,
Sow the seed, and reap the harvest with enduring toil,
Storing yearly little dues of wheat, and wine and oil;

Till they perish and they suffer – some, 'tis whisper'd – down
    in hell
Suffer endless anguish, others in Elysian valleys dwell,
Resting weary limbs at last on beds of asphodel.
Surely, surely, slumber is more sweet than toil, the shore
Than labour in the deep mid-ocean, wind and wave and oar;
Oh rest ye, brother mariners, we will not wander more.

Ulysses

It little profits that an idle king,
By this still hearth, among these barren crags,
Matched with an agèd wife, I mete and dole
Unequal laws unto a savage race,
That hoard, and sleep, and feed, and know not me.
I cannot rest from travel; I will drink
Life to the lees. All times I have enjoyed
Greatly, have suffered greatly, both with those
That loved me, and alone; on shore, and when
Through scudding drifts the rainy Hyades
Vext the dim sea, I am becoming a name
For always roaming with a hungry heart;
Much have I seen and known, – cities of men
And manners, climates, councils, governments,
Myself not least, but honoured of them all;
And drunk delight of battle with my peers,
Far on the ringing plains of windy Troy.
I am a part of all that I have met;
Yet all experience is an arch wherethrough
Gleams that untravelled world whose margin fades
For ever and for ever when I move.
How dull it is to pause, to make an end,
To rust unburnished, not to shine in use!
As though to breathe were life! Life piled on life
Were all too little, and of one to me

Little remains; but every hour is saved
From that eternal silence, something more,
A bringer of new things; and vile it were
For some three suns to store and hoard myself,
And this grey spirit yearning in desire
To follow knowledge like a sinking star,
Beyond the utmost bound of human thought.

This is my son, mine own Telemachus,
To whom I leave the sceptre and the isle –
Well-loved of me, discerning to fulfil
This labour, by slow prudence to make mild
A rugged people, and through soft degrees
Subdue them to the useful and the good.
Most blameless is he, centred in the sphere
Of common duties, decent not to fail
In offices of tenderness, and pay
Meet adoration to my household gods,
When I am gone. He works his work, I mine.

There lies the port; the vessel puffs her sail:
There gloom the dark, broad seas. My mariners,
Souls that have toiled, and wrought, and thought with me –
That ever with a frolic welcome took
The thunder and the sunshine, and opposed
Free hearts, free foreheads – you and I are old;
Old age hath yet his honour and his toil.
Death closes all; but something ere the end,
Some work of noble note, may yet be done,
Not unbecoming men that strove with Gods.
The lights begin to twinkle from the rocks:
The long day wanes; the slow moon climbs; the deep
Moans round with many voices. Come, my friends,
'T is not too late to seek a newer world.
Push off, and sitting well in order smite
The sounding furrows; for my purpose holds
To sail beyond the sunset, and the baths
Of all the western stars, until I die.

It may be that the gulfs will wash us down;
It may be we shall touch the Happy Isles,
And see the great Achilles, whom we knew.
Though much is taken, much abides; and though
We are not now that strength which in old days
Moved earth and heaven; that which we are, we are:
One equal temper of heroic hearts,
Made weak by time and fate, but strong in will
To strive, to seek, to find, and not to yield.

Tithonus

The woods decay, the woods decay and fall,
The vapours weep their burthen to the ground,
Man comes and tills the field and lies beneath,
And after many a summer dies the swan.
Me only cruel immortality
Consumes: I wither slowly in thine arms,
Here at the quiet limit of the world,
A white-hair'd shadow roaming like a dream
The ever-silent spaces of the East,
Far-folded mists, and gleaming halls of morn.

   Alas! for this grey shadow, once a man –
So glorious in his beauty and thy choice,
Who madest him thy chosen, that he seem'd
To his great heart none other than a God!
I ask'd thee, 'Give me immortality.'
Then didst thou grant mine asking with a smile,
Like wealthy men who care not how they give.
But thy strong Hours indignant work'd their wills,
And beat me down and marr'd and wasted me,
And tho' they could not end me, left me maim'd
To dwell in presence of immortal youth,
Immortal age beside immortal youth,
And all I was, in ashes. Can thy love,

Thy beauty, make amends, tho' even now,
Close over us, the silver star, thy guide,
Shines in those tremulous eyes that fill with tears
To hear me? Let me go: take back thy gift:
Why should a man desire in any way
To vary from the kindly race of men,
Or pass beyond the goal of ordinance
Where all should pause, as is most meet for all?

A soft air fans the cloud apart; there comes
A glimpse of that dark world where I was born.
Once more the old mysterious glimmer steals
From thy pure brows, and from thy shoulders pure,
And bosom beating with a heart renew'd.
Thy cheek begins to redden thro' the gloom,
Thy sweet eyes brighten slowly close to mine,
Ere yet they blind the stars, and the wild team
Which love thee, yearning for thy yoke, arise,
And shake the darkness from their loosen'd manes,
And beat the twilight into flakes of fire.

Lo! ever thus thou growest beautiful
In silence, then before thine answer given
Departest, and thy tears are on my cheek.

Why wilt thou ever scare me with thy tears,
And make me tremble lest a saying learnt,
In days far-off, on that dark earth, be true?
'The Gods themselves cannot recall their gifts.'

Ay me! ay me! with what another heart
In days far-off, and with what other eyes
I used to watch – if I be he that watch'd –
The lucid outline forming round thee; saw
The dim curls kindle into sunny rings;
Changed with thy mystic change, and felt my blood
Glow with the glow that slowly crimson'd all
Thy presence and thy portals, while I lay,

Mouth, forehead, eyelids, growing dewy-warm
With kisses balmier than half-opening buds
Of April, and could hear the lips that kiss'd
Whispering I knew not what of wild and sweet,
Like that strange song I hear Apollo sing,
While Ilion like a mist rose into towers.

Yet hold me not for ever in thine East:
How can my nature longer mix with thine?
Coldly thy rosy shadows bathe me, cold
Are all thy lights, and cold my wrinkled feet
Upon thy glimmering thresholds, when the steam
Floats up from those dim fields about the homes
Of happy men that have the power to die,
And grassy burrows of the happier dead.
Release me, and restore me to the ground;
Thou seest all things, thou wilt see my grave:
Thou wilt renew thy beauty morn by morn;
I earth in earth forget these empty courts,
And thee returning on thy silver wheels.

To Virgil
*Written at the Request of the Mantuans for
the Nineteenth Centenary of Virgil's Death.*

Roman Virgil, thou that singest
    Ilion's lofty temples robed in fire,
Ilion falling, Rome arising,
    wars, and filial faith, and Dido's pyre;

Landscape-lover, lord of language
    more than he that sang the Works and Days,
All the chosen coin of fancy
    flashing out from many a golden phrase;

Thou that singest wheat and woodland,
    tilth and vineyard, hive and horse and herd;
All the charm of all the Muses
    often flowering in a lonely word;

Poet of the happy Tityrus
    piping underneath his beechen bowers;
Poet of the poet-satyr
    whom the laughing shepherd bound with flowers;

Chanter of the Pollio, glorying
    in the blissful years again to be,
Summers of the snakeless meadow,
    unlaborious earth and oarless sea;

Thou that seest Universal
    Nature moved by Universal Mind;
Thou majestic in thy sadness
    at the doubtful doom of human kind;

Light among the vanish'd ages;
    star that gildest yet this phantom shore;
Golden branch amid the shadows,
    kings and realms that pass to rise no more;

Now thy Forum roars no longer,
    fallen every purple Caesar's dome –
Tho' thine ocean-roll of rhythm
    sound for ever of Imperial Rome –

Now the Rome of slaves hath perish'd,
    and the Rome of freemen holds her place,
I, from out the Northern Island
    sunder'd once from all the human race,

I salute thee, Mantovano,
    I that loved thee since my day began,
Wielder of the stateliest measure
    ever moulded by the lips of man.

Morte d'Arthur

So all day long the noise of battle roll'd
Among the mountains by the winter sea;
Until King Arthur's table, man by man,
Had fallen in Lyonnesse about their Lord,
King Arthur: then, because his wound was deep,
The bold Sir Bedivere uplifted him,
Sir Bedivere, the last of all his knights,
And bore him to a chapel nigh the field,
A broken chancel with a broken cross,
That stood on a dark strait of barren land.
On one side lay the Ocean, and on one
Lay a great water, and the moon was full,
    Then spake King Arthur to Sir Bedivere:
'The sequel of to-day unsolders all
The goodliest fellowship of famous knights
Whereof this world holds record. Such a sleep
They sleep – the men I loved. I think that we
Shall never more, at any future time,
Delight our souls with talk of knightly deeds,
Walking about the gardens and the halls
Of Camelot, as in the days that were.
I perish by this people which I made, –
Tho' Merlin sware that I should come again
To rule once more – but let what will be, be,
I am so deeply smitten thro' the helm
That without help I cannot last till morn.
Thou therefore take my brand Excalibur,
Which was my pride: for thou rememberest how
In those old days, one summer noon, an arm
Rose up fom out the bosom of the lake,
Clothed in white samite, mystic, wonderful,
Holding the sword – and how I row'd across
And took it, and have worn it, like a king:
And, wheresoever I am sung or told

In aftertime, this also shall be known:
But now delay not: take Excalibur,
And fling him far into the middle mere:
Watch what thou seëst, and lightly bring me word.'

　　To him replied the bold Sir Bedivere:
'It is not meet, Sir King, to leave thee thus,
Aidless, alone, and smitten thro' the helm.
A little thing may harm a wounded man,
Yet I thy hest will all perform at full,
Watch what I see, and lightly bring thee word.'

　　So saying, from the ruin'd shrine he stept
And in the moon athwart the place of tombs,
Where lay the mighty bones of ancient men,
Old knights, and over them the sea-wind sang
Shrill, chill, with flakes of foam. He, stepping down
By zig-zag paths, and juts of pointed rock,
Came on the shining levels of the lake.

　　There drew he forth the brand Excalibur,
And o'er him, drawing it, the winter moon,
Brightening the skirts of a long cloud, ran forth
And sparkled keen with frost against the hilt:
For all the haft twinkled with diamond sparks,
Myriads of topaz-lights, and jacinth-work
Of subtlest jewellery. He gazed so long
That both his eyes were dazzled, as he stood,
This way and that dividing the swift mind,
In act to throw: but at the last it seem'd
Better to leave Excalibur conceal'd
There in the many-knotted waterflags,
That whistled stiff and dry about the marge.
So strode he back slow to the wounded King.

　　Then spake King Arthur to Sir Bedivere:
'Hast thou perform'd my mission which I gave?
What is it thou hast seen? or what hast heard?'

　　And answer made the bold Sir Bedivere;
'I heard the ripple washing in the reeds,
And the wild water lapping on the crag.'

To whom replied King Arthur, faint and pale:
'Thou hast betray'd thy nature and thy name,
Not rendering true answer, as beseem'd
Thy fealty, nor like a noble knight:
For surer sign had follow'd, either hand,
Or voice, or else a motion of the mere.
This is a shameful thing for men to lie.
Yet now, I charge thee, quickly go again
As thou art lief and dear, and do the thing
I bad thee, watch, and lightly bring me word.'

Then went Sir Bedivere the second time
Across the ridge, and paced beside the mere,
Counting the dewy pebbles, fix'd in thought;
But when he saw the wonder of the hilt,
How curiously and strangely chased, he smote
His palms together, and he cried aloud,

'And if indeed I cast the brand away,
Surely a precious thing, one worthy note,
Should thus be lost for ever from the earth,
Which might have pleased the eyes of many men.
What good should follow this, if this were done?
What harm, undone? deep harm to disobey,
Seeing obedience is the bond of rule.
Were it well to obey then, if a king demand
An act unprofitable, against himself?
The King is sick, and knows not what he does.
What record, or what relic of my lord
Should be to aftertime, but empty breath
And rumours of a doubt? but were this kept,
Stored in some treasure-house of mighty kings,
Some one might show it at a joust of arms,
Saying, "King Arthur's sword, Excalibur,
Wrought by the lonely maiden of the Lake.
Nine years she wrought it, sitting in the deeps
Upon the hidden bases of the hills."
So might some old man speak in the aftertime
To all the people, winning reverence.

But now much honour and much fame were lost.'
    So spake he, clouded with his own conceit,
And hid Excalibur the second time,
And so strode back slow to the wounded King.
    Then spoke King Arthur, breathing heavily:
'What is it thou hast seen? or what hast heard?'
    And answer made the bold Sir Bedivere:
'I heard the water lapping on the crag,
And the long ripple washing in the reeds.'
    To whom replied King Arthur, much in wrath:
'Ah, miserable and unkind, untrue,
Unknightly, traitor-hearted! Woe is me!
Authority forgets a dying king,
Laid widow'd of the power in his eye
That bow'd the will. I see thee what thou art,
For thou, the latest-left of all my knights,
In whom should meet the offices of all,
Thou wouldst betray me for the precious hilt;
Either from lust of gold, or like a girl
Valuing the giddy pleasure of the eyes.
Yet for a man may fail in duty twice,
And the third time may prosper, get thee hence:
But, if thou spare to fling Excalibur,
I will arise and slay thee with my hands.'
    Then quickly rose Sir Bedivere, and ran,
And, leaping down the ridges lightly, plunged
Among the bulrush-beds, and clutch'd the sword,
And strongly wheel'd and threw it. The great brand
Made lightnings in the splendour of the moon,
And flashing round and round, and whirl'd in an arch,
Shot like a streamer of the northern morn,
Seen where the moving isles of winter shock
By night, with noises of the northern sea.
So flash'd and fell the brand Excalibur:
But ere he dipt the surface, rose an arm
Clothed in white samite, mystic, wonderful,
And caught him by the hilt, and brandish'd him

Three times, and drew him under in the mere.
And lightly went the other to the King.

    Then spoke King Arthur, drawing thicker breath:
'Now see I by thine eyes that this is done.
Speak out: what is it thou hast heard, or seen?'

    And answer made the bold Sir Bedivere:
'Sir King, I closed mine eyelids, lest the gems
Should blind my purpose, for I never saw,
Nor shall see, here or elsewhere, till I die,
Not tho' I live three lives of mortal men,
So great a miracle as yonder hilt.
Then with both hands I flung him, wheeling him;
But when I look'd again, behold an arm,
Clothed in white samite, mystic, wonderful,
That caught him by the hilt, and brandish'd him
Three times, and drew him under in the mere.'

    And answer made King Arthur, breathing hard:
'My end draws nigh; 'tis time that I were gone.
Make broad thy shoulders to receive my weight,
And bear me to the margin; yet I fear
My wound hath taken cold, and I shall die.'

    So saying, from the pavement he half rose,
Slowly, with pain, reclining on his arm,
And looking wistfully with wide blue eyes
As in a picture. Him Sir Bedivere
Remorsefully regarded thro' his tears,
And would have spoken, but he found not words,
Then took with care, and kneeling on one knee,
O'er both his shoulders drew the languid hands,
And rising bore him thro' the place of tombs.

    But, as he walk'd, King Arthur panted hard,
Like one that feels a nightmare on his bed
When all the house is mute. So sigh'd the King,
Muttering and murmuring at his ear, 'Quick, quick!
I fear it is too late, and I shall die.'
But the other swiftly strode from ridge to ridge,
Clothed with his breath, and looking as he walked,

Larger than human on the frozen hills.
He heard the deep behind him, and a cry
Before. His own thought drove him, like a goad.
Dry clash'd his harness in the icy caves
And barren chasms, and all to left and right
The bare black cliff clang's round him, as he based
His feet on juts of slippery crag that rang
Sharp-smitten with the dint of armed heels –
And on a sudden, lo! the level lake,
And the long glories of the winter moon.

    Then saw they how there hove a dusky barge,
Dark as a funeral scarf from stem to stern,
Beneath them; and descending they were ware
That all the decks were dense with stately forms
Black-stoled, black-hooded, like a dream – by these
Three Queens with crowns of gold – and from them
    rose
A cry that shiver'd to the tingling stars,
And, as it were one voice an agony
Of lamentation, like a wind, that shrills
All night in a waste land, where no one comes,
Or hath come, since the making of the world.

    Then murmur'd Arthur, 'Place me in the barge,'
And to the barge they came. There those three Queens
Put forth their hands, and took the King, and wept,
But she, that rose the tallest of them all
And fairest, laid his head upon her lap.
And loosed the shatter'd casque, and chafed his hands,
And call'd him by his name, complaining loud,
And dropping bitter tears against his brow
Striped with dark blood: for all his face was white
And colourless, and like the wither'd moon
Smote by the fresh beam of the springing east;
And all his greaves and cuisses dash'd with drops
Of onset; and the light and lustrous curls –
That made his forehead like a rising sun
High from the daïs-throne – were parch'd with dust

Or, clotted into points and hanging loose,
Mix'd with the knightly growth that fringed his lips,
So like a shatter'd column lay the King;
Not like that Arthur who, with lance in rest,
From spur to plume a star of tournament,
Shot thro' the lists at Camelot, and charged
Before the eyes of ladies and of kings.

   Then loudly cried the bold Sir Bedivere,
'Ah! my Lord Arthur, whither shall I go?
Where shall I hide my forehead and my eyes?
For now I see the true old times are dead,
When every morning brought a noble chance,
And every chance brought out a noble knight.
Such times have not been since the light that led
The holy Elders with the gift of myrrh.
But now the whole ROUND TABLE is dissolved
Which was an image of the mighty world;
And I, the last, go forth companionless,
And the days darken round me, and the years,
Among new men, strange faces, other minds.'

   And slowly answered Arthur from the barge:
'The old order changeth, yielding place to new,
And God fulfils Himself in many ways,
Lest one good custom should corrupt the world.
Comfort thyself: what comfort is in me?
I have lived my life, and that which I have done
May He within Himself make pure! but thou,
If thou shouldst never see my face again,
Pray for my soul. More things are wrought by prayer
Than this world dreams of. Wherefore, let thy voice
Rise like a fountain for me night and day.
For what are men better than sheep or goats
That nourish a blind life within the brain,
If, knowing God, they lift not hands of prayer
Both for themselves and those who call them friend?
For so the whole round earth is every way
Bound by gold chains about the feet of God.

But now farewell. I am going a long way
With these thou seest – if indeed I go –
(For all my mind is clouded with a doubt)
To the island-valley of Avilion;
Where falls not hail, or rain, or any snow,
Nor ever wind blows loudly; but it lies
Deep-meadow'd, happy, fair with orchard-lawns
And bowery hollows crown'd with summer sea,
Where I will heal me of my grievous wound.'
　So said he, and the barge with oar and sail
Moved from the brink, like some full-breasted swan
That, fluting a wild carol ere her death,
Ruffles her pure cold plume, and takes the flood
With swarthy webs. Long stood Sir Bedivere
Revolving many memories, till the hull
Look'd one black dot against the verge of dawn,
And on the mere the wailing died away.

Crossing the Bar

Sunset and evening star,
　And one clear call for me!
And may there be no moaning of the bar,
　When I put out to sea,

But such a tide as moving seems asleep,
　Too full for sound and foam,
When that which drew from out the boundless deep
　Turns again home.

Twilight and evening bell,
　And after that the dark!
And may there be no sadness of farewell,
　When I embark;

For tho' from out our bourne of Time and Place
　The flood may bear me far,
I hope to see my Pilot face to face
　When I have crossed the bar.

ROBERT BROWNING
(1812–1889)

The Lost Leader

Just for a handful of silver he left us,
 Just for a riband to stick in his coat –
Found the one gift of which fortune bereft us,
 Lost all the others she lets us devote;
They, with the gold to give, doled him out silver,
 So much was theirs who so little allowed:
How all our copper had gone for his service!
 Rags – were they purple, his heart had been proud!
We that had loved him so, followed him, honoured him,
 Lived in his mild and magnificent eye,
Learned his great language, caught his clear accents,
 Made him our pattern to live and to die!
Shakespeare was of us, Milton was for us,
 Burns, Shelley, were with us, – they watch from
 their graves!
He alone breaks from the van and the freemen,
 – He alone sinks to the rear and the slaves!

We shall march prospering, – not thro' his presence;
 Songs may inspirit us, – not from his lyre;
Deeds will be done, – while he boasts his quiescence,
 Still bidding crouch whom the rest bade aspire:
Blot out his name, then, record one lost soul more,
 One task more declined, one more footpath untrod,
One more triumph for devils and sorrow for angels,
 One wrong more to man, one more insult to God!
Life's night begins: let him never come back to us!
 There would be doubt, hesitation, and pain,
Forced praise on our part – the glimmer of twilight,
 Never glad confident morning again!

Best fight on well, for we taught him – strike gallantly,
　　Menace our heart ere we master his own;
Then let him receive the new knowledge and wait us,
　　Pardoned in Heaven, the first by the throne!

My Last Duchess

That's my last Duchess painted on the wall,
Looking as if she were alive. I call
That piece a wonder, now: Frà Pandolf's hands
Worked busily a day, and there she stands.
Will 't please you sit and look at her? I said
'Frà Pandolf' by design, for never read
Strangers like you that pictured countenance,
The depth and passion of its earnest glance,
But to myself they turned (since none puts by
The curtain I have drawn for you, but I)
And seemed as they would ask me, if they durst,
How such a glance came there; so, not the first
Are you to turn and ask thus. Sir, 't was not
Her husband's presence only, called that spot
Of joy into the Duchess' cheek: perhaps
Frà Pandolf chanced to say, 'Her mantle laps
Over my lady's wrist too much,' or 'Paint
Must never hope to reproduce the faint
Half-flush that dies along her throat:' such stuff
Was courtesy, she thought, and cause enough
For calling up that spot of joy. She had
A heart – how shall I say? – too soon made glad,
Too easily impressed; she liked whate'er
She looked on, and her looks went everywhere.
Sir, 't was all one! My favour at her breast,
The dropping of the daylight in the West,
The bough of cherries some officious fool
Broke in the orchard for her, the white mule
She rode with round the terrace – all and each

Would draw from her alike the approving speech,
Or blush, at least. She thanked men, – good! but thanked
Somehow – I know not how – as if she ranked
My gift of a nine-hundred-years-old name
With anybody's gift. Who'd stoop to blame
This sort of trifling? Even had you skill
In speech – (which I have not) – to make your will
Quite clear to such an one, and say, 'Just this
Or that in you disgusts me; here you miss,
Or there exceed the mark' – and if she let
Herself be lessoned so, nor plainly set
Her wits to yours, forsooth, and made excuse,
– E'en then would be some stooping; and I choose
Never to stoop. Oh, sir, she smiled, no doubt,
Whene'er I passed her; but who passed without
Much the same smile? This grew; I gave commands;
Then all smiles stopped together. There she stands
As if alive. Will 't please you rise? We'll meet
The company below then. I repeat,
The Count your master's known munificence
Is ample warrant that no just pretence
Of mine for dowry will be disallowed;
Though his fair daughter's self, as I avowed
At starting, is my object. Nay, we'll go
Together down, sir. Notice Neptune, though,
Taming a sea-horse, thought a rarity,
Which Claus of Innsbruck cast in bronze for me!

Meeting at Night

The grey sea and the long black land;
And the yellow half-moon large and low;
And the startled little waves that leap
In fiery ringlets from their sleep,
As I gain the cove with pushing prow,
And quench its speed i' the slushy sand.

Then a mile of warm sea-scented beach;
Three fields to cross till a farm appears;
A tap at the pane, the quick sharp scratch
And blue spurt of a lighted match,
And a voice less loud, thro' its joys and fears,
Than the two hearts beating each to each!

Home-Thoughts, from Abroad

Oh, to be in England
Now that April's there,
And whoever wakes in England
Sees, some morning, unaware,
That the lowest boughs and the brushwood sheaf
Round the elm-tree bole are in tiny leaf,
While the chaffinch sings on the orchard bough
In England – now!

And after April, when May follows,
And the whitethroat builds, and all the swallows!
Hark, where my blossomed pear-tree in the hedge
Leans to the field and scatters on the clover
Blossoms and dewdrops – at the bent spray's edge –
That's the wise thrush; he sings each song twice over,
Lest you should think he never could recapture
The first fine careless rapture!
And though the fields look rough with hoary dew,
All will be gay when noontide wakes anew
The buttercups, the little children's dower
– Far brighter than this gaudy melon-flower!

Porphyria's Lover

The rain set early in to-night,
    The sullen wind was soon awake,
It tore the elm-tops down for spite,
    And did its worst to vex the lake:
    I listened with heart fit to break.

When glided in Porphyria; straight
   She shut the cold out and the storm,
And kneeled and made the cheerless grate
   Blaze up, and all the cottage warm;
   Which done, she rose, and from her form
Withdrew the dripping cloak and shawl,
   And laid her soiled gloves by, untied
Her hat and let the damp hair fall,
   And, last, she sat down by my side
   And called me. When no voice replied,
She put my arm about her waist,
   And made her smooth white shoulder bare,
And all her yellow hair displaced,
   And, stooping, made my cheek lie there,
   And spread o'er all her yellow hair,
Murmuring how she loved me – she
   Too weak, for all her heart's endeavour,
To set its struggling passion free
   From pride, and vainer ties dissever,
   And give herself to me for ever.
But passion sometimes would prevail,
   Nor could to-night's gay feast restrain
A sudden thought of one so pale
   For love of her, and all in vain:
   So, she was come through wind and rain.
Be sure I looked up at her eyes
   Happy and proud; at last I knew
Porphyria worshipped me; surprise
   Made my heart swell, and still it grew
   While I debated what to do.
That moment she was mine, mine, fair,
   Perfectly pure and good: I found
A thing to do, and all her hair
   In one long yellow string I wound
   Three times her little throat around,
And strangled her. No pain felt she;
   I am quite sure she felt no pain.

As a shut bud that holds a bee,
    I warily oped her lids; again
    Laughed the blue eyes without a stain.
And I untightened next the tress
    About her neck; her cheek once more
Blushed bright beneath my burning kiss:
    I propped her head up as before,
    Only, this time my shoulder bore
Her head, which droops upon it still:
    The smiling rosy little head,
So glad it has its utmost will,
    That all it scorned at once is fled,
    And I, its love, am gained instead!
Porphyria's love: she guessed not how
    Her darling one wish would be heard.
And thus we sit together now,
    And all night long we have not stirred,
    And yet God has not said a word!

Rabbi Ben Ezra

Grow old along with me!
    The best is yet to be,
The last of life, for which the first was made:
    Our times are in His hand
    Who saith, 'A whole I planned,
Youth shows but half; trust God: see all, nor be
        afraid!'

Not that, amassing flowers,
    Youth sighed, 'Which rose make ours,
Which lily leave and then as best recall?'
    Not that, admiring stars,
    It yearned, 'Nor Jove, nor Mars;
Mine be some figured flame which blends, transcends
        them all!'

Not for such hopes and fears
    Annulling youth's brief years,
Do I remonstrate: folly wide the mark!
    Rather I prize the doubt
    Low kinds exist without,
Finished and finite clods, untroubled by a spark.

    Poor vaunt of life indeed,
    Were man but formed to feed
On joy, to solely seek and find and feast;
    Such feasting ended, then
    As sure an end to men;
Irks care the crop-full bird? Frets doubt the
       maw-crammed beast?

    Rejoice we are allied
    To That which doth provide
And not partake, effect and not receive!
    A spark disturbs our clod;
    Nearer we hold of God
Who gives, than of His tribes that take, I must believe.

    Then, welcome each rebuff
    That turns earth's smoothness rough,
Each sting that bids nor sit nor stand but go!
    Be our joys three-parts pain!
    Strive, and hold cheap the strain;
Learn, nor account the pang; dare, never grudge
    the throe!

    For thence, – a paradox
    Which comforts while it mocks, –
Shall life succeed in that it seems to fail:
    What I aspired to be,
    And was not, comforts me:
A brute I might have been, but would not sink
    i' the scale.

What is he but a brute
Whose flesh has soul to suit,
Whose spirit works lest arms and legs want play?
To man, propose this test —
Thy body at its best,
How far can that project thy soul on its lone way?

Yet gifts should prove their use:
I own the Past profuse
Of power each side, perfection every turn:
Eyes, ears took in their dole,
Brain treasured up the whole;
Should not the heart beat once 'How good to
        live and learn'?

Not once beat 'Praise be thine!
I see the whole design,
I, who saw power, see now love perfect too:
Perfect I call thy plan:
Thanks that I was a man!
Maker, remake, complete, — I trust what Thou
        shalt do!'

For pleasant is this flesh;
Our soul, in its rose-mesh
Pulled ever to the earth, still yearns for rest:
Would we some prize might hold
To match those manifold
Possessions of the brute, — gain most, as we did best!

Let us not always say,
'Spite of this flesh to-day
I strove, made head, gained ground upon the whole!'
As the bird wings and sings,
Let us cry, 'All good things
Are ours, nor soul helps flesh more, now, than
        flesh helps soul!'

Therefore I summon age
To grant youth's heritage,
Life's struggle having so far reached its term:
Thence shall I pass, approved
A man, for aye removed
From the developed brute; a god though in the
germ.

And I shall thereupon
Take rest, ere I be gone
Once more on my adventure brave and new:
Fearless and unperplexed,
When I wage battle next,
What weapons to select, what armour to indue.

Youth ended, I shall try
My gain or loss thereby;
Leave the fire ashes, what survives is gold:
And I shall weigh the same,
Give life its praise or blame:
Young, all lay in dispute; I shall know, being old.

For, note when evening shuts,
A certain moment cuts
The deed off, calls the glory from the grey:
A whisper from the west
Shoots – 'Add this to the rest,
Take it and try its worth: here dies another day.'

So, still within this life,
Though lifted o'er its strife,
Let me discern, compare, pronounce at last,
'This rage was right i' the main,
That acquiescence vain:
The Future I may face now I have proved the
Past.'

For more is not reserved
To man, with soul just nerved
To act to-morrow what he learns to-day:
   Here, work enough to watch
   The Master work, and catch
Hints of the proper craft, tricks of the tool's true play.

   As it was better, youth
   Should strive, through acts uncouth,
Toward making, than repose on aught found made:
   So, better, age, exempt
   From strife, should know, than tempt
Further. Thou waitedst age: wait death nor be afraid!

   Enough now, if the Right
   And Good and Infinite
Be named here, as thou callest thy hand thine own,
   With knowledge absolute,
   Subject to no dispute
From fools that crowded youth, nor let thee feel
     alone.

   Be there, for once and all,
   Severed great minds from small,
Announced to each his station in the Past!
   Was I, the world arraigned,
   Were they, my soul disdained,
Right? Let age speak the truth and give us peace
     at last!

   Now, who shall arbitrate?
   Ten men love what I hate,
Shun what I follow, slight what I receive;
   Ten, who in ears and eyes
   Match me: we all surmise,
They, this thing, and I, that: whom shall my
     soul believe?

Not on the vulgar mass
    Called 'work', must sentence pass,
Things done, that took the eye and had the price;
    O'er which, from level stand,
    The low world laid its hand,
Found straightway to its mind, could value in a trice:

But all, the world's coarse thumb
    And finger failed to plumb,
So passed in making up the main account;
    All instinct immature,
    All purposes unsure,
That weighed not as his work, yet swelled
        the man's amount:

Thoughts hardly to be packed
    Into a narrow act,
Fancies that broke through language and escaped;
    All I could never be,
    All, men ignored in me,
This, I was worth to God, whose wheel the pitcher
        shaped.

Ay, note that Potter's wheel,
    That metaphor! and feel
Why time spins fast, why passive lies our clay, –
    Thou, to whom fools propound,
    When the wine makes its round,
'Since life fleets, all is change; the Past gone, seize
        to-day!'

Fool! All that is, at all,
    Lasts ever, past recall;
Earth changes, but thy soul and God stand sure:
    What entered into thee,
    That was, is, and shall be:
Time's wheel runs back or stops: Potter and clay
        endure.

He fixed thee mid this dance
Of plastic circumstance,
This Present, thou, forsooth, wouldst fain arrest:
Machinery just meant
To give thy souls its bent,
Try thee and turn thee forth, sufficiently impressed.

What though the earlier grooves
Which ran the laughing loves
Around thy base, no longer pause and press?
What though about thy rim,
Skull-things in order grim
Grow out, in graver mood, obey the sterner stress?

Look not thou down but up!
To uses of a cup,
The festal board, lamp's flash, and trumpet's peal,
The new wine's foaming flow,
The Master's lips a-glow!
Thou, heaven's consummate cup, what need'st
thou with earth's wheel?

But I need, now as then,
Thee, God, who mouldest men;
And since, not even while the whirl was worst,
Did I – to the wheel of life
With shapes and colours rife,
Bound dizzily, – mistake my end, to slake Thy thirst:

So, take and use Thy work,
Amend what flaws may lurk,
What strain o' the stuff, what warpings past the
aim!
My times be in Thy hand!
Perfect the cup as planned!
Let age approve of youth, and death complete
the same!

Prospice

Fear death? – to feel the fog in my throat,
    The mists in my face,
When the snows begin, and the blasts denote
    I am nearing the place,
The power of the night, the press of the storm,
    The post of the foe;
Where he stands, the Arch Fear in a visible form,
    Yet the strong man must go:
For the journey is done and the summit attained,
    And the barriers fall,
Though a battle's to fight ere the guerdon be gained,
    The reward of it all.
I was ever a fighter, so – one fight more,
    The best and the last!
I would hate that death bandaged my eyes, and forbore,
    And bade me creep past.
No! let me taste the whole of it, fare like my peers
    The heroes of old,
Bear the brunt, in a minute pay glad life's arrears
    Of pain, darkness, and cold.
For sudden the worst turns the best to the brave,
    The black minute's at end,
And the element's rage, the fiend-voices that rave,
    Shall dwindle, shall blend,
Shall change, shall become first a peace out of pain,
    Then a light, then thy breast,
O thou soul of my soul! I shall clasp thee again,
    And with God be the rest!

ARTHUR HUGH CLOUGH
(1819–1861)

'Say not the struggle nought availeth ...'

Say not the struggle nought availeth,
    The labour and the wounds are vain,
The enemy faints not, nor faileth,
    And as things have been they remain.

If hopes were dupes, fears may be liars;
    It may be, in yon smoke concealed,
Your comrades chase e'en now the fliers,
    And, but for you, possess the field.

For while the tired waves, vainly breaking,
    Seem here no painful inch to gain,
Far back, through creeks and inlets making,
    Comes silent, flooding in, the main.

And not by eastern windows only,
    When daylight comes, comes in the light;
In front, the sun climbs slow, how slowly,
    But westward, look, the land is bright!

MATTHEW ARNOLD
(1822–1888)

Requiescat

Strew on her roses, roses,
    And never a spray of yew.
In quiet she reposes:
    Ah! would that I did too.

Her mirth the world required:
    She bath'd it in smiles of glee.
But her heart was tired, tired,
    And now they let her be.

Her life was turning, turning,
    In mazes of heat and sound.
But for peace her soul was yearning,
    And now peace laps her round.

Her cabin'd, ample Spirit,
    It flutter'd and fail'd for breath.
To-night it doth inherit
    The vasty Hall of Death.

The Scholar Gipsy

'There was very lately a lad in the University of Oxford, who was by his poverty forced to leave his studies there; and at last to join himself to a company of vagabond gipsies. Among these extravagant people, by the insinuating subtilty of his carriage, he quickly got so much of their love and esteem as that they discovered to him their mystery. After he had been a pretty while well exercised in the trade, there chanced to ride by a couple of scholars, who had formerly been of his acquaintance. They quickly spied out their old friend among the gipsies; and he gave them an account of the necessity which drove him to that kind of life, and told them that the people he went with were not such impostors as they were taken for, but that they had a traditional kind of learning among them, and could do wonders by the power of imagination, their fancy binding that of others: that himself had learned much of their art, and when he had compassed the whole secret, he intended, he said, to leave their company, and give the world an account of what he had learned.' – GLANVIL'S *Vanity of Dogmatizing*, 1661.

Go, for they call you, Shepherd, from the hill;
  Go, Shepherd, and untie the wattled cotes:
    No longer leave thy wistful flock unfed,
  Nor let thy bawling fellows rack their throats,
    Nor the chopp'd grasses shoot another head.
      But when the fields are still,
  And the tired men and dogs all gone to rest,
    And only the white sheep are sometimes seen
    Cross and recross the strips of moon-blanch'd green;
    Come, Shepherd, and again renew the quest.

Here, where the reaper was at work of late,
  In this high field's dark corner, where he leaves
    His coat, his basket, and his earthen cruse,
  And in the sun all morning binds the sheaves,
    Then here, at noon, comes back his stores to use;
      Here will I sit and wait,
  While to my ear from uplands far away
    The bleating of the folded flocks is borne,
    With distant cries of reapers in the corn –
    All the live murmur of a summer's day.

Screen'd is this nook o'er the high, half-reap'd field,
  And here till sun-down, Shepherd, will I be.
    Through the thick corn the scarlet poppies peep
  And round green roots and yellowing stalks I see
    Pale blue convolvulus in tendrils creep:
      And air-swept lindens yield
  Their scent, and rustle down their perfum'd showers
    Of bloom on the bent grass where I am laid,
    And bower me from the August sun with shade;
    And the eye travels down to Oxford's towers:

And near me on the grass lies Glanvil's book –
  Come, let me read the oft-read tale again,
    The story of that Oxford scholar poor,
  Of pregnant parts and quick inventive brain,
    Who, tir'd of knocking at Preferment's door,

One summer morn forsook
His friends, and went to learn the Gipsy lore,
    And roam'd the world with that wild brotherhood.
    And came, as most men deem'd, to little good,
      But came to Oxford and his friends no more.

But once, years after, in the country lanes,
    Two scholars whom at college erst he knew
      Met him, and of his way of life enquir'd.
Whereat he answer'd, that the Gipsy crew,
    His mates, had arts to rule as they desir'd
      The workings of men's brains;
And they can bind them to what thoughts they will:
    'And I,' he said, 'the secret of their art,
    When fully learn'd, will to the world impart:
      But it needs heaven-sent moments for this skill.'

This said, he left them, and return'd no more,
    But rumours hung about the country side
      That the lost Scholar long was seen to stray,
Seen by rare glimpses, pensive and tongue-tied,
    In hat of antique shape, and cloak of grey,
      The same the Gipsies wore.
Shepherds had met him on the Hurst in spring:
    At some lone alehouse in the Berkshire moors,
    On the warm ingle bench, the smock-frock'd boors
      Had found him seated at their entering,

But, mid their drink and clatter, he would fly:
    And I myself seem half to know thy looks.
      And put the shepherds, Wanderer, on thy trace;
And boys who in lone wheatfields scare the rooks
    I ask if thou hast pass'd their quiet place;
      Or in my boat I lie
Moor'd to the cool bank in the summer heats,
    Mid wide grass meadows which the sunshine fills,
    And watch the warm green-muffled Cumnor hills,
      And wonder if thou haunt'st their shy retreats.

For most, I know, thou lov'st retired ground.
  Thee, at the ferry, Oxford riders blithe,
    Returning home on summer nights, have met
  Crossing the stripling Thames at Bablock-hithe,
    Trailing in the cool stream thy fingers wet,
      As the slow punt swings round:
  And leaning backwards in a pensive dream,
    And fostering in thy lap a heap of flowers,
    Pluck'd in shy fields and distant Wychwood bowers,
      And thine eyes resting on the moonlit stream.

And then they land, and thou art seen no more.
  Maidens who from the distant hamlets come
    To dance around the Fyfield elm in May,
  Oft through the darkening fields have seen thee roam,
    Or cross a stile into the public way.
      Oft thou hast given them store
  Of flowers – the frail-leaf'd, white anemone –
    Dark bluebells drench'd with dews of summer eves –
    And purple orchises with spotted leaves –
      But none has words she can report of thee.

And, above Godstow Bridge, when hay-time's here
  In June, and many a scythe in sunshine flames,
    Men who through those wide fields of breezy grass
  Where black-wing'd swallows haunt the glittering Thames,
  To bathe in the abandon'd lasher pass,
      Have often pass'd thee near
  Sitting upon the river bank o'ergrown:
    Mark'd thy outlandish garb, thy figure spare,
    Thy dark vague eyes, and soft abstracted air;
      But, when they came from bathing, thou wert gone.

At some lone homestead in the Cumnor hills,
  Where at her open door the housewife darns,
    Thou hast been seen, or hanging on a gate
  To watch the threshers in the mossy barns.
    Children, who early range these slopes and late

For cresses from the rills,
Have known thee watching, all an April day,
The springing pastures and the feeding kine;
And mark'd thee, when the stars come out and shine,
Through the long dewy grass move slow away.

In Autumn, on the skirts of Bagley wood,
Where most the Gipsies by the turf-edg'd way
Pitch their smok'd tents, and every bush you see
With scarlet patches tagg'd and shreds of grey,
Above the forest ground call'd Thessaly –
The blackbird picking food
Sees thee, nor stops his meal, nor fears at all;
So often has he known thee past him stray
Rapt, twirling in thy hand a wither'd spray,
And waiting for the spark from Heaven to fall.

And once, in winter, on the causeway chill
Where home through flooded fields foot-travellers go,
Have I not pass'd thee on the wooden bridge
Wrapt in thy cloak and battling with the snow,
Thy face towards Hinksey and its wintry ridge.
And thou hast climb'd the hill
And gain'd the white brow of the Cumnor range,
Turn'd once to watch, while thick the snowflakes fall,
The line of festal light in Christ-Church hall –
Then sought thy straw in some sequester'd grange.

But what – I dream! Two hundred years are flown
Since first thy story ran through Oxford halls,
And the grave Glanvil did the tale inscribe
That thou wert wander'd from the studious walls
To learn strange arts and join a Gipsy tribe:
And thou from earth art gone
Long since, and in some quiet churchyard laid;
Some country nook, where o'er thy unknown grave
Tall grasses and white flowering nettles wave –
Under a dark red-fruited yew-tree's shade.

  – No, no, thou hast not felt the lapse of hours.
    For what wears out the life of mortal men?
      'Tis that from change to change their being rolls:
    'Tis that repeated shocks, again, again,
      Exhaust the energy of strongest souls,
        And numb the elastic powers.
    Till having us'd our nerves with bliss and teen,
      And tir'd upon a thousand schemes our wit,
      To the just-pausing Genius we remit
        Our worn-out life, and are – what we have been.

Thou hast not liv'd, why should'st thou perish, so?
    Thou hadst *one* aim, *one* business, *one* desire:
      Else wert thou long since number'd with the dead –
    Else hadst thou spent, like other men, thy fire.
      The generations of thy peers are fled,
        And we ourselves shall go;
    But thou possessest an immortal lot,
      And we imagine thee exempt from age
      And living as thou liv'st on Glanvil's page,
        Because thou hadst – what we, alas, have not!

For early didst thou leave the world, with powers
    Fresh, undiverted to the world without,
      Firm to their mark, not spent on other things;
    Free from the sick fatigue, the languid doubt,
      Which much to have tried, in much been baffled, brings
        O Life unlike to ours!
    Who fluctuate idly without term or scope,
      Of whom each strives, nor knows for what he strives,
      And each half lives a hundred different lives;
        Who wait like thee, but not, like thee, in hope.

Thou waitest for the spark from Heaven: and we,
    Vague half-believers of our casual creeds,
      Who never deeply felt, nor clearly will'd,
    Whose insight never has borne fruit in deeds,
      Whose weak resolves never have been fulfilled;

For whom each year we see
Breeds new beginnings, disappointments new;
　Who hesitate and falter life away,
　And lose to-morrow the ground won to-day –
　　Ah, do not we, Wanderer, await it too?

Yes, we await it, but it still delays,
　And then we suffer; and amongst us One,
　　Who most has suffer'd, takes dejectedly
　His seat upon the intellectual throne;
　　And all his store of sad experience he
　　　Lays bare of wretched days;
Tell us his misery's birth and growth and signs,
　And how the dying spark of hope was fed,
　And how the breast was sooth'd, and how the head,
　　And all his hourly varied anodynes.

This for our wisest: and we others pine,
　And wish the long unhappy dream would end,
　　And waive all claim to bliss, and try to bear
　With close-lipp'd Patience for our only friend,
　　Sad Patience, too near neighbour to Despair:
　　　But none has hope like thine.
Thou through the fields and through the woods dost stray
　Roaming the country side, a truant boy,
　Nursing thy project in unclouded joy,
　　And every doubt long blown by time away.

O born in days when wits were fresh and clear,
　And life ran gaily as the sparkling Thames;
　　Before this strange disease of modern life,
　With its sick hurry, its divided aims,
　　Its head o'ertax'd, its palsied hearts, was rife –
　　　Fly hence, our contact fear!
Still fly, plunge deeper in the bowering wood
　Averse, as Dido did with gesture stern
　From her false friend's approach in Hades turn,
　　Wave us away, and keep thy solitude.

Still nursing the unconquerable hope,
   Still clutching the inviolable shade,
      With a free onward impulse brushing through,
  By night, the silver'd branches of the glade –
     Far on the forest skirts, where none pursue
       On some mild pastoral slope
  Emerge, and resting on the moonlit pales,
    Freshen thy flowers, as in former years,
    With dew, or listen with enchanted ears,
      From the dark dingles, to the nightingales.

But fly our paths, our feverish contact fly!
  For strong the infection of our mental strife,
    Which, though it gives no bliss, yet spoils for rest;
  And we should win thee from thy own fair life,
    Like us distracted, and like us unblest.
     Soon, soon thy cheer would die,
  Thy hopes grow timorous, and unfix'd thy powers,
    And thy clear aims be cross and shifting made:
    And then thy glad perennial youth would fade,
      Fade, and grow old at last, and die like ours.

Then fly our greetings, fly our speech and smiles!
  – As some grave Tyrian trader, from the sea,
    Descried at sunrise an emerging prow
  Lifting the cool-hair'd creepers stealthily,
    The fringes of a southward-facing brow
     Among the Aegean isles:
  And saw the merry Grecian coaster come,
    Freighted with amber grapes, and Chian wine,
    Green bursting figs, and tunnies steep'd in brine;
     And knew the intruders on his ancient home,

The young light-hearted Masters of the waves;
  And snatch'd his rudder, and shook out more sail,
    And day and night held on indignantly
  O'er the blue Midland waters with the gale,
    Betwixt the Syrtes and soft Sicily,

To where the Atlantic raves
Outside the Western Straits, and unbent sails
There, where down cloudy cliffs, through sheets of foam,
Shy traffickers, the dark Iberians come;
And on the beach undid his corded bales.

Rugby Chapel

NOVEMBER 1857

Coldly, sadly descends
The autumn evening. The field
Strewn with its dank yellow drifts
Of withered leaves, and the elms,
Fade into dimness apace,
Silent, – hardly a shout
From a few boys late at their play!
The lights come out in the street,
In the school-room windows; – but cold,
Solemn, unlighted, austere,
Through the gathering darkness, arise
The chapel-walls, in whose bound
Thou, my father! art laid.

There thou dost lie, in the gloom
Of the autumn evening, But ah,
That word, *gloom*, to my mind
Brings thee back, in the light
Of thy radiant vigour, again;
In the gloom of November we passed
Days not dark at thy side;
Seasons impaired not the ray
Of thy buoyant cheerfulness clear.
Such thou wast! and I stand
In the autumn evening, and think
Of bygone autumns with thee.

Fifteen years have gone round
Since thou arosest to tread,
In the summer-morning, the road
Of death, at a call unforeseen,
Sudden. For fifteen years,
We who till then in thy shade
Rested as under the boughs
Of a mighty oak, have endured
Sunshine and rain as we might,
Bare, unshaded, alone,
Lacking the shelter of thee.

O strong soul, by what shore,
Tarriest thou now? For that force,
Surely, has not been left vain!
Somewhere, surely, afar,
In the sounding labour-house vast
Of being, is practised that strength,
Zealous, beneficent, firm!

Yes, in some far-shining sphere,
Conscious or not of the past,
Still thou performest the word
Of the Spirit in whom thou dost live –
Prompt, unwearied, as here!
Still thou upraisest with zeal
The humble good from the ground,
Sternly repressest the bad!
Still, like a trumpet, dost rouse
Those who with half-open eyes
Tread the border-land dim
'Twixt vice and virtue; reviv'st,
Succourest! This was thy work,
This was thy life upon earth.

What is the course of the life
Of mortal men on the earth?

Most men eddy about
Here and there – eat and drink,
Chatter and love and hate,
Gather and squander, are raised
Aloft, are hurled in the dust.
Striving blindly, achieving
Nothing; and then they die –
Perish; – and no one asks
Who or what they have been,
More than he asks what waves,
In the moonlit solitudes mild
Of the midmost Ocean, have swelled,
Foamed for a moment, and gone.

And there are some, whom a thirst
Ardent, unquenchable, fires,
Not with the crowd to be spent,
Not without aim to go round
In an eddy of purposeless dust,
Effort unmeaning and vain.
Ah, yes! some of us strive
Not without action to die
Fruitless, but something to snatch
From dull oblivion, nor all
Glut the devouring grave!
We, we have chosen our path –
Path to a clear purposed goal,
Path of advance! – but it leads
A long, steep journey, through sunk
Gorges, o'er mountains in snow.
Cheerful, with friends, we set forth –
Then, on the height, comes the storm.
Thunder crashes from rock
To rock, the cataracts reply,
Lightnings dazzle our eyes.
Roaring torrents have breached

The track, the stream-bed descends
In the place where the wayfarer once
Planted his footstep – the spray
Boils o'er its borders! aloft
The unseen snow-beds dislodge
Their hanging ruin! alas,
Havoc is made in our train!
Friends, who set forth at our side,
Falter, are lost in the storm.
We, we only are left!
With frowning foreheads, with lips
Surely compressed, we strain on,
On – and at nightfall at last
Come to the end of our way,
To the lonely inn 'mid the rocks;
Where the gaunt and taciturn host
Stands on the threshold, the wind
Shaking his thin white hairs –
Holds his lantern to scan
Our storm-beat figures, and asks:
Whom in our party we bring,
Whom we have left in the snow?

    Sadly we answer: We bring
Only ourselves! we lost
Sight of the rest in the storm.
Hardly ourselves we fought through,
Stripped, without friends, as we are.
Friends, companions, and train,
The avalanche swept from our side.

    But thou would'st not *alone*
Be saved, my father! *alone*
Conquer and come to thy goal,
Leaving the rest in the wild.
We were weary, and we
Fearful, and we in our march

Fain to drop down and to die.
Still thou turnedst, and still
Beckonedst the trembler, and still
Gavest the weary thy hand.

If, in the paths of the world,
Stones might have wounded thy feet,
Toil or dejection have tried
Thy spirit, of that we saw
Nothing – to us thou wast still
Cheerful, and helpful, and firm!
Therefore to thee it was given
Many to save with thyself;
And, at the end of thy day,
O faithful shepherd! to come,
Bringing thy sheep in thy hand.

And through thee I believe
In the noble and great who are gone;
Pure souls honoured and blest
By former ages, who else –
Such, so soulless, so poor,
Is the race of men whom I see –
Seemed but a dream of the heart,
Seemed but a cry of desire.
Yes! I believe that there lived
Others, like thee in the past,
Not like the men of the crowd
Who all round me to-day
Bluster or cringe, and make life
Hideous, and arid, and vile;
But souls tempered with fire,
Fervent, heroic and good,
Helpers and friends of mankind.

Servants of God! – or sons
Shall I not call you? because

Not as servants ye knew
Your Father's innermost mind,
His, who unwillingly sees
One of his little ones lost –
Yours is the praise, if mankind
Hath not as yet in its march
Fainted, and fallen, and died!

See! In the rocks of the world
Marches the host of mankind,
A feeble, wavering line.
Where are they tending? – A God
Marshalled them, gave them their goal.
Ah, but the way is so long!
Years they have been in the wild!
Sore thirst plagues them, the rocks,
Rising all round, overawe;
Factions divide them, their host
Threatens to break, to dissolve.
– Ah, keep, keep them combined!
Else, of the myriads who fill
That army, not one shall arrive;
Sole they shall stray; in the rocks
Stagger for ever in vain,
Die one by one in the waste.

Then, in such hour of need
Of your fainting, dispirited race,
Ye, like angels, appear,
Radiant with ardour divine!
Beacons of hope, ye appear!
Languor is not in your heart,
Weakness is not in your word,
Weariness not on your brow.
Ye alight in our van! at your voice,
Panic, despair, flee away.
Ye move through the ranks, recall

The stragglers, refresh the outworn,
Praise, re-inspire the brave!
Order, courage, return.
Eyes rekindling, and prayers
Follow your steps as ye go.
Ye fill up the gaps in our files,
Strengthen the wavering line,
Stablish, continue our march,
On, to the bound of the waste,
On, to the City of God.

Dover Beach

The sea is calm to-night,
The tide is full, the moon lies fair
Upon the Straits; – on the French coast, the light
Gleams, and is gone; the cliffs of England stand,
Glimmering and vast, out in the tranquil bay.
Come to the window, sweet is the night air!
  Only, from the long line of spray
Where the sea meets the moon-blanched land,
Listen! you hear the grating roar
Of pebbles which the waves draw back, and fling,
At their return, up the high strand,
Begin, and cease, and then again begin,
With tremulous cadence slow, and bring
The eternal note of sadness in.

  Sophocles long ago
Heard it on the Aegean, and it brought
Into his mind the turbid ebb and flow
  Of human misery; we
Find also in the sound a thought,
Hearing it by this distant northern sea.

 The sea of faith
Was once, too, at the full, and round earth's shore
Lay like the folds of a bright girdle furled;
 But now I only hear
Its melancholy, long, withdrawing roar,
 Retreating to the breath
Of the night-wind down the vast edges drear
And naked shingles of the world.

 Ah, love, let us be true
To one another! for the world, which seems
To lie before us like a land of dreams,
So various, so beautiful, so new,
Hath really neither joy, nor love, nor light,
Nor certitude, nor peace, nor help for pain;
And we are here as on a darkling plain
Swept with confused alarms of struggle and flight,
Where ignorant armies clash by night.

DANTE GABRIEL ROSSETTI
(1828–1882)

The Blessed Damozel

The blessed Damozel leaned out
 From the gold bar of Heaven;
Her eyes were deeper than the depth
 Of waters stilled at even;
She had three lilies in her hand,
 And the stars in her hair were seven.

Her robe, ungirt from clasp to hem,
 No wrought flowers did adorn,
But a white rose of Mary's gift,

For service meetly worn;
And her hair lying down her back
  Was yellow like ripe corn.

Herseemed she scarce had been a day
  One of God's choristers;
The wonder was not yet quite gone
  From that still look of hers;
Albeit to them she left, her day
  Had counted as ten years.

(To *one*, it is ten years of years.
  . . . Yet now, and in this place,
Surely she leaned o'er me – her hair
  Fell all about my face . . .
Nothing: the Autumn fall of leaves.
  The whole year sets apace.)

It was the rampart of God's house
  That she was standing on;
By God built over the sheer depth
  The which is Space begun;
So high, that looking downward thence
  She scarce could see the sun.

It lies in Heaven, across the flood
  Of ether, as a bridge.
Beneath, the tides of day and night
  With flame and blackness ridge
The void, as low as where this earth
  Spins like a fretful midge.

She scarcely heard her sweet new friends:
  Playing at holy games,
Softly they spake among themselves
  Their virginal chaste names;
And the souls, mounting up to God,
  Went by her like thin flames.

And still she bowed above the vast
  Waste sea of worlds, that swarm;
Until her bosom must have made
  The bar she leaned on warm,
And the lilies lay as if asleep
  Along her bended arm.

From the fixed place of Heaven, she saw
  Time like a pulse shake fierce
Through all the worlds. Her gaze still strove
  Within the gulf to pierce
Its path; and now she spoke, as when
  The stars sung in their spheres.

The sun was gone now. The curled moon
  Was like a little feather
Fluttering far down the gulf. And now
  She spoke through the still weather.
Her voice was like the voice the stars
  Had when they sang together.

'I wish that he were come to me,
  For he will come,' she said.
'Have I not prayed in Heaven? – on earth,
  Lord, Lord, has he not prayed?
Are not two prayers a perfect strength?
  And shall I feel afraid?

'When round his head the aureole clings,
  And he is clothed in white,
I'll take his hand and go with him
  ·To the deep wells of light,
And we will step down as to a stream
  And bathe there in God's sight.

'We two will stand beside that shrine,
  Occult, withheld, untrod,
Whose lamps are stirred continually

With prayer sent up to God;
And see our old prayers, granted, melt
   Each like a little cloud.

'We two will lie i' the shadow of
   That living mystic tree,
Within whose secret growth the Dove
   Is sometimes felt to be,
While every leaf that His plumes touch
   Saith His Name audibly.

'And I myself will teach to him,
   I myself, lying so,
The songs I sing here; which his voice
   Shall pause in, hushed and slow,
And find some knowledge at each pause,
   Or some new thing to know.'

(Ah sweet! Just now, in that bird's song,
   Strove not her accents there
Faint to be hearkened? When those bells
   Possessed the midday air,
Was she not stepping to my side
   Down all the trembling stair?)

'We two,' she said, 'will seek the groves
   Where the Lady Mary is,
With her five handmaidens, whose names
   Are five sweet symphonies,
Cecily, Gertrude, Magdalen,
   Margaret, and Rosalys.

'Circlewise sit they, with bound locks
   And foreheads garlanded;
Into the fine cloth white like flame
   Weaving the golden thread,
To fashion the birth-robes for them
   Who are just born, being dead.

'He shall fear, haply, and be dumb;
    Then I will lay my cheek
To his, and tell about our love,
    Not once abashed or weak:
And the dear Mother will approve
    My pride, and let me speak.

'Herself shall bring us, hand in hand
    To Him round whom all souls
Kneel, the unnumbered ransomed heads
    Bowed with their aureoles:
And angels meeting us shall sing
    To their citherns and citoles.

'There will I ask of Christ the Lord
    Thus much for him and me: –
Only to live as once on earth,
    At peace – only to be
As then awhile, for ever now
    Together, I and he.'

She gazed, and listened, and then said,
    Less sad of speech than mild,
'All this is when he comes.' She ceased.
    The light thrilled past her, filled
With angels in strong level lapse.
    Her eyes prayed, and she smiled.

(I saw her smile.) But soon their flight
    Was vague in distant spheres;
And then she laid her arms along
    The golden barriers,
And laid her face between her hands.
    And wept. (I heard her tears.)

Index of Authors

Arnold, Matthew	388	Johnson, Samuel	196
Blake, William	233	Jonson, Ben	77
Breton, Nicholas	27	Keats, John	327
Browning, Robert	375	Lamb, Charles	280
Bunyan, John	171	Lodge, Thomas	51
Byron (George Gordon		Lovelace, Richard	156
Noel Byron), Lord	289	Lyly, John	51
Campbell, Thomas	285	Marlowe, Christopher	58
Campion, Thomas	73	Marvell, Andrew	162
Carey, Henry	178	Milton, John	106
Chatterton, Thomas	227	Pope, Alexander	180
Chaucer, Geoffrey	15	Ralegh, Sir Walter	46
Clough, Arthur Hugh	388	Rossetti, Dante Gabriel	404
Coleridge, Samuel Taylor	254	Shakespeare, William	59
Collins, William	206	Shelley, Percy Bysshe	303
Constable, Henry	55	Sidney, Sir Philip	49
Cowley, Abraham	158	Southey, Robert	277
Cowper, William	222	Southwell, Robert	55
Crabbe, George	232	Spenser, Edmund	28
Crashaw, Richard	149	Suckling, Sir John	147
Daniel, Samuel	56	Surrey (Henry Howard),	
Donne, John	82	Earl of	26
Drayton, Michael	57	Tennyson (Alfred Tenny-	
Dryden, John	173	son), Lord	348
Dyer, Sir Edward	53	Thomson, James	192
Fitzgerald, Edward	338	Vaughan, Henry	165
Goldsmith, Oliver	210	Waller, Edmund	104
Gray, Thomas	197	Wither, George	90
Herbert, George	102	Wolfe, Charles	302
Herrick, Robert	92	Wordsworth, William	239
Hood, Thomas	334	Wotton, Sir Henry	75
Hunt, James Henry Leigh	288	Wyatt, Sir Thomas	21

Index of First Lines

A Clerk there was of Oxenford also 18
A good man was there of religion 20
A good wife was there of besidë Bath 19
A Knight there was and that a worthy man 15
A little learning is a dang'rous thing 190
A slumber did my spirit seal 241
A sweet disorder in the dress 95
A Yeoman had he, and servants no mo 16
Abou Ben Adhem (may his tribe increase!) 288
Ah, Sun-flower! weary of time 238
All is best, though we oft doubt 147
All kings, and all their favourites 84
All the world's a stage 59
And did those feet in ancient time 238
And wilt thou leave me thus? 21
As I in hoary winter's night stood shivering in the snow 55
As you came from the holy land 46
Awake! for Morning in the Bowl of Night 338
Awake, my St John! leave all meaner things 180

Behold her, single in the field 246
Bid me to live, and I will live 97
Blest pair of Sirens, pledges of Heaven's joy 106
But see the fading many-coloured woods 193

Care-charmer Sleep, son of the sable Night 56
Charis one day in discourse 78
Cherry ripe, ripe, ripe, I cry 92
Close by those meads, for ever crown'd with flow'rs 188
Coldly, sadly descends 397'
Come Sleep, O Sleep, the certain knot of peace 49
Consider this small dust, here in the glass 81
'Courage!' he said, and pointed toward the land 356
Cupid and my Campaspe play'd 51

Death, be not proud, though some have callèd thee   89
Degree being vizarded   68
Diaphenia like the daffadowndilly   55
Drink to me only with thine eyes   78

Earth has not anything to show more fair   247
Even such is Time, that takes in trust   48

Fair Daffodils, we weep to see   96
Fair pledges of a fruitful tree   98
Fear death? – to feel the fog in my throat   387
Fear no more the heat o' the sun   71
First follow Nature, and your judgment frame   189
Five years have passed; five summers with the length 242
Follow a shadow, it still flies you   81
Follow your saint, follow with accents sweet   73
Forget not yet the tried intent   22
From Harmony, from heavenly Harmony   176
From pole to pole the rigid influence falls   195
From the moist meadow to the wither'd hill   192
Full many a glorious morning have I seen   62

Gather ye rose-buds while ye may   96
Get up, get up for shame, the blooming morn   93
Go and catch a falling star   82
Go, for they call you, Shepherd, from the hill   390
Go, lovely Rose   104
Grow old along with me   380

Had we but world enough, and time   164
Hail, holy Light, offspring of Heaven first-born   144
Happy those early days, when I   165
Has heaven reserv'd, in pity to the poor   196
He that is down, needs fear no fall   171
Hence loathed Melancholy   107

Hence vain deluding joys   111
Her eyes the glow-worm lend thee   95
Here, a little child, I stand   100
High in front advanc'd   146
How happy is he born and taught   76
How many thousand of my poorest subjects   66
How sleep the Brave who sink to rest   206
How vainly men themselves amaze   162

I am monarch of all I survey   223
I bring fresh showers for the thirsting flowers   305
I can love both fair and brown   83
I cannot reach it; and my striving eye   170
I grant indeed that fields and flocks have charms   232
I had a dream, which was not all a dream   295
I have had playmates, I have had companions   280
I have lost, and lately, these   92
I loved a lass, a fair one   90
I met a traveller from an antique land   311
I remember, I remember   334
I scarce believe my love to be so pure   85
I struck the board, and cried 'No more   102
I travelled among unknown men   240
I wandered lonely as a cloud   239
I was angry with my friend   236
I weep for Adonais – he is dead   312
I went to the Garden of Love   237
I wonder, by my troth, what thou and I   84
If aught of oaten stop or pastoral song   206
If to be absent were to be   157
In that same Garden all the goodly flowers   42
In the first rank of these did Zimri stand   175
In the hour of my distress   100
In the merry month of May   27
In Virginè the sweltry sun 'gan sheene   227
In Xanadu did Kubla Khan   274
Indeed I must confess   158

Is it possible 25
It flows through old hushed Egypt and its sands 288
It is an ancient Mariner 254
It little profits that an idle king 361
It was a summer evening 277

Just for a handful of silver he left us 375

Let me not to the marriage of true minds 64
Little Lamb, who made thee? 234
Lord, what is man? why should he cost Thee 154
Love bade me welcome; yet my soul drew back 103
Love, thou art absolute, sole lord 149
Loving in truth, and fain my love in verse to show 49

Mark when she smiles with amiable cheer 28
May the Babylonish curse 280
Milton! thou shouldst be living at this hour 247
Most glorious Lord of life, that on this day 29
Much have I travelled in the realms of gold 327
Music, when soft voices die 312
My days among the Dead are passed 277
My friend, the things that do attain 27
My heart aches, and a drowsy numbness pains 327
My heart leaps up when I behold 247
My lute, awake, perform the last 23
My mind to me a kingdom is 53
My Mistress' eyes are nothing like the sun 64
My Phillis hath the morning sun 52
My true-love hath my heart, and I have his 50

Nature, that fram'd us of four elements 58
Not a drum was heard, not a funeral note 302
Not marble, nor the gilded monuments 72

O joys! infinite sweetness! with what flowers 166
O Life, thou Nothing's younger brother 160

O Mistress mine, where are you roaming?   61
O Rose, thou art sick   237
O Thou, by nature taught   208
O what can ail thee, knight-at-arms   332
O wild West Wind, thou breath of Autumn's being 303
O Winter! bar thine adamantine doors   233
Of all the girls that are so smart   178
Of Man's first disobedience, and the fruit   121
Of these the false Achitophel was first   173
Of your trouble, Ben, to ease me   79
Oh! sing unto my roundelay   229
Oh that those lips had language! Life has passed 222
Oh, to be in England   378
On either side the river lie   350
On Linden, when the sun was low   286
One day I wrote her name upon the strand   29
Our bugles sang truce, for the night-cloud had lower'd 285
Our revels now are ended. These our actors   72
Out upon it! I have lov'd   148

Peace to all such! but were there One whose fires 192

Roman Virgil, thou that singest   365
Rose-cheeked Laura, come   74
'Ruin seize thee, ruthless King   202

Say not the struggle nought availeth   388
Season of mists and mellow fruitfulness   331
Shall I compare thee to a summer's day?   61
She comes! she comes! the sable Throne behold   191
She dwelt among the untrodden ways   242
She walks in beauty, like the night   290
Since there's no help, come let us kiss and part 58
So all day long the noise of battle roll'd   367
So, we'll go no more a roving   298
Some Atheist or vile Infidel in love   57

Stay, stay, sweet Time; behold, or ere thou pass 57
Still to be neat, still to be drest 77
Strew on her roses, roses 388
Sunset and evening star 374
Sweet Auburn! loveliest village of the plain 210
Sweetest love, I do not go 88

That time of year thou mayst in me behold 63
That which her slender waist confin'd 105
That's my last Duchess painted on the wall 376
The awful shadow of some unseen Power 308
The barge she sat in, like a burnish'd throne 70
The blessed Damozel leaned out 404
The curfew tolls the knell of parting day 197
The earth, late chok'd with showers 51
The Frost performs its secret ministry 276
The grey sea and the long black land 377
The Hag is astride 99
'The isles of Greece, the isles of Greece 298
The lunatic, the lover, and the poet 65
The quality of mercy is not strain'd 65
The rain set early in to-night 378
The sea is calm to-night 403
The soote season, that bud and bloom forth brings 26
The twentieth year is well nigh past 225
The woods decay, the woods decay and fall 363
There is a garden in her face 73
There was a sound of revelry by night 293
There was a time when meadow, grove, and stream 248
There was also a Nun, a Prioress 17
They are all gone into the world of light 167
Thou art not fair, for all thy red and white 75
Thou still unravish'd bride of quietness 330
Thou, who dost flow and flourish here below 169
Three years she grew in sun and shower 240
Tiger! Tiger! burning bright 235
Time hath, my Lord, a wallet at his back 69

Tired with all these, for restful death I cry 63
To be, or not to be: that is the question 67

Well then; I now do plainly see 159
What is beauty, saith my sufferings, then? 59
What should I say 24
When God at first made Man 103
When I consider how my light is spent 146
When Love with unconfined wings 156
When my grave is broke up again 87
When the lamp is shatter'd 310
When the moon is on the wave 291
When to her lute Corinna sings 74
When to the sessions of sweet silent thought 62
When we two parted 289
Whenas in silks my Julia goes 99
Where then shall Hope and Fear their objects find? 196
Whether on Ida's shady brow 234
Who would true valour see 172
Whoever comes to shroud me, do not harm 86
Why, all delights are vain; but that most vain 60
Why so pale and wan, fond lover? 147
With blackest moss the flower-plots 348
With fingers weary and worn 335
With him there was his son, a young Squire 15
With how sad steps, O Moon, thou climb'st the skies 50

Ye learned sisters which have oftentimes 30
Ye Mariners of England 287
Yet once more, O ye laurels, and once more 116
You meaner beauties of the night 75
Youth of delight, come hither 235